A CON AFFAIR

JOE GLASS

For all the missed opportunities along the way

I don't know what I'm doing here.

I thought maybe it was time to try a big show, but I've been sat here since 10am and I haven't had a single person stop at my table. A few furtive glances as they walk by, a few times having my table blocked by excited cosplayers who haven't seen each other in ages and decide to catch up right in front of the table, but otherwise, nada.

I mean, it's been six years? I've made a few issues and the smaller comic cons I've done, people are starting to recognise me, to come back to my table. And after I uploaded the issues of *The surREALS* onto Comixpedia everything seemed to take off. It's been incredible, so I figured it was time to take this little experiment out of South Wales and into the Big Smoke of London. Surely this would be the next big step on my rise to comic book superstardom?

It was a risk, don't get me wrong. The hotels in London are insanely priced, everything is double what it costs back home, and then there was getting here. Packing as much stock as I could into my suitcase, which is not designed to hold nearly 35 kilograms of comics judging by the way the wheels started scraping along the pavement as I dragged it; a weekend bag of clothes, a roll up banner, and dragging it all myself from London Paddington out to the Docklands, I arrived more sweat than man. I must have looked crazy, a slightly chunky (okay, maybe more than slightly), dishevelled white man lugging an overpacked suitcase, a carryall, a backpack, long carry case strapped across the suitcase handle, making me awkwardly wide (not just me this time, I swear, I've not put on that much weight) flinging my eyes around everywhere to make sure I'm going the right way. But then, maybe that's common in the big city.

And honestly, it's the 21st Century, how the hell are there Tube stations with no escalators or elevators?

But I thought it would be worth it. I figured I was ready. I figured I was wanted.

I guess I figured wrong.

Look, I'll be honest with you: half the time I don't know what I'm doing. I just know that there's this thing I'm good at that most people think is silly, or hell, they're surprised is even still a thing, and doing it is fun. It's also frustrating as all hell, not knowing what I'm doing, but hey, who does these days, right? I'm just trying to get by, doing something I enjoy for reasons that make no sense to me, so I can't even begin to explain them to anyone else, because God knows I can't stick with working retail all my life. And comic cons can be a lot of fun too…when people are actually showing interest, anyway.

Still, the cosplay around here is some of the best I've ever seen. Like, don't get me wrong, I could never do cosplay of any level, I just don't seem to have it in me, and I love it all. But some of the ones I've seen today have been incredible. So detailed and intricate, or huge and elaborate. Mitch (he's exhibiting on the other end of the hall, so I haven't seen him since we bought our morning coffees before the doors opened) says that it just gets better as we get into the weekend too: that the Thursdays and Fridays tend to be quiet at the show. Which I guess I should keep in mind…but it cost so much to get here, to even get a table. I need to make a killing this weekend.

Doesn't help that I'm boxed in between a girl whose towering stand is just filled with tons of prints of characters from Marvel and DC (I checked, she's not an artist at either company, and she's not done any comics, near as I can tell. Just hundreds and hundreds of prints of intellectual property she has had no hand in) and then a booth selling JoyCo Vinyl Dolls, thousands of perfect cube boxes creating a practical fortress of inevitable landfill that the punters are flocking to in droves.

(I can't be too critical: I'd be lying if I said I didn't have a few of them at home myself, but when you're being outsold by a lump of mass produced plastic, it's hard not to take it personally).

The hardest part of doing these comic cons is the not knowing how things will shake out. I mean, you have to pay out up front and for all you know you might not get a single sale all weekend, leaving you in the hole with no way out. It's the hardest part of comics as a whole, to be honest. The money. The fact that everything costs so much, and just seems to get higher all the time, so even if you do start doing well it always feels like you need to do better. I have no idea what I'm going to do if this weekend is a bust: I still have to pay Gertie, my artist, for the latest issue, and I was really hoping that sales from this would cover it, but now I'm not so sure, and savings…ha! I'm from Swansea, my friend, I've never had the privilege of having 'savings' to play with.

Still, I can't imagine doing anything else. If I just sat in a call centre taking calls forever, these stories, these characters, I dunno, feels like they'd split my head open just to find some way into the world without me. It's the release I need. The tension of not writing them down, finding the artists, making them real - it would be too much.

And that's just the thing: I tried that. After university, I was so scared that maybe I didn't have it in me to make the whole writing thing happen, I took the safe option. Retail job after retail job, with a few brief stints in call centres too. It didn't take long for me to realise they weren't for me. The endless drudgery of meaningless conversations, the continual push for ever higher sales and targets that if you achieve, the next day are raised higher, making you feel like every achievement is hollow and worthless.

They provided security, sure, and a little extra money, so I tried the writing thing again. Applied for jobs in publishing and even TV, only to be met with the age old response of 'we're looking for someone with experience', though how anyone is supposed to get that experience when no one will hire a new person in the first place is beyond me. The frustration compounded with each rejection, and instead of feeling safe, I felt...stuck.

So, I had a little money put away, and figured go big or go home: I packed in the day job to pursue writing full time (albeit with the odd stint in temp work or seasonal work to supplement where needed, of course), and just make the bloody things myself. Luckily, from uni and some lucky encounters at comic cons as a punter, I met some likeminded folks who thought it would be cool to make my inane scribblings into something. And so, *The surREALS* was born, after a few bumps along the way.

So here I am now, trying to bring that up to the next level and suddenly getting those feelings of rejection seeping into my head again.

Maybe that's just it. I'm too tense, need to try not to think about it and relax.

Of course, easier said than done.

The other hard part of doing a comic con, at least for me...let's just say I never realised spandex and lycra was my 'thing' until I came to my first show.

Which is wild to think about, right? Here I am, a gay man who voraciously devours superhero comics of all kinds, who even makes his own, and it never occurred to me I may have a thing for men in skintight costumes that leave little to the imagination. And yet, when I found myself head height to some extremely obscene VPL (visible penis lines) courtesy of a, I guess, very happy Spider-Man who came to check out my books, it was like a door suddenly opened in my mind and was like 'this is what the rest of my adult life is going to be about'.

Of course, I've never done anything about it. It feels like it would be wrong, and I'm not here to hook up. I'm here on business, and if they are fans of my books already it would just feel way out of line (something I wish more comic creators would agree with, to be quite honest). But I got eyes in my head, an appreciation of a man's form and a sex drive that never seemed to quite understand the notion of decorum, so you can see my difficulty.

Still, I can look. Respectfully. And hell, even when I see some gorgeous Superboy walk down the aisle, it's a 90% 'that cosplay is just amazing' with just a 10% of 'oh, man, that is so hot!'.

Fuck. It's not like I'm getting any other distraction now. Maybe if I did hook up while I was in London tonight it could relieve some of this tension? Maybe I'm giving off a vibe? No one's spoken to me in nearly four hours now, so I resolve to open Grindr and see if I can get some conversation on there and maybe find someone to take me up SoHo later (and take me up wherever else he wants).

Big mistake. I forgot the Grindr Law of Fresh Meat: if you open up the app in a new city or town, be prepared for the deluge as the only new piece of ass on the market. Within a minute, I've had ten new messages, all of which are picture messages. I'm surrounded by people, and I swear at least one person turned their head when they heard the telltale trill of a Grindr notification. I hate having notifications hanging over me though, so I decide to check them. Maybe it's a bunch of nice face pics?

I'm greeted by a dozen photos of rigidly engorged cocks or stretched out holes, as I quickly bounce out of the messages and hit block on some of the grossest offenders. Don't get me wrong: I'm horny, I want to get laid later, but an unsolicited dick pic (or worse, hole pic) is never welcome at the best of times, and certainly not when I'm surrounded by my colleagues in the middle of a convention. Consent is sexy, and if you didn't even say 'Hi' first, then I sure as hell didn't consent to a Dutch Angle of your booty-hole.

Maybe if I updated my profile details, make it clear that I'm not in the space to be affronted by smut right now.

> USERNAME: BORED ARRAN
> DETAILS: NEW IN TOWN FOR THE WEEKEND FOR THE
> SHOW. NOT AVAILABLE UNTIL AFTER THE CON.
> CHAT, HANGS AND DTF

It takes about half hour more, but then I get a notification. I pull it up and it's a cute guy, only eighty-three metres away? He must be here in the comic con. I scan through the rest of his pics, and sure enough it's a selection of him in cosplay. He's actually a really good cosplayer too to be honest, some of these costumes look really well done.

HI.

Hey.

You at the comic con?

Yeah. You?

Yup. Wanna come round my hotel room for a quickie. Could use some fun :D

Oh, sorry. I'm, uh, actually exhibiting. I can't really meet during con hours

Ooooh. Maybe I could come over under your table. Bet you won't be bored then

Thanks but I'm pretty positive that's a surefire way to get me banned from every con in the country

Come on. It'd be so hot

I roll my eyes and put the phone face down on the table. Why should I be surprised? A horny gay in cosplay is still just a horny gay. And on that app, horny takes over all sense of, well, common sense and decent conversation. Time for a new update.

> USERNAME: BORED ARRAN
> DETAILS: NEW IN TOWN FOR THE COMIC CON.
> LOOKING FOR SOME GOOD CONVERSATION. GEEKS,
> NERDS, COMMUNISTS, SOCIALISTS AND CREATIVES
> TO THE FRONT OF THE Q. TERFS AND TORIES NEED
> NOT APPLY.

I take a break from the, well, nothing really, and go and get myself another coffee. On my way back, I briefly stop at the JoyCo booth and begrudgingly buy myself an Iceman JoyCo to add to my gay superheroes collection (yes, I know, I'm a hypocrite). I settle back in behind the table, take a sip and take out my phone to play a game or something. That's when I realise I had another message and didn't feel it vibrate.

Huh. Just a lightning bolt emoji for his username. Cute guy. Cosplayer again, so probably here at the show too. He's got a really sweet smile in his main photo. Which, okay, I know I'm looking for some fun later, and a smile isn't a hugely important factor, but I dunno. It's charming and I feel like it would make me feel at ease?

I decide to stop falling in love with a photograph on a hookup app and actually read the message.

As much as I love them, comic cons are probably the absolute worst place for communist socialists right?

Lol, too true. Late Stage Capitalism: The Live Event.

HA!

Though this place is crawling with socialists nonetheless.

Well, it's the superheroes. They're all social justice warriors at the end of the day.

OMG exactly! I can't believe there are some fans out there that don't get that.

It seems obvious right?

So, you cosplaying here too?

Ah, not me. Love cosplay, but I've never done it.

No, I'm actually exhibiting. In the Artists Alley.

Oh cool. Are you an artist?

Nah, I'm the writer. I write the comics. I hire people with actual talent to draw them.

Ah, don't sell yourself short. Writing is a cool talent too.

So what comics are you into?

Oh, I'm a basic gay comic book fan, so X-Men, Batman, Superman, Wonder Woman. I read a lot of Indies too. Got to know what my peers are up to, y'know.

You?

Oh, pretty much the same, tbh. I like keeping up to date, and I love the movies too. But I like seeing more independent ones too, even superhero books. Like Invincible, Blackhole Son or Thunderman.

OMG I love Thunderman! It's such a brilliant take on the genre!

Ha, well, not to sound like a total creeper, but it's nice to see you smiling now.

What?

Look up.

I look up. Standing before me is Thunderman. A white and blue, skintight outfit, highlighted by a shiny golden bolt from one shoulder down to the crotch. Which I never realised until now is kind of like a big arrow pointing right down at the hero's junk, because I'm suddenly very aware of the large bulge pointed right at my face. I return my gaze up before I make it too obvious, and I realise underneath the cowl is the guy I've been talking to on Grindr.

"Oh my god, you look amazing! I've never seen someone cosplay Thunderman before!" I manage to blurt out.

"Thanks. I was a little worried I wouldn't get it done in time for the show, but it all came together well, I think." He smiles as he looks down at me and it turns out I was right: that smile makes me feel unreasonably comfortable. After all, I don't even know this guy's name.

I stand up so we can be at the same level, though I realise he's actually about a good three inches taller than me still.

"Hi. I'm Arran."

"I know. You had it on Grindr. Thankfully, I didn't think your first name was 'Bored'"

I laugh and then stand there a little awkward, realising that I'm extremely attracted to this guy in the costume of one of my favourite characters and I can't tell if it's just because it's Thunderman or because even with half his face covered up this guy is insanely cute.

"Oh! I'm Cameron, by the way. Sorry, I can be a bit of a ditz in social situations."

"Ha, I know just what you mean. This is why I normally keep a table between me and other human beings."

He laughs and it's got this casual spirit with a sprinkling of an awkwardness to it that is actually endearing.

"Oh, hang on," he says, as he starts lifting the neck of the cowl and pulling the whole thing over his head in a singular piece, revealing a shock of loosely curled pink hair that despite being flattened under a hood for hours still has bounce and life to it. He ruffles his own hair with a gloved hand, before smiling that smile and flashing some brilliant white teeth. He puts out his hand out to shake mine.

"Again. Hi, I'm Cameron."

"Arran. Nice to meet you."

"So how is the con going for you?" The urge to lie and say I'm having a great time is strong, but for some reason I decide I don't want to lie to him.

"I'll be honest, not great. Thus the 'bored'. I've barely seen anyone all day. I dunno, maybe this convention just isn't the scene for my work."

"Are you kidding? These look great! It's probably just because it's the Thursday, man. Not many people get the whole event off work, so you'll probably see a much better day over the week-end." He's right. Just like Mitch was. But he's also a stranger, and I guess hearing someone who doesn't have a reason to be false to spare my feelings means I take it better.

"Yeah. Yeah, maybe. Doesn't help much with the boredom, though. Thus the Grindr." I try to laugh, but it kind of comes out like a broken sigh, and I hate that I'm so awkward.

"Ah, that's what that's all about. Well," he bows his head forward and tilts it slightly to one side, looking up at me with those deep blue eyes, looking at me passed a loose tuft of pink curls that has fallen slightly in front of them and oh damn, it is undeniably gorgeous. "Maybe I could help with that?"

I feel a flush of heat rise to my face, and would be lying if I said I didn't also feel a rush of heat somewhere else too.

"Uh, I dunno. I kinda feel like it would be weird, or frowned upon maybe, if I did that with a fan at the show, you know? Not that-I just...oh god, kill me now, I am so awkward."

He smiles at me sweetly, then bites his lip. "Heh, I totally get it. But, you know, I asked you. And if it helps, I actually never heard of your books until just now."

It shouldn't really help, and really should feel a little like an insult maybe to be honest, but I'm looking at this incredibly cute guy who's being unashamedly forward but in a charming and smoother way than anyone I've met off a dating app in God knows how long and I have to say...

"Yeah. Yeah, that helps."

When the show came to a close, I head back to my hotel room to stash away my cash box and things. We'd said we'd meet later.

In fact, Cameron and I continued talking on and off via Grindr all the rest of the day. Which was a plus, as it was still incredibly slow for me. But now, I dunno...it didn't seem to bother me so much. After all, if nothing else, I did get to meet a cute guy.

We chatted about comics, of course, but also films, and where we're from and politics. Cameron is really a lot smarter about that than I am. I'm much more of a 'I don't know how to explain to you that you should care about other people' kind of a guy, but Cameron is much more up to speed on it all. Which is cool. But obviously, similarities in personal tastes and politics is not what is really on my mind as I rush through a commiseratory McDonald's alone in my room.

I check myself in the mirror before I leave: I'm in shape, if the shape is round. I guess I can't say much about it given I spend most of my time writing, or trying to market my comics online, and eating MaccyDs. My brown hair is boring compared to Cameron's, but I don't dare dye it. My dad is bald, and that is the last thing I can deal with. It's a mess, but at least I can try and do something with it. I could probably use a shave. Do I have time? Screw it, he saw me earlier, so I guess it'll do. I shake off my image crisis and head out the door.

He told me his hotel and room number.

Just after 9pm, I'm standing outside his door. There's still a few people in cosplay walking up and down the corridors heading back to their rooms, or out into the night in London, which really won't be the oddest looking thing in London, I suppose. I wait for the hallway to get quiet before knocking.

The door opens and Cameron is stood there wearing a white, fuzzy hotel bathrobe and as near as I can tell little else. He has glasses on now too, subtle golden framed spectacles that are round in shape and compliment his features well.

There is a split second where I have to admit I feel disappointed that he isn't still dressed as Thunderman, or in some other kind of form-fitting suit, but it's a fleeting feeling as I stare at this gorgeous guy who for some reason wants to roll in the hay with me.

"Hey," he greets me brightly.

"Hey," I just about manage to squeak out.

I swear I'm not normally this completely without game, but I'm still kind of in shock. After the business of the day was so dire, I was so sure that this whole day, heck, this whole trip would be an absolute write off, but instead, this stunning man wants me and I'm just a little dumbfounded. Clearly, we're stood on the doorway with me awkwardly staring too long when he says, "I'm not normally into public reveals, but if it gets you to come inside..." and pulls the cord on his dressing gown and lets it fall open.

He isn't wearing anything underneath.

Without thinking, I'm through the doorway and on him. Our lips almost smashing together as he walks backwards into the room, pulling me with him as the door slams shut. My hands cradle his face as he has one hand on the small of my back, drawing me close to him. I feel him swell against me, kicking off a chain reaction with my own, as I begin to strain against my jeans.

We bump into the end of the bed, but right ourselves before we fall onto it. I'm not done worshipping him yet. As he goes to take my shirt off, I lean in and kiss his neck, prompting a deep moan to escape his lips: I guess I found one of his favourite spots. I'm determined to find them all.

I slide the dressing gown off, letting it fall to the ground in a heap and a soft thump. I keep kissing across his smooth chest as I let my hands slowly move down his back, pausing briefly in the soft curve at the base of his spine.

He's completely naked, bar his glasses, but I'm fully clothed and on my knees, inspecting every inch of his body with my lips. I trace a line of musculature around his back with my index finger, gently caressing the subtle V-line of his Apollo's belt. I glance my eyes upward, my lips not leaving his tense abdominals, to see the effect I'm having. Cameron is looking straight up, lips barely parted as he lets out a series of low moans. As subtle as that display of his appreciation is, a far more obvious one comes into my grasp.

His cock is solid, thick and long, my hand wrapped around it and the large head still uncovered. I gently run my tongue along the tip, then under the head before planting a slow, soft kiss on it. The gasp from Cameron is enough to make me smile and push further, taking all of him into my mouth to the base. His legs buckle and he falls back onto the bed as he lets out a sharp sigh. But before I can bring him back into my mouth, he places a hand over his privates and props himself up on his elbows.

"As good as that feels, man, I'm starting to feel a little over-dressed here. Get your clothes off. I want to see you."

"Okay," I say a little hesitantly. How can I compare to this practical adonis? Clearly he works out and takes good care of himself, whereas I can go for days without moving from my desk and then wonder why my back hurts so much…at just thirty-three years of age.

That said, there's something about someone so beautiful eager to see someone like me naked that turns me on, and I find myself taking the clothes off slowly not out of hesitancy, but because I want to savour the moment. The way his eyes never leave me once, I feel like he wants it to last too.

As I throw my shirt to the ground, I run a hand into my chest hair and ruffle it, wondering if he likes the hair compared to his smooth chest. With a bite of his lip he lets me know that he does.

As I slide off my jeans, his eyes widen.

"A jockstrap?" he asks, with a hint of amusement to his tone.

"I find them comfortable…"

"Oh, no complaints from me." He says as he pushes himself to the foot of the bed and stops my hands as I reach for my jock. He runs his tongue along the pouch, running the length of my shaft through the material. "Let me."

He pulls my jock off in one swift motion, and as I step out of them he brings his hands back up to grab my butt cheeks in a firm grip. Drawing me closer, he buries his face into my crotch and I hear him inhale, which makes me twitch in anticipation and from his closeness. Feeling this, he turns his attention to my cock and it's my turn to almost buckle.

His mouth feels warm, wet and soft as he moves along me with skill and a kind of firm tenderness that is distressingly hard to come by. It's like he's devouring me but with care and gentleness, his tongue tickling at my tip.

He slowly stands back up, both of us stood in the middle of the beige hotel room, naked to the world. He stands a little taller than me, and his body is almost completely smooth apart from a furry patch at the base of his penis and the slight peach fuzz of his ass. What hair he has is fair, compared to my thicker, darker hair that spreads all across my chest and rounded stomach, legs, butt and arms. Our cocks are both hard now, and brush side by side gently as we take each other in.

He's all muscle, but not in an overdoing it at the gym kind of way, more like a lithe and natural way, like he was born this way, just naturally athletic in physique. I'm soft, rounder at my edges, and could probably stand to hit the gym a little more than I do, but it doesn't seem to bother Cameron. His hands explore every inch of me, slowly caressing along the side of my shaft, gently brushing my balls before following the shape of me up my body until his hand comes to rest in the crook of my neck, cradling my cheek. He leans in and kisses me, and it's sweet and gentle, before he moves his lips to my ear and quietly breathes a request.

"I want you to *fuck* me."

I don't know if it was the sharpness with which he uttered the word 'fuck', or the feeling of his breath on my earlobe, but all sense of control leaves me. I immediately spun him on the spot and pushed him onto the bed, dropping over him so I could run slow, deep kisses down his spine, moving down an inch at a time, my cock between the cheeks of his ass sliding back until my face finds the mound of his buttocks. I kiss each cheek in turn before pulling them apart and burying my face between them. Eyes closed, I lick and suck, listening to Cameron moan and giggle ecstatically.

I may not always trust that I'm good at things, but I know I'm good at rimming. Cameron's breathless confirmations just urging me to keep going, deeper, harder, until I think he may just come from this alone. His dick feels wet as I take it in my hand, pulling it back so I can run my tongue from his hole, over his balls, down the length of him and then suck at the end.

Cameron flips over and signals me to come join him, and I lean over him, kissing him as I meet his eyes. As our lips are locked together, I can feel him reaching for the bedside table. When I pull back, he has a bottle of lube in his hand, and he squirts a generous amount into the palm of his other hand before using it to stroke my cock. He moves up and down, slowly coating my whole length, before taking another quick squirt and moving it between his cheeks.

I kiss him again, slow and passionate, as with one hand I hold myself over him and with the other, I manoeuvre myself until I can feel the tip of my dick against him. He looks into my eyes and subtly nods as I attempt to push inside. With no success, he grabs me by the back of my neck and pulls me back into an embrace, moving his leg to rest against my shoulder. I find him again and thrust.

We both gasp, lips locked. I feel him let me in, tight around me, his gasp for that initial pain that comes with the promise of ecstasy.

"Slowly, slowly…" he breathes, as I push myself deeper within him. He moves his other leg over my shoulder, crossing them at the ankles and drawing me in, his eyes rolling up into his head as a smile spreads across his face.

"Fuuuuuck me."

"Planning on it." I joke, because I have to ruin every moment with jokes. But he just gives me an impish grin and a playful look, driving me wild.

We go at it like animals. We go at it like lovers. We lose track of time and sense, just in this moment. One moment it's slow and tender, the next, hard, fast and desperate. I don't know how long it was, it didn't matter, we both loved every second of it. But all good things.

"Where do you want-?" I start to ask, letting him know I'm ready.

"Inside," he purrs, and I lean back and push into him harder, feeling him tense around me, until finally I release and feel myself filling him.

As I do, he also spends himself across his own stomach, and I collapse down on top of him, feeling the dampness between us. We lie there holding each other for a moment, panting ragged breaths. For a moment, I feel something that feels like peace, until Cameron coughs and breaks the silence.

"Christ, I know they say the pen is mightier than the sword, but have they seen your dick?"

I groan and roll off him, laughing.

"Oh my god, that is so cringe!" But I'm laughing too much to care. It didn't break the mood, it exemplified it. We were comfortable in each others presence in a way that was maybe strange for a random hookup.

Laughing, he kisses me on the forehead and rolls me into a hug. We lie there for a few minutes, sated and smiling. When he rolls back, I figure I take the hint and sit up on the bed, surveying the mess of the room for all my items of clothing. I find my jock and pick it up and stand to put it on.

"Hey," Cameron says, leaning up on an elbow, looking up at me with earnestness and a gentle smile, "You don't have to go anywhere. Unless you want to. I've got no other plans tonight.

"You can stay. If you want."

And so I threw the jock to the ground and I stayed.

LONDON EXCELSICON
SUMMER 2018 DAY TWO

The next day was a completely different beast. Not only was the Friday a lot busier than anyone seemed to be expecting, but my table suddenly got very busy.

At first, I thought it would wind up the same as yesterday. But then I remembered the changes Cameron suggested for my Grindr. My book had LGBTQ+ interest; I was a gay author and the story features a queer leading character (I gave him a rundown of the book, which was the first time I've done that bollock naked), so he said to me, laying there in the afterglow of perhaps one of the most exquisite fucks of my life, "Why not use it to advertise?"

"Grindr? Don't I already do that?"

"Not your dick - sell your book. Instead of telling people you're horny, tell them where to find you. There's loads of gay guys here at the con, and they're always going to check the app. Throw up some directions."

And well:

USERNAME: ARTISTS ALLEY TABLE 14
BIO: COME CHECK OUT THE SURREALS! AN
INDEPENDENT SUPERHERO COMIC FOR THE
KOOKIEST AND CRAZIEST #LGBTQ #SUPERHEROES

For the first half hour, nothing seemed different. But then I had my first notification.

Oh, gay comics? Sweet! I'll be right over!

Then another.

Oh, I think I saw that on comixpedia. I didn't
know it was in print too.

And before I could answer, the first real life customer stopped by my table and started flicking through the issues. I started telling him about the story and characters, and why I made the book, and then another person, dressed in the costume of some anime I hadn't the faintest inkling about (I've come to realise if I don't recognise a cosplay, it's most likely from anime), listening in as they pick up another issue. Before I knew it, I was struggling to keep up the pace, and starting to wish I wasn't doing the show on my own.

Around lunch time, things started to quiet down for a bit.

"Looking better today, huh?" The girl from the table next to me looked over with a smile.

"Uh, yeah. Seriously better. I thought I was a goner after yesterday."

"I could tell. You seemed really down. But you came in today looking a lot brighter. It's a nice vibe to bring people in."

"Yeah. Sorry for being a downer…"

"Oh, I didn't mean it like that. People are going to buy this stuff no matter what," she humble-bragged, waving towards her prints of tentpole Marvel and DC characters. "But it does help to try and be positive. If nothing else, for your own wellbeing. These things are hard enough, especially alone."

"God, ain't that the truth."

"I'm Emily," she said, putting out her hand to shake. I take it and feel a momentary pang of guilt for judging her yesterday in my low moments.

"Arran. You're doing well too?"

"Oh sure, but this is still one of the quieter days. Most people can't get the time off work. Just wait until tomorrow, it's something else. Your first show?"

"Oh, no. I mean, my first one of these, but I've been doing smaller shows all over for about five…god, six years, maybe."

"Oh wow. You're an old hand," she laughs, and I'm suddenly conscious of how young she looks. "What brought you out of your funk yesterday, anyway?"

Dicking down the hottest man I've ever had the pleasure to in my life, I think. "Oh, just spent the night hanging out with a friend, venting."

It was technically true. Cameron and I hung out for hours after our bit of fun. We talked more about comics, favourite movies. What kind of music we're into. He told me about his cosplay a bit, how he makes a lot of his own stuff, but has to order in some of the base elements. Watching him talk about that was adorable, he got enthusiastic and his eyes lit up in such a way, I just lay there and watched him.

I told him about my years making my comic, and how I'd love to write for the big publishers some day, but things didn't seem to be going anywhere fast with it.

"Well, it's still early days," he said, running his slender fingers down my side, as we lay face to face.

"Ha, feels like I've been at it forever. It's been like five years or so already."

"Sure, but that's not a long, long time. And you're making your own stories, that's got to be more rewarding, right?"

"Well, yeah." It was more rewarding, or near as I could tell given my lack of experience writing for an established IP. But when people came up to me and told me how much they loved *The surREALS* it always made me feel really proud, if only for moment. "I just wish, I dunno. I see guys my age breaking in and I feel like, how? Ya know?"

He rolls onto his back and bounces the bed purposefully and playfully. "I get it. But hey, you're not going anywhere anytime soon. Just enjoy the ride, make what you want to make when you can, and someday, I'm sure it will all work out."

We talked until it was really late, and I said I had to get back to my hotel room so I could get ready in the morning before the show. As I sat at the foot of the bed, putting on my shoes, he sidled up next to me, naked still, and kissed me on my cheek and wished me good night and a better day tomorrow.

I guess the wish worked, because I am doing incredible.

I decided to treat myself to some hot food from the concourse in the convention centre, and after I managed to source an exorbitantly overpriced hamburger and fries, I sat back at my table and watched the flow of people moving around the convention.

Part of what I loved about these shows was the energy. Everyone was excited about something, and even if it wasn't always the exact same thing, it was close enough that everyone just fed off everyone else's buzz and kept going. A perpetual motion machine of joy, about the comics they read, the cartoons they watch, the friends they make. And of course, it's a place where people's enthusiasm has the most outward expression, as people mill around dressed as their favourite characters, acting like them or just marvelling at the work of fellow journeymen in the game of costume-making and extreme nerdery.

If you're a fan too, like me, it's even exciting just looking around, playing a mental bingo of the cosplays you see. There's a Superman. A Batman there. A kaleidoscope of Harley Quinns, each a different style or version to the last. And a near infinite number of Spider-Men flooding your view.

In fact, the one in front of me looks familiar, and not just in the sense of the more niche Spider costume choice only a real nerd like me would get, having opted for the 90s *Clone Saga* era Ben Reilly Spider-Man costume. No, something triggers a sense of memory in my mind, and it takes me a second until I realise it's his butt that looks intimately familiar to me.

"Cameron?"

The webbed-wonder in front of me turns, and then bounds over towards my table. Stopping in front, he whips off his mask revealing the tumble of pink curls and twinkling blue eyes from my memorable night before.

"Hey! I figured I was around the right place! I wanted to show my friends your book." As he explains, a Batman, a Doctor Who and a Supergirl file in around him, smiling at me. "This is Brian, Vince and Carrie."

They all say hi, and I return a slightly meek response. How did he describe how we know each other exactly? Does it really matter?

"I was telling them about your book, and they're keen, so come on, tell 'em what you got," he says, flashing a smile at me.

I return the smile and then break into salesman mode, giving my full spiel about the comics, the story, world and why I make them. They actually all pick up a copy each, and Carrie buys a pin badge too, marvelling at the glittered enamel I had it made with.

"So how's today gone?" Cameron asks as the others slowly mill over to the adjoining tables, Vince heading to the JoyCo booth next door.

"Honestly, so much better than yesterday. I've struggled to keep on top of everyone at times. You were right." I give the last part with a sheepish tilt of my head, and he smiles at me.

"I'm glad. I knew it would be."

We stand there for a few beats, a silence passing between us that isn't entirely awkward, but also pregnant with things left unsaid (or maybe not yet done). Then a realisation dawns on me.

"Wait, Cameron…have you been sending people over? Telling them where to find me?"

"Nope. Not me," he laughs. "It's just you putting yourself out there more, probably. Not feeling so defeated."

My shoulders relax, and I guess he's right.

"That, and it is a really great comic."

"Wait, I thought you said—"

"I hadn't read it. Until last night," for a second, it almost looks like he's blushing too and sinking back, but he pushes forward and meets my eyes, "After you left, I got curious. Found them online and read them all on my tablet. They're genuinely great stuff, Arran. You should be more confident in what you've done."

It's my turn to flush with heat, and I slowly lower myself into my chair. I've had a few people come up and tell me how much they liked the series today, some bought it online, some grabbed it at some other con in the country. And it always felt nice, a moment of pride. But this time feels a little…different.

"Hey, what you doing tonight?" Cameron asks, as I see his friends waving at him to join them and continue wandering the halls.

"Oh, um, I'm having a meal with my friend Mitch. He has a table on the other end of Artists Alley. But he doesn't tend to stay out so then I guess I have nothing."

"Come join us tonight! You can meet some of the other cosplayers, get them into your comic too. Think of it like pre-gaming for the con tomorrow.

"Plus, you can spend another night with me," he says, balancing on one foot, the other hooked around his ankle in a faux-display of of shy innocence.

Well, how could I refuse.

"So better day today, huh?"

Mitch fixes me with his cool eyes from across the table, a dark eyebrow arched inquisitively. I met Mitch at a con in Bristol two years back, and we've tabled next to each other more often than not.

Interesting thing about Mitch: he's crazy good at the whole 'business' side of this whole comics making lark, way more than I have ever been. It just seems to come naturally to him. The truly weird thing about it though, is I find myself always wanting to try and impress him, not by doing something huge and great, but just by getting better at this whole gig or trying to be more professional. Don't know why, he just pulls that need out of me, somehow.

"You could say that, yeah. Like, I actually had people buy things today, so that's good."

"Ah, so I guess you can actually eat tonight then?"

"Very funny." But also true.

The waiter comes over with our drinks: Zombie cocktails, served in these gorgeous skull tiki glasses. I have a weird love for skulls and skull things, especially everyday objects like glasses. A bizarre memento mori fascination that I really can't explain, but I find myself wondering if I can somehow pocket the glass to take home.

Mitch suggested we come to this Thai restaurant, having tried it the last time he did Excelsicon. I deferred to his experience, though I've never eaten Thai food before. I wound up just ordering the only thing on the menu I'd ever heard of before, Pad Thai, but daren't admit I haven't the foggiest what it is.

"So how was it for *you* today?" I ask, taking a long sip of Zombie. Good lord, this is going to get me wasted fast.

"Not too bad, not too bad. Busier than I usually expect for a Friday. Will be needing to restock from the extra stock in my car boot, which is good."

"Yeah, I sold out of my copies of issue one I brought."

He looks at me from under his fringe, eyebrow cocked. Oh no.

"You didn't bring enough stock?"

"Well, I didn't know what to expect. And I had to drag it on the Tube, I couldn't really bring much, and..." he continues to glare at me. "Yeah, okay, I fucked up."

He takes a long swig of his cocktail, like he's measuring how to respond in his head.

"You know what, you'll be fine." He points a finger down on

the table. "Your book has done well digitally, right? You'll still have potential sales from people who read it online. 'Course, it's not ideal. If you had more issue ones you could get more sales of all the comics in a bundle, which is a better sale. But whatever, you live, you learn.

"But, you know, learn." He grins at me. He knows I'm now feeling like an idiot, and he loves it.

"Fine. Ass."

"You're the one who didn't bring enough stock."

I roll my eyes as the waiter brings the food and sets it down. It looks and smells delicious, so maybe my good luck today is still going.

We wind up talking through our meal about all things business of making comics as small press, independent, self-published creators: what we're working on at the moment, how're things going, who is acting like a jackass at the moment, thinking they're the next Mark Millar or some shit.

(Pad Thai, it turns out, is fantastic, and I think I may love Thai food now).

I order a second Zombie as Mitch turns to talk about his career.

"I have a few crowdfunding campaigns this year, but I'm putting a bit more focus on the production work with the TV studio. It's steady work and keeps the lights on more than the comics, to be honest. And with the family getting bigger…"

My eyes widen. "Another one? My god, Mitch, how many is that now?"

He smiles, proudly. "Third. What can I say, the Connell seed is just too potent."

"Ew, gross" I gag. Mitch is actually a year younger than me, having turned thirty-three myself last year, but he's been a proud dad now for the last six years, and just keeps going. Of all the parents I know (and I know more and more by the month it seems lately), he's one of the only ones who actually still looks younger than me. Which I kind of envy him for. You know what they say about hitting thirty on the gay scene: it's the gay death.

As my second cocktail arrives, he asks me the dreaded question. "What about you? Where do you see yourself in five years time?"

I hate this one. I can barely guess where I'll be in one weeks time, let alone years. Everyone romanticises living in the moment, but what they don't mention about that is when you focus on just the now, the future and even the past fail to exist to you. I can barely remember the steps I took to get to where I am, and I have no plans, no safety nets for any eventuality in the future. I'm just the now. Always the now. And the now can be a really depressing and lonely place.

"Oh, I dunno. I kinda hoped I'd be getting some Marvel or DC work by now, but I'm just getting no interest there at all. Still, it's where I hope to end up one day…"

"Why?' he asks, a confused expression on his face. "I don't mean to rain on your parade, but it's just your books are doing well. Independent work is all you, you don't have to worry about someone trying to force you into something you're not. Why would you want to work for them so much? I mean, you've probably heard more of the horror stories than I have, I don't see what you see in it."

"I dunno. Sure, I've heard bad things here and there, but also plenty of good too. It's like any job I guess. There's good and bad anywhere you go, isn't there?"

"Sure," he considers for a moment. "But not so big a bad that stifles your creativity, or screws you out of your own ideas. I mean, hell, what if you create some new character for Marvel and then it appears in a movie. You know you'll see barely a penny for it, but Marvel, or really Disney, will make millions. More even. If you just kept that idea and did it yourself-"

"It probably wouldn't get optioned. I don't have an agent, or representation, and I haven't the first idea how to get someone to look at my stuff that way. I dunno. Plus, hell, you know me. I love superheroes. That's where superheroes live. Of course I'd want to play in that sandbox sometime."

Mitch leans back in his chair and raises a hand to get the waiters attention, before ordering himself another cocktail too. "I don't know, man. Not me. Can't say they appeal to me at all."

"Really? If Marvel or DC came up to you right now and offered you a gig, you'd say no?"

"I'm not saying that, per se. It would depend. If the deal was good, I'd be an idiot not to go for it." He tilts a head to the side and fixes me with his eyes, clocking how confusing it is to me that someone doing what I do wouldn't want to work with the Big Boys someday. "But it's not a goal of mine, I guess. I get more enjoyment and thrill out of working on my own properties, I don't feel a desire to work on someone else's."

"Huh." I guess it makes sense. Of course, it also makes sense that not everyone would have the same dreams and aspirations too. I guess not all of us in this industry are chasing after the same things.

We finish up and split our bill, each paying exactly for what we had and leaving a small, but decent, tip. About all we can really afford to be honest.

"What you up to tonight, anyway? Don't suppose you'll be being sensible like me and retiring to the hotel room to watch footie and check figures."

"Heh, no. No, nothing like that." I smile, keeping a little secret to myself. "I'm, uh, meeting up with a friend to hang out."

He cocks an eyebrow at me. "Okay. Well, don't get him pregnant or anything, dude."

I tell him he's gross, but secretly smile in my mind thinking how it wouldn't be for lack of trying.

I head to the Hermes Hotel, where I arranged to meet Cameron in the bar. Ascending a small spiral staircase, I find my mind racing wondering what we might get up to tonight.

I'm mildly deflated when I see him at the bar…with his friends from earlier, and a few others. Some are still in cosplay, others have changed into normal clothes. Cameron is one of the latter, changed into a smart shirt tucked into some tight low-rise jeans, the kind that perfectly hug the curve of his ass. The deflated sensation soon vanishes.

"Arran! Hey. You made it," he calls, making a path to me, his friends politely following with their eyes to where he's heading and smiling at me. "Everyone, this is Arran. He writes a comic! It's called *The surREALS*…"

"Wait, you're Arran Wilson?" asks a bulky, muscled man dressed in a Green Lantern outfit. He's not wearing a mask and his hair has been spray dyed orange, so he's a clear Guy Gardner. Not the immediate type I'd assume would like my work.

"Uh, yeah, that's me. You've read the book?"

"Dude, that shit is hilarious! I love it! Yo, Maggie! You should check out his comic, you'd love it."

Cameron quickly makes introductions for the whole group. Guy (or Ben, as it turns out), Maggie, Brian, Vince, Carrie and Alex. Alex is a lot younger looking than the others, an attractive skinny twink of a guy with short brown hair. He's wearing a Spider-Man one-piece suit that hugs in places but looks loose in others, and loose in places no one else seems to have, suggesting he needs to grow into it almost.

Whatever sense of let down I had swiftly goes as the alcohol begins to flow. Alex, it turns out, is younger than anyone here, but still of legal drinking age (which I had genuine doubts about at first). It turns out that it's his first show.

"I mean, you can probably tell. I know my cosplay isn't fitting right, and it's just one I bought, I didn't make anything." he tells me, self-deprecatingly. Brian grabs his shoulder.

"Ah, don't beat yourself up, it's your first time. You'll grow into it. Or hell, you'll start picking up some tips from these guys, I'm sure." I hope I reassure him.

"I hope so. I bumped into them at the show and it blew my mind. I've been following Brian and Carrie on Instagram for ages." He gushes, a level of enthusiasm that honestly would match someone meeting a Hollywood celebrity. It catches me off guard, but I suppose I can see it. The guys start showing me their Instagram profiles, and some of the shots are genuinely really impressive, both in terms of the costumes and the poses and photography.

"Do you have a social media too?" I ask Cameron.

He smiles. "I have a twitter account, but I barely use it to be honest. Mainly to talk politics now and then, but it's a hellhole, so I don't spend much time on it. I tend to use instagram a lot more for cosplay stuff. You can follow me if you want."

We swap handles on social media, when he leans in, devilish grin on his face and whispers in my ear, "Why? Looking for an alt account?" I feel myself flush, and cover my burning cheeks with my pint glass, hoping no one notices.

We giggle and flirt like this for a while, among the group, but everyone is excitedly talking comics, cosplay and swapping stories of conventions past that I don't think anyone really notices us. But as well as the flirting, we also spend some of the time actually getting to know each other better. I tell Cameron about my crappy day job to help cover the bills, and where I went to university. He tells me that actually, he's an accountant out in the real world.

"Wait…an accountant accountant, or like what someone on TikTok means when they say they're an accountant?" I smirk.

"You spend way too much time on social media," he laughs, assuring me he spends more time looking through log books than pulling his pants down to stroke his log online. "Besides, doubt I'd make much money doing that."

"What?" I can't believe he even could think that. "Dude, you do realise you are stupidly hot, right?"

Cameron blushes and smiles, a flash of teeth showing, but revealing a side to him I hadn't seen yet. Like he's a little embarrassed, but happy too. "Thanks. I mean, I don't think so. But that's very kind of you to say."

My eyes are wide with pure shock. "Are you kidding? You are one of the most beautiful guys I've ever seen. I can't believe you seem so shy and anxious, I never saw that in you before."

"I guess. I mean, you've pretty much only seen me in cosplay…"

I look around us and make sure no one's paying attention to us at the moment. "I've also seen you in considerably less."

He flashes me that devilish grin that drives me wild. "Well, social anxiety goes out the window when there's someone trying to get in my pants."

"I don't recall any pants."

He pokes me. "Play your cards right, mister, and there won't be any pants later too."

We giggle like kids, but I can't tell a lie, I also find myself already firming up at the thought.

"In cosplay, I dunno. I guess I lose all my anxieties? I mean, it's like I'm me, but this other me, someone who's more confident. I don't really do the whole 'in character' thing, but there's something freeing about hiding behind another identity like that."

"Huh. I guess I can see that. It's like drag in a way."

He laughs. "I've never really thought of myself as a drag queen, but I guess it fits."

"More of a drag superhero, I guess."

Alex grabs our attention and asks us to join him outside, he wants to make some content for his TikTok account, and wants us all to take part.

"Oh, I dunno, man. I'm a bit old for all these TikTok things, haven't got the flexibility for them these days." I joke. Though only half joke, as I definitely am not as spry as I used to be, and a lot of these moves amaze me but I cannot even fathom how to do them.

Cameron grabs me by the hand and lifts me up off the chair. "Come on, old man. I know there's more flexibility than you're letting on." I brush away the coming blush to fire back.

"Hey, who're you calling old. I can't be much older than you."

"I dunno. I'm twenty-four, how old are you?" I fail. The blush comes on. I didn't realise how much of an age gap there was between us.

"I'm, uh, I'm thirty-three. Oh my god."

Cameron laughs. "So? That's nothing! Come on, you're not dead yet."

Outside, the area is still filled with cosplayers. Many of them are congregating in big groups, making social media content in the form of photos and videos, or just drinking out on the street. It's a good thing the convention centre is so far out from the centre of London, I doubt they'd get away with it there.

As our group starts to join in, I find myself hanging back. I suddenly feel really out of place and my brain starts falling down a rabbit hole.

"Hey, what's up?" Cameron notices, and looks concerned.

"I really didn't realise you were so young, and I'm so old and I totally understand you'd not want to do anything with me, I'm so sorry if…"

"Hey," he shuts me down with a serious look. "I flirted with *you*. I asked you to my room. I don't care about this age difference, because fuck me, it's not even a big age difference. There's fourteen years between my folks…"

"Nineteen between mine." I admit.

"There you go," he says, throwing an arm around my shoulders, smiling again. "You've got a bad habit of getting in your head a bit too much, you know that." He leans in close, his lips brushing my ear. "Besides, maybe I like a Daddy."

I am not normally into being called that, it normally is an immediate turn off. But right now I feel my cock press against the inside of my jeans almost immediately.

"The fuckin' cheek." I say, as if to make sure Cameron can't tell the effect he just had on me.

We join the others and laugh and drink some more. Alex makes his videos. He's nice enough to tag me and mention my comics, as does Vince, who it turns out has almost five times the amount of followers as me. I stifle a sense of jealousy over something as daft as that.

Before too long, Cameron takes my hand again, and when I look at him, he jerks his head towards the hotel. We walk away, the group too engrossed in their games and discussions to even see us leave.

Before I know it, we're bursting through his hotel room door, our lips on each others again, rolling against the wall as we awkwardly make our way deeper into the room.

There's something primal and hot as we rush into what we want to take from each other. By the bed, I fall to my knees and yank his jeans down, my fingers brushing down his thighs. His cock springs up to face me, already hard. I want it, more than I've wanted anything it feels like, and I swallow it down to the base, feeling him hit the back of my throat and causing my eyes to water.

I hear him let out a sudden groan, the shock of it sending shivers up him as he rolls his head back. I keep sucking his cock, hard and fierce, as I open my own jeans and pull them down. When he sees my dick out and hard, Cameron tries to lift me and starts moving down to return the favour, but I stop him.

"What?" He asks, but I just give him a sultry look as I get on the bed and lay across the width of it on my back. I hang my head over the edge, looking at him upside down in my vision, his cock hovering above my chin, a glistening drop of precome dribbling from the tip. Cameron understands exactly what I want.

He bends his knees and pushes his cock past my lips, down into my throat, reaching depths we'd not explored yet. I cough briefly, before regaining my breath and start working his cock, my hands reach up and around, grabbing his ass and pulling him deeper. I want to feel him as deep inside me as I can.

All of a sudden, I feel a wet stroke down the length of my own cock, from head to balls, and I realise Cameron is leaning over me and sucking my cock now. He's working it slowly, but he's so good at it, I know I'm going to lose it sooner rather than later.

We go like this with a sense of urgency that doesn't detract from the heat of the moment, instead it intensifies it. As we keep going, I feel Cameron thrusting harder and he twitches inside my mouth. I know it's coming and if I could speak right now, I feel like I'd pray for it.

He shoots bitter come directly into my throat, and as he does so I feel myself come too as Cameron jerks me off beside his cheek. As he pulls out from me, his come somehow goes from bitter to sweet as I gasp to take in more air. A last small blast hits my chin, and I move it with my fingers to my lips as I look up at Cameron, his own face covered in me.

He drops to his knees and kisses me, slow and deep, the taste of each other intermingling.

Minutes later, cleaned up and refreshed, we rejoin the group. They didn't even notice we were gone, as we look at each other with a shared grin at what we got away with.

LONDON EXCELSICON
SUMMER 2018 DAY THREE

Saturday at Excelsicon is a whole different convention again. The sheer number of people wandering around feels like it has quadrupled today, and it dwarves the number of people I've seen at any single other comic con I've ever been to before. Hell, maybe all of them put together! The only places I'd say I've seen more is at some of the US shows, but those I've only ever seen online on Twitter or Instagram. Being right in the middle of it is a whole new experience.

I'm swamped, and again I'm really wishing I had someone else covering the table with me. Staying on top of the people coming over and checking out the table is a mission like no other, and I know I'm losing sales from folks I haven't had a chance to speak to directly. That said, it's not like the show isn't going well for me: I'm selling hand over fist, and I think I'll probably wind up sold out of most stock by the end of the day at this rate.

It's a couple hours in when I realise I made a huge mistake.

I decided to lie in a little today, and skip grabbing lunch and supplies from the nearest supermarket before heading in for the day: I figured things had been going so much better, I might treat myself to something from the convention centre's concourse again, filled as it is with interesting (if expensive) food options.

What I didn't count on was half the geek population of the UK being here today. When I tried to take a bathroom break earlier, I wound up away from table for forty-five minutes, as the crowds move sluggishly, or people stop dead right in front of you to pose for a picture. In fact, impromptu cosplay photoshoots happen left and right, making manoeuvring around the convention extra difficult, despite the wide corridor spaces.

On my way back from the toilets, I pop my head out into the concourse briefly, and see a number of the food stalls with lines running down for dozens of metres and doubling back on themselves. If I go to get any food or drink there, I think I'll probably lose another hour or more away from the table, so I have to write the whole Saturday treat off.

"I've got some biscuits left, if you'd like some?" Emily offers, between serving a constant stream of customers. They're ginger nuts, which I'm not into (well, not these kind of ginger nuts anyway), but at this point I'm so ravenous I accept this lifeline with overflowing gratitude.

Of course, the next shoe drops pretty soon after. Talking pretty much non-stop all day, I begin to find my throat closing up, and even halt mid-conversation or sales pitch as the air catches in my mouth. I desperately need a drink, some water, anything, but again, I can't lose so much time at one of the stalls, and getting out of here and heading to the supermarket now would take just as long or longer. Honestly, running this whole thing solo has never felt like such a challenge, and it leaves me feeling like I could pass out.

As an ebb in the flow settles around me, I make a desperate bid for some help. Or two, really. I pop on my phone, open Twitter and post a status update:

@ARRANWILSONCOMIX: WHOO BOY, IT IS WILD AT LONDON EXCELSICON TODAY! AND NUMPTY THAT I AM, I DIDN'T BRING ANY WATER. IF ANYONE WANTS TO SAVE ME BEFORE I PASS OUT, I'M IN ARTISTS ALLEY, TABLE 14 - IF YOU BRING ME A WATER, I WILL PAY YOU BACK AND LOVE YOU FOREVER

I then update the Grindr profile too, adding a 'send 💦' to the end of my profile info. I very quickly realise that one was a mistake when I start getting a few messages from guys at the con and in the surrounding area of London sending me dick pics and photos of them coming. I cut the addition out of that profile pretty damn fast.

"I thought I gave you more than enough of that last night, to be honest." I look up to find a smirking Magneto with a familiar face under the iconic helmet: Cameron gives me a wink that immediately brings back memories from last night and a flush of heat through my body.

"Heh. Sadly, I don't think that's going to help me out in this situation. I'm an altogether different kind of thirsty," I choke out, coughing briefly at the end.

"Fear not, mutant. I bring you hope in the darkest times, for one of the Brotherhood." Before I can question his sudden penchant for the amateur dramatic and over the top soliloquy, he pulls a bottle of water from within the recesses of his cape. Magneto was right, he has indeed saved me at my darkest hour.

After I gulp down a big swig of water and sigh with relief, I thank Cameron for yet again saving my day. "See, evidently putting that call out on grindr did help."

"Actually, I saw the tweet first. I started following you earlier and saw your cry for help. Luckily, I had a spare."

"Oh cool. Well, how much do I owe you for it?"

He pushes my hand holding my wallet away, and just smiles. "Put that away. Your money is no good here." He takes a quick glance up the aisle, then fixes me with a devilish glint in his eye. "Other things, however, very good here. Fancy coming round mine later again?"

"Why, Cameron! My body cannot be so easily bought!" It's my turn for the feigned dramatics, before I return his smile. "Sounds good to me, though. I'll be there with bells on."

"Okay. As long as I can take them right off." And with a flourish of his cape he's away, and as cool as it looks, I can't help but wish the cape wasn't there as it means I don't get to watch his perfect butt in that spandex as he walks away.

Though I guess I'll get plenty chance to see it in a lot less later.

When the show wraps up, I make a beeline for Cameron's hotel room. I don't even go back to mine first, I'm so eager to see him again and get up to who knows what. But more than that, I'm actually kind of excited to tell him about my day.

I shouldn't throw myself into this too eagerly though; I've been known to do it before. A guy shows a passing interest in me and I start thinking this is the next big love affair of life. The fact that touch is definitely my love language doesn't help, as there's been a lot of touching. But, come on: he's a random guy I met at a comic con, coming from somewhere else in the country, and I may never even see him again. I should enjoy whatever this is while it lasts.

Except I may have already jumped the gun there.

I knock on Cameron's door and wait for a response. Nothing. Oh my god, did I beat him to his own hotel room? Oh god, this looks so desperate, I should go, I should turn and head back to mine and shower, then maybe head back in an hour or so, maybe have dinner. I turn to go and too late - Cameron comes round the corner and catches me waiting outside his room.

I am mortified, he must think I'm a freak. I spend a second that feels like an eternity falling through an anxiety haze, when I catch his smile. He's smiling. At me.

"Someone's eager," he says, making a beeline for me, and when he meets me he lands a massive kiss on my lips, holding the side of my face, the momentum pushing me back into the door as his cape swings over us and his helmet drops to the ground.

"Hi." I manage to stutter out when we come up for air.

"Hi."

"I just…I wanted…I…"

"It's cool. I wanna hear all about it too. And get all those clothes off you as well." He fixes me with his eyes in an intense stare looking up past his eyebrows and right into mine. I normally hate making eye contact for any extended period of time, but I don't want to move a muscle now.

Except for the fast flurry of motions as he whips out a keycard, opens the door, I grab his helmet (not a euphemism), and we're inside his room and making out in seconds flat.

"Stop, stop, stop" he pants, pushing me back.

"What's wrong? Is this not okay? Did you change your mind?"

"What? No. Don't be silly. I just got to shower first. This get up really does not breathe, and after eight hours packed in that building…it is not good."

I honestly can't tell at all, because he looks as good as he always does, but I'm suddenly also very aware that I am not my freshest and I try to subtly take a sniff to see if I should have maybe showered too. He turns, his back to me, before he looks over his shoulder at me and says, "Little help?"

There's a zip in the fold of his lycra costume, running the length of his spine from Cameron's neck right the way down to the tight curve of his butt. I shake myself out of being hypnotised by the sight and slowly pull the zipper down, the lycra pulling apart across the taut muscles of his shoulders and back. They have a sheen to them, the sweat that must have been building after a day wrapped in skintight material and jostling with thousands of other geeks, but in this moment it looks so sexy.

As I reach the top of his buttocks, Cameron steps forward, away from me and moving to the bathroom. As he does, he pulls his arms free of the costume and slides it over the mound of his ass and then casually lets it fall to the floor, stepping out of it so smoothly I can't help but imagine that this was a practiced move. He turns into the bathroom doorway, naked but for this crazy tight thong looking thing, before pausing and looking back at me.

"Coming?"

Oh, we will be.

I wish I could say I calmly followed, but I hurtled towards the bathroom, shedding clothes as I go. By the time I catch up with him, Cameron has turned on the shower and faces me, nude, a grin on his face as he looks at the awkward mess of a man with legs tangled in his jeans and underwear still firmly on (even if they are feeling tighter than they were a few minutes ago).

"You're a little overdressed," he snickers, and he goes on his knees in front of me and helps free my ankles from my trousers. He then focuses right at my crotch, slowly reaching for the waistband of my boxer shorts before easing them down my legs until I'm as naked as he is. Freed from its cover, I feel myself rise a little and stroke his chin.

"That's better."

And that's pretty much the last thing we say for the next half hour or so, as we enter the shower and spend the time getting each other clean. We don't fuck, we don't suck, we barely kiss except for a few furtive, gentle brushes of our lips. Instead, we slowly wash the water down each others bodies. I run soap over Cameron's smooth, tight skin, while he massages it into the hair on my chest and butt. I kiss his shoulder as I stand behind him, running my hand with the suds in along the peaks and troughs of his muscled stomach and into the thicket of hair under his waist, and gently let it wash over his cock.

We giggle and laugh as we wash each others hair, the shampoo foaming up and letting us sculpt our hair into strange new shapes as the soap suds almost get in our eyes. It's childish, it's charged, it's relaxed. It's the sexiest time I've ever had that doesn't involve any actual sex.

It's bliss.

When we got out of the shower, we jumped straight into the bed. But unlike the last couple nights, we don't jump right into making our deepest, most pornographic fantasies a reality. Sure, we fooled around a bit, but it was more…playful. Fun. Literally just enjoying each other, before the exhaustion of a long and busy day finally got the better of us.

We didn't sleep either, though. We lie there, together. The sheets are on top of us, but pushed down to our waists. Our hands that are nearest each other slowly tracing lines up and down each others bodies, like we're exploring each other lazily. Sometimes he runs the back of his knuckles gently over the length of my shaft, sometimes I entwine our fingers, feeling the measure of them.

And all the while we're just…talking.

"So, mister big shot comic writer guy. Where do you see your-self in ten years time?" Cameron sighs, lying on his front, his face pressed against my shoulder as I stroke the mound of his ass with the back of my hand. I can feel his eyelashes against my skin, and it tickles in the most electrifying way.

"Oh, man, I hate that question. Honestly, I don't know where I'll be in ten years time. I'm certainly not where I wanted to be by now ten years ago."

He looks up at me, with actual interest. He kisses my shoulder before asking, "Well, where did you want to be by now?"

I normally wouldn't tell anyone this, I just hold it inside. But Cameron just…relaxes me.

"Well, I been doing these comics for, what, nearly ten years now? If we round up, like," I add, noting the arched eyebrow confronting me. "But I'm still just self-publishing. Sure, I got it on a platform that gets it all around the world, and there's people reading my work on, as near as I can tell, every continent, but I've still never had a single publisher ask me to pitch or show any interest.

"I know it may sound dumb, but I thought I'd be writing *X-Men* by now, or some shit. I dunno. Not like, *Uncanny* or *Adjective-less*, like, but maybe a mini or one of the smaller books. And I see these guys getting these gigs, these folks who interned at Marvel or DC or Image, and they're twenty-five and still full of fresh ideas and energy and I can just feel it all slipping away. Like maybe I missed my time, but I'd never had a chance."

"Come on, Arran, you're being silly. Thirty-three isn't old. You're still young too." He scoffs as he picks the sheets back up over us, but keeps his hand under them so he can stroke my belly.

"I know, like, on the surface of it, I know that. But when I was a kid, I had this, like, roadmap. By thirty, I'd be working at Marvel, I'd have travelled all over America, I'd have a nice house or flat, maybe in London or Cardiff or Manchester.

"I'd have a boyfriend, who adored me and I adored him and we'd be getting a cat."

"Ah, so you're a cat person then?"

"Yeah, why? You not?"

"I like cats. They don't like me. Don't know why. I have a pet dog at home with my parents, but my flat doesn't allow pets, so..."

"That sucks."

"Yeah. But also, that's life, I guess? And your thing...I get it. I mean, when I was a kid, I thought my life would go one way too, but when we're kids we don't know how the world works. Not to mention it keeps changing out from under us. Our parents were getting mortgages and getting married in their early twenties, but these days, getting on the property ladder is next to impossible for anyone, even stable married couples in their thirties."

He leans over me, looking me square in the face with the most serious expression I've seen all weekend. "Trust me, I'm an accountant. I know these things." And then he blows a raspberry on my nipple.

"Argh, you bloody freak." I laugh at him.

"The point is, I think you're being unfair on yourself. You can't measure your life based on the dreams you had before you had any experience. Before you made your comics, did you even know anything about the industry you were getting into, or is that something you learned as you got into it?"

I consider for a brief moment, "The latter."

"Exactly. Your dreams can't hope to match up to reality when you don't really know how to tailor them to fit. Look at what you do have: you have this great comic that people love, and that means a lot to them too. You have fans. You are building a reputation. You're really kind and sweet, and it's getting more people into your stuff. You also have a handsome young man with a totally bomb ass butt laying in bed next to you who thinks you're hecka hot. You may not be where you thought you were going to be, but where you are seems pretty great too, right?"

"I can't argue with that," I admit, "but come on, you've only known me for a couple days. How can you say you know so much about me already."

He rolls onto his back and looks at the ceiling, as the lights through the curtains dance over us. "Because last night you were complimentary to Alex and raved about his cosplay, even though he's clearly got a lot to learn. You didn't do it because you wanted something from him, you didn't even lie really, you genuinely made him believe he was doing good and was going to do better no matter what."

He turns to look at me. "That's how I know you're a good guy, Arran. Because you just are. And it's refreshing."

I feel myself get glassy eyed, but I'm not going to have a breakdown in bed with a hottie. I look up to the ceiling. "Thanks, man. I can kind of get into my head sometimes, and get low on myself and everything. Thanks for pulling me out of there."

"That happen a lot?"

I sigh. "More often than I'd like, yeah. I dunno, being a writer can be pretty lonely at times. Not many live around me, so I always feel like I'm doing it by myself. It's easy to get a little... *isolated*."

Cameron puts a hand on my cheek and turns my head towards him again, and kisses me gently on the lips. "You're not alone right now." I feel the words so strongly it's like they resonate in my heart as well as my head, and I pull him in and kiss him more intensely.

He swings a leg over me and sits up, reaching a hand behind and guides me inside.

We don't stop until we're both slick with sweat and panting and thoroughly here in the now.

Lying under the sheets, streetlights fall across us from the crack in the curtains, as his arms are wrapped around me, my back against his chest.

"So what are you doing after the show tomorrow?"

"Leaving. Sorry. My friend is giving me a lift back to Swansea. I'll be going straight from the show."

We lie there in silence for a minute. I can't see him, but I wonder if he's frowning as much as I am.

"Shame. I was going to say, maybe we should get dinner. It's a Bank Holiday Monday so I booked the extra night in the hotel to have a more chill trip back down then."

"Well, how about next time? What's your next show?" Please be where I'm going, please be where I'm going.

"I don't really know yet. How about you?"

"Hm, I got a small little thing in Swansea in July, then Bristol in August. Speech Balloon in November is my next big, big show though, I guess."

"I've never gone there. Heard good things, but someone said there's not so much cosplay?"

"There's some, but yeah, not as much, I guess."

We lie there in the dark.

"I have some friends in Bristol. I'll have to pay them a visit."

Yes!

LONDON EXCELSICON
SUMMER 2018 DAY FOUR

Sunday at Excelsicon is a lot quieter. Don't get me wrong, it's still busier than Thursday, but it's nothing compared to yesterday. But it's still a Bank Holiday tomorrow, so people have a long weekend to have fun and are enjoying the last day of the show.

The show is also free to kids under twelve today, so there's a lot more families around. It's meant having to explain whether the comic is suitable for kids a lot more today, and having to weigh it up based on the age of the kid. My comic isn't mature content by any length of the imagination, but I guess really young kids won't get it much too.

Also, I have to tentatively let the parents know that the book contains LGBTQ+ content. I'm always a little scared that maybe someone will throw the book down in disgust when I mention that, but that actually doesn't happen at all. In fact, if anything, as soon as I mention it, a lot of parents get more excited, either for their kid or someone else they know. I guess comic cons don't attract too many bigots and 'phobes, which is nice.

Quieter or not, it's still busy enough that I'm not bored, and I'm doing okay.

Cameron even swung by again. This time by himself, and he

wasn't in any kind of cosplay. Instead, he's wearing a simple white t-shirt, tight across his torso, with a loose shirt over the top. Skinny jeans cling to his legs. And his butt. His pink curls bounce at the top of head, over his glasses and a beaming smile.

"Going well today?"

"Yeah, it's been a great weekend!" I'm not lying. This might be the best show I've ever had in the end. And also, "And, uh, you've actually been a big part of that, Cameron."

"Awww, you'll make me blush." He says it with a sly tone and wicked smile, but he actually does flush. I love that I did that.

He chatted with me for about half hour, before moving on, and I'm a little surprised that I'm already wondering if I'm going to ever see or hear from him again. And how much I'm hoping I do.

I'm so wrapped up in stupid, teenage-style feels that I almost ignore some people at my table, so I shake it off and throw myself into the comic con fully for the rest of the day.

Before long, things start drawing to a close. In the last two hours, I barely see a single person at my table. Some folks start breaking down their tables already, even though the convention centre won't let them bring any trollies or anything in until after the show is over. I don't have much, so I figure I'll wait until the end.

When it does finally wind down, a voice blares out over the tannoy letting us all know and wishing us a safe journey home. Weird little quirk, everyone behind their tables applauds, like they're congratulating the organisers, other exhibitors, or themselves for just making it through the whole thing.

"Hey, how did the con go for you?"

I look up from packing books into boxes to see Sarah, my friend who's giving me a lift home.

"Yeah, it's been great, thanks! I was a little nervous at first, but honestly, it's been the best show I've ever done." And I met a gorgeous guy who for some reason wanted to spend naked time with me and made me so goddamn horny all weekend I felt like a dumb hormonal kid again, but I figure I'll keep that to myself. "How about you?"

"Oh, yeah, pretty good, thanks. It was a little crazy yesterday, I could have done with a break at one point, but there was no getting out of here." She dances foot to foot, a medium suitcase next to her and a slightly exhausted look. Though that's a look that's going around today.

"How were your friends?" The reason I hadn't spent much time with Sarah during the weekend, despite her very kindly giving me a lift home, was she was actually staying with some friends in London. She hadn't seen them in a while, so doubled up this weekend as business but also to catch up with old buddies.

"Oh, we had a wicked time. They took me to this amazing burger place in SoHo, and then we hit G-A-Y for a bit before finding somewhere quieter. I haven't had a night like that since uni!"

I load up my own suitcase, and we start making moves down to the underground car park. We're not the only ones, so we have to queue for an elevator, but we use the wait to catch up on each others weekend. Sounds like Sarah had a weekend of business and pleasure too, though maybe not quite the same as mine (though as far as she knows, I just made a bunch of new friends in the cosplay community, which isn't a lie, just not a whole truth I guess).

When we finally get on the road, we sit in comfortable silence, Sarah focused on the road while I take a nap. I'm almost dropped off into slumberland when I feel the familiar gentle buzz of my phone in my lap. It's a notification from Grindr.

hey, remember to follow me on instagram, okay.

Lol, first thing I do when I get back to Wales

You're waiting until you cross the bridge?
Savage.

I figured, you being you, you might be waiting for
my consent to start following my insta, so here I
am, consenting hard

Okay, you know me far too much already lol. I
was, I didn't wanna seem like a stalker

Lol, you spent a whole weekend face first in my
butt and you still want consent to follow a
cosplay account. You're so weird

Oh my god, why are you like this?!

I wanted the pleasure of imagining how you just
squirmed when you read that :P

Well, you succeeded

And in my defence, it's a damn good butt

Damn right

I immediately follow the instagram link in his Grindr profile and hit follow.

IN BETWEEN DAYS...

"So how many more issues until the end of the series?"

Gertrude "Gertie" Milton is the artist on *The surREALS*, and sometime after getting back from London she came down to discuss the series plans. It's a welcome visit, as I haven't seen Gertie much since she started her transition. I know she has a great support network at home in Cambridge, but I also know how lonely comics making can be, so it's good to see her in person. I'm relieved that she's doing great, and seems really happy.

For my own part, it's only been a couple weeks, but the high of London is already wearing off. I know I should just focus on the good, but I want to keep moving forward and I'm not anywhere near where I want to be, so there I was getting down on myself again. Gertie's visit couldn't come at a better time.

"Well, after issue four, there's two more issues to this story arc. Then, I have other stories I want to tell with them, but obviously I'm not gonna hold you to those." Oh wait! "Not that I'm holding you to do any more! Obviously, only if you want to."

"You're good, dude. I'll finish the series with you." She smiles, knowing how much I probably just went down an anxiety hole in seconds flat. "So, how was London?"

"Oh, it was great! The sales were *crazy*, I've never shifted so many books at a single show before."

"People seemed into it?"

"Yeah. I actually had a lot of great feedback and praise, which was nice. Heck, one of Cameron's friends acted like I was Chris Claremont or something."

"Cameron?" Shit. I hadn't told anyone about Cameron. He's been pretty much just my secret.

"Uh, yeah…" Fuck it. "Okay, I met someone while I was there. And we had a lot of fun. A lot."

"Oh my god, only you could wind up hooking up at comic con, Arran. How did you meet him?"

"Well, Grindr. Obvs. But he was there cosplaying. He's really awesome at it."

Gertie looks at me with a mixture of shock and amusement. "You fucked a cosplayer? Arran!"

"Hey…he fucked me too." I sheepishly grin.

"You know that's not what I mean. Just be careful, you don't want it to turn out you smashed a crazy fan who becomes obsessed."

"It's not like that," I'm pretty positive it's not anyway. "We spoke on Grindr before we even realised that we were both at the show." Kind of. "And he'd never read my comics until that weekend, actually."

Gertie eyes me with concern. "Just don't make a habit of it. You don't want to get cancelled because you're nailing cosplayers left and right."

Rolling my eyes, I feel myself get flustered. "Again, it's not like that. I'm not going out hunting down cosplayers at the show. I just happened to hook up and get along with this one. And Cameron's really cool, actually. He's sweet, and funny, and stupidly hot. It was just two adults getting a little extra fun at the show."

"Oh my god, you really like him don't you?" She smiles at me, and I feel my face get even redder.

Because I do like him, I guess. We've spoken nearly every day since London on Instagram, and he's really helped me with the negativity in my head. And yeah, there's been other stuff too. "Yeah, I guess I do. I mean, obviously, nothing can ever come of it. I'm too focused on this, and we don't live anywhere near each other. I'm really not into the long-distance thing. But he's a nice guy, and I at least made a new friend. With benefits."

"You know, distance doesn't have to stop you. It didn't stop me with Emma." Emma is Gertie's girlfriend, who started dating her after meeting her at one of our early comic cons, and prior to her transition. They've made the distance work until Emma moved over to Cambridge with her and stood by her through it all. She's honestly amazing people.

"Yeah, I guess. I just don't know. Juggling this career is a lot of work as it is. I don't know if I have it in me to pursue adding this kind of emotional work on top."

Gertie pulls a face and sighs, before we move things back to the comic and discussing the next issue.

Instagram buzzes at me.

Hey, how you doing?

I'm feeling awful. In bed, full of cold. I need something to cheer me up.

Send noods etc etc

I don't see how even my sexiest pics can cure you of a cold lol

Dopamine. Serotonin. Adrenalin. Take your pick, but it will help flush this out of me

It'll definitely flush something somewhere in you :P

But who am I to question your advanced medical knowledge. Must come with age.

Oi

A photo of a steaming bowl of ramen arrives.

Haha, very funny

(Though they do look really good rn tbh)

See. Just leave it to Doctor Cameron. I know how to make you better

Seriously though, wish I was there to bring you chicken soup and help you, man

But in the meantime

Cameron standing with a domino mask on. With only a domino mask on.

That's the stuff

I lie in bed scrolling through twitter, obsessively thinking how I've clearly forgotten to do something important, but not able to remember what it even is. Twitter definitely isn't what I've forgotten. I've been on it most of the day. But here I am, scrolling so much I'm starting to see the same posts over and over again.

The hardest part of being a comic writer (or I guess a creative of any kind, really) is you have to also be your own brand manager and PR team all the time. At least when you're making independent, self-published stuff. And the thing is, that doesn't come naturally to me, or most of us to be entirely honest.

I never wanted to get into marketing, it feels like sales, a job I left behind a while ago and never really cared for how it made me feel anyway. I don't know what are the best times to post or on which social media platform and when. Most of the time I'm just blindly throwing random tweets and instagram posts out in the hope that they'll be useful and get some extra sales.

I tend to get lost in a cycle of doing this, and feeling like I'm missing something hugely important, whenever I'm feeling down. So here I am.

It's been a few quiet weeks now on my online store, and I haven't had any cons now since Excelsicon a couple months back. Sure, the comics latest issue went up on Comixpedia, and they did a sale on the first issue too. I figure that will boost sales a bit, but I don't know exact figures. But it just feels too quiet. These in-between days, when my scripts are in to Gertie, and I don't have much to do besides market myself - I just hate them. I hate having to sell myself.

But it's the nature of the beast.

I find myself rolling over on my bed and distracting myself by checking in on Cameron's instagram again. He's got a few new updates: a progress shot of a new cosplay he's 3D printing, armour plates that I haven't quite worked out what they're going to be part of yet, but he seems happy with them. A shot of him next to a standee for the latest Marvel film (he obviously loved it). And a new spandex costume shot, with him striking a superheroic crouched pose, looking fiercely at the camera. The material hugs his muscles and it makes him look intensely strong and badass.

As if he knew I was checking him out again (I didn't like anything, I swear he's just psychic for it), Cameron slides into my DMs on Instagram.

Hey mister! How you doing today?

Ugh, not great

What's up?

Just feeling like I'm going nowhere again. I'm struggling to think of new ways to get new audience for the book, and it just all feels so hard

Maybe I'm not cut out for this

Dude.

You have so many people who love your work.
I've read it, it's good stuff

And I'm not just saying that because I think your
butt looks great

Lol, thanks (on both counts)

But I dunno…if it was so good, wouldn't I be
getting some attention from publishers by now?
I'm just feeling like people say nice things but I
question whether they mean them

There's a pause where Cameron doesn't reply. I switch out of the app and stare at twitter again, scrolling and scrolling through doom post after doom post, and I don't know what to do about anything. My work, my marketing, myself, the world. Everything is just feeling too big.

I stare at the ceiling, a dense feeling in my head: not a headache, not pain, just…full. Like there's too much in there and it's all crowding around and nothing can get out properly.

A buzz as my phone vibrates on the duvet next to my head.

Have you been outside at all today? Spoken to
anyone?

No. Nowhere to go.

But I have spoken to people today

Online doesn't count

No fair. It totally counts. Online people are
people too, you know :P

You're deflecting. I'm calling you.

We'd swapped numbers a while back. Made it easier to send each other certain videos. Turns out, even separated by hundreds of miles, we're still horny as fuck for each other.

My phone starts ringing. I look at it for a second wondering if I should answer. I kind of hate taking phone calls. All those years in a call centre I reckon. But I haven't heard his voice (bar his moans off camera in some of those videos. They're really good videos) in months, and I really want to.

"Hey" I say, unmoved from the bed.

"Hey yourself. Tough love time, mister. I'm not cool with you vegging in the dark in your room."

"How do you know I'm in the dark? I could have my lights on."

"Do you?"

I look around as if someone can see me, but the answer is obvious. "Okay, I'm in the dark. But I don't need the lights on. The way sales are going lately, I can't afford to have them on."

"Stop being melodramatic." Cameron chastises me, but I swear I almost hear the hint of a smile flash across his face. "Such a drama queen."

I lie there for a second, and we just listen to each other breathing, like we both don't know what to say next. It's not awkward or uncomfortable, but for some reason I feel the need to apologise.

"Sorry for being such a downer."

"Hey, don't you apologise. You're allowed to feel down. I just don't think your brain is being very good to you, and you don't need to feel down.

"Look, maybe this isn't my place, and you can tell me to fuck off -"

"I'd never tell you to fuck off," I interject, because it's true.

"-but have you ever thought that maybe you have depression?"

I'm taken aback a little by the statement. Not offended, even though it sounds like an accusation, but thankfully the logical part of my brain is louder today so I don't let it feel that way. Nothing to be ashamed of after all. "It's in my family, but I never really presented that way. I could never say I felt anywhere near as bad as my cousin and mum. I'm just low."

"Maybe you're burned out. Trying too hard and not lying back and enjoying where you are enough."

"I'm alone in my bedroom on a Saturday night, in a tiny flat I can barely afford, and my career feels like it's going nowhere. What's there to enjoy about right here?"

"I dunno," he mumbles. "Maybe the fact you're talking to someone who cares about you and likes you. Who thinks you're insanely hot and sweet. And your career is moving, even if it feels slow to you."

I wave of guilt washes over me. He's right - I am spending time, albeit long distance, with someone I like being around. But then that's just it. I like being around him, and he isn't here right now.

"I wish you were here right now." I tell him, because it's true.

"I do too. If only to hug you and then smack some sense into you."

"Kinky."

"Oi. We'll get to that. But right now, I want you to do something for me."

"Oh yeah?" I breathe luridly, a grin spreading on my face.

"Hey, stop trying to distract me."

"Sorry." I sigh, rolling over onto my side. "I probably shouldn't be pushing things that way, anyway. It's kinda manipulative. Sorry. It's no excuse, I'm just feeling down and I guess I do need company. But I shouldn't be forcing-"

"Whoa, now, hold up. You're not *forcing* anything. I like doing that stuff with you, I am consenting and desire it, and I know you do too."

"Of course. I just-"

"No, no. Here's the thing. You always seem so ready to believe this stuff about yourself, when it's just not there. That you've somehow taken advantage of my attraction to you, or your work is failing when it really isn't.

"I think you know that you're a good person, and I think on some level you know that you're doing good stuff. I just think that maybe you don't like yourself very much, for whatever reason, 'cause it makes no sense to me. I think you need to learn to like yourself too, and maybe you won't find yourself getting dragged down into one of these self-pity holes so often."

I'm sitting on the bed now, knees up to my chest with one arm wrapped around them, fidgeting with the edge of a hole in my jeans. I'm hit with the clarity of what Cameron said…maybe I have been being cruel to myself. Not liking who I am for whatever reason. I have to work that out. "You're right. Maybe it *is* depression. Maybe it's something else. But I guess maybe I haven't been the nicest to myself."

"I'm not saying that it isn't hard. What you're trying to do, with no backing or support, hell, it must be so hard. And you have to do so much more than just write your stories, I can't imagine having to juggle it all like that. But you shouldn't take that difficulty and turn it into a way to attack yourself. It'll just make you feel bad, and you don't deserve that."

I breathe down the phone and let the beat pass between us, Cam waiting for a response. It doesn't push me, doesn't feel like he's pushing me to respond, just waiting for me to catch up. I wipe at my eyes.

"Yeah. Thanks, Cam. I think this helps. You saw something I guess I didn't see myself."

"'Cam'? We're doing cutesy shortened names now, huh? Wait, would that make you Ron?"

A sharp intake of breathe passes through my teeth. "Don't you dare."

Cam laughs, and it sounds amazing. "Well, anyway. You probably spend too much time online too. Go outside, touch some grass or whatever. It will help."

"Okay, I will."

"But before you go," Cam whispers down the phone, as I hear him shifting in his seat. "Let me help you feel even better."

My zip is down before I can even say, "Okay."

When is your next con now?

Swansea. In three weeks.

You coming?

Wish I could be there, but I have a conference with work.

Sadly, I will not be wearing lycra there

Well, at least, nothing visible :P

Okay, you are going to have to show me

Of course ;)

The day of Swansea Comic Con comes around, and I'm just about to head out the door, boxes of comics strapped onto my trolley and a bag with everything else in it, when my phone beeps.

Good luck today. You're gonna smash it!

Despite all the bags and boxes weighing me down, I smile.

SWANSEA COMIC CON 2018
DAY ONE

Lugging the stuff over to the convention hall, being held in the relatively small room of the Swansea Council Hall, was harder than I thought it'd be. Sure, I didn't bring much, but this July has been crazy hot, and the sun even at 9am felt like it was beating down on me as I wheeled several boxes on a trolley over to the building.

Once there, set up was easy, so I had enough time to run to Costa and grab an iced coffee and settle in ready for the day ahead. Sarah is actually tabling next to me, and arrived a little later seen as she had to drive over from Cardiff. She's still setting up, so I leave her to it while I try and cool off and make sure I'm ready and presentable for the day ahead. After all, no one's going to want to approach a sweaty, hassled looking man, are they.

I sit and open my change box, making sure the money is separated into different sections of the tray, and notes are in ascending order of value. Most folks probably don't have to do this, but for me I find it helps me find the right change faster, and if it wasn't in its right place it'd make me feel indescribably anxious for some bizarre reason.

Next, I open my small notebook, noting the date and event name at the top, then in the left hand column, I list all the issues and items I have on sale here. I have three issues of *The surREALS* and a couple pins. I brought a few prints of the series too, but I'm not really expecting them to move. I found that prints are great sellers…if they're of well-known, established characters from Marvel or DC or something. Otherwise, it doesn't matter how good the art is, if people don't know the characters they won't really be interested. It's a shame, but it is what it is, I guess.

"Hey, is your friend coming for the show?" Sarah looks over to me with a smile, her blue eyes glinting knowingly past her thick red framed spectacles.

"Friend? Who do you mean?" I'm only half playing dumb here, because if she does mean Cam, I'm kind of surprised. We didn't talk much about him after London did we?

"Come on, you know. The cosplayer. The one you…" she looks around, as if about to share in some great conspiracy, before leaning in towards me and whispering, "The one you hooked up with."

My eyes almost bulge out of my head. "How do you know about him?"

She straightens up and continues fussing with her table, a smirk forming at the corners of her mouth. "You are not as subtle as you think, you know. I saw how much you messaged him on Grindr and Instagram on the drive home from Excelsicon."

"You were driving! You should have had your eyes on the road!"

"I couldn't help it. That glaring grin on your face as you were messaging each other was more distracting than any oncoming headlights."

I groan and put my head in my hands. "Ugh, stop. And no, he isn't coming," I whine. With a sigh, I pick up the latte to take another sip as I wonder how his day is going, if it's even started. "He's got another thing this weekend, with his day job. A conference for accountants."

"He's a spicy accountant? I, err, noticed some of the photos. Wait, spicy accountants have cons too?"

"No!" I manage to choke out past my latte, as it abruptly and dangerously bubbles in the cup with the blowback. "No, no, regular accountant. Though, now I'm wondering if spicy accountants do have a con too. What would that be like?"

"Demonstrations of ideal camera and lighting set ups in the bedroom? Panels about marketing and anal bleach?" Sarah ponders as she sidles into her seat on our 'exhibitor side' of the tables.

We both sit there for a moment contemplating how an Only-Fans convention might look, as I casually suck on the straw of my latte. Rich, one of the SCC organisers, comes over then and wishes us a good morning.

"Ready for the day?" He booms at us, and I wonder how someone has this much energy already, especially seen as he had to have been up long before us to get this place set up.

"Yeah, all good. Thanks for inviting me, by the way. I appreciate it." I stand so we're eye level, as I watch him take off his glasses to clean them on his bright pink convention shirt, the logo that emblazoned all the posters and flyers also printed on it. "Expecting a big crowd today?"

"We sold a whole bunch of tickets, yeah, so hopefully should be good. Though the family day tomorrow will probably be busier."

"You think?" Sarah sounds surprised, and I don't blame her: Sunday's are pretty universally slow at any con.

"Yeah, we tend to find a lot more people come in on a Sunday, what with the free entry for kids. The family zone makes for an easy activity for them, I guess. Saturday tends to be more hard-core geeks and fans, but we've been growing. It's so nice to have you both here for this one. Next year should be even bigger again."

He fills us in a bit more on the history of this convention, and hints at some of the plans: a new venue is opening up next year, so we're expecting much bigger crowds with the bigger capacity, apparently. It makes sense. While this venue is nice, and it makes for a chilled location, it is tiny in comparison to Excelsicon. Part of me, the ugly part that speaks too loudly in my head sometimes, can't help but think this will be a complete washout of a show for me, after the huge, busy London show.

But the truth is, smaller shows is how I started. How any of us start, to be honest. We do these small, local gigs that have minimal or no set up, travel or accommodation costs. Sure, they're in the lobby of a hotel, or community building of some kind, and you have barely two dozen exhibitors, but it's something to build on.

I'd been doing this for five years before Excelsicon. I'd gone there once as a punter early on, and I immediately knew it was too big for me then. But now, as the series has grown, as more people are aware of it, and with a couple other small one shot comics behind me, it was worth it.

And yeah, Cameron being there definitely helped make it worth it too, but for wholly other reasons.

But these smaller shows are still worthwhile, especially this one. It's pretty much on my doorstep, the costs of doing it are absolutely negligible. I could sell one book here and technically I'd be in profit (though, gods of comics, please let me sell more than one book). And I know that sounds pretty mercenary, and not what some people think is in a creatives head, but honestly, if a creative wants to make a go of it as a career, as they make their bread and butter? It's kind of how you have to think.

Sure, for me, the main reason of making the comics is because I love them. I have loved this medium since I was small, grabbing copies of *Sonic the Comic* at the newsagents and devouring all the stories inside within an hour. I read them more voraciously than I ever did books, and heck, it helped me in school too, because I learned words like 'voraciously'. In a way, comics were the first downtrodden minority identity I was part of. No one considered them real literature, no one thought they were intelligent, these were just things for kids etc. But there I was, doing well in school because I'm using words I picked up in an issue of *X-Men*, or understanding complex social issues because there was an analogy or they were outright included in *Superman*.

I think it was the art for me, of course. Having that amazing, colourful, bombastic artwork to look at as I progressed through the story helped keep my attention hooked, and pushed me to keep going. I liked reading books too, sure, but without the pictures, I guess I found it harder. I guess I just needed something to hold my attention better, as no matter how much I enjoyed a book, I read it slower than I did a comic (though if I was really enjoying a story, which was generally if it was fantasy or sci-fi, then I read that a lot faster too).

So yeah, I make comics because I love them. And I write about the things I do, and include the characters and identities I do, because I didn't see them in the comics I love, so I figured I'd better do them. It just made sense to me.

I guess it started as a hobby, and a laugh, but then I realised how much I loved doing it as well, and so I started to get more serious. Make sure I was tracking sales figures, making sure I had a separate account for money made on the comics side of things, doing my tax return as self-employed. Treating it not just as something I loved, but as my business.

I still love it. I do. But I won't lie, the lustre has worn away a bit. Now, nine times out of ten I'm worried if I'm doing the right thing, or I'm freaking out about the money, especially as juggling finances for making new books while keeping a roof over my head has proved…challenging. Which is why we have to be a little mercenary about comic cons too. Will this one make me enough money? What should I bring? What costs should I keep in mind first? Should I skip it?

It all goes into the decision process now past a simple 'this should be fun! I can't wait to see the cosplay!'

We're broken out of our chat when one of Rich's volunteers walks into the hall and yells to get everyones attention, letting us know the doors will now be opening. Rich wishes us luck and bids a hasty goodbye, while me and Sarah made sure we're ready and looking good. I grab the shiny, multicoloured poncho made out of a rainbow of sequins and throw it over my shoulders. Sarah lets out a snort.

"What is that?"

"It's something Cam suggested, kinda, actually. A lot of *surREALS* audience comes from the LGBTQ+ community, so why not make it obvious. Advertise my presence more, that kind of thing."

"Well, it certainly does that," she grins. "You look fabulous."

"Honey, I know." I retort, flicking back my hair and giving her my best sassy hips.

And with that, the crowds start coming in.

Don't get me wrong, it's no Excelsicon. I can still see through the crowds, but the initial rush to get in is always a nice cluster. And again, while the cosplay maybe doesn't quite meet the standards of a big show like Excelsicon, there's some genuinely impressive looks being served.

And you know what, the numbers may not be anything in comparison too, but it's going alright. People seem very enthusiastic and happy, and they're checking out the book. Sarah's doing well too, her series about an anthropomorphic bakery drama really drawing crowds. In fact, oddly, our crowds seem to be quite well matched, and often people who checked out her work are moving onto mine, and vice versa. I guess the content doesn't need to be similar, so much as the vibe, and we both have the inclusive vibe going for us.

In fact, I have had so many people compliment me on my look, and tell me they had to come and speak to me when they saw the sparkles. I guess Cam was right. I figure I'll tell him when I get a free moment.

Things start to wind down around lunch time, most people having successfully done a couple laps of the hall, now they're either shopping or heading out for some food before (hopefully) coming back. Cosplayers are standing outside in the sun, using the better natural lighting to take photos for their social media and generally just enjoying themselves.

I settle down back on my chair and fish out the sandwich I picked up at Tesco from my bag, and whip out my phone. I'm delighted as soon as I see the screen, as among my notifications, I see a DM from Cam.

How's it going?

Really well actually! Hey, I meant to let you know, your sequins plan? A roaring success! So many people stopped by because they couldn't take their eyes off me!

Imagine how many more would be there if you were just naked :P

blush I'm not sure that would have the same effect.

Someone's feeling frisky.

Agh, I'm just pent up

This conference is just so dull. Most of the folks here are just so rattled by my hair, I can't imagine what they'd do if I showed up in costume

I can't tell if it's the pink tips or the fact my roots are showing. I really should redo it

Wait, your hair won't be pink anymore?

...you do realise pink is not my natural colour, right?

Noooo, I figured you were some weird, sexy mutant, and this was just the phenotypic expression of your frightening and awesome mutant sex powers

….you have have been reading way too many comics

No such thing

I know, but still. Not decided what colour to go, maybe you can help me choose? What's your fave colour?

Mine? Green. Reminds me of home

Aw, that's sweet. But green is so not my colour, so we'll see.

I munch on my sandwich for a bit, and help a customer find the latest issue of *surREALS* (they picked up the first two at Bristol a year ago apparently, and when they say that a vague recollection of the face comes to mind. I think they had a beard then?). We talk for a little bit about the new issue and when I hope to have it out, before they move on and I refocus on my sandwich, and new notifications from Cam.

What's the cosplay like?

…

Sorry, customer. Yeah, it's pretty good! A lot of Spider-Men and Deadpools, I guess they're easier to start, but a couple really look the part.

You mean they have Parker Butt ;)

NO. (I mean, they do) but I mean they just look movie quality, I guess. High end. I'm not ALWAYS looking at the booty you know

Unless it's mine

Unless it's yours :P

Well, any cosplay cuties there?

You realise I don't make a habit of hooking up with cosplayers, right? You're an exception that proves the rule

Awww, I'm special <3

Well, any cuties at all? Maybe you'll have a mid-con party tonight?

I reiterate: someone is feeling frisky

And no, I don't think so

You know you can hook up with other people, right. Like, you know we're not exclusive or anything right?

LOL I know! My god, I'm not some fresh twink hitting the scene for the first time. I know we were just some fun

Well, hopefully a bit more than that

I flush, and quickly look around, partly to make sure no one can see me getting flustered, and partly to make sure I'm not about to be interrupted.

Well, yeah…more than just fun. I like you. We're friends. Friends who do stuff.

Omg I thought you just said you weren't some new young thing :P you sound like a teenager. 'Do stuff'

We're friends who fuck each others butts

OMG that's just crass (but yes :P)

So, anyone gonna smash you tonight? Some balding, grey accountant daddy ready to…

…I was trying to think of a sexy accountancy pun, but then realised I know nothing about accountancy

Thank god. And ew, no. well, yes. there's this one guy here, tattoos visible through his shirt, trying to play his edginess more down low than me I guess.

But I'm thinking I'm gonna smash him actually :P

Nice. Tell me all about it tomorrow?

Of course

Okay, well, I better get on with the show. Don't want to miss a sale. Or accidentally pop a boner.

HA! Nice to know I still have that effect, even from all the way over here

Always

Good luck with the show!

Good luck with the man!

;D

The rest of the show goes off without either a hitch, or a highlight either. Not a bad thing, it was just steady and low key, but I make a good amount of sales. What's more energising though is the positivity. It's just what I needed, and I find myself making notes in my ideas book throughout the day too.

The fog in my head feels entirely lifted, and as the show comes to a close, it's great to feel enthusiastic about what I do again. I wish I could feel this way all the time.

"Coming to the pub?" Sarah smiles as he shoulders her backpack. Her friend, Rhian, has joined her. She's crashing at her's for the night, saving Sarah the drive back tonight and tomorrow morning, which means we can actually catch up post-con too.

"Sure! Let me just stash the money box, and I'm good to go."

As I stuff the money box, portable card payment device and note books in my bag, I feel the familiar vibration in my leg. I see a new message from Cam.

> Operation: Punk Rider is a go!

I grin before it quickly turns into a brief frown. I'm happy he's having fun, and I'm kinda excited to hear all about it (and I mean ALL about it) but...

I also feel a little sadness. Just this tiny little pang, like when an ice cube grazes your tooth and you get a flash of sensation that goes as quickly as it came.

I shake it off and head out into the warm summer night with the girls.

SWANSEA COMIC CON 2018
DAY TWO

My head rests against the table. I swear this happens at too many comic cons: we all go out on the first night, celebrating or commiserating the day, and sure we'll be sensible for tomorrow. Only for a couple drinks to turn into a bunch of shots, and then some karaoke and then some chilled drink and conversation at one of the local creators' houses or the hotel bar.

Needless to say, the paracetamol isn't working fast enough.

"Morning!"

I flinch as something softly thuds onto the table. Tearing my eyelids open, I look up to see a beaming Sarah bearing a godsend of a gift: piping hot coffee.

"You're an angel."

"Ta muchly." She sips her own as she settles in behind her table. "Went a bit all out last night, huh?"

"It couldn't be helped. I hadn't seen Brian since last Bristol Comic Con, and we wound up chatting all night. Unfortunately, chatting with Brian until 3am also involves whiskey."

"I shall endeavour not to be smug about my sobriety and thus cool head today." I pull a mocking face of gratefulness as she smiles at me. "So, think it's going to be busy today like Rich said?"

"Oh god, I actually kinda hope not. I don't know if I can take a bunch of screaming, crying kids today." I put the disposable coffee cup to my lips and pray for life.

"Oh, come on, it won't be that bad. Hopefully, they'll be too happy for tears anyway. Everyone loves comics now!"

True. In the last decade especially, it seems like everyone now loves comics. Or more specifically, comic book characters. Though this is mainly in movies and TV, and hasn't exactly circled back to the comics themselves.

Still, it's a better state of affairs than it used to be, I guess. Even if comics sometimes feel harder to come across than they used to, thanks to a rampant monopolisation and narrowing the market of where to find them. Gone are the days you can pick up a cheeky US Marvel or DC issue in the local newsagents…then again, gone are newsagents to be honest. Digital markets are helping though.

It was a godsend when Comixpedia opened up to accept independent and self-published titles on their platform. It's certainly gone a long way to getting *The surREALS* as big of an audience as it has. Outside of sales at comic cons (where I still make the most money), the monthly royalties I get from Comixpedia are the second largest source of income from the books. Sales through my own webstore are trickling at best, and when Brexit comes into play, I can't imagine it will get much better.

The doors open and the crowds start to trickle in. It's not the mad rush of yesterday, but it's steady, and constant, and there's a lot more families too, as predicted.

Sarah's book does a bit better today, it's a bit more accessible to younger readers. *The surREALS* skews a little more teen and up, I guess. I always feel a little bad about not having something more All Ages and appealing to younger kids, but I honestly don't feel like I know how to write for them. I was a mess as a kid, jumping from one obsession to the next, so I don't think I could ever hope to know what will grab a child's attention and keep it there.

After a few quiet browsers and as the coffee starts to make me feel more of a human being, I feel the vibration of my phone on the table, where it sits next to my card reader. It's Cam.

Okay, so last night was a success

Yeah? Got your end away then?

Ha, you could say that. Let's just say, I feel sorry for the people staying in the hotel room next to him

Nice.

…you okay?

Yeah, yeah. Just hungover. Con's started and I guess I'm just trying to stay upright lol

We don't have to talk about this if you don't want to

I do. I like talking to you, and this will definitely be a fun thing to talk about. But maybe now isn't the best time

Loud and clear. I'll save it for tonight if you're up for a FaceTime :P

Lol, we'll see how I survive the day

Business at the table is slower today, but it's okay. Yesterday was good, and as I say, it's all basically profit as I could stay at home. Doesn't help the staying awake when I'm hungover though. Thankfully, I have Cam for that.

The cosplay still good?

Yeah it's pretty good. Not as many today, it's a lot more kids in halloween costumes and the like, but there's a few

Show me :)

I can't just take a photo of a random stranger

Why not?

It's creepy, isn't it?

Arran, we're cosplayers. Do you think we do the cosplay just so we see it ourselves? No, we want everyone to see how awesome we look and feel!

Just ask! If they really don't want a photo taken, they'll say no. it's fine, it happens a lot

I'm a little anxious, but I scan the room looking for anyone who I think looks really good. Luckily, just as I'm about to sit back down, a man in a fur loincloth and worn leather harness and dusted in white facepaint all over his bare chest walks past. I just about remember the video game character and call out the name, mildly amazed that he turned to it.

"Hi! You look amazing! Can I take a picture of your cosplay for my friend?"

"Sure, man. If you post it online, do you mind tagging me?"

"Uh, sure, no problem." He poses, pulling out a hefty looking battleaxe and looking sternly at the camera. After I take the shot, we swap socials and he heads off on his way. I send the photo straight over to Cam.

Wow. He can call me 'Boy' any day!

Cam!

I'm kidding, I'm kidding. Kinda. He really looks the part.

Yeah, he was really nice too. Get this though, he asked if I post it online to tag him

Well, yeah, duh

This happens a lot?

Sure! It's nice to see your hard work get out there. It's a bit like your books, man. We spend ages on the costumes, and sometimes a lot of money. It's really nice to see it spread and the feedback people give

Even if it's a bunch of lecherous comments?

Well, that can be a mixed bag, yeah. It's annoying. Obviously, we're not cosplaying to look sexy or to get anyone off

But that's not to say some of us aren't into a little of that role play too, you know

As long as there's consent and no one's taking it too far, it's okay

I dunno. I feel weird posting it.

Well, you don't have to. But he seems open to it. And hey, it might help people find you and your stuff too

Think of it: lotta people look up cosplay on instagram and Tumblr - maybe a little virtual cosplay parade from you will make them look through your other posts and see the comics you make too

I guess. I don't want to be using someone though

Dude, I know you. You wouldn't be. You'd be celebrating them. Go for it!

I take a few more shots of cosplayers as they come by my table. Some stay and check out the comics too, otherwise give me their business cards. I was a little surprised at that, these totally professional looking cards with their social handles and sometimes websites with full bios and credits for the piece makers for their costumes. I guess I didn't realise how much of a whole business cosplay really was.

As the day wears on and starts to quiet down, I decide to post the cosplay pics on my instagram. I try and tag everyone I can, and try and use hashtags for the characters and the event I'm at. See how it goes. Before long, I have people at my table again and I forget about it.

It isn't until we're all wrapped up and breaking down to head home (another good day, not as good as yesterday, but still) that I check my phone again. And my notifications are through the roof.

Instagram is blowing up. People liking all the cosplay photos, but more than that: my followers have shot up too!

I wave goodbye to Sarah and make my way back to my flat, swiping through new followers and likes and comments. Thankfully, there's only a couple of my gay friends making slightly innuendo laden comments about some of the guy cosplayers (especially the video game barbarian daddy) but it all seems to be taken in jest.

As I get into my flat, I even get a couple of new sales through my webstore, and I can't help but feel it has to be connected.

"You were right!" I tell Cam on the phone. "The posts are blowing up! Probably some of the most popular posts I've ever done on instagram, which I will choose not to take as an insult to my selfies and comics posts."

"Told you. And the cosplayers in them are happy too, right?" He sounds smug. I don't hate it.

"Yup. A couple asked to be tagged in when they found them if I hadn't already, but generally everyone was just very kind and thankful for my posting them. I think a few of my gay mates are following that barbarian guy now."

"Ha, to be expected."

I crash down on my bed, phone still held to my ear. I'll worry about food and sorting my stuff out later, I just want to chat with Cam right now.

"Thank you. You're always looking out for me and trying to help me get out there more. I appreciate it."

"Hey, of course. I just want you to get all the good things you deserve. And if I get to feel like I was there with you too, all the better."

"Hopefully next time you will be there with me." It just slips out, before a tone of panic squirms into my voice. "If you want to, like."

"I do." I hear him just about cover up a giggle under his breath. "What's next for you?"

"Bristol. In about three weeks. Always a nice show, and I like Bristol itself."

"Not been before. Might be worth a visit."

"Please do. I'd love to see your face again."

"Ah, well you don't have to wait for that. Switch to FaceTime? I want to show you exactly what I got up to last night."

I flip onto my front and turn FaceTime on. The screen turns into a dimly lit bedroom, nondescript, white bed linen and beige walls, but kneeling on the bed is Cam. Wearing a jock strap. Just a jock strap.

And then he shows me exactly what he got up to last night.

BRISTOL COMIC AND GAMING CON 2018 DAY ONE

"Oh wow, you have the new issue out!" says the somewhat skinny looking Thor in front of our table, picking up the latest issue of *The surREALS*. "I picked up the first three at this show, like, two years ago! That was one helluva cliffhanger to leave it on."

"Yeah, sorry about that. Kinda my bad, sort of." Gertie looks kinda bashful as she apologises, but really there's nothing to apologise for. We're not Marvel or DC, we never promised a monthly release schedule, and we're still having to make ends meet around this. But it's more than that, the break was down to personal reasons, which no one needs to know about.

"Oh, are you the colourist? I know Arran from last time, and I met the artist G-"

"Yeah, no, this *is* the artist, actually." I cut in fast.

"Oh, you had to get a new artist? What happened with the other guy?" It's not this guy's fault, but I kind of wish he'd drop it.

"Um, yeah, nothing happened as such. I remember you, actually. I think you were doing a really rad Mechanoid Man cosplay, right?" Gertrude fixes him with a gentle smile, but her eyes are firm, like she's trying to telepathically pass along the message. The look on Skinny Thor's face tells me he's not getting it.

"Uh, yeah, I was, how did you-?"

"Yeah, I thought it was really cool. Always loved that game, it was nice chatting to you about it. I actually went back and played the third one again while I was recovering from surgery." Gertie looks at him from under her eyelashes. I watch the exchange with a mixed bag of feelings myself, flop sweat breaking out on my forehead as I try to figure out what I'm supposed to do here.

"Oh, righ— Oh, OH! Oh my god, I'm so sorry, I didn't-"

"It's cool, don't worry about it. But yeah, I'm the artist. Same one from the first three issues. We actually reprinted the first three too, with my name on it properly now. I'm *Gertrude* Milton, nice to see you again." She offers her hand, and the poor guy takes it with gusto, if ever there was a thing as an apologetic handshake I think this is it in spades.

"So you enjoyed the first three issues, then?" I butt in, now that I think I can't make the situation any worse.

"Oh yeah, it's so fun, dude. I like the main character, he's so funny. And the art is amazing, Gertrude, really. Better than half the stuff Marvel is putting out lately, I can tell yer." He's got a kind of manic enthusiasm thing going on, probably left over adrenaline from the awkward situation, but he seems really genuine.

"Thanks, man. I appreciate it. And please, call me Gertie." Gertie relaxes again and chats with the guy a bit more about drawing the book, before he buys a copy and makes us promise to do another one. He even buys the first three issues again, now they have Gertie's real name on them. "Collectors Items,", he says. "Look forward to the next issue, then. Hope there's not so big a gap after another cliffhanger," he laughs, and I try not to think of it as a dig. Try, and part of me fails, but there we are.

"Don't worry, I'm actually most of the way through the fifth and final issue now, actually." Gertie assures him.

"Final for now, at least," I jump in. "I have plans for plenty more with our guys, don't you worry." I smile to Skinny Thor, but for a second out of the corner of my eye I'm sure I see Gertie shoot an anxious glance at me before looking away.

As Skinny Thor moves along to catch up with a group of other Asgardian heroes and villains, someone new comes up to the table and hands a coffee cup each to me and Gertie. "You okay, hun?"

Emma stands the other side of the table, her dyed blue hair falling in waves against her denim dungarees. She's been growing out her hair lately, and the blue is really only starting from halfway down now, but it really works for her, her chestnut brown roots showing through. Her concerned eyes don't leave Gertie though.

"I'm good, babe. It happens. Probably will for a while, with anyone who knew me from before. Especially people who only knew me in passing. Honestly, it's nothing." She gives a smile, but we both see the quavering edge to it, as she quickly hides it behind her latte.

"Hey, look. Sorry I didn't jump in. I just-"

"Didn't know what to say. It's cool, dude. It's not your place to tell people I transitioned anyway, that's up to me if I want to. Seriously, I'm okay."

"You know what? Why don't you take a break and go for a walk. It's not crazy busy here, I can man the table by myself. Go have a wander for a bit, eh?"

Gertie looks to Emma, who smiles, before looking back. "You sure? I don't want to put you under pressure."

"Honestly, it's all good. Not my first time doing it on my own, innit. Go chill. I promise, I'll text if I suddenly get swamped."

She makes me promise to that last part, but then Gertie and Emma head off into the crowds of the old Station building, looking to get some air or space. Whatever she needs.

The con's been pretty steady actually. Bristol is always a good show, its main drawback being a lack of consistency in location.

The last two have been in the old Station building, but it's been held at hotels in the past too, and I think it will be again next year.

Despite this, it's a good mix of 'regulars' (people who come to this show every year) and new folks, so the comics are selling well. Not Excelsicon well, of course, but I don't think anywhere in the UK does as well as that.

I'd also say this show has had the most cosplay of any other I've been to in the UK besides Excelsicon too, which is awesome. The usual Deadpools and Spider-Men fill the halls, along with a ton of teens in beige and brown militaristic-style uniforms and hulking metallic boxes on their thighs - I'm not really sure what that one is, so I assume anime. Manga and anime are still a bit of a blindspot for me, and I don't know much beyond the bigger and older ones that have had a chance to leak into my consciousness via cultural osmosis.

It's also easy to tell which Marvel movies have come out lately due to an increase in cosplays of characters from those, and Harley Quinns seem to be multiplying, each one a different style or variation on the character, which is cool. There's even a lot of really cool crossplay and genderbent cosplay, which is pretty awesome. Cam filled me in on those terms: basically, crossplay is when a cosplayer cosplays as a character of a different gender to them, and genderbent is when you take a character of a different gender and create a version that matches your gender. So, we get a lot of boy Harley Quinns or Phoenixes (cool note: a lot of those are queer guys too. Obviously not exclusively, but a lot - I guess the gays really relate to smart, powerful women who go a bit crazy now and then), and even a really awesome drag Rogue, who looked absolutely badass.

I'm sat back enjoying the people watching from behind the table when a tall, spandex-clad Spider-Man approaches the table and stands looking at me.

"Hey, thanks for stopping by! Would you like me to tell you about the comics?"

Spider-Man tilts his head quizzically. "Actually, I was kind of wondering what you think of my costume?"

I look him up and down, smiling. It's a really good Spidey costume, to be sure. In fact, it's the Scarlet Spider costume, which to be honest I always had a soft spot for, the cut off blue hoodie just giving me grunge vibes. "I'm loving you went with the Ben Reilly one, I don't see that often. You look really cool."

"Uh huh. And do you like my web shooter?" he says.

I raise an eyebrow. I really don't know where this is going, he can't have meant that to have sounded as lewd as it did, did he? "Uhhh…"

He leans forward, closer to me. "I know you never had any complaints about it before." With that, he stands back up, his gloved hands reaching up to his mask, drawing behind and clutching at the zipper that must be there. He lifts the mask from where it tucks under the main torso of the costume and pulls it off.

Cam is standing before me, skintight red lycra emphasising his physique, a fact I'm suddenly able to appreciate. But what actually catches my breath away from me is the long, thick shock of silvery white hair that has just tumbled down from his head as he took off the mask. Now, with his free hand he swoops it all off to one side, letting it cascade and frame the right hand side of his face, partially covering his eye on that side.

"Cam! I…I didn't know you were gonna be here!"

"Surprise!" He gives me a quick flourish of jazz hands. "I saw you'd be here and I figured why not come down. I still owe you that dinner, after all."

A smile pulls across my face, my cheeks feeling warmer. Before we can carry on talking, I usher him around the table to come join me on my side and as he steps around, I pull him into a hug.

"Ha, careful! I probably reek, it's mad hot in here, and spandex is not as breathable as you might think."

"Don't care. Glad you're here." I inhale while I'm holding him, and actually, he smells amazing. He smells like Cam.

He parks up in the chair next to me and we start chatting. Catching up on what he's been up to, work, last shows etc. He asks about the book, and how it's going, and even if he doesn't fully understand the ins and outs of it all, he's interested, or at least looks it. Occasionally someone stops to ask for a photo of his cosplay and he runs back around to pose for the camera, or someone checks out the comics and has some questions. Cam even helps out when we had a bit of a busy spell, and I sneak a photo and post it to twitter, bragging about the Scarlet Spider selling my comics.

We're mid-conversation, conspiring like a couple of teenagers, when we're next interrupted. "Hey," Gertie says, a look of bemused amusement on her face, Emma backing her up.

"Hey, Gertie! Emma! You guys doing okay?" I ask, before I remember that Cam is in her seat. "Oh crap, right. Gertie, Emma, this is Cam. Cam, Gertie is the artist on *The surREALS*, and Emma is her girlfriend."

"Oh my god, it's so nice to meet you! I'll get out of your seat now."

"No, no, it's all good. So you're Cam, huh? I hear a lot of good things." Gertie says, grinning evilly as my cheeks hit meltdown. Emma barely stifles a snort.

"All good, I hope." Cam says as he makes his way back around the table.

"Judging on the smile on Arran's face whenever he talks about you, I'd say really good, yeah." Emma throws in, impish giggles punctuating.

Oh my god, kill me now.

"Well, what can I say: he gives as good as he gets." Cam joins in. Why! Why is my life like this?

I sink into my chair as the girls come back around.

"You don't have to go on our account, it's all fine honestly." Gertie smiles.

"Yeah, it would be nice to get to know the cosplayer of Arran's dreams." Emma adds, poking her tongue out at me as I scowl at her.

"I'd like that, but maybe later tonight? I should catch up to my friends, I left them hunting for Minimon ages ago." Cam smiles, fussing with his Spidey hood in his hands. "I hope you ladies don't mind, but I'd like to snatch Arran away for a bit later, buy him dinner."

"Oh, you don't have to buy me—"

"Oh, don't worry. We'll find a way to entertain ourselves, I'm sure. But meet us for drinks after?" Gertie genuinely seems amused.

"Sure." Cam waves bye to the girls, then pulls his hood back on, tucking his hair into the face shell before zipping up. He turns to me, those massive lenses staring at me. "I'll see you later, tiger. I'll text when I swing by your hotel."

And with that parting pun, Cam spins off into the crowd…for about eight feet before someone stops him for a photograph.

***

About an hour after the show, I'm sat in the hotel lobby waiting for Cam. He's staying in another hotel in Bristol, but said he'd come meet me at mine, so I rushed back, hopped in the shower and threw on some fresh jeans and a nice shirt and headed down. I didn't know where we'd be going, so I figure the best bet is to dress fairly smart casual, just in case. Right?

I run straight back up to my room and throw on a t-shirt. I don't want to come across as thinking we'll be doing anything super posh, right? Ten minutes later, I've thrown on another shirt, and realise that at this point I'm out of options even if I wanted to, exhausting the contents of my travel bag.

Back in the lobby, a tasteful (ish) colourful short-sleeve shirt on, I sit on one of the artfully arranged sofas just as the automatic revolving doors start up again and in walks Cam.

Gone is the Spider-Man look from earlier, replaced by black

skinny jeans, a tight black t-shirt and a beautiful silk short sleeve shirt thrown over. His hair is swooped to one side again, but this time he's wearing his round, gold-rimmed spectacles, one lens partially covered by his sweeping fringe.

"Hey! You been waiting long?" he beams a smile at me as I stand to meet him.

"Oh, no, not at all. Just got down here." I figure a small white lie is okay, and saves my dignity.

"He's been up and down about three times, actually!" I turn to see Emma and Gertie at the hotel bar, waving, a devious grin on Gertie's face. I drop my head in exasperation as Cam bursts out laughing.

He nudges me and leans in to my ear. "Don't worry. I couldn't decide what to wear, either."

"Really?"

"Yeah. I mean, jock strap, thong, briefs...nothing at all." Deviousness is spreading, it's now rising across Cam's features too.

I gulp hard, mind racing. I'm half tempted to say screw dinner and just take him upstairs, but I dunno. I kind of want to do this too much.

"Come on," he says, taking my hand and dragging me towards the doors as they come to life turning again. "What do you fancy? Anything in mind?"

Oh yes. "Um, I actually don't mind. And I don't really know what's around to be honest. Shall we just wander and see what jumps out to us?"

We walk through Bristol, ostensibly to look for somewhere to eat, but in truth we're barely paying attention. Instead, we're chatting like friends who haven't seen each other in ages, despite the fact we're talking online, on our phones, on FaceTime almost daily at this point. We talk about the con today, talk about the cosplay. Turns out Cam knows what some of the ones I didn't know were, and he winds up extolling the virtues of anime. Seems it's another facet of pop culture he loves.

"I'll have to make you a list of titles I think you'll like. Anime and the manga. Open you up to whole new horizons."

"What is with you and always opening me up?"

"Hey now, *filthy*," chidingly, he bops me on my arm. "That was a bad pun worthy of me there. Besides, I think if we tallied things up, you've done a lot more of that than me."

We decide to take a break from our ambling and stop in a bar called The Village Tavern for a drink. I stare at the barman a little too long as Cam orders, unable to shake the feeling he looks familiar somehow. It's only when we sit down that we notice a rainbow flag. A couple guys decked out all in leather kissing in the corner.

"Huh. Trust us to accidentally find a gay bar."

"Well, good. Means I can do this with no worries." He leans in and plants a kiss on my lips, running his tongue along my lower lip, lingering in the closeness before slowly taking a seat back. "Been wanting to do that all day."

I feel myself flush, but can't help but agree. "Yeah, me too. Though I daresay we'd have got some stares at the show. You in your cosplay, me selling my books."

"Let them stare, we're not doing anything wrong. I've seen worse at a comic con anyway."

"Really?"

Cam starts filling me in on a whole other side of comic con I never knew about. Relating stories of secret trysts, long distance cosplay relationship dramas and even a couple FansOnly collabs arranged here and there. I marvel at this whole other aspect to a culture event I've loved for years but knew nothing about, realising that things you love sometimes have depths you never quite find yourself until someone else shows you. Meanwhile, part of me can't stop flicking glances over at the barman, racking my brain to figure out just why he seems so damn familiar.

"Oh!" I exclaim I little too loudly, derailing Cam mid-sentence.

"What? I mean, I've never starred in one or anything...have been asked though..."

"No, no, not that. Though I am not at all surprised. No, the barman. I just realised how I know him."

"Oh god, you haven't slept with that twink too, have you? Do I have competition?"

"Ha! As if. No, I think I follow him on TikTok." I started checking the app more after I got roped into attempting (and failing) TikTok dances at Excelsicon. My brain switches to a different tack as what Cam said registers. "Why, you jealous, Mister Perkins?"

"Not at all," he smiles, but I swear I see his cheeks flush pinker. "He should be though. After all, I've got to see you naked and he hasn't."

"I think few would find that the grand prize you seem to think it is."

He lets go of his glass and takes my hand on the table. "Hey, stop that. You're a catch. Don't ever think otherwise. For real."

I blush furiously and change the topic of conversation, returning to the idea of food. It's then I think some local knowledge might be handy.

"Hi," I call out to the barman as I wave and start walking over. "Me and my friend are looking for somewhere to eat. I don't suppose you can recommend somewhere?"

The barman seems to think for a second, looking over me and Cam as if trying to work out what cuisine will be to our taste by sight alone. "Actually, there's a really great taco place a few doors down from here. It's small, so might not have any room left, but it's amazing food for a first date."

I freeze, flustered as I stumble over words I can't seem to quite find. "Oh, we're, um, we're—which is to say, it's not, uh…"

Cam strides up beside me, placing the empty glasses back on the bar, before taking my arm and giving me a big, theatrical kiss on the cheek. "Sounds perfect. Thanks so much! Come on, stud!"

As he drags me out into the slowly setting sunlight of the day, I give him my deepest glare. "You enjoyed that."

"Yes, yes I did," as he pulls me in the directions of tacos. "It's nice to see you floundering like a hot mess on our date."

He strides on as I watch him, stunned, and feel a grin spread across my face.

"God, I need to work out how to make these." I manage to get out in between bites of the most delicious taco I've ever eaten in the history of my life. It's also technically the first taco I've ever eaten in my life, but who's checking.

"You cook?" Cam has a pleased and surprised look on his face. I guess we haven't spoken too much about our other hobbies besides comics, cosplay and cocks.

"Yeah. I really enjoy it. It relaxes me, I guess. And when I finish something and sit down to eat it, I have this sense of accomplishment." I've never really given it much thought, but that seems like an accurate assessment. "I mean, I'm hardly a cordon bleu chef or anything, I tend to make comfort food more than anything else. Mac and cheese, shepherd's pie, brownies, things that make you feel not just full, but I guess safe and warm too? That probably sounds silly."

"Not at all." Cam leans across the table, and looks me in the eye. "Cook for me sometime?"

Blushing, I nod quickly, and then take a swig of my lager. "What about you? I know about the cosplay, but what else do you do for fun?"

"Besides you?" he grins.

"Look, not even your dick is big enough to get me from home. I'm sure you do other stuff besides cam sex with me."

He leans back and plays with his quesadilla thoughtfully. He takes a crunch of it, swallows and then, "Hm, I'm a big gamer, I guess. I have all the current consoles, and I stay pretty up to date on the releases. I also design some cosplay stuff for other people.

Nothing major, most of the time it's as favours, but occasionally I'm selling a commissioned piece."

"So cosplay is like a business for you too?"

"Hm, no, not quite. It's still not really what I go in it for. It's a nice bit of extra money now and then, but I worry if I pursued it full time it'd kill my passion for it, you know?"

I do know. Over the years, I've had spells where making comics, which had always been my dream, feels like more of a challenge than it's worth. Bringing me more pain than happiness. Like Kirby is paraphrased as saying, "'Comics will break your heart.'"

"Excuse me?"

"Oh, nothing. It's a quote that gets attributed to Jack Kirby all the time. It's not one hundred percent accurate, or even all of what he said, but the soundbite is snappier and it catches with a lot of people. Essentially, it's about how comics is a hard business.

"All of which is to say, yeah, I get you. I've felt the same thing now and then. I push through because I can't really imagine myself doing anything else."

He leans into one of his hands, elbow resting on the table, eyes never leaving me. "I can imagine. It's actually kind of inspiring that you stick with it, the determination of it all."

I laugh, embarrassed. "Ah, it's not all that. I'm just not smart enough or strong enough to do a normal job."

Tilting his head, Cam says, "You always find a way to be self-deprecating, don't you."

"It's my skill. That and eating ass like a champion."

He laughs, loud and unexpected, the table next to us turning their heads slightly. "Yeah, okay, that's definitely up there too."

"What about you? What are your goals for the future?"

"Where do I see myself when I grow up, you mean?" He smiles that devilish smile again, and then relaxes. "I don't know, truth be told. I don't think I can see myself working for the firm forever. Don't get me wrong, I could, I could rise up the ranks there easy enough, if I gave it that much of my life. But I don't think I'd be happy to make that my career, wholly as it is.

"Not that I don't like accountancy. I actually do, it's a lot of fun really."

"More for you than me, I reckon. Me and numbers have never been friends," I joke, and we keep eating for a few minutes more, just enjoying each others company. And fully clothed for once.

Before long, Cameron breaks the silence.

"I like this, you know. Spending time together that isn't…you know."

"Oh, look who's getting shy now! This is a wholly different colour on you." I tease, enjoying the role reversal.

"Who's shy? Time together that isn't sweaty, nude and oh so horny." A flash of teeth through that naughty grin of his, the blood rushing to my cheeks and other places. "But I like spending time with you. I hope it's not too presumptuous to think that we're a bit more than a random hook up now."

"No, not at all. I haven't thought of us that way since…" since we actually met, I thought it was more than just that, I hoped it was. "Since ages ago, I guess. We're friends. Friends who don't get to see each other anywhere near as much as they should."

"Awesome," he smiles, finishing his drink. "So, you hooked up with any other horny cosplayers since I last saw you?"

"You know I don't exclusively shag cosplayers, right? I'm not even looking for that. I mean, you don't think—"

"Relax, I'm teasing. I hit on *you*, remember. I know you're not after one thing." He smiles as my heart rate returns to a normal pace. "Why were you on Grindr that time in London, anyway?"

"Well, I wasn't hunting cosplay dick, if that's what you mean." I defend myself, and he laughs.

"It wasn't. Again, I know you're not like that. Geez, you worry too much about what other people think, you know that?"

"I do," I admit, though I don't really know where that comes from. "I was just having a hard time. Sales we drying up after the lengthy dry spell in the books release. Don't get me wrong, I don't blame anyone for that, especially not Gertie, it is what it is. But that day, the show wasn't going well for me.

"I guess…I guess I was feeling like a failure? Like the dream was dying in my hand, that I'd soon have to admit defeat and get a 'real job'. I was feeling low, and I needed a pick me up.

"I've always turned to sex for that, I guess. I know I'm no looker," Cam gives me a stern look and looks like he's going to interrupt, "but I know I can make other people happy, and that feels weirdly like an accomplishment too, you know? So I guess I was needing a win, and sure, I was horny, so I figured I'd let London know I was around and available. Maybe find someone after the show."

"And then I came along."

"And then you came along. Honestly, I wasn't trying to find someone at the show, or a cosplayer, or whatever. It's not what I was there for."

"You know, we're all adults. You can hook up with whoever you want, it's just about consent. Don't take this the wrong way, but you're not like a celebrity or anything. And remember, again, I hit on you."

"I know," I admit, "but it doesn't *look* great. And in this industry, there have been far too many stories of guys taking advantage of, if not fame in the way you mean, their position in the industry or as someone that's looked up to. Not that I'm saying I'm there yet, and I know that's not me, and it's not what we did."

"And again you're worrying *too much* about what other people think…"

"Sure. But also, when I go to a comic con, I'm not just there for fun? Like, it's my business. My career. I don't go there with the purpose of hooking up, like, say, some of my gay friends in Wales when they visit the Big City. I'm there to make sales, meet new potential fans, network maybe. I love them, I have so much fun at them, I guess a natural byproduct of comics making being a largely lonely and solitary work, but it's also work for me."

Cam purses his lips in consideration. "I can see that. It's funny,

I guess I never considered it that way before. Like I said, some cosplayers use con's for business too, they've made a career out of it. But for me it's *just* fun, it's a way to relax. I guess I forget sometimes that for others, it is work."

"Yeah, exactly. So, you know, I don't really make a habit of hooking up with people at shows, or at the very least *from* shows. It's not necessarily a goal for me."

"Okay," he leans in, "So why were you horny that day?"

I think of material stretched tight over the round shape of a perfectly toned butt. Images of shirtless men like characters from my favourite comics and games. The tell tale line down a thick thigh. I gulp hard.

"I dunno. It had been a while, I guess."

Cam looks at me, a knowing expression on his features, but he lets it pass. "Mhm, *that's* all. Well, hopefully it won't be too long again this time, because after wining and dining you, I really am hoping to—"

My hand shoots into the air, startling a waiter as she walks past our table. "Bill please!"

Cam settles the bill (refusing my attempts to help out, and taking my card and pocketing it when I place it on the tray before the waiter can take it), and we head off to meet the girls for a couple of drinks before ticking off the final part of Cam's checklist of things to do today.

It did not stay 'a couple of drinks'.

We meet the girls at a craft beer bar, where they were trying to work their way through the whole menu of beers, lagers and ciders. As we get through the door, they call us over to their table, and I can already tell they're well on their way.

Within seconds of sitting down, Emma and Gertie give me recommendations for drinks they think we'll like and send me off to get them, keeping Cam captive for an interrogation. I try to get served as quick as I can to get back, but it's busy and the barman is apparently confused by my cloak of invisibility or something. Eventually, I get served and bring the drinks back to the table. All three of them are laughing their heads off, and I honestly can't decide if this is a good sign or a bad one.

"You never told me you tried to do a TikTok dance!" Gertie manages to wheeze out as she calms down.

Oh no. "You didn't."

"I did," Cam says sheepishly, before holding up his phone and playing a video from Excelsicon. It's me very badly trying to dance outside the hotel in the middle of the night and tripping over my own feet before face planting into the ground.

I sigh into my hand. "I am not made for movement. I am all head."

"So we hear!" Emma snorts. Amazingly, Cam blushes, but then bursts out laughing. Seeing him laughing and getting along with some of my closest friends somehow completely disarms me, and I start laughing too.

Somewhere around the third pint, any remaining hangups and concerns are washed away, and we're all talking openly like we've all known each other for years. Gertie and Cam wind up getting on like a house on fire, talking about a mutual love of table top gaming. Emma keeps asking about how I'm feeling, and isn't it nice having Cam around. It is, but I feel like she's pushing toward something and after a fourth pint I have no idea what it is.

We head back to the hotel bar and another round is bought. We talk comic cons, Cam educating the girls on the secret ins and outs of the cosplay community, with Gertie paying special attention, curious as to what design elements in characters appeal most to cosplayers, what really gets them to go viral etc.

"Why you so interested, Gert? I love our book, but I don't think we're going viral any time soon."

Gertie bites her lip as she thinks for a second, taking a glance at Emma who just shrugs at her. She looks back at me and Cam.

"Okay, I'll tell you something, but you have to promise to keep it a total secret."

Me and Cam look at each other, before nodding our promise to her.

"I got a gig with Marvel. It's early days, but I'll be doing a little mini-series with them next year."

"Oh my god, that's amazing news, Gertie! Congratulations!" Cam says enthusiastically. "You know what, we need to celebrate. Next rounds on me!" And before anyone can say anything, he's off to the bar.

"Arran? You okay?" Gertie looks to me, a small bundle of nerves building in her head and showing on her face.

"Of course! Congratulations!" I say, but I hear the tinge of sadness in it. If she's taken by Marvel, does that mean I'll need to find someone else to finish *The surREALS*? What about the future of the series? And, the thoughts I'm most ashamed of, that I'm most disgusted about: what about *me*?

Marvel has been one of my dreams for years, and if they saw Gertie's work in the book and decided they want her but not *me*, does that mean they don't rate my work at all? Is that the case with everyone? Is it just the art everyone likes, and not what I'm bringing to it?

Gertie must be able to sense exactly what's going through my mind. "I'm still committed to finishing *The surREALS*. I'm mostly done with this issue, and there's just the last one of this arc left. But I probably won't be able to do another arc, if you were wanting to continue it.

"Honestly, I've loved every minute working on it, man, and I really wasn't expecting anything to come of this Marvel gig. I just took a chance and sent in my portfolio to an editor there, and they liked my pages of *surREALS*, and well, they found something for me to start on."

"So they just saw some pages?"

"Well, a bit more than that. But the editor, Jess, she asked me to send some digital copies of the comic then too. She loves it, by the way. Thinks you got a real great way with storytelling. I think it's just, like, easier to find a space for an artist in the schedule than a writer. And maybe there's more they need to see, where as I can show a lot in the portfolio and the comic. But hey, someone at Marvel loves the book. You're on the radar too, man."

I shake my head, annoyed that I made it all about me, whether I intended to or not. "You're right. I'm so sorry, Gertie. This is incredible news. I am really happy for you. And I totally understand if you need to leave *The surREALS...*"

She places a hand on my shoulder and looks me dead in the eyes, "Hey. No. I'm committed. We're finishing this. Marvel can wait."

Cam appears next to us, leaning down and placing a bucket filled with ice, a bottle of champagne and four glasses on the table, before running back to the bar and returning with four small glasses of black liquid. "Shots!"

"Shots?" I say, making a face in protest.

"Shots!" The girls yell in unison.

Another two rounds of shots and a bottle of champagne later, and the girls are splitting off from us to head to their room as Cam, arm over my shoulders, guides me to the elevator.

In the elevator, just the two of us, intoxicated by far too much alcohol and far too much lust, I grab Cam by the waistband and drag him towards me, slurring out what I must think is the sexiest phrase ever uttered by man, only for Cam to laugh in my face.

"You're drunk, mister"

"And you're sexy as fuck," I mumble, as I pull him in and nibble his ear lobe.

The doors slide open and I pull my hand from his pants. Cam takes it and pulls me out into the hallway, "Okay, handsy man, which room number again?"

"'s 235."

We stumble and laugh down the halls, shushing each other exaggeratedly, probably loud enough to wake anyone in the rooms. As we reach the door, I fumble with the key card before swinging the door wide open and tripping inside. The door isn't even closed as I start throwing off my clothes, almost falling over my jeans around my ankles. When I'm down to just my jockstrap, I dive on the bed, only for the room to somersault around me and I land with a thud face up on the floor with a groan.

Laughing, Cam drops down, leaning over me, "Oh my god, are you okay? You bounced right off the bed, you dumbass."

"S'okay. I'm on my back down here too. Take me, Thunderman!" Wrapping my legs around him, I grab his belt and fumble with the clasp.

Amazingly, and with a groan of his own, Cam stands, lifting me with him and throwing me on the bed. "Uh uh, I think it's better if we just go to sleep, buddy. Besides, I've drunk enough to put paid to that plan now, I think."

"Awwww," I moan. "But I wanted you to make me your sex toy. You wined and dined, it gotta —"

"Go to sleep," he interrupts. "Come 'ere."

He gets me into the covers, actually tucking me in. I grab his arm as he stands up. "Stay. We don't have to do anything, but I want you to stay."

"Good, because I have every intention to." He says as he stands in front of me and takes his shirt off, throwing it onto a chair in the room. He undoes his belt and the top two buttons of his jeans, and slides them over his ass before just letting them drop. He's not wearing any underwear. He walks around the bed and climbs in behind me, kissing the back of my neck as he brings me in to a cuddle.

"Mmkay. But if we're cuddling, we're doing it right." I say, awkwardly reaching under the blankets and fidgeting until my hand comes back out, holding my jockstrap. I toss it across the room, and push my butt back into Cam's groin, feeling him react with the contact.

"Tha's better," I mumble, before falling into an abyss of rolling darkness and warmth inside and out.

BRISTOL COMIC AND GAMING CON 2018 DAY TWO

"Oh my god, I think I'm dying,"
Cam sits on the chair across the room, the kettle freshly boiled and a coffee in his hands, a smile on his face. "Yeah, I hear hangovers are really bad when you get over a certain age."

"Quiet, you." I glare at him, before throwing my head back onto the pillow. "Did you make one of those for me too?"

"Of course. Though I haven't added milk and sugar yet, as I didn't know."

"Milk and two sugars, please," I call back, muffled as my face is buried in the pillows. "Two of those weird little milk pot things, if they left us enough, actually."

A minute later and Cam cheerily, and far too enthusiastically for this time on a Sunday morning, says, "There, all ready for you."

"Ugh. I don't think I can even get up." I hurl the quilt off me, and lay there, exposed, spread out on the mattress. "That was all the energy I had, I'm done for. Save yourself. Or bring me a paracetamol. Or five."

"Mm, I got something better, actually." I look down as Cam stands from the chair. He's still naked, and he's very hard. It's then I notice that I am too.

"What're you…"

"Shhh…"

Cam moves to the edge of the bed, and crawls on. He runs his tongue along my balls, up my shaft, before taking it in his hand and lifting my cock so it's pointing at him. He gives me one last look from under his dishevelled hair, before taking me in his mouth.

I gasp and arch my neck back as he works me, slow and deep at first, like he's studying every inch, every vein with his tongue. I let out a sigh, letting him know I like this plan of his (even if I can't quite figure out how this solves my headache dilemma).

As I relax into it, Cam surprises me by taking me in deeply, making me gasp in exhilaration. When he comes off me, he sighs, takes a deep in take of breath, grabbing my shaft in his hand and pulling at me.

He starts giving me head again, but now he's using his hands too, picking up the pace with each stroke, a subtle twist of his wrist each time he pulls down. The intensity mounts, as I run a hand through his hair, holding him into my groin.

"I'm gonna come…" I pant, and Cam takes that as cue to start getting faster again, ploughing forward until with an almighty groan, my back arches, pushing my cock forward into his mouth and I'm spent.

I lie there, panting, as if I'd been running or more than just a submissive, laid back participant in this. Cam crawls up the bed, over me, until we're face to face and he kisses me. His lips taste slightly salty and bitter, a mixture of caffeine and me. He leans onto his elbow, trailing circles in my treasure trail below my bellybutton.

"Bet the headaches gone now, huh."

He looks assured, and amazingly, he's right. "Yeah. What're you, some kinda sex mutant?"

"Yup. My gift is healing orgasms. It comes in handy. Or blowy. Or fucky." He gets up, heading back over to the small coffee table, and brings me my coffee as I sit up in the bed. "Old trick I learned: orgasms help ease headaches. Doesn't do much for the rest of the hangover, but it helps with that at least."

We sit there in a post-coital domesticity, drinking our coffees and smiling at each other, idle chit chat about the day ahead. When we finish, Cam stands to go get his jeans, but I stand up behind him, grabbing his shoulders and spinning him around.

"Not going yet." I push him onto the bed. "Your turn."

And I drop to my knees.

***

"Well, you're looking well rested." Gertie grins, eyebrow raised and full of implications. She comes round the table and gives me my cup of coffee she picked up on her way in.

"What can I say, getting to be an old hand at these Sunday con day hangovers now. Take it in stride." I deflect, drinking my coffee and not meeting her eye.

"Mmhm. And I'm sure Cam was a lot of help too." I spit coffee back into my cup, managing to get some on myself. Brushing it off, I give her a glare that lasts just seconds before turning into a smile.

"Well, he has his uses."

The con goes pleasantly enough. Quieter than yesterday, and the sales are slow, but I had an okay day yesterday, and my head isn't wholly on the comics sales anyway.

Instead, I find myself spending a lot of time wondering what the future holds for my writing. It had taken me a while to find an artist who wanted to work with me on *The surREALS* originally, and now I will have to do it all again. Whether for something new or to continue *The surREALS*.

It's times like this I wish I had an editor involved. Someone who could help me make those connections, help me work out the marketing and business movements. It's not my strongest suit, at the end of the day. I'm a creator, a writer, not a PR guy or businessman - but doing this by yourself makes you have to wear many hats. From what I hear, that's the same to some extent when working with a major publisher too, but at least then you have a few more hands to help with the lifting.

Even with a few commissions to work on, Gertie notices. Between drawing famous characters for fans, she reassures me that she's here to see *The surREALS* through. As she finishes up a commission of Psylocke from Marvel, I reassure her too that it's not about her, not really, and I am so happy for her and her big shot.

Gertie heads off with Emma for a walk just after 1pm, as I sit and stew some more. However, before I can sink too deeply into worry, my stomach gurgling prompts me to remember I didn't pick up anything for lunch today. I contemplate leaving the table unattended and making a run for a Tesco when as if by magic, a sandwich lands on my table in front of me.

Cam is standing there wearing sandy coloured robes, a long brown hooded robe over the top of them. The silver hair actually really works with it all.

"Was that some kind of Jedi mind trick? Did The Force tell you I was fucking starving?"

"Nope, good ol' fashioned attentive lover, that is," I blush, causing Cam to grin before coming round to join me behind the table, "I'll say this for the Jedi though…they sure make comfy outfits for a nice, comfortable Sunday cosplay."

We chat over lunch, occasionally interrupted to talk with con goers and buyers. The tension I was feeling this morning at the show bleeds away, I just laugh with Cam and check out the cosplay, talking about who's costume looks best, trying to work out what the most popular cosplay of this con is. It's nice. It feels chill, peaceful. I'm able to focus on the fun again.

"Hey, so I was thinking…" Cam leans back, turning slightly to face me, a much more serious expression on his face.

"Oh no, what were you thinking about? Am I going to have cover up your lightsaber?"

"Maybe later," he winks, the impish grin back for a flash, "But

I was thinking, maybe I could come and visit you? Like, not just see you at the next comic con…maybe we could meet up in a non-comic con related environment. I got some time off to use and I've never actually been to Swansea."

"I'd love that!" He looks a little startled that I answered so quickly, and I suppose I am too. But I didn't need to think about it, I just felt it: it would be lovely to have some time, just the two of us, no concerns distracting, and not just because the idea of a debauched weekend in my bedroom sounds like absolute perfection.

"Awesome. Well, cool, let's do it then."

"Yeah, totally. Work out when you can get the time off, I'm free pretty much every weekend that isn't a comic con. I'll be more than happy to host."

"Maybe you can cook for me?"

A swallow hard. "Yeah, yeah, I could do that. What would you like?"

"Anything you'd like to give me." He smiles.

I do too, as I fix him with a look under my brows. "Oh, I can think of something I'd love to give you."

He meets me at my level, grabbing my thigh with his hand. "Oh, I think I'll take plenty of that, too. As much as we can manage in a weekend, eh?"

We sit there conspiring a dirty weekend at my place for the rest of the hour before Emma and Gertie come back. They take one look at us, roll their eyes, and say they'll come back when the air is less filled with the stank of horny schoolboys. Cam laughs, gives me a peck on the cheek and heads around the table.

"I'll text you later to sort out the deets, now get back to selling your comics, you horndog." He waves back as he heads into the crowds.

Oh man…I gotta figure out how to keep him entertained with just me now.

THE VISIT

I stand just outside the great big greyish brown building of Swansea train station, hands in my pockets as I watch the world go by. The September sun beats down, as we have yet another unseasonably warm day ahead of us. I'm even still wearing shorts, after two weeks of colder weather making it feel like that period had ended already for another year, I had to pull them back out of the wardrobe.

I don't want to be a mess of sweat for Cam after all. Though the nerves filling my stomach seem to have other ideas, the small of my back already feeling sticky with flop sweat for reasons I can't really fathom. What is there to be nervous about?

It may not be Cardiff Central, but Swansea station still gets its busy times. A Saturday in the sunshine being a good example. Mixes of families coming for the day out, maybe with a picnic basket to head down to Mumbles and sit along the coast. Hen parties blaring out into the sun through the automatic doors, laughing as the light hits them as they come to the edge of the entrance awning. Teenagers meeting up before heading into the city centre to do not much of anything at all. Cars slowing to pick up passengers just arrived, or parking to the side to wait, the traffic interspersed with cyclists and electric scooters, their riders either decked out in tight, form fitting lycra or heavy duty coats and giant cube backpacks, taking meals out even this early.

It's just after 11am, and already this strange carnival of human activity is in full swing. I find myself people watching, though never taking my view too far from the doors, bouncing from one foot to the next. My fingers flex and relax, until I become conscious of them and grab my phone instead, checking twitter, Instagram and Facebook for the twentieth time in a row.

Finally, a shock of brilliant white hair catches my eye, and my spine goes straight as I look to the door head on.

Cameron steps into the light wearing light grey denim shorts, that look like they used to be jeans cut-off ready for the summer. A low cut green vest just about covers his chest, the neckline plunging so low I find myself biting my lip. Even from here, the sheen of a slight sweat plays with the light as it hits him, sending my mind racing. He's wearing large, round glasses, with a pinkish tint to the lenses, a light green jacket, loosely clings around his shoulders, supported by a backpack slung over his left. I run up to meet him, waving.

"Hey, you." As I reach him I stutter in my step, unsure what to do in greeting, pulling myself away from reaching in to kiss him at the last moment, switching into a hug.

"Hey, you too," Cam laughs, catching my awkwardness and kissing my cheek, as much to let me know that public displays of affection are in fact on the table as to greet me.

It's only as I'm up close that I realise he's cut his hair again. Still that same shocking white colour, but he's shaved at his temples, the short buzzed hair looking more dark grey as a result. His naturally wavy curls nestle at the top of his head, looking at once perfectly manicured and effortlessly natural. I run my hand up along his left temple.

"Oh, yeah. Had a moment and got a fresh cut. You like?"

I smile, the sensation of the shaved hair feeling oddly pleasurable at my fingertips. "Oh, I like."

"So, Swansea..." he looks around like someone seeing the city for the first time. Wait, this is his first time, isn't it?

"Oh, you've not been to Swansea before, right?" I ask, as I offer a hand out to take his bag. He bats it away playfully, with a look telling me not to be daft.

"First time. Always wanted to visit, but never had a reason to. Until now." He butts my shoulder with his as we walk side by side.

"Well, far be it from me to be a bad host! I shall have to show you all the wondrous sights of my fair city. Come on, you must be hungry after all the trains, let's get some chips."

We skip the city centre for now and hop on a bus to head out to Mumbles Pier. From there, we walk up and down the coastal paths, stopping to grab some chips from a small cafe and eat them as we chat and throw the odd one out for the seagulls. Being local, I should know better, because this of course turns us into prime target for the birds, as they gather in hordes and start swooping at us greedily for more. We laugh as we run from these homophobic gulls, ruining a couple of guys sweet afternoon stroll like this, and at the last I dump the remainder of my chips behind us to distract them. Bursting down stone steps to a thin strip of sand, Cam leans into me, pushing my back against the wall.

Laughing, we stay there, his arm over my head, leaning against the wall. Against me.

"Fancy a hot one?" he grins.

"What? Cam, I'm as kinky as the next guy, but I draw the line at certain arrest." I laugh him off, but look at him warily...and aroused.

Instead, he pulls out the crumpled paper cone of chips from under his jacket. "Hope you like salt, I think I went a bit mad with it."

I playfully punch his shoulder, before snatching a salty chip. "You dirty bugger. You had me going then."

"Oh, I'm not saying sex on the beach is out of the question... but maybe when there's not so many people around, eh?"

"Aye, aye. I'd sooner keep it in my bed, thank you. Last thing I want up my arse is half the sand of Mumbles."

"Oh yeah? That a promise then?"

I blush, but try to play it cool, ignoring the heat in my face. "Patience, boyo. We'll get there, eventually."

"Oh my god, you're even Welsher when you're in your home town." He bites his lip for a second mid-laugh as he eyes me, the sun behind him framing him in blue and bouncing from the white curls atop his head.

"You love my accent, so consider it foreplay." I tease, letting my hand brush quickly over his butt before I give it a slap.

"Oof, you planning on edging me all day like this then?"

"We'll see."

We head back into town as I show him around. It's really kind of a whistle stop tour, the longest time spent in the gay bar that I tell him was my first and still my favourite, even though it's changed hands several times over the years. We finish our cold drinks, gently poking at each other with our feet under the table, before heading back into the world.

The shopping centre. The greenhouse gardens. The old castle ruins. We barely spend any time at any, spending more time with our eyes on each other than anything I'm supposed to be showing him. I'm hardly being the perfect tour guide, but then, the visit isn't really about Swansea. Cameron's not here for ruined fortresses or sweltering indoor forests. He's here for me.

As the sun begins to set, bathing us in glowing orange and pink, I take a chance and grab his hand, leading him back down the streets.

"Come on. I think there's one last place to show you, and then you can take a load off."

"Oh? Where's this?"

I lean in, so my lips are near his ear. "How about my place?"

He smiles broadly. "I was starting to think you'd never ask."

I warned Cam before opening the door that my flat wasn't much to write home about. Cam rolls his eyes, and I hope he's not really disappointed by the reality of being a writer and earning next to nothing. I flick the light switch by the door on, light flooding into the room to reveal the inside of the flat.

Cam casually looks around as we walk in. I take his jacket and hang it with mine on the hooks as he drops his bag on the floor, looking at the prints I have on the wall between the front door and the kitchenette. I can't do much to decorate in here, but I try to add some touches here and there that speak to me and who I am.

I take a few steps forwards, past the kitchenette, standing just behind the two-seater couch in front of the TV. Cam comes to join me, surveying the short space from my 'living room' to the bed and the small work desk next to the wardrobe, on the side nearest the window.

"So this is where the magic happens." I say, waving my arm haphazardly in the general lay of the land that is my meagre studio flat. I immediately regret it. "Oh my god, that was so cringe! That sounded like a line."

Cameron just about manages to cover up a laugh. "Well, it *is* a line."

"Okay, but I didn't mean it *that* way." I really didn't. "I just meant 'this is where I make my stories'. And I guess where I live overall, like."

"It's really nice, Arran." He smiles earnestly.

"But…?"

"Why do you always think there's a 'but'?"

I let out a huff as I crash down on the couch. "I dunno. Like, I'm okay with the place. It does the job. I just wish I could get something bigger, maybe. A nicer kitchen, maybe? Somewhere where I'm not living around boxes of my stock, maybe put them in a room of their own…" trailing off, wistfully, imagining the kind of place I'd like to live.

Cam settles into the couch next to me, brushing up against me, and I tell myself it's not because the couch is so small. "Yeah, but why worry about that now?" he asks, and not judgementally or harshly, instead filling his voice with a sensitivity and care that let's me know he understands. "Just be thankful for what you have now, when you need it. Bigger and better can always come later, there's no rush." He smiles at me, and gently strokes the back of my neck.

"You do this to yourself a lot, you know. I think it's all measuring yourself up to others, or the rubric others set out for you. Or worse, the goal posts that Kid You set out. But Kid You didn't know what the world was going to be like when you were grown. Hell, Kid You didn't know what the world was really like then, either, and the bit of him still living in that head of yours exclusively wears rose-coloured glasses about it all. You can't measure yourself against a fantasy.

"And honestly, Kid You was kind of a dick." He grins at me, and we both laugh.

"How the hell did you get to be so much wiser than me?"

"I know. It's so odd considering you are *so* much older than me -"

"Oi!"

"-but I dunno. I think being the oldest of five kinda did it."

My mouth drops in a gasp. "You have four siblings?"

"Have we never talked about that? I guess not, I don't remember if you have any." Cam muses, as he looks at me with a mix of thoughtfulness and surprise.

"Only child, apple of my parents' eye. It's a lot of pressure." I blurt out.

"That...explains a lot, actually." He smirks as he leans into me, resting his head on my shoulder. I'm struck for once by how much younger than me he is, but it doesn't make me anxious or insecure. I just want to wrap him up in my arms and protect him, from what I don't know. "Yeah, oldest of five. I have a younger sister, Jess. She's just two years younger. My parents got divorced when I was six, started new families a few years after. I have another sibling on my mother's side, Ari. Their full name is Ariella, but they came out as non-binary a few years back and prefer to just go by Ari now. It feels right for them."

"Well, yeah, it sounds so cool."

"Heh. They'd love that. Found out a few months back that they read your book, by the way."

"Oh my god, that's so cool!" A thought suddenly flashes through my brain. "Oh my god, do they know I..."

"Railed their brother within an inch of his life? Oddly enough, that hasn't come up. But I did say I know you, which earned me some Cool Bro points." He smiles at my blushing.

"My dad has another two sons, Michael (never call him Mike) and Brian, the youngest of the lot. Brian still tears around the place like he's invincible. Michael is quieter, hitting that awkward age. He asks for more advice than anyone else. Wouldn't be surprised if he turns out to be another baby queer in the family, to be honest, so I try to give him the best advice I can. I know how hard it can be coming to that realisation.

"The divorce was amicable and we're all close. Family gatherings can be huge. So I'm always feeling, as the oldest, I have to, I dunno, take charge of all the Perkins-Warnock brood. No one put that on me but me, I guess but it's fine. I can take the responsibility.

"I think that's why I like the cosplay, you know? I get a chance to just *play*. No one's looking up to me beyond a superficial 'dressed as their hero' thing. I get to just have fun."

He catches it as the smile on my face from how adorable he is turns into a subtle frown. Subtle, but he never misses it. "Uh oh, I know that look. Why are you in your head now?"

"You've had to be the wise and responsible one and give advice all your life when you're growing up. And now you're having to do it for me too because my head is always so busted up over everything. I hate that I do that to you."

Cam seems thoughtful for a moment as he looks into my eyes. He smiles and bumps my shoulder with his.

"The difference is, with them I feel I *have* to. With you, I *want* to."

I blink past the burn in my eyes, and lean in and kiss this amazing young man. He turns on the couch, pushing into me, pushing the kiss deeper.

His hands go under my shirt, his thumb brushing against my nipple as he wraps his arms around me, leaning in. I lay back, our lips furiously locked, tongues brushing against each others lips, his hair falling against my head.

We stay like this on that awful, awkward, painfully small couch for an hour, just kissing each other and looking at each other.

Despite everything we've done together though, this is the closest we've ever felt.

We lay on my bed, the lights off, a tangle of sweat-sheened limbs, knotted together as the street lights gently glisten against us, lighting us in warm reds and oranges.

Despite Cam being the slightly taller of the two of us, tonight he's being little spoon, nestled in the crook of my shoulder, gentle kisses pecking lazily against my neck, the top of my arm. Warm, soft fingers trail through my chest hair and down to my groin, making lazy circles in our aftermath. He never takes his eyes off mine.

"I love this. This thing we have," Cam breathes.

"I do too. I love...this." I said. Because I meant it.

Later, lying in each others arms, Cam's head resting on my chest as he softly snores, asleep. I stare up at the ceiling in the dark, unable to rest.

Because, oh god, I meant it.

The next day we spend most of it in bed. Naked. Holding each other. Kissing each other. Fucking each other.

We don't stop when we finally get out, showering together and taking it in turns to make each other come again. Even when we sit on the couch, 'watching' a movie, we spend most of it with our hands all over each other, quick, desperate breaths…long, exhausted, happy sighs.

The longest time we spend not fooling around or riding each other is when I finally cook for Cam.

I made tacos.

"So tell me," Cam says, as he looks up at me in bed from where he's nestled himself in my armpit. "Why comics?"

We're lying in bed again. Our last night together before Cam leaves on the train in the morning. I brush his hair with my free hand, the sweat from our last activities drying out in it, and look down at him awkwardly. "What do you mean?"

Cam rolls over, leaning into me, kissing me on my chest. Then with a playful smile, he straddles me and rests his hands on my chest, leaning in for a kiss on my lips. Leaning back, I can feel him resting against me, but it looks like he isn't going to try for round two just yet…or whatever round we're actually on at this point.

Instead, he looks down at me with an almost concerned expression. "It's just, it seems really hard—"

"Choice phrasing right now."

"Deflecting," he says, grinning at me. "You seem to find the whole thing frustrating a lot of the time, even though you make this thing that people love, and it just makes me wonder: why do you do it?"

The room is quiet around us, the bedside lamp our only illumination. In the soft lighting, the shadows play across Cam's tight form as he sits, mounting me, and I lose myself in the absolute shock of the moment: this gorgeous man is here, with me, like this. And he wants to know more about me still, he doesn't find me a bore, or tedious, just…fascinating.

"I guess…well, ever since I was little, I used to like making up stories. I had this active imagination, and would always create these little story books for my classmates in school. Nothing crazy good, you know, just the idle play of a kid. But they enjoyed them, liked colouring in the awful little illustrations I did, and thought the stories were funny or crazy, and I remember them laughing or asking me what would happen next.

"I guess I really loved the attention. Odd, I know. A single child, it's not like I was short on attention from my parents. And heck, they really loved them too, they encouraged it. Even as I got older, as long as I was still doing good in school, they didn't mind me telling my stories. My schoolbooks were covered in doodles and barely legible story notes, but no one cared, long as my grades were okay.

"And then I found comic books. American comics, I mean. And there were these superheroes, and their adventures were huge, and crazy and filled with possibility. So I decided, I want to be part of that. I got older, realised I can not draw for shit, but I can tell a story. So why not comics.

"And sure, they're frustrating, but most of that isn't the story-telling. Most of it is the fact that, doing it alone, or at least without a publisher, it means I'm also doing the press, the marketing, the production, the shipping, the sales. It's like I have to wear a ton of different hats, pulling me in all sorts of directions, sometimes away from the actual writing. That's what I find frustrating.

"But then someone reads the comic you made, and they laugh, or they show awe, and they ask what happens next, and it's like that spark when I was a kid all over again. So I do it to find those moments. They're few and far between sometimes, but when they happen, dude, it means everything to me."

Cam leans in for a kiss, this time lingering, more passionate, and I feel him inhale, breathing me in. Then he gets off me, returns to my side and hugs me.

And in that moment, biting my lip, I wonder if I can leave it at that. At that stock answer I trot out in some variation to anyone who asks why I make comics. And I don't think it's enough this time.

I turn the tables and roll over him, hands either side of his head, my hips resting between his legs, holding them apart.

"And they're also so fucking sexy," I say, leaning in and biting his earlobe. "Like, even when I was in my early teens, I recognised that. The superhero is hot, their whole world is sexy, more than anything in my world, and I just wish my world was as full of colour, and brightness, and action as that. And maybe, by playing at making these stories, I can be. Maybe if I get to play in the big leagues, my life will feel as sexy as those little paper worlds."

I stop grinding my hips into his, and sigh. "And then there's the other thing…"

"What's the other thing?" Cam whispers.

I look down into his face, my hair hanging loose between us, falling towards him. I lean on one hand, brush it back with the other, before returning to pinning Cam in place.

"I get them. Superheroes. The crazy worlds they live in. All the disparate and crazy timelines and shenanigans, and insane family trees - they make sense to me. More than anything else in the real world. They're big and loud and really shouldn't make any sense at all, but to me they do. And that feels…

"…that feels safe. And just like them, maybe by doing what I do, I can make a difference. Maybe I'll feel safe, and someone else out there who needs it will too."

We stay there in silence for a while. A passing lorry's headlights briefly flash by, illuminating Cam's face, and his brilliant blue eyes sparkle for a moment, and I feel like I could fall into the icy pools of them forever.

"Thank you for telling me that, Arran. I think you already do that, and I really wish you could know that more often than you do. I want you to feel safe with me, too, you know."

I stare into his eyes and whisper, "I do…" because I really do, and I don't quite know what that means yet. Is he just my very own superhero, made flesh, that I get to tag along with, or am I…

He leans forward, lips inches from my own, never once leaving mine.

"But right now, I really want you to fuck me."

Twenty sweaty ecstasy filled minutes later, we lay there again in each others arms panting. I opened myself up to him more than I ever have to anyone before, and my mind races trying to figure out exactly what that means.

But that doesn't matter right now. He goes in the morning. I don't want it to happen, but it will. So as if to stop him, at least for now, I throw the duvet over us again and wrap my arms around him and bury my head in the pit of his arm, and hold onto him for dear life.

SPEECH BALLOON 2018
DAY ONE

The air in Leeds is thick with fog when I come in to get ready for the first day of Speech Balloon Comic Art Festival. There's a chill stronger than anything back home yet, making me wish I'd packed a scarf and gloves with me, but too late to worry about that. Instead, I grab a warming cup of pumpkin spice latte on my way in, and hold it between both hands to try and absorb the heat before drinking it.

(Yes, I am *that* basic and need the pumpkin spice when the season hits).

Speech Balloon isn't like other shows. While it does include a comic con element, it's much less about the celebration of fandoms and pop culture so much as a celebration of the art form of the comics medium. As well as exhibitors selling their work, there's a lot more speeches and talks than any other UK shows, and there's usually a highlight seminar by one of the big names of comics. This year's no different in that regard, with the head speaker being none other than Gary Clarkson, veteran of the British Invasion of US comics of the 80s and 90s. Honestly, if I wasn't exhibiting, I'd be going along to that one.

What is making this one different is the show is sponsored for the first time by Comixpedia. To make matters more interesting, last month they announced they'd be starting their own line of original releases, making them not just a digital distribution platform but an actual publisher now too. Apparently, we'll get the first line of titles announced here, so it's going to be a big newsworthy weekend for anyone who follows the ins and outs of the industry.

I walk into the convention hall, welcomed by smiling Blue Shirts, the 'uniform' of the many volunteers Speech Balloon employs to help run the show smoothly. Honestly, they've always got the best attitude of any convention staff I've ever known. It's part of why I love doing this show, even if I never sell much here.

"Hey, Arran Wilson, right?" A large, burly American man waves me over from behind a table as I pass. I don't need to look at his banner to know it's James Grayson. I follow him on Twitter, sure, but there's also all of his work at DC Comics. One of the other benefits of Speech Balloon, their guest list has more names from the big publishers than any other UK show. In fact, there's often editors and creative talent scouts here too.

"Er, hi, yeah, that's me."

"James Grayson. It's so nice to finally meet you, man." He reaches out a large hand to shake mine, with gusto.

"Oh, I know. I'm kind of surprised you know who I am, if I'm honest." I try to be good at networking, but I rarely know what to say really. However, I play a good game, I think.

"You kidding, man? I love *The surREALS*! Been reading it since it landed on Comixpedia. Found it after we chatted on Twitter a while back. Honestly, that's some solid work, man." I try to hold back how much I'm geeking out at this. My mind reels between elation that this guy who's work *I* love loves *my* stuff, shock that he even remembers our conversation from online, to the nasty little bugger in my head telling me he's just being kind, or worse, actually making fun of me for some reason. "You exhibiting here?"

"Yeah, I'm just across in the other hall. Got the new issue launching here so hoping to make a big splash."

"You got the next issue out already? That's cool! I'll try and swing by. What's your table number?"

"Uh, table 123. Just up in the back corner, I think."

"Awesome. Well, I'll leave you to it, man. Good luck, today," I turn to head out, wishing him luck too, when he shouts after me. "Hey, you'll be at the party later, right?"

"Oh, sure! See you there!"

I move through the large archway into the next hall still kinda buzzing, when a familiar voice pulls me out of my head.

"Well, someone's popular." Mitch glances at me with some side eye, then smiles as we move into the hall.

"Ah, he was just being nice," I say.

"Selling yourself short again, I see. You realise it makes more sense that he was being honest right? What would it benefit him to lie about that." He fixes me with a look waiting for my head to reach the conclusion he did. He sounds serious, almost like he's admonishing me, but I know that this is his way of trying to pull me out of my head. He's a good friend.

"Yeah, yeah." I tilt my head in his direction. "Cheers."

We head to our tables (Mitch is just a few tables down from me) and finish setting up ready for the day. I got myself some new stands and light boxes to create some verticality and add colour and light to the table display. Hopefully bring some more attention. I get the new issue front and centre of the display, then settle into the chair to write up my price lists in my sales tracking book.

The show gets started shortly after, and enthusiastic, happy looking people all start filing in, checking out stalls and grabbing new comics by the numerous independent and big name creators stationed throughout.

Speech Balloon has never been a wild seller for me, but it is worth doing, and I couldn't imagine not coming. As well as selling the comics, the show is really the most powerful networking show in the whole UK. Not just because of big names and editors who may be doing the rounds, but also so much of the UK independent and small press scene comes to this show, whether as exhibitors or as just weekend ticket holders, doing the rounds to see their friends and colleagues and party in the evening. A kind of event for camaraderie and catching up as much as anything like sales and marketing and making a name for oneself.

As such, throughout the day I wind up seeing many people I've worked with on the comic, or who have been doing shows the same as me. Sarah is up here with her books, a new collected edition that she seems genuinely enthusiastic about and says is selling really well (her kind of book always does better here, I find). Gertie and Emma are here too, helping me out on the table, but we also carved out half of the table to give them space to sell some prints and small zines that they've been working on together.

"So, is Cameron coming this weekend?" Emma asks, as Gertie talks with a customer about the art making process for our comic.

"Nah, I don't think so. It's not really a cosplay show, is it. He'll probably see me next at one of the London shows, or maybe we'll arrange a get together or something."

It's not wrong: it's not that there isn't cosplay here at Speech Balloon, but more that it's not really a focus element like it is at other comic cons. Mainly because this show is not really about fandom, as I say. It's much more about the art, the process, the actual nature of the creative industry, rather than the stories and characters made in it. There's some cosplayers here, and some of it is really good, but the volume is a lot less than you typically find at a comic convention, I find.

"Wait, weekend get togethers? Have you guys been spending time together outside of comic cons?" I'd forgotten I hadn't really told anyone about Cameron's weekend visits to Swansea…or that I'd been planning to go and see him for a weekend at his place in the new year.

"Um, yeah. He's been down to mine, spent the weekend."

"Or in you, you mean?" Gertie winks at me, having finished with the customer.

"Ha ha, very funny. Though, admittedly, partly true too."

"Ew, that was a little too far for me." Emma makes a face, as Gertie laughs.

"Ah, don't be such a prude. Well, Ar, is it official or anything now?" They both turn to me with an expectant look on their faces, smiling.

"Is what official?"

"Are you bloody boyfriends now or what?" Emma says, rolling her eyes at me.

"No, no, we're just friends who like to fuck, love to actually, but we're not…"

"Why the hell not?" Mitch jumps in, having snuck up to the table without us noticing. He casually sips on a coffee, not taking his eyes off me.

"Mitch, we were just talking about…"

"Your cosplay boyfriend, I know. Except you don't seem to know that yet. So why not? He married or something? You his bit on the side?"

"No! Wait, what? How do you know about…?"

"Tall, skinny and has a fascination with lycra? Come on, man, everyone knows. You've been inseparable at most of the comic cons of the last year. You get that giddy look on your face when you're with him too, even *I've* bloody seen it."

"Wait, so everyone is talking about me and Cameron?" I try to keep the sound of trepidation out of my voice, but fail. As much as I want to make a name for myself, the concept of being the object of gossip is really uncomfortable.

"I wouldn't say that," Gertie says, diplomatically, "More that people have noticed you guys and have been assuming you were a couple. Some folks think it's kind of cute when they find out he's a cosplayer too, like some grand convention romance. It's sweet."

"And other folks?" Of course my mind immediately zeroed in

on the implication in her sentence. Gertie and Emma share an awkward look.

"Who gives a fuck what those other folks think. The people that matter know what it is, that's all that matters." Mitch sips his coffee again as a thought seems to hit him, "Well, all except for you, apparently."

"Well, it's not like that, if anyone tries to suggest otherwise. He'd never even heard of my book until we started…hooking up. And it's not like he's a wannabe creator, or I'm some huge big shot holding promises of future success over him. I mean, for fuck sake, I'm just about scraping by myself." I feel my skin heating up, my face surely flushing red, a combination of embarrassment and anger and indignation. But also shame.

Emma grabs my shoulders and shakes me until I face her, as she leans in locking me to look her in the eyes. I have the over-whelming urge to pull away, I have always found direct eye contact so weirdly uncomfortable. "Hey, stop spiralling. None of that matters. Don't waste your time fretting what others think about your relationship. You think me and Gert haven't had similar shit ourselves? You're a good man, and all the people that are important know that. Just focus on that. We didn't mean to make you feel bad."

"Yeah, sorry, kid. Not the intention." Mitch looks genuinely heartbroken for a moment, before remembering his usual guard and popping the guise of stoic, aloof observer again.

"'Kid'? Aren't I older than you?" I raise my eyebrow at him, leaning into the change in conversational direction.

"You don't act it most of the time, to be fair. Though come to think of it, I dunno, I think I'm a year older than you, aren't I?"

I sit back down into my chair, and sigh. "In answer to the orig-inal point - we're not boyfriends, we're just friends. Long distance is messy, and neither of us is really thinking of making those kind of big moves right now. I'm focusing on my career, and I wouldn't be much of a boyfriend right now anyway."

"Well, that's bullshit and you know it. Just because you're

trying to 'break into comics' doesn't mean you can't also have a life. If it did, I wouldn't have the kids now, would I." Mitch cuts through my shit with brutal facts, their rigid truth slicing through to the core where in truth, I'm not really sure *why* I'm holding back.

"That's great, for you. But I dunno. I think I would struggle to juggle it all at once. I just need one thing to work, one big break and then maybe I can focus on everything else. I just need to take things one thing at a time, you know?"

"Well, fine. But I'm just saying, if you get too tunnel-visioned on one thing, you're going to miss a lot of the stuff skirting by you."

"Yeah," Gertie nods, taking Emma's hand in hers.

"Anyway, I'll leave you to have a think on that bombshell, you're welcome by the way. I better get back to my table. I'm doing amazing, by the way, thanks for asking. The crowds blocking my table as they queued for that Detective Comics guy have started actually looking at my table too, and it's paying dividends now. This show might not be a total crapshoot after all." And with that, Mitch spun on his heel, drinking coffee, and marches back to his table next to the crowded table of a *Batman* artist.

The three of us left behind talk about something else, anything else, planning what we might do for dinner tonight before the party. The girls offer for me to join them, and I'm about to take them up on it, when I'm aware of a figure in the corner of my vision standing over me. I turn to see a smart dressed man with a lopsided smile and the most brilliant white teeth I've ever seen staring down at me before putting out a hand in greeting.

"Arran Wilson! Good to see you, man. How's it going?" Chuck Everleigh, the CEO of Comixpedia, says as he shakes my hand. Gertie looks on barely masking a faint look of surprise, while Emma simply looks confused, eyebrow cocked.

"Yeah, hi, Chuck. I'm good, thanks. You know how it is, plugging away." I met Chuck briefly at a show last year, a similar but much smaller version of Speech Balloon down in the south of England somewhere (I always forget what that town was called, but some pretty and rather surprising town for holding a small comic art festival with some surprisingly big names in it). We talked about Comixpedia's independent, small press submission platform, and how *The surREALS* was doing really well on it.

"I see that, man, yeah. You got a couple new issues out, huh?"

"Yeah, up to the penultimate issue, and the final issue should be out at the start of the year, to be honest." I smile, pretty proud at the speed we've been getting the latter half of the series out.

"Last issue? That's a shame, actually. We love the book over at Comixpedia, you know. Was thinking maybe we could have a talk later? About what your plans are?"

"Oh," I say, taken aback. Gertie's eyes widen in surprise, and Emma continues to look really confused. "Uh, sure, I'd like that."

"Awesome, man. Let's say 6:30pm, after the show closes? At the cafe around the corner? We've kind of set up shop in there to do a few chats."

"Sure, sounds good."

"Awesome. And hey, lemme grab some issues off you. I don't think I have any of these in print yet, so lemme grab the run to date, yeah?" As he says this, he pulls out his wallet and starts rifling through the most insane wad of notes I've seen at a con before. You'd think he was buying some extremely rare collectible at San Diego Comic Con, not my small press fare out of South Wales.

He buys the comics, flashes another dazzling smile and salutes casually as he leaves, with me and Gertie more than a little bit gobsmacked.

"Okay, what the fuck was that all about?" Emma can't hold back her consternation any more.

"That was Chuck Everleigh, he's the CEO of Comixpedia." Gertie fills her in.

"And I think, if I recall the press release right, he's the head of content for the new line of original material Comixpedia is going to start putting out. They're calling them Comixpedia Premiers I think. And he wants to talk to me…"

"Is he always so…?"

"What?"

Emma shakes her hands out at her sides and flashes her best Hollywood smile. "Flashy?"

I tilt my head, like if I pour it from one ear to the other, somewhere in the middle the question might make sense to me. "How do you mean?"

"He came across very Hollywood, if you get my drift." Emma elaborates, eyebrows raised, but no more elucidating than before.

"Not really. But he is kind of a big deal, I guess. Maybe it just comes with the status."

"What do you think he wants to talk about?" Gertie chimes in, breaking the course of the conversation to something my brain feels more equipped to ponder about.

"I dunno. Maybe he likes my writing, and wants me to come up with something for Premiers? Or maybe it's something about the small press submissions?"

"He seems pretty keen on *surREALS*, man."

"Not that he asked *you* about that at all." Emma points out, with more than a little heat in her tone.

"I'd never go into more of that without you, you *made* that book, Gert."

"Ah, shut up. I don't mind, honestly. You were great to work with and we made something fun, and honestly, I think that book has a lot to it. If you got more to tell, and you want to keep it going, you go find someone else and do it, man. Honestly. You have my total blessing."

I smile a trembling smile, struggling to keep the emotions from reaching my eyes where I know they'll come flooding out. I really want to continue telling this story, but I didn't want to step on

Gertie's toes, so she just saved me from having to make a painful decision. Emma softens as she sees my reaction.

"Thanks, Gertie. I...I really appreciate it. I really would love to do more in that world."

"No worries. And hey, look, I know a few folks I think would be a great fit, so I'll help you find someone to take over if that's what this all turns out to be."

"That would be awesome. But hey, let's not count our chickens, yeah? It might be nothing at all."

"Hey guys, what did I miss?"

We turn in unison, I almost expect Mitch to have come back, but that bright, jovial tone didn't feel right. And I see why. Instead of Mitch with his tired expression of worldweary wisdom and expectation, dark hair and dark eyes, I'm met with a tall, slender frame, a face filled with glowing youth and exuberance, a shock of blue curls tumbling down to lighter blue eyes, behind round gold rimmed spectacles. Decked out in smart jeans, clean white trainers, and a thin ochre turtleneck, wrapped warm in a knee length puffer jacket. Warmth outside and in, shared across the table by a gentle smile and a devilish sparkle behind the eyes.

Cameron stands there, a cardboard tray of Starbucks in hand with four coffees.

"Surprise!"

Cameron fills me in on his journey and surprise appearance as we wander the rows of exhibitors and stalls in Speech Balloon's halls. Gertie and Emma said they'd be more than happy to cover the table, and I should go as I never get time to check everything out any more, which technically is true.

We sip at our coffees, my lips playing into a small smirk when I realise Cam bought me a pumpkin spice latte even though he bemoans how 'basic' that makes me.

"I swear, I'd have got here sooner but the train delays were insane. I must have been stuck just yards outside of Leeds station for 45 minutes. I thought I'd miss today entirely."

"I'm glad you didn't," I nudge him, with a smile. "But I really didn't expect to see you. This con isn't a huge cosplay one near as I can tell. It's not like the shows we usually see each other at."

"Sure, but I like more things than just cosplay, you know. The guest lineup here is insane, and some of the panels sound really interesting. Plus, you know," he grins at me, with a soft smile in his eyes, "you're here too."

We continue walking down the row, looking at this comic or that acrylic charm. I occasionally nod a hello to a familiar face, only sometimes getting a flash of embarrassment when I realise I can't remember their name because I haven't seen them in so long (when Cam asks about one of these folks and I have to reply 'I have no idea' despite being locked in conversation for five minutes straight, he just laughs). We smile, content in each others company as we wonder at things. For a brief moment, I twitch the fingers on my free hand, dangling between us towards his own, making to connect. Our fingers a mere breath apart, as I imagine them tangling together to hold, but then pull back overcome by a shyness I can't explain.

The things we've done together, and I can't hold his hand?

"Oh, hey, Arran, dude, it's been too long." I'm broken from my reverie by a strong American accent, a touch of a Southern drawl clinging in there but heavily masked by years of practice in enunciation and vocal clarity. I look up to see the skinny frame and edgy cool smile of Kenny Taylor.

"Hey, Kenny, I forgot you were going to be here! How's it going?" I met Kenny briefly last year at a show in London, when we shared a cheeky joint out on a hotel bar balcony, and talked all about the comics industry. He gave me some pointers in what he thinks I could try to get noticed by the Big Leagues, but admitted that it may not work…he understood how lucky he was to have made it there.

"I'm good, man, good. Show's been going well, how about you?"

"Yeah, man, pretty good. It's never a big seller for me, this one, but I always have a great time." I suddenly remember I'm not alone, having caught Kenny's heavy hints as he flashes glances to the person at my side. "Oh, damn, yeah, Kenny, this is C-"

I turn to look at Cam in introduction mode, but I was not ready for what I see. Ever cool, ever confident Cam is stood frozen stiff and rigid like a board, eyes wide and mouth hanging open as he stared at Kenny. It's then I realise: Cam is a fan.

I can barely hold back a giggle. "Uh, this is Cam. Cam, this is Kenny-"

"Kenny Taylor! Oh my god, sir, I am such a *huge* fan! I have, like, every issue of your *Spider-Man* run, and the *Doctor Strange* mini, and I am so psyched for your new Image book! I'm just-"

"Okay, Cam, cool your jets." I laugh.

"It's cool, it's cool. Nice to meet you, Cam, was it?" Kenny grins, giving me a sideways glance as he puts out his hand for Cam, which he takes with gusto.

"Cameron Perkins! Or Cam! Arran calls me Cam, you can call me Cam too! Oh my god, I am being so unbelievably cringe right now, I'm so sorry."

"It's cool. Seriously, swing by my table later, I'll sign any books you have." Kenny turns to me, giving me a small nod as he makes his goodbyes. "Anyway, man, I better jet. I'm supposed to be at a panel. You'll be at the party later?"

"Never miss it."

"Cool. See ya later!" Kenny peels into the crowd to look for his panel room, Cam watching after him slack jawed before looking back at me with the shock still on his face.

"You never told me you know Kenny fuckin' Taylor." I am finding this *way* too amusing.

"I didn't know you were a fan of his. But yeah, me and Kenny met at a show last year, hit it off. Spoken a few times by email and WhatsApp since. I helped him with some advice when we got targeted by those loony fringe comic fans, the crazy ones. I get them enough for having the audacity to be gay and making comics, but he got it off them when he said he voted Democrat or something."

"Yeah, I'm a fan of his! His *Spidey* run was immense! And did you ever read his debut series, *Sword Lords*?"

"Yeah, that was a great series. I wasn't expecting to have as much pathos as it did, actually made me cry first time I read it."

"Right!" Cam runs a hand through his hair, and takes a swig of his coffee. "Jeez, I knew you were going to make it huge someday, but I didn't know you were already well on your way."

"You think I'm going to make it?" It's strange how much him thinking that means to me. Even when I struggle to believe it myself.

"Of course, Ar. You've got such great ideas, and you're all heart. You got this."

"That's...really nice to hear, thanks Cam." I kiss him on his cheek, and blush. "But honestly, knowing a few big name creators doesn't really mean much, if I'm honest with you. They're not the ones hiring, the end of the day. It's editors and creative talent execs you need ins with and I dunno, I struggle with them. So much easier talking to other writers and artists. They're just... colleagues and contemporaries, you know? Even if they're far more successful and well known, we're all working to the same thing. Editors, however, they scare me.

"Won't lie though, when I first met him, I geeked out a little bit too. I just did my geeking out all in my head."

Cam groans, palming his face. "I just made a total tit out of myself, didn't I?"

"Don't be daft. It was adorable."

"He is fucking *hot* too, though."

"...Yeah, okay, I'll give you that. But don't ever tell him I said so."

We carry on walking, having made a lap of everything, we make our way idly back towards my table.

"What's this party he mentioned?" Cam asks.

"Oh, Speech Balloon does an official party after the first night. It's held in this Street Food hall in the city centre, great food, great music, a bunch of comic creators DJing…it's stupid fun. We'll probably all wind up at the con's official hotel for drinks afterwards too, into the early morning."

"And die a death at the show tomorrow?" Cam smiles.

"Yup. We're all going. You get entry to the party just by having a ticket, so you need to come with us. Please."

Cam grabs my free hand in his and smiles at me. "Of course I will," he says and his smile brings my own out onto my face too.

Then I remember that weird meeting earlier. "Oh, though I have this meeting after the con first. With the CEO of Comixpedia."

"Dude, really? What about?"

"I actually don't really know. I'm kind of confused about it, to be honest."

"Maybe this is the big break, Ar! Be positive, it'll happen."

I look at this impossible man holding my hand, this stupidly cool dude who is also a nerdy goofball and I can't help but feel he's right.

***

I'm standing in the cafe looking around but Chuck is nowhere to be seen.

My mind starts cycling through the possibilities: he thought better of it and decided not to show up; it was all an elaborate joke, he thinks I'm a terrible writer really; I must have misheard him, and I've made a horrible mistake. But then I see a table with a small Comixpedia logo taped to it, and a slightly nervy, bespectacled, shirt-with-a-pocket-protector wearing skinny kid sat at it. He gives the air of 'intern' if ever you saw one, and I wonder if he works for Comixpedia.

"Uh, hi. Chuck said I should come round for a chat after the con. I'm Arran-"

"Arran Wilson!" Chuck's voice booms ahead of him as he sweeps into the cafe, slapping a hand on my back and taking my hand in his with his other. "Sorry I'm late, man, got caught up in a deep talk with Scott, then there was some stuff at the office I needed to check over while our time zones lined up enough. Never mind, all done now. Sit, sit! You want a coffee?"

"Uh, sure, I guess I'll order a latte," I stutter, hovering over the seat unsure whether to sit down or head over to the counter to order first.

Chuck sits down, throwing his houndstooth jacket off his shoulders casually, and inclining his head towards Intern. "Ben, grab Arran a latte, and a black coffee for me, thanks. Use the card."

Intern Ben nods, throws a smile at me, and then hurries off to the counter, leaving me and Chuck at the table.

"So! How was the show for you today, man?" Chuck leans back in his chair, a smile fixed to his face as he crosses one leg over his knee.

"Yeah, it was good. We did okay today, and hopefully tomorrow will be the same again."

"Sweet, sweet. But *The surREALS* is coming to an end, right?"

"Uh, yeah. Looks like the next issue will be the last. It's already the last in this arc, but Gertie has got a gig at Marvel, so…" I trail off, but Chuck keeps staring at me, waiting for me to divulge more info, though what exactly he's looking for I don't quite know.

"I mean, I'd like to do more. I have ideas. And Gertie gave me her blessing, but I'd have to find an artist good enough to follow on from her, otherwise it just wouldn't feel right. But I've got other ideas too, you know. Other stories to tell, so it's not the end of the road for me." I feign a smile.

Ben comes back with our coffees, and then sits down, pulling out a tablet and looking like he's ready to take notes. Chuck leans in, takes a sip of his coffee, and then fixes me with his smile again.

"That's cool, man. Cool. And we love *The surREALS* over at Comixpedia, you know we do. And if I'm honest, we'd love to see more of it too."

"Oh, cool. That's, uh, really nice of you to say."

"Mhm. So. What do you know about Comixpedia Premiers?"

"Only what I've read online. It sounds interesting. Congratulations on the launch, by the way."

"Thank you, man. Did you hear about our first wave of books?"

"Uh, not yet. Not had the chance to check the news." I'm still at a loss for where this is going.

"That's fair. Well, we got Snyder, Clooney, Carey and Smith-Janson on the first books." I'm at once wowed by the names he's dropping, as it's quite the lineup, but also a little thrown with the almost commodification of their names. "And that's just wave one. Wave Two we're hoping to bring in some new voices, people we think could shake up the industry, people making stories no one else is."

"That sounds cool, Chuck. Not many opportunities for new voices out there, so that would be nice to see."

"Totally. And we want Comixpedia to be that publisher, lifting up new voices. Maybe voices like yours?"

What? "What?"

Chuck's smile returns again, locking onto me and the surprise clearly evident on my face.

"For real, man. We want the next big thing from Arran Wilson in the lineup. And we'd really love for that to be more of *The surREALS*."

I can't believe this is happening. "You really do?"

"Absolutely. But hey, let me give you the lowdown: Premiers is a digital first marketplace. We'll pay you an advance, you just build your team, tell us what you need and send us your pitch, and we'll green light and back you. The book sells on the app, with sales making back the advance. By the end of the first quarter, you should see the advance paid back in full, and then it's a straight split between Comixpedia and you on all sales afterwards. That's 60-40, favouring you too, as *you're* the creator."

"Wow, that sounds…"

"That's not the end of it either, man. We're digital first, not digital *only*. When your story arc is complete, we'll do collected editions, and we're partnering a print market publisher too, who'll print a physical edition of the trade, making it available for comic shops worldwide to order. Think of it: *The surREALS* not just accessible globally via Comixpedia, but also in every single comic shop in the world. And you'll get a share in those sales too."

The fantasy being drawn into focus before me has me enthralled. My books, sitting on the comic shelves next to *Justice League*, *Batman*, *Avengers*, the *X-Men* (well, alphabetically, probably more likely next to *Spider-Man* and *Thor*, but you get the idea). My little idea, my baby, in stores everywhere, for anyone to find and read and see this silly little thing I had bouncing around my brain since I was old enough to read comics. And I could finally be part of it.

"What do you say, man? That sound like something that would interest you?"

"Yes. Oh my god, yes. Where do I sign?"

Chuck smiles. "We'll draw up the contracts and send them to you after the show. Enjoy yourself for this weekend, you've earned it. Have your people check it out, we'll make any concessions you need, we just want to work with you. So excited to have you aboard, man."

"My 'people'?" I ask.

"You know, your agent or lawyer, whoever you use for that boring stuff. I want you to know exactly what you're going into, so I recommend you show it to them first, as I say, there's no rush. We'll get there in time." Chuck smiles.

As if I have 'people', I'm barely affording to make the comics, let alone legal representation. But whatever, he doesn't know that and the world he lives in, this is probably the norm. I'm sure I can ask some friends with more sense for those kind of things to nose it over and we can work out any contract legal jargon together.

"Sounds good, Chuck. Thank you. Honestly, thank you so much, you have no idea what this means to me."

Chuck puts his hand out, and I grab it, squeezing firmly to show how invested in this I am. Chuck smiles at me and laughs, those brilliant white teeth flashing.

THE PARTY

I knock on the door when I get back to my room. Cam wanted to wait for me before heading to the party so we could go in together, so I gave him my keycard to wait in my room, thinking it would be nice to see someone while I'm getting ready and either celebrate or commiserate whatever happened.

For some reason, it takes a second longer for him to open the door than I would have thought, but when it swings wide I see why. He must have been checking through the peephole to make sure I was alone in the hallway, because I'm greeted by Cam stood there, smiling, and wearing nothing at all.

"Well, how did it go?" he asks.

I don't even say a word, I don't know what's come over me, the high I'm feeling, the elation, or just the sight of his gorgeous, tight body greeting me in my room, but I barge in and grab him by the face, throwing my backpack into the room as I do, and start kissing him. Fierce, ferocious, wanting. He's surprised, but leans into it, pushing my jacket off me as my hand runs down his back until I have a fistful of his ass cheek and squeeze like I'm making to take it with me. He gasps into my mouth, and this fills me with a thrill.

I barely register the door closing behind us as I throw my shirt off and barrel right back into Cam, tasting his lips as I run my tongue along them before snatching them in my teeth. He gives as good as he gets, as while I undo my belt and drop my trousers to the floor, he bites my neck like he wants blood, making me moan. Then he laughs gently into my neck.

"We don't have time for this, you need a shower before the party."

"Fine," I practically grunt it out as I grab his now raging hard cock and drag him with me into the bathroom. He whimpers like a slight protest, again shocked by the forcefulness with which I'm handling him, but I can tell he's eager to join me too. "Then *you're* coming with me."

We're in the shower and have the water running in seconds, barely able to keep our hands and lips off of each other. I worship every inch, every centimetre, of his body like I may never have it again. As I suck on the hollow of his collarbone meeting his neck, I inhale deep, wanting to breathe him in like air. He's gasping and panting, trying to keep up with this wild animal that's taken me over, laughing with surprise with each unexpected grab and push as I take what I want, what I need right now.

I turn him around, back to me, sliding my left hand down his side, following the water as it cascades down his body and then using my right, I push his shoulders, making him bend over. I bang my knees on the bathtub as I hit the floor, but I don't care, again an electric volt shooting through my body as my tongue meets his asshole and he gasps in pleasure. I go to town down there, every moan he lets out urging me to push deeper, to kiss harder, to make him squeal again until I can't take it anymore.

I stand, taking my cock in my hand and slapping it against his backside, teasing it with my head until Cam whimpers out a 'yes', before placing a hand on my waist and looking back.

"We...we really don't have time for this," he gasps out between breaths, "We'll be late."

"Then they can wait," I say, and he smirks in response before leaning back onto me. I feel the pressure as I push against him give way, my head breaching inside. Cam lets out a breath before slowly pushing further onto me, until his cheeks are pressed against my stomach. I start a rhythm with my hips, back and forward, slowly letting him feel every bit moving out and inside him.

But it's not enough. I start speeding up, my thrusts more forceful, harder, Cam letting out a moan with each slap against him. I keep picking up speed, grunting as I struggle to keep my own breath up.

Eventually, my knees buckle and I fall to them again in the bath, pulling Cam with me, not letting him get a respite from my being inside him. He's on his knees too, straddled across me, as I pound upwards into him. I grunt with each thrust, feeling myself coming to an end, before finally, explosively, I let out a yell and feel him filling up with my come. I lean back, my spent cock drawing out of Cam, who collapses backwards onto me, the pair of us lying there panting as the water falls over us, Cam barely able to open his eyes when he tries to look up at me.

"So it went well, then?"

We laugh, each of us surprised by whatever this was that just took over me. I make to apologise for being so forceful, but Cam shuts me down. "Don't you dare. That was fucking hot, Ar. We can do that again anytime."

We get clean together and dry and dress, as I fill him in on the meeting and the huge step forward in my career I'm finally going to be getting to make. He can tell I'm excited, and nods along smiling, but I get the sense there's something he's not quite saying.

"So yeah, they'll work up a contract, but that's just a formality really. I'm going to be able to take *The surREALS* to the next level, see it in actual comic shops and everything. It's going to be amazing!"

"Sure," he says, smiling. "But, like, be careful when reading the contract, man. I know you're excited, and this is potentially a really great opportunity, but you have to be careful any time a contract gets involved."

I'm a little taken aback that Cam sounds so reticent. Can't he see what this means for me? "I get what you're saying, but come on. I've been working with them for years at this point, and Chuck seems really excited about the book and bringing a new voice into the market. This is a good thing."

"I know. It really does look like that, and I'm happy for you, I am. I just…I don't want you rushing into something because you're so excited, and miss out anything that might not actually be as perfect as you want for your book. You know the stories, creators in the industry have been screwed over all the time."

"I know, I know," I wave off the concerns, annoyed at him for not just being excited with me. This is important to me, why is he raining all over it. "But, like, I have worked for this for so damn long, you don't think I know to make sure it's all right and okay?"

Cam takes a breath, motioning with his hands for me to settle. "I know, and again, I am really happy for you. I'm just saying don't leap before you look, you know? It's exciting, it's what you've been working towards and wanting, and I'm sure that Chuck isn't out to take advantage…but we don't know what his bosses want. It's a big company, with serious money behind it if they're able to throw it around like that, and you're just one little guy. You have to be careful with that kind of power dynamic is all I'm saying."

I huff, "'Throw it around'? What, you don't think my book is good enough?"

Cam gives me a stern look, tilting his head and pulling his lips thin, almost like he's considering a child. It makes me mad, but also mad at myself because I'm aware I am sounding pretty petulant. "You *know* I think your work is great. You know how I feel about you, or at least, I hope you do." He crawls across the bed to where I'm sitting, the look on his face turning from stern to soft, and I swear his eyes look wet for a moment. He puts his hands on my tensed shoulders, and I let them relax, as he leans in to envelop me in his arms.

"I care about you. I just want what's best for you. I don't want to see you get hurt."

I take three deep breaths, closing my eyes. I feel my heart slowing down, and the heat that had risen to my head start to fall. Finally, I open them again, and lean my head into Cam's where he's holding it in the crook of my neck. "I know. I understand. I'm…I'm sorry for getting worked up, I just…

"I'm just really excited, and I want you to be happy with me." I say as I turn to meet his eyes, wiping a tear from them, startled for a second that I did this to him.

"I *am* happy for you. And with you. I'm just always going to look out for you too, because you're too important not to." Cam kisses my thumb where I'd wiped away his tear, before leaning in and kissing me. "I'm sorry too. Let's just enjoy the news tonight. I shouldn't have brought a damper on it tonight."

I say it's okay as we get our jackets and head out of the hotel to go find the party, but part of me still feels hurt and I worry if I'm being unreasonable, or if Cam's right after all.

***

We get to the central Leeds shopping centre and head up the escalator outside leading right next to the food court. I low key (okay, very high key) love this place: a collection of street food vendors, many permanent residents but also a few that swap and change so there's always something new here, so you can try a bit of everything from burgers to pho, from bao buns to freshly made ice cream and more.

There's a large space made which I imagine during the day is filled with tables and seating, but now is a massive dance floor that is already filled with dancers from the con. Fans and creators are packed on the dance floor, as the Yorkshire-based comics writer Brian Grint throws them for a loop by playing a track from the *War of the Worlds* soundtrack. There are faces I recognise among the crowd, from the few cosplayers that are here every year, to colleagues in the comic making scene, and even a few folks who just love the con and medium so much you will find them at Speech Balloon every year, coming from anywhere from London to Ireland to Israel.

Dai is already bouncing on the floor with wild abandon, backed up by the block of pure muscle that is fellow indie writer Shahid Qazi, a pair who are inseparable on the dance floor every year. I briefly wonder how long it will be before they start trying to re-enact the lift from *Dirty Dancing* again.

Cam and I search through the crowd and find Gertie and Emma sat in a little tucked away alcove, with a couple new faces plus Mitch and Sarah in tow.

"What kept you guys? We thought you were gonna miss the annual *War of the Worlds* dance-off." Gertie asks, a knowing grin flashing across her face.

"And please, *do* spare the details," Mitch deadpans.

"Sorry, err, my meeting thing overran a little and it held us both up." My excuses sound as fake as they are, clearly, as not a single face shows any belief in them, even the new ones.

"Yeah yeah. Anyway, this is Arthur and Liana. Liana came over from America, she's been drawing indie books with that new publisher we were talking about before. And Artie's working on his first comics after today. They're sound!"

We say hello and make introductions before Cam excuses himself to go and get us some drinks. Artie tells me how he's been coming for years and just thought he was a fan, but he watched this panel talk today that has really inspired him to get writing himself, which he'll somehow work on in-between completing his PhD. Liana from America is the epitome of cool, but in a super friendly way. She just exudes a quiet confidence that is immediately disarming and welcoming; I like her, she's going to be huge, I can tell. Cam gets back with our drinks, and the conversation returns to my unexpected meeting.

"So, spill. How did it go? What did Chuck want?"

"Chuck Everleigh?" Liana asks, eyes widening with interest.

"Yup. Called our boy in for a chat after the show, but we don't really know why, and he's sitting far too coolly on this information for my liking. Knowing Arran he's fit to burst."

"Yeah, yeah, laugh it up. But yeah, it's good news," I flash a glance at Cam, and I'm relieved to see him smiling and in no way disagreeing with that assessment. I fill everyone in on what was said and the potential future for *The surREALS*.

"Dude, that is amazing! I definitely need to get you in touch with my friend Michael, he'll be perfect for it, I promise." Gertie smiles, as she jumps up and throws her arms around me.

"Cocktails! We need cocktails!" Emma declares, to a wave of agreement, and we're swept into the enlarging crowd on the hunt for something bright, colourful and exceedingly alcoholic.

Me and Cam do eventually get some food (bao buns and a mini-kebab for me, a burger and fries for him), but the rest of the night is given way to drink, celebration and dancing.

A slightly more raunchy number comes on, and while the others go looking for more drink, Cam grabs my arm and pulls me in close to him. He's grinding on my thigh to the rhythm and I am suddenly very thankful that I have my loose fit jeans on tonight. Throwing my arms around his shoulders, I realise we've never had the chance to do this. To go out dancing, that is. Drinking we've done, even a dinner date, but we've never got to cut loose. At least, not with clothes on and in public. Eyes are definitely on us, but right now, I don't give a shit. I'm on a high, this hot guy who keeps fucking me good for some reason is all over me, and the future feels promising and in my grasp.

Somewhere close to midnight, the venue finally switches the lights on, officially ending the DJ set of the greatest British comic creators of the millennium, and moving this strange mishmash of usually socially averse comic makers, exuberant fans and perpetually high energy social butterflies into the streets, and the party is not over.

"Where we going now?" Cam asks.

"Dunno, just follow Kieron and Jamie, we'll wind up where everyone else is then. Works every year." I answer, smiling as Cam realises who I'm talking about, and waving my arms in the air as the marching crowd of late night comics revellers breaks into an impromptu rendition of *Total Eclipse of the Heart.*

Where we wind up is the official con hotel of Speech Balloon, where many of the Guests of the show are staying. The bar is already a who's who of many of the international guests, and I make my hellos to the few I've met before. In turn, they introduce me to others, and I'm amazed at the people I'm meeting, some of whom are making my favourite comics right now or even the ones that made me want to make them in the first place.

Even more surprising to me is how many of them have heard of my little book. It's so strange to me still. *The surREALS* was just a hobby at first, but incredibly close to my heart. I've picked at and played with it since I was a teenager, until I finally had the balls to actually try and make it, and sure, it's got bigger. I'm aware it's out there and been read, and I'm invested in it so much it's become more than a hobby but an actual business for me, but still. It's this silly little thing that rattled around my head while I was bored in Swansea, and it amazes me that anyone could possibly think anything of it beyond disinterest, condescension or an 'aww' at how I'm trying.

Thankfully, at this stage of the night I'm filled with so much alcohol and adrenaline from this high of good news I'm on that I'm able to play it cool, and my fanboying is kept to a distinct minimum. After all, these are my colleagues now, or soon will be. I'm finally breaking into the comics industry. I'm one of *them.*

Cam smiles at me, and I can tell he's also trying his best to keep his cool, but it's clear from his eyes when we start talking to someone new that he's read their work or loves their art and is biting his tongue to not just rave about it endlessly.

In fact, I practically see him pinching himself when Kenny turns up, and joins us, a tumbler of iced amber liquid in hand.

"Arran! Man, how's it going? I thought that was you two I saw on the floor earlier! Keep it for the bedroom, eh?" he laughs.

"Ha, what can I say, I'm irresistible, I guess."

"We're just celebrating," Cam adds, clearly trying to keep the topic on me instead of launching into raving about Kenny.

"Oh yeah, what for?"

"I dunno if I should say, nothing's set in stone, I haven't signed a contract yet."

"It's cool, man. It's a party, this is Hotel Con now, you can talk shit and it stays here." Kenny means the kind of weird after show con experience, which tends to refer to US shows more than it does here in the UK. Outside of the con, creators and editors sometimes make business connections at the hotel bar, talking shop and revealing things to colleagues, but also occasionally making connections that will lead to opportunities later. It's not an ideal way to run business, everyone's inebriated and buzzing, but it happens.

"So I might be continuing *The surREALS* after all. As a Comix-pedia Premiers."

"Dude, that's amazing! I'm doing a book with them too next year, we're gonna be publisher buddies!"

We celebrate our mutual news and then start talking about books we've been reading and who's doing what. Cam joins in too, and Kenny seems to warm to him more as Cam relaxes and stops seeing him as this amazing man on a pedestal to just this guy, doing what I do.

"I'm really proud of him, you know? I think he's going to smash it, and I can't wait to see how it all turns out." Cam says about my potential future as a big muckity muck writer hitting the big times.

"I just feel like I'm finally breaking into this industry, you know. Finally breaking into comics." I laugh, but I mean it.

"Babe, you already broke into comics. You're making them, that's all it takes to break in." Cam says, kissing me on the cheek, and I feel my heart flutter and I can't tell if it's what he said or his eyelashes brushing against the side of my face.

Kenny watches us, his smile straightened out across his face slightly. There's a seriousness there that wasn't there a second ago. Then he slams back the last of his whiskey and makes a move to leave. "Time for a refill for me, boys. You guys want anything?"

I try to say no, I couldn't possibly, but he bats my hands away and makes me give him an order. Cam gratefully accepts too and Kenny makes a move for the bar.

In the hectic line of events of the whole day and this evening, I realise we lost Gertie and Emma, but then seeing it's now nearly 2am, I know they've probably headed back to their hotel and bed.

"You tired?" Cam asks, seeing me checking the time on my phone.

"Nah. I'm still buzzing. You?"

"I'm good if you are."

"Well, I am busting for a piss, I'll say that. You okay here for a minute?"

"Oh sure, I'll just gawk at all these amazing comic writers and artists I'm somehow in the middle of." He looks at me as I raise an eyebrow. "I'm kidding, I'm fine! Go piss before you get it on me."

"Like you never thought about it," I joke, kissing his cheek.

"Hey now, let's keep kink talk for a conversation later, eh? Don't want the great and mighty Kenny Taylor knowing we're a pair of degenerates now, do we?"

"Oh, that ship has sailed, babe. We're all freaks here!" I say as I peel off and head to the bathroom.

I'm standing at the urinal, minding my own business, when someone comes in, and moves straight for the urinal next to me. My first thought is this is weird, as there's a few more with plenty of space that someone wouldn't have to stand right next to me as I shake myself off, but then I realise who it is: Kenny.

"Hey man, had to let the lizard out too. I left the drinks with your man."

"Ah, cool," I say awkwardly. I dunno why, I have always found bathroom conversations, especially around a urinal, really strange. This should be a quiet place. I guess except for all those times at gay bars where there's been fucking in the bathrooms, but whatever.

I finish up and move away to the sink to wash my hands in silence, but Kenny looks around and breaks it when he realises we're the only ones in here.

"So, hey man. Where did you meet Cam anyway? How do you guys know each other?"

I grab some paper towels and dry my hands, my eyebrow twitching slightly in the sudden interest, but figure it's just normal smalltalk. "Uh, we met at another comic con, actually. Down in London."

"And he's a cosplayer, right? A fan?" Immediately, I start to get a sinking feeling about where this is going.

"Well, yeah, he's a cosplayer, a really good one actually. And sure, he's a comics fan. But he's not a fan of me, per se. Or at least, when we met, he'd not ever read any of my stuff."

"He has *now* though, yeah? He sure talks like he has." Kenny says as he zips himself up and makes his way to the sink.

"What are you getting at, man?" I hate confrontation, especially with someone I admire, but I can't help feel the heat rising in my words.

He seems to consider his next words carefully as he dries off his hands, and then he throws me with the look on his face as he leans against the sink, tossing the used tissue into the trash: a look filled with concern. "Look, maybe it's not my place, and I'm sorry if I'm crossing a line. But I'm just thinking, you need to be careful. You don't want some random gossip tanking your career before it's had the chance to really take off."

My shoulders slump, and the anger building in me is replaced by a sickly sensation of worry. "What gossip?"

"That comics creator Arran Wilson has been bedding fans at comic cons? That maybe someone decides they feel used? That maybe they're just some starfucker looking to meet all the creators they love by sleeping with someone on their way up?" Each accusatory phrase ends like a question, like he's reeling off possibilities. Ones that I'd be lying if I said my head hadn't swam in before in my deepest, darkest moments.

I feel giddy and bump into the stall frame as I lean back into it. "Are people saying that about me? About us?"

Kenny stands, and walks over to me, placing a hand on my shoulder. "No, man, I've not heard anything like that. Not yet anyway. But so much of this gig is *perception* now, and the perception of what we do carries more weight than how things really are sometimes. And we all know that there have been guys doing *exactly* that shit for years, more than the public at large probably knows about even.

"The way this whole industry is now, the way things are linked to gossip rag websites and social media, it'd be so easy for someone to take one look at you guys and where and how you met and jump to a conclusion that could follow you for years.

"I'm just saying be careful, is all. Think about the optics and if what you guys are doing is worth the risk."

I pull myself upright, energised by a new sense of indignation. "We're not just fucking around, you know. I'm not using him, and he's not using me, we're..."

"Aren't you? You're, what, boyfriends? More? Because that's not how you talk about him, and he's sure proud of you, but he doesn't use those loaded words either."

I sag again. What *are* we doing? Am I risking the career of my dreams on some fun? It's the best sex I ever had, but is that all it is? Is that worth losing it all?

Kenny pats my shoulder, before making for the exit. "Hey, don't listen to me, you know. Maybe I know nothing. It could all be fine, maybe no one would give a fuck. Maybe *you* shouldn't."

His accent thickens, the South coming out in earnest. "But just remember: people on social media, they're not so big on context and when they see two black birds they tend to think that all birds are blackbirds, y'know?"

He pauses at the door. "He is right though, you know. You already broke into comics, man, just by making them. Don't make the measure about whether you get work with a publisher or not, that's bullshit."

He leaves me alone in the bathroom, as I pick myself up again and head back to the sink and look in the mirror. The energy and buzz of the night is gone, and part of me just wants to go back to the hotel room and slip into the dark.

I must be taking too long, as the door swings open and I see the reflection of Cameron walking in.

"Hey, you okay? You've been in here a while? You haven't puked have you?" He laughs.

"Nah. No, I'm fine. Think the night just hit me and I'm getting kinda tired now, is all."

He walks up and puts his hands on my shoulders, watching my reflection in the mirror. "You sure you're okay? What did Kenny say to you?"

"Nothing," I lie, and pray it doesn't show on my face. "I'm good. Let's just finish these drinks and head back to the hotel, yeah?" I turn and force a smile, looking Cameron straight in the eyes, hoping that the thousands of questions and scenarios reeling through my brain aren't written across my own for him to see.

"Okay. Come on, let's get your energy back up out there," he says, taking me by the hand, and we leave and try and enjoy the rest of the night.

SPEECH BALLOON 2018
DAY TWO

Light breaks in through a crack in the curtains, falling across my face. I open my eyes to meet this chill grey light, and immediately feel a throbbing rush through my head to the back of my eyes. Thinking better of it, I roll over to the body of warmth behind me: Cam, still sleeping, peaceful, serene.

His left arm, the one nearest me, is lifted over his head, angling at the elbow and lightly resting on the pillow. His lips are slightly parted, as he breathes in and out smoothly, a slight snore escaping his lips that I'll tease him for mercilessly later. It's surprisingly warm in here, which explains why he's pushed the covers down in his sleep, so I can follow down with my eyes, his smooth chest with it's barest tuft of light blondish hair, his stomach, smooth and hiding the hard muscles underneath when he's not flexing, a trail of furry hair leading down under the quilt.

I look back up to his exposed armpit, dark hair neatly trimmed there, and I press my face into it and inhale deeply, filling my nostrils with the scent of him before kissing him gently there as I wrap my arms around him.

"Unhhh," he moans, "I've not showered yet, I smell like booze."

"You smell sexy, just like everything else." I mumble.

He rolls over and pushes down so his face meets mine. "Well, if you like that, here, have some morning breath too," and he embraces me in a kiss. Which tastes off stale booze and a cheeky cigarette or two.

"Ugh, on second thoughts." I stick my tongue out as I pull away and he punches my shoulder, grinning.

Rolling onto my back, a fresh wave of pain shoots through my skull. "Ugh, my head."

"Head? Yeah, I can do that." He flashes me his devil eyes, before slowly kissing down my chest.

"I didn't mean...oh, what the hell." I throw the covers to the floor so I can watch his ass angled up into the air as he descends my body, stopping at my nipples to playfully bite them, then down, down towards my...

Then everything from last night comes crashing down into my head, and I put my hand on his cheek. "Wait."

"What's up?" He looks up at me, for all the bleariness of sleep, I see the concern in them.

"We...we don't have the time. I have to get ready for the show, doors open in about an hour, and I'm definitely going to need to shower after last night."

Cam rests his chin on my grown, his Adam's apple resting against me, considering. "Yeah. Yeah, I suppose you're right. Shame though. I do normally start the morning with a dose of protein."

"Oh, dude, that was gross." I make a retching face.

He looks just as disgusted in himself. "Yeah, not my best. It's early, and I'm hungover, leave me be."

We get up, have a coffee together, and he gets dressed while I get in the shower. He's left his bag of clothes at his hotel when he checked in, so he's going to head over and get ready there, and I'll see him at the con. After I kiss him goodbye at the bathroom door, I close it and lean against it, waiting for the telltale click of the front door closing behind him and wonder what I'm going to do.

The con goes well again, despite everyone having the worst hangover in history, as if it were some mass outbreak. Sunday is a chill day though, and sales are slow and steady, so no one is feeling especially pressured.

Gertie and I are talking about this artist friend of hers she's recommending for *The surREALS* when Cam comes up to the table, looking fresh faced and snazzily dressed, a scarf loose around his shoulders and a light zipped hoodie instead of the thicker winter coat from yesterday.

"How's the head?" he asks, smirking.

"Never had any complaints before," I fire back, and give him a smile back. "I could use a coffee though, you want one? Gertie, want one?"

"Uh, sure," she says, giving Cam a quizzical look, and he just shrugs.

"I'll come with," Cam offers, but I wave him off. "No, no, it's all good. Wait here, I'll be right back."

I leave them both looking confused as I rush out from behind the tables, awkwardly apologising as I squeeze past busy or broken comic creators. I march down the hall and out to the small cafe around the corner, and get in line.

My brain is telling me that I don't want Cam to have the ammunition to fire one day, that I was using him or taking advantage. My brain is also screaming that that wouldn't ever happen, that he likes me, that maybe he even-; before a third part of my brain (seriously, how many hemispheres does mine have?) tells me that I'm going to miss out on potential sales the longer I muck around playing childish games of avoidance.

I almost miss that I've reached the front of the queue, the server having to say hello to me twice before I place my order. As I fret waiting for the coffees to come, I jump as a strong hand lands on my shoulder.

"Sorry there, partner! Didn't mean to startle ya," Chuck says, his broad smile beaming down at me.

"Oh, Chuck. Sorry, hi. No worries, I guess I'm still a little discombobulated from last night."

"Ha, that good, eh? A little too good maybe. Still feeling the effects myself. How's the show going? Selling out yet?" Oh my god, is he lining me up to cancel the deal? I feel the rug pulling under me already.

"Heh heh, no, not yet, but I'm sure I will! Just early days yet." I hate how the speed of my answer goes all over the place, from slow and steady to tumbling out of my mouth like a runaway boulder.

The server gets my attention again, and I nod to Chuck an excuse me. I take the tray of coffees and turn, not to Chuck anymore, but Gertie.

"Okay, what the hell is going on?"

Sighing, I walk back slowly, filling in Gertie on everything running through my head. Or rather, not everything. I don't tell her what's been said to me to make me feel like this, just that I don't want Cam to think I'm taking advantage of him or ever be able to say I was. She takes her coffee from the tray, and sips it thoughtfully.

"Do you honestly think he would? I mean, you know each other pretty well now, right?"

"Well, how well does anyone know anyone? Maybe I think it's all going well and he'd never do that, but he feels like I'm using him?"

"Now you just sound neurotic," she glares at me. "Look, I left him manning the table, because I have not been riding that young man like a bronco but I still trust the fuck outta him. I'm going to go wake Emma up, and I'll see you back here after lunch. I want you to not be a weird lunatic by the time I get back, okay?"

I nod quickly, my cheeks burning from the cold and from how genuinely stupid I feel. She thanks me for the coffee and heads off, so I make my way inside.

I find Cam sat behind the table, looking genuinely nervous. Not because he's unsure of himself behind the books. I know it's because of me.

"I'm sorry," I say, holding out his coffee as a peace offering.

He takes it and I make my way around and come sit next to him. "Accepted. But I don't know what you're being sorry for? What's up?"

I take a deep breath and tell him how I'm freaking out that maybe I've been taking advantage of him and how maybe it looks bad, because he's a fan, and I'm a creator, and he's young and I'm old, and he's hot and I'm not…

"Okay, okay, I get it, but please, don't take offence when I say this to you earnestly," he places his hands on my arms, looks me dead in the eyes, "Please, shut the fuck up."

I was not expecting that response.

"You're not whatever you were just about to say: you're fucking gorgeous, and I love every inch of you, and no, not just those very valuable ones. Don't belittle me by saying I'd be wasting my time with someone I didn't find attractive enough to want to be with." He says, not angrily, not harshly, just calmly and pointedly.

"You're not old, there's not even a decade between us, and even if there was, so what? You're not my boss, not my teacher, not my role model or in any position over me, age can just be a number, and you keep up with me plenty where it counts." I go to make a smutty joke and for once Cam stops me.

"And I may be a fan, but I am not *your* fan, or at the very least I wasn't when I met you. And when we met, it may have been at a comic con, but it was not in the dynamic of a fan and a pro. Not to make you feel bad, but you were, and still are, just rising through the industry, you're not some superstar yet, but trust me you will be. It was just two horny gay guys who happen to have similar tastes meeting at the same event.

"So I don't *care* what anyone says, or what anyone thinks, I just want to spend time with someone I like. And I would hope that was the same for you, and if you don't like me anymore, you can just say so, no hard feelings."

I practically jump towards him, as my mind jumps out of the convoluted morass it's been mired in. "No, no, I haven't stopped liking you, and I never will, Cam. I love spending time with you, it's been one of the highlights of this whole fucking year for me. I just...I get all in my head sometimes, and I think, in some ways, I maybe don't like *myself* very much, so I always just wait for the other shoe to drop with other people. Because if *I* don't like me, then how can anyone else like me?"

Cam gets on his knees in front of me, tilting his head up and looking at me earnestly. "You very nearly quoted RuPaul then, you know that?"

I burst out laughing, but feel the sting of tears prickle my eyes. Cam pulls me down the the floor in a hug, and we kneel there, laughing at my stupidity until someone above us clears their throat.

"You know, you probably shouldn't do the gay sex here at the con. They'll definitely ban you for that on family day," Mitch says dryly. "At least, I can only assume this is how the gay sex starts."

We both look up at him with raised eyebrows. "You have a very weird idea of what gay sex is, Mitch." I let the words drip out of me with mock venom.

We laugh it off, and have a brief chat with Mitch, who is not at all hungover, as like a sensible man he left the party early and came back to his hotel room to watch football and then have a good nights sleep. He lords the lack of hangover over us for another ten minutes before making his rounds, and me and Cam fall back into our usual rhythms of conversation.

"Oh my god, what is that?" Cam says, looking up the aisle with a look of horror.

Moving slowly down the aisle, and seemingly making a beeline for us, is a broad man in a thick, waxy duster coat. A black wide brimmed hat sits upon his head, lank, greasy looking black hair cascading out.

"Is-is that cosplay?" I ask Cam.

"If it is, I don't know the character and I know everything," he says, transfixed by this entity like something straight out of *The Ring* if it were entirely about Northern farmhands moves towards us.

They arrive at the table and don't utter a word, just stare downward at the books on the table. "Hi," I squeak. "Did you want me to tell you what the books are about?"

The figure draws a hand out from their pockets, revealing fingernails that clearly haven't been clipped in at least six months. I'm not talking false nails, I mean actual human nail growth, chipped and ragged by being roughly caught in everyday use. They move their hand over one of the books covers, the nails a fraction of a millimetre from the book. Cam watches aghast, mouth hanging limp, unable to say anything.

The figure lifts their head and looks at me, gives me a brief nod, before turning away and moving off into the distance to haunt someone else's nightmares for time immemorial.

"What. The fuck. Was that?" Cam finally squeals.

"I swear to god, every comic con, you get at least one interaction like that, man. Being a comic maker takes nerves of fucking steel, I tell you."

"What the hell happened to you two?" We turn to see Gertie and Emma. We fill them in on the out of body experience we just shared, and we all laugh and start sharing stories about the weirdest interactions we've ever had at a comic con.

"You guys okay now?" Gertie asks quietly, while Emma and Cam are deep in their own conversation.

"Yeah, yeah, we're good. My brain was just being fucked up. Probably overtired."

The rest of the day goes by uneventfully, until they call the end of the show. Applause breaks out through the halls, from creator and fan alike, as everyone moves out into the winter darkness of Leeds.

"Have you guys got to rush off now?" Cam says, loading a box onto a trolley for me.

"Oh, nah. The drive is a bitch in the dark, so we stay an extra night, to head back tomorrow. We'll probably just have a chill night in the hotel.

"You heading back tonight?"

"Nope, got my ticket for tomorrow too." He smiles.

"Wanna join us at the bar?" I ask, bumping shoulders with him.

"Always," he says.

The bar is a pleasant and generally uneventful night. I spend the night catching up with other creators like me, talking about the show, what ones we did this year, and if anyone's got anything booked for next year yet.

Speech Balloon is also the last show of the UK calendar, so the bar on a Sunday is often a hive of creators taking stock, figuring out what worked, where we think would be good shows for who, which shows to avoid (like the ones being run by a member of the English Defence League), and the like.

It's chill and perfect, as I sit on a couch talking and laughing, Cam nestled in the crook of my arm, laughing at jokes and befriending these people who are part of my comic life at least.

Then I look over at the bar and see Kenny, looking over, and he raises his whiskey to me and nods.

I'm left with the echo of something he said last night. I don't call Cam boyfriend, neither does he do that for me. So what *are* we doing? Do I *want* that? If I do, would that be wrong?

"Hey, can I stay with you again tonight?" Cam purrs into my ear, pulling me out of my head again.

"That hotel room of yours was a total waste of money, you've barely spent any time there." I laugh, and then kiss him. "Of course you can."

And he did.

THE QUIET SPELL

Christmas is an interesting time of year for me, because on the one hand, I do love the festivity, the general sense of joy and happiness, and I love buying people presents. On the other, there's too many people everywhere, it's too noisy, and I *hate* buying people presents.

It's also a sign of a long, tough time for comic creators, especially in the UK: there are no comic cons at all, people don't tend to use your online store so much, and in January, you have to submit your tax return and may owe a bunch of money. All this when there's nothing bringing money in, but everything seems to be taking money out.

As such, I tend to take on a seasonal job or two to supplement my income for a while. This year I'm being extra bar staff at my local gay bar, so my evenings have been pretty busy.

Not that that is the real reason I've barely spoken to Cam since Speech Balloon.

Yes, I've been torturing myself about it. But my head just feels so…full? Like a constant scraping buzz that is just filled with endless, dystopia-level fantasies about how everything could go wrong, how the world could come crashing down, how my dreams could be crushed.

On top of this, I'm trying to buy presents for my parents, who are notoriously difficult to buy for ("Ah, you don't have to buy me anything, you could use the money" etc etc), and the contract came through from Chuck and Comixpedia. It took everything I had not to sign it immediately and send it back, but I'm taking Cam's advice (and yes, I'm aware of how hypocritical I am).

I'm reading over the contract for the second time, realising that everything still sounds so completely alien to me it might as well be a different language.

I tried asking Chuck about it after the first reading. "I can't really give you advice on it, man. End of the day, I work for the other party in the contract, so I can't advise you. Just show it to your lawyer, take all the time you need, seriously. No rush."

I haven't the heart to tell him that I don't have a lawyer, because come on, like I can afford that? I dunno, at times I think he thinks I'm way further along in my career than I actually am.

I find myself getting baffled by language that seems to have too many commas and too few all at once when my phone goes off.

"Okay, what the fuck is going on with you and Cam now?" Gertie sounds pissed, not least because she didn't even say hello, and she's a real stickler for good phone etiquette.

"Hey Gertie. What do you mean?" I try to act dumb, but the guilt is already making me nauseous.

"You haven't spoken to him in weeks. He doesn't know what he's done. He's home for Christmas, and is acting like he isn't hurting, but I can hear it in his voice. You know you're my ride or die, mate, but you're being a top class cunt right now."

"I know," I sigh, exasperated and collapsing on my bed. "I just…I'm getting all up in my head, and I dunno, maybe it's for the best if whatever this is was over."

There's silence on the other end of the line for a long minute, making me wonder if she's just hung up on me. "What's this all about, man?" she asks, calmer. "Ever since Speech Balloon, you've been talking some weird fucked up shit about you and Cam, and honestly I don't see any of this actually coming from him. So fess up. What happened? Is it the Comixpedia gig?"

"No. At least, not entirely. But that is fucking with my head too. I've been reading this contract and the legal mumbo jumbo is just incomprehensible to me. Between that, Cam, everything Kenny said, I'm just feeling buried. Like, everything feels on top of me, and my head feels, like, actually full. Like there's no space for anything more. And Cam doesn't deserve that. He deserves someone who can give him more."

"Okay, two things," I hear the ire in her voice rising again. "A relationship, whatever that relationship is, involves more than one person. Don't you think Cam gets a say in what he 'deserves' too? And second, just what the fuck did Kenny say to you?"

I fill her in on what Kenny said to me in the bathroom, about how whatever this thing is between me and Cam, from the outside looking in it could look a certain way, and make it look like I'm just as bad as so many other men in this industry and could ruin me before I begin.

Gertie seems to think about it for a second, before starting back up again, calmer and warmer this time. "Okay, who gives a fuck what anyone else thinks?"

"But what if one of those someone elses is an editor who won't hire me because they think I'm some sort of predator or some shit?"

"For fuck's sake, Arran, you aren't though! Cam isn't a kid, honest to god, he's more mature than you are to be entirely blunt. And if some theoretical editor made that kind of judgement on you based on the opinion of some random twitter user who's never met you and knows nothing about your relationship with Cam, then that editor isn't someone you'd want to work with anyway. They're not gatekeepers like that, man, they want to find people to work with. They're in the collaboration too."

I realise by this point, Gertie knows a lot more about that than me, having worked with editors now while I still never have.

"But look, I also get where you're coming from. You think I

didn't have similar concerns when I came out and started my transition? What people might think about what I'm doing to Emma by putting *her* through this; what they might think about her because of me? Worse, what she might think of me?

"That fear held me back for so long, and I get it. Emma means so much to me, the thought of losing her was too much. But the weight of the maybe is too much to bear too, and if I had let the fear keep me from moving forward, no matter what, I wouldn't be as happy as I am now.

"And yeah, it's a risk. I won't lie to you. But not trying because of what someone might say or think isn't ever worth it, trust me."

Gertie doesn't really talk about her transition with me much, and I don't pry. I can understand how unbelievably personal that journey is, and it should always be her choice who she shares that with.

"Thank you for sharing that with me, Gertie. I appreciate you. And I'd never equate my journey with yours, but…"

"Oh, fuck that! It's not the same, but doesn't mean you can't relate. There's too many people in this world who act like the lives of others are so alien, so strange, that they cannot fathom how someone could choose that path, and look where that's led this world. You are one of the most empathic people I've ever met, you can relate, and I can relate to your fears, and I'm telling you: they are fucking stupid, Kenny fucking Taylor can fucking piss off, and you are going to fuck up something really potentially great for you if you don't pull your fucking finger out right now, mate."

I know she's getting serious when all the 'fuckings' start flying. My vision goes blurry, so I sit up and feel the warm path of a tear going down my cheek. "I know. I'm just…it's all so much, and I don't know what to do."

"Okay, first thing: send that contract to me. I know that's probably breaking the rules, but Emma deals with legal stuff all the time with her job, so between us we can work it out. Then, message Michael - he's also been waiting to hear from you."

"I checked out his art, it's great stuff."

"I know, I told you, I only recommend the best. Then, with that distance, you call Cam and explain what happened and get your act together. We'll get on top of this together, and then you can call it a Christmas miracle or something."

"Ha. Thanks, Gertie. I think…I think I have some work to do. I better get to it."

"Damn straight. Now, I'll speak to you soon, good bye." She hangs up the phone, and all is right with the world as her phone etiquette returns.

Michael really is a great guy, enthusiastic and eager. He's based out of Italy, and occasionally his sentence structure in emails takes a little deciphering, but he seems like a nice guy. And his artwork is just phenomenal. Different from Gertie's, sure, but it still fits well with what came before.

I pitch my ideas for the next arc with him, and he's fully on board. He makes some suggestions of things he'd love to draw, and I think we can make this work.

Likewise, Emma's breakdown of the contract makes so much more sense to me. They even made allowances to let me continue to sell stock I already have, which sounds really reasonable of them.

It's times like these I remember how this industry and career can feel so isolated at times, but it really is a team, whether it be the people making the books, or those out there wanting to see you succeed. You just have to reach out to them, because despite the things we write about, no one is psychic. They won't know you're struggling unless you let them know. Of course, I'm also incredibly aware that I'll probably make the same mistake again in the future.

Case in point, I left it another few days before finally plucking up the courage to speak to Cam. I ping him a FaceTime request and take a deep breath.

After nearly a full minute, I see him pop up on my phone's screen, in a room that looks strange to me and with a look on his face which I can tell is him trying to look measured and calm, but I can see the sadness.

"Hey."

"Hey," he sighs back at me.

"Um, where you to at the moment? Whose room is that?"

"It's mine. I'm back home for the holidays."

"Cool." I fidget in my chair, biting my lip. "Look, I'm sorry. I've been an ass."

Cam lets out a deep sigh, and I see a tear drop down his cheek. Shit. "Yeah, yeah, you have. But what I want to know is why you've been a complete ass, man."

Okay, full honesty time. I tell him all about Kenny and the bathroom intervention. About how my head has felt insanely heavy with nonsense and craziness and I felt like I'd be a nightmare to be around, and maybe it was best if I let him go, but apologised for ghosting him as that wasn't the way to have dealt with it at all.

"Kenny Taylor can get fucked." Cam finally sobs, angry through his tears. "I can't believe he'd make you think that about me. I can't believe *you* would think that about me!"

"I didn't! Not really. But sometimes, my brain runs away and I can't help but get caught in the negative and it makes me so scared I get stuck in the fear. But I know that you're not the kind of guy who'd want to use me like that, and I know that I'm not using you. I care about you too much to do that to you."

"You do?" he asks, and my heart breaks that he had to wonder about that. "Because I like you, Arran. I don't know what we are to each other, and I was cool playing things as they were, but I think we're more than just fuckbuddies at this point. There's definitely feelings there for me.

"I hope there are for you too?"

I take a deep breath. It feels like I'm making a massive step, but at the same time, I don't know why, because this is Cam. Of course I do. Of course. "Yes, yes, Cam, there definitely are." I wipe away tears and probably snot too, and I kick myself that this 'romantic moment' comes from me having to apologise for being a complete asshole and now looking like a blubbering mess.

"I don't care what anyone else thinks, and if you want to play things cooler in public so it doesn't affect your career, I get it. But I don't want this to end right now, because I still want you."

"I still want you too."

"Good. Then bloody show it with a text sometime, yeah?" he laughs, and wipes his tears away on the sleeve of his jumper. I do the same as there's a knock at his bedroom door.

"Hey, Cammy! Can you help me wrap mum's present?"

"I'll be right there, Ari." He turns back to me. "Sorry, I better go. Big brother duties."

"Wait a second," I jump forward, smiling. "Tell them to come in."

He looks at me through the phone and grins. "Ari, come in." The door opens, and in comes his sibling. "Let me introduce you to someone. Ari, this is Arran Wilson. Arran, this is Ari."

Ari's eyes go wide and they rush forward to the camera, covering their open mouth with their hand wrapped up in their sweater sleeve. "Ohmigod, no way! I freakin' love *The surREALS*! I was so sorry it ended."

"Well, Merry Christmas, there's going to be more." Cam gives me a look from behind, and I tilt my head in a silent 'I'll fill you in later'. Ari looks ecstatic.

"Hell yeah! That's awesome news!"

"Alright, alright, that's enough fanboying over Arran. Let's get those presents wrapped." Ari waves goodbye and wishes me a Merry Christmas. "Thanks for that, you probably made their Christmas, you know."

"Ah, I was just getting you Big Brother Points. A small present, but Merry Christmas all the same." I give him a weak grin, that feels like another apology as much as my happiness to finally have all this crap off my chest.

"Nah, you already made my Christmas, Ar. Merry Christmas."

We hang up, and on the high of finally taking whatever this is with Cam a step forward, I open the email to Chuck, upload a signed copy of the contract and send it straight off.

Next year is going to be amazing.

CARDIFF COMIC EXPO 2019
DAY ONE

Christ, the start of this year has been such a ball ache.

We got the ball rolling on the new *The surREALS* series, and things have been going pretty well. But it's not all been plain sailing.

About eight pages in, Chuck messaged us to let us know they've had to tweak the format specifications, to optimise for all tablets or something. It meant having to adjust the pages already done, which was a bit of a frustration for Michael, but he laughed it off well enough.

Not so much when it happened again in February, after he'd drawn the whole first issue. Still, we got it done, and the first payment of the advance came in, and man, that was a relief. There's barely any shows this time of year, at least here in the UK, and so things have been pretty tight for me. So when that money came through like mana from Heaven, honestly, I could have wept.

Now, thankfully, I have my first show of the year too. Cardiff Comic Expo is a small, hotel con. That is, it's held in an events room in a local hotel. So it's not huge, a fairly cosy affair all in all. But as it's a bit more central for the Cardiff and Bristol comics lot, we all get to come together and see each other.

I said hey to Sarah when I first got in, and caught up with her a bit about her upcoming gig: she's pivoting into animation and is working on a show that's being prepped for Channel 4, which is pretty awesome. It all sounds cool as hell, and she's seeming a bit more relaxed in herself.

"Not giving up this lark, though, don't you worry," she assures me with a laugh that genuinely sounds light for her. "I'll keep making the comics, it just isn't my only bread and butter any more. Takes off a lot of the pressure, you know."

"It's not a lot of extra work, though?" I ask as I set up one of my book stands ready for the day.

"Well, yeah, but if anything, it gets me kinda energised, to be honest. Like, the creative juices get flowing at work, and then I can play with them when I get home on things I want to make myself." She smiles as she thinks about it. "It's just making it all fun again, you know? Like, I think..."

She trails off and her fingers fidget over the plastic lid of her takeaway coffee cup. I stop what I'm doing to focus on her, and it's like she's trying to think of how to say it...or whether to say it at all.

"I think I basically stopped enjoying making the comics for a bit there," she sighs, holding her arms about her. "Like, I'm still super proud of it all, and the story is always churning away in my head, wanting to get out. But the constant hustle, the push to try and make it bigger and sell better and find new audiences, it just...sucked a lot of the joy out of it all. Because I needed it to get bigger constantly, so I could keep making it and keep the lights on.

"And every time things got a bit rough, I started wondering 'Is it because I'm not good? Do I need to work harder? Is it just not for me?' And I dunno, I think I just got tired. I actually did consider packing it all in."

"Sarah, no, that would be—"

"It's all good, not going to. I took a break, let myself focus on me for a bit, and started applying for creative jobs. Something to keep the money coming in. Then this gig came about, and honestly, I've never felt more energised." She smiles again. "Honestly, I'm sure it's just how you've been feeling with the Comixpedia gig, man. It's so awesome it's happening for you, just like you wanted."

I simply agree with her. She doesn't need to know how stressful it's been so far. But then, it has also felt like a step in the right direction too. Sure, money has been tight at times, the back and forth has been frustrating, but they've also been really supportive, letting me know how they plan to market the book and keeping me in the loop. We're hoping to announce it officially in May, when half the series is completed and ready, and launch shortly afterwards in June or July, which will be so awesome.

It's been like a rocket ride after how long it took me and Gertie before, and faster than I can keep up with at times, but a great learning experience, right? Like, this is how it'll be when more projects start launching and maybe if other publishers get interested in me too, so I should learn all I can from this time.

We wish each other luck as Sarah heads to her table and the con officially opens. Local cosplayers and fans pile into the conference hall, and things get under way.

It's a pretty chill day, and I see a lot of people who've bought from me before, at shows from all over the country. The energy is positive and quickly starts to rub off on me as I settle into a rhythm.

I text Cam to see how his weekend is going, but he doesn't reply. I guess he must be busy.

Cam's been great over these last few months, too. Whenever I'm feeling confused or frustrated, he's been a great sounding board and talked me off the anxiety precipice more than once. I still think he has his reservations about the whole deal, but he's happy to see me so happy, I think. Which is great. It's great to have this *friend* in my corner, helping me out whenever I need to vent. A friend who knows how to cut through my bullshit.

Yeah. A friend.

It's about lunchtime when I get a text message back from Cam. I finish up a sale with a rather diminutive Thor, and check my phone.

Behind you

I spin around and sure enough, there's Cam: light blue hair, just long enough for the natural wave in it to start really showing, turtleneck jumper over his broad shoulders and smiling at me in that casual way of his.

I run from behind my table and pull him into a big hug as we both laugh.

"I didn't know you were coming!"

"I figured I'd keep it a surprise. How's it going?" Cam's hand brushes down into the small of my back before slowly sliding away. We head over to my table and he comes and sits behind with me as I fill him in.

"How long you staying for?" I finally ask.

"Just today, I'm afraid. I have a big work thing on Monday, so I can't risk getting stuck out of the city. I have a ticket for the last train tonight."

"Ah, that's a shame," I say, genuinely meaning it.

Cam leans in and breathes into my ear. "Why? What were you planning on doing with me this time, mister?"

I laugh, feeling my cheeks and ears flush red, and playfully slap his shoulder. "Get your head out of the gutter, man. I was just thinking it would be cool to hang out too. It's not always about your dick, you know."

"Yeah, well…you do like that a lot too though," he grins and I shrug with a 'you're not wrong' kind of admission. "Anyway, I said 'last train'. I can hang after the show for a bit, we can get a drink and you can show me what's good in Cardiff."

"Ha, I don't get out here much myself, to be honest. But Sarah will happily show us both around, I'm sure. And Gertie is coming down too, so we can all hang out."

"Sounds awesome," he says, smiling brightly at me. "Right, I best let you sell some of these AWESOME COMICS then," he says, volume increasing drastically at the last part and turning heads towards us as he leaves the table. "See what else is at this show, even if THE BEST STUFF IS RIGHT HERE!"

I shoo him off, laughing. "Oh my god, you are such a dork."

Works though. I turn around to five people at my table, all checking out the books.

The night out is great.

Sarah takes us to a few spots, including an underground rock bar that plays all the 00s classics, but unfortunately smells horrifyingly like wet feet. But we don't care as we're all dancing and laughing and drinking, and it's honestly like being a teenager again.

Especially when the handsome man always at my side sneaks in a peck on my cheek, or grabs my hand, or dances with me, or is just smiling at me.

As we get pushed close together in the crush on the dance floor, I throw my arms over his shoulders, letting my slightly shorter than his own frame nestle naturally into him. His hands drop further down until they're cradling my butt cheeks, and he leans in until I can feel his breath on my ear.

"Wish this wasn't as physical as we could get tonight." He grins.

I kiss him and as I pull away I gently nip his lower lip. "Behave, you. The girl's are watching."

Sure enough, I glance over to see Gertie rolling her eyes and Sarah retching over dramatically.

As we get closer to midnight, Cam has to take his leave. I walk him to the train station, and stand just outside the large, sandy coloured stone front.

"See you at the next one?" Cam says.

"I hope so," I smile at him, stroking his hand.

"Or hey, if you can spare some time from making the next comic masterpiece, come down to my neck of the woods maybe?"

My smile falters and I rub the back of my neck. "I'll have to see what I can do. Money is tight and the book is more work than I thought it would be, everything keeps happening so fast—"

Cam puts his thumb on my lips, and I look right up at him.

"Don't worry about it, I understand. Some day. But I'll just see you at the next show, okay?"

I nod. "Text me when you get home safe?"

He leans in and kisses me, then smiles. "I'll text you then, and every day in between, Arran."

He heads into the station, one last parting wave before he heads up to the platform. I head back out giddy at how everything is finally coming together.

CARDIFF COMIC EXPO
DAY TWO

Sunday is a lot slower, which is useful, because I'm absolutely hanging. I'm not sure which pint was the pint passed the line, but I think I went over it and then some in the end.

But all in all, it's been a nice weekend. A gentle but much needed start to the con year, and hopefully a sign of things getting on an upward trajectory in the near future.

As we're breaking down at the end of the day, Sarah comes and checks in with me to walk me to the train station.

"Well, you and Cam are definitely getting closer, huh?" She says after we cross the road and head into the city centre.

"Yeah. Yeah, I guess so."

"So…what are you to each other? Boyfriends?" We both laugh at how ridiculous that word sounds when it's two thirty-some-things talking about it.

"We've not really put labels on anything. And with everything how it is right now, maybe it's too early to? Like, I'm a bit scatty at the moment, with the comic and navigating this whole 'being published' deal. No one tells you how different it is from just self-publishing your stuff."

Sarah nods. "True. It's a whole other ball game, that's for sure. Wish I could say I had any pointers, but everything I've had up until now kind of fell through." We walk in silence for a little while, letting the busy city sounds fill the lull. "But hey, you got friends, you got a successful book, a new deal and a man who, I think, really is keen on you. You really do have it all, man. You should enjoy that."

"Yeah. Totally." I say, smiling. And I think it too. Everything is working out. It's all going well.

So why do I always feel like I'm just waiting for the other shoe to drop?

THE ANNOUNCEMENT

They announced the new series of *The surREALS* today. A press release went out to all the big comics news sites, and most of them ran it. Newsarama, Bleeding Cool, ComicsBeat - I never thought I'd see my name on those sites if it wasn't in the comments section or message boards, but here I am. Exclusive interview went out on io9, and finally the word is out: *The surREALS* have graduated from small press, self-published to one of the most successful digital publishers to ever exist.

Social media quickly followed, with posts on instagram, Facebook and Twitter. Twitter's where I live though, so those ones I followed more. I got some congratulations messages, which was nice. Mostly from people I'd expect, but I even had one or two from some pretty big name creators, people whose work I follow rabidly, so that blew my mind.

But then the other messages started.

I sit in my flat, checking my phone every few minutes. I try to ignore it, but the notifications are coming thick and fast, and the constant buzzing is like a drill inside my head. I try putting the phone on Do Not Disturb, but it's like the sound of it vibrating on the arm of my couch with every new barb, every new insult or insinuation, and very few positive messages is going off in the depths of my head.

I pick it up and click on the notifications again.

> YOU EVER SEEN THIS GARBAGE BY
> @ARRANWILSONCOMIX? WHY THE FUCK WOULD
> ANYONE PICK UP THAT TRASH TO PUBLISH?
> HONESTLY, HE SHOULD JUST THROW HIMSELF OFF
> A ROOF NOW

As I'm staring at thirty messages telling me I suck, my work sucks, I should go away, or even die, and the four new messages congratulating me, my phone lights up with a different notification. A text from Gertie.

> Hey, I hope you're okay, buddy. I know you're probably staring at the phone right now, so I'm telling you, from experience. Go outside. Leave your phone at home. Walk away. Trust me. Call me when you get back.

My foot taps out an aggressive rhythm at three times tempo, and I bite my lip.

> WE SHOULD BOYCOTT COMIXPEDIA. WE DON'T
> NEED THEM PUSHING THEIR AGENDA ON US, JUST
> LIKE MARVEL AND DC. JUST READ THE REAL
> COMICS BY COMICSRIGHT! #GOWOKEGOBROKE
> #MAKECOMICSGREATAGAIN #CUSTOMERMOVEMENT

I throw the phone down, throw myself to my feet and head out the door. I'm outside in seconds flat, marching down the street with my hands in my pocket. I go to put my earbuds in to drown out my thoughts with some music, but then I remember my phone is in the flat, so that's a no go.

I stop at a cafe and grab a coffee, just to do something. I head towards the city centre, thinking the noise of people around me might distract me, but it doesn't.

Instead, I wonder if any of these strangers around me are the minds behind the faceless profiles online. Their words stick in my head, like an inescapable news feed of abuse.

YOU KNOW WHAT WE NEED? A GOOD WAR.
SENDING THEM OFF TO WAR ALWAYS THINNED EM
OUT, OR FIXED THEM. IF THEY GET KILLED IN DUTY,
WELL, LEAST THEY WERE USEFUL FOR SOMETHING
THEN

I head to the park - what is it they say, 'walk in nature'? Maybe seeing some green will switch this crap off in my head.

I walk into the denser parts of the park, trees towering over me towards the grey skies above. I inhale the scent of grass and leaves, trying to let nature wash my brain clean, reset, refresh. I find a bench and sit down, and try to zone out all the sounds around me, the birds, the passersby, I just focus on my breathing.

In. One, two, three, four, five. Out. One, two, three, four.

My breathing is starting to slow when I feel the first raindrops hit my head. I realise I don't have a jacket on, I ran out of the flat so fast I didn't grab it.

By the time I get back inside, I am completely drenched through. I throw my sodden clothes off and straight into the washing machine, walking naked across my flat towards the bathroom when I stop at the couch. The corner of my phone pokes out from under a cushion, staring up at me as it lights up again.

Shaking my head, I jump in the shower and turn the heat up as high as it will go. My skin burns for a second but then I get used to it and I just let the heat wash over me, hoping to clean everything off me. What, I don't know. I just feel...covered.

Finally, I sit on the couch in a towel and grab the phone.

There's one hundred and sixteen notifications from Twitter alone. An email reply from Chuck after I asked him what we should do about all these hateful messages. 'Just ignore it' he says, as if it's as easy as that.

Three texts from Gertie. One from Sarah. WhatsApp messages from Mitchell. Three missed calls from Cam.

Before I work through them, I go to check out the Twitter notifications. More of the same, but now some of my followers are arguing with the trolls posting hateful stuff about me or my comics too, and I'm tagged into whole threads of their endless back and forth. And then I notice the DMs.

No one wants your faggy comics, leave comics alone

You're gonna die penniless and forgotten. Just hope you know.

The Lord will find you, and you'll burn. I hope I'm there to watch it.

No one will read it. You should just give up now. Not much point in you being around.

Keep your homo agenda away from kids, you fucking pervert

We'll see you at the next comic con. best make a will

Fucking fruit

Faggot

Just die already

The phone lights up again and begins vibrating. The light looks weird and that's when I realise there are tears in my eyes.

It's Cam calling again. I answer before I even have a moment to think about what a mess I must look.

"Help!" I cry to him as he comes into view. I try to hold back a sob, but seeing his face, I just wish he was here right now and I just can't hold it in.

"Hey, hey, Arran, babe, are you okay? Shh, calm down," I see the panic in his eyes, like he wasn't expecting to see me like this, and then I realise he never really has.

"It's just-it's so much-the things they're saying, and it's all the time, and—"

"Hey, look at me. Look at me and just let it out." He stares right at me through the camera and I do as he says. I bawl and wail, the phone tumbling from my hand as I lose my grip.

This was supposed to be a happy day. I was supposed to feel like I'd reached the next step, that I was on the rise. This was my moment, my victory.

But instead all that's around me is hate and anger and it's like it's seeping into my head and now it's all I can see.

The tears start to dry up and my breathing slows down, only hitching in my throat now and again. I fumble for the phone and lean it up against a mug on my coffee table. Cam is still there, tears in his eyes, but looking grim and stoic.

"Okay, what is it about all of this that's getting to you?"

"Have you seen the tweets, Cam? I mean, come on!"

"I have seen some of them, yeah. But trust me, walk through this with me. What is it that is getting to you?"

I wipe my face as I try and think of how to explain it to him. "I - I just wanted this to feel like a win, you know? To just have this, this celebration, and instead—"

"What's stopping you?" Cam interrupts. I look at him and am about to come at him with a defence of 'hundreds of bigots and vile messages' when he stops me. "Never mind those messages, there's also been people congratulating you. Your friends probably have too, right? Have you gone out to celebrate your personal victory yourself at all? Or did you just stay inside looking at tweets from strangers on your own?"

Defensive, I stammer out that I went outside, but Cam looks me dead in the eye and I have to admit that my mind never left the app.

"But Cam, I'm getting them everywhere. My mentions, even in my DMs, and the things they're saying…"

"Is any of it an actionable threat?" I focus on my breathing and think about them and I realise none are in any way credible. They don't know my address, they're all just bravado and bullshit.

"They still hurt though. It still feels like they're…in my head, under my skin…" I trail off.

Cam takes a deep breath and looks at me with soulful, calm eyes. "I'm sure they do. Because I know you, Arran, and I know how much you take this all to heart.

"But I'm telling you, you're focusing on the wrong thing. There's so much love for what you do."

"I know," I admit. Mixed in with all the pain and anger is a ball of shame, sitting in my gut, because I'm focusing on the haters instead of those that support me. "But people online hardly ever say anything when it's positive. It's always the hateful people posting, a dozen posts at a time, and it just becomes this constant…noise."

Cam smirks. "Welcome to the internet."

I laugh, and wipe the tears from my face.

"End of the day, you have to try and change your point of view of it all. Because as sad as it is to say, hateful people aren't going anywhere, and there's always going to be people out there who like nothing more than throwing shit. But there's people who do love you and love your books, and isn't it kind of rude to spend all your time worrying about some asshole who hates your work instead of the fan you've met or chatted to who loves it?"

The shame turns in my stomach. "Yeah, when you put it like that, I guess I am. But it's so easy to just say 'ignore it' or 'change how I look at it' and so much harder to put in action."

"Look, Arran, we've talked before about how you let this all get to you. Social media can become a bit like an addiction, and for different people, it can affect them in different ways.

"I think you should really think about taking a break from the apps. Step back."

"But-"

"I know you're going to say that you need to be on there to market your books, but let Comixpedia handle that for a bit. You need to think about *you*, and your health. And right now, the way these messages from sad, lonely, pathetic assholes on the other side of the planet are getting to you is *not* healthy."

I breathe in and close my eyes. "You're right."

We talk for another half hour or so, talking through some options on how I can handle this better. Make the apps work for me, instead of working me over. I close my DMs, switch off my notifications. Cam really wants me to delete the app from my phone, but I'm not there yet. I post a thank you tweet for all the kind words, and then shut the app down. He says he'll send me a link to an application and guide that will show me how to block the worst offenders en masse, so it doesn't have to become a chore.

"Thanks, Cam. I'm sorry I'm such a freak with this stuff."

"You are not a freak! Anyone would feel just as alone and battered by that crap, you just need to learn to focus passed it. Otherwise it could overwhelm you.

"And I don't ever want to see that happen to you."

I smile at the beautiful young man on the phone screen. "I'm so lucky I got someone sensible and peaceful like you to calm me down."

"Are you kidding? I want to find each and every one of these sad-ass chuds and beat the ever-loving shit out of them. Ain't no one makes my man feel like this on his special day."

I blush when he says 'my man' and almost knock over the phone.

We sit in silence for a few minutes, until I break it. "I wish you were here."

"I wish you were here, too," he smiles. "And hey, I didn't get to say it before, but congratulations. This is amazing. I knew you could do it."

I feel the tension drop from my shoulders and move to the bedroom and get into bed with him, digitally at least, and wish him goodnight. Turning over, I rest my hand on the empty half of the bed and imagine it not being so barren and cold there someday.

MANCHESTER ULTRA CON 2019
DAY ONE

"So I went up to the Green Room for a bit, because I decided I needed a break. Good thing about being a guest at shows it turns out, is you get access to the green room, if the show has one, and means you sometimes find yourself side by side with stars of TV and film as you all peruse the cheap supermarket sandwiches and coffee that they'll give you for free.

"I grab a coffee and sit down. I just wanted to have a few minutes away from the hustle and bustle, you know, it was kind of a busy one today.

"That's when I hear these two comic creators talking about some of the cosplayers. In particular some of the women cosplayers. Now, I'm not going to name names, because maybe it was a one off, but given what this industry can be like at times and the elements it seems to sometimes attract, I wouldn't be surprised if it's far from the first time they've had these kind of attitudes. But needless to say these are two guys who are pretty damn popular, who've worked with some of the bigger publishers, and have a *lot* of fans.

"'Did you see what some of these cosplayers are wearing?' The one guy, let's call him Bill, asked the other, let's say Elliot.

"'It's the heat, man. Got them making them as skimpy as possible. And the cosplay gives them an excuse to slut it up.' And they're laughing, like the most lads lads bullshit I've ever seen at a comic con. I thought better would come out of these guys, but instead it's the same old, toxic masculinity, raging machismo, misogynistic crap.

"'But some of it was pretty hot, right? Honestly, some of it is gonna stick with me, make me have to have a long hard look at why I love the things I do' Elliot laughs.

"'Aw, you mean that slutty Freddy Krueger lass? Christ, mate, if she cut those shorts any shorter I'd be able to see right up her Elm Street!'

"'Never thought I'd be able to knock one out to Freddy Krueger' and they keep laughing and elbowing each other in their corner, like schoolboys talking about which 'bird' has the biggest tits now. I dunno, I think that's when I saw red.

"'Excuse me, you realise that's another human being you're talking about, right? And a fan, no less. And here you guys are, sexualising a girl who is probably half your age.' I yelled at them.

"'Oi, now, mate, no need for that. We're just having a laugh.'

"'I hope so, I'd hate to hear you'd been taking advantage of these fans you're calling sluts and 'knocking one out' over. Enough of that going round this industry as it is, don't need any more trash clogging it up.'

"Well, that's when I think I got a rise out of them, as they stood up from their table and headed over to me. But I stood my ground. We don't need another story of a creator taking fans to their hotel room to 'show them new pages' when really it's to pull out their flaccid lonely-looking knobs.

"'Now, you shut the fuck up, you little pissant shit. Don't you know who I am?'

"'Oh yeah, I know exactly who you are, and that's why listening to you slut shame that young girl is such a let down. For shame, you should know better, a man your age and working in this industry as long as you have.

"'Even if she was dressed in a sexy, evocative way, she's not doing it for you, or to get you off.'

"Ah, she knows what she's doing…' Elliot rounded, and that's when I stood up too.

"'Yeah, she's dressing as a character that she loves, in her own creative way. And maybe she is making it sexy to enjoy her body, but that's not for anyone else but her.'

"'Listen, kid, you better shut it now. I know the organiser for this show, I can make sure you never get a table here again. And I won't stop there, I can make sure you can't get in at any show in the country. I've been at this game for years now, mate, and I can make your little 'career' very bloody short.'

"'Go on, then,' I say, 'Let's go talk to the organiser. Let's go tell them all about how you think the women at this show are sluts, how they're dressing provocatively to turn you and all the other men here on. Let's go talk to them about where this con stands on consent and the sexualising of cosplayers, eh?' And I grabbed my coffee and tossed it in his face and spun on my heel and marched right out of the Green Room and to my table, and well, if I got kicked out, then so be it."

"Or, at least, that's what I wish I had the guts to have done," I tell Cam, as we sit in an American Diner-style restaurant in Manchester.

He lifts an eyebrow at me. "Why didn't you?"

I squirm in the leather seat. "I dunno. Too cowardly, I suppose. You know me, I hate conflict. And he probably *could* make my career very hard for me, I guess I was scared that standing up for what's right, shutting down that deeply misogynistic bullshit, it could have caused more problems for me than him." He stares at me from across the table, sipping on his extravagant looking milkshake. "That, and…"

"'And', what?"

"And I'd be a total hypocrite, wouldn't I? Here I am with a cosplayer I'm actually fucking every comic con, who am I to tell someone off for taking advantage and sexualising someone whose cosplay turns them on?"

His straw makes a noise as it battles to get every last bit of milkshake he's sucking in, while he stares at me dead on and deadpan, before he finally sits up and takes a deep breath.

"Okay, Arran, listen here, and listen good, and don't interrupt.

"It's probably good that you didn't say any of those things, because technically, that guy wasn't doing anything wrong. Was it crass and demeaning? Yes. But it was in the privacy of his safe space with a friend, and nothing more. Do he and his friends have garbage opinions and messed up ideas about women, sex and personal clothing choices? Yes. But as long as he's not putting that on another person; not wolf-whistling women, or forcing himself on them, he's entitled to his bullshit.

"Secondly, that you didn't shut them down doesn't make you a coward. You can want to stand up for others, and you can be an ally, but that doesn't mean you have to show up every time. If it's not safe, if you need space, if it's not something you're good with, you can step back. Be vigilant, and step in when you have to, but no one is expecting you to swoop in every single time.

"And thank you for standing up for cosplayers and consent, honestly. We do get sexualised way too often for just doing what we love and what makes us feel comfortable. And even if we do wear something provocative, we do mainly do it for ourselves and how it makes us feel.

"But we're not ignorant of how that might make others feel, and how they may perceive it. But as long as there are boundaries and respect, everyone can think and feel what they like, it's all good."

He pauses, dips his finger in the pink foam coating his milkshake glass, and puts it in his mouth, as he continues to stare at me. Yes, it is as hot as it sounds, but the look also carries a question, I can feel it.

"Lastly, why do you think you'd be a hypocrite? You fuck a cosplayer, and that cosplayer fucks you plenty too, I might add, but you do so because *I* want you to. We have consent, and more than a fair share of feelings involved too. I want you to sexualise me, because I sexualise you too, mister. You think I don't think nasty thoughts about you when I'm staring at the back of your head as you bash the fuck out of that poor keyboard on your MacBook? Trust me, I do. Filthy, filthy thoughts. And it's okay, because I know you like that and want that, and if that ever changed, you'd let me know. So, why oh why would you be a 'hypocrite'?"

I bite my lip and flush thinking about everything he just admitted, but also about the admission I have to make. Will he think less of me? Am I the asshole?

"I…because…because I've had some dirty thoughts about you, and others, too. In your cosplay. So I guess I'm just as bad." I feel myself shrink into myself.

"So?" He says, matter of factly.

"What do you mean, 'so'? I mean, you I guess is okay, but when someone walks up to me in a spandex outfit and his package staring right in my face through it, I shouldn't be looking at it or thinking anything about it. It's not what he's there for!"

"How do you know? He might be a bit of an exhibitionist. He might get off on people looking."

"Cam!"

"Hypothetical cosplayer aside, again, if you have had naughty thoughts after seeing someone in cosplay, they're just thoughts. You're only human. You have desires and kinks, just like they probably do. I know I do."

"But…"

"Have you ever acted on one of these little fantasies?"

"Well, no…"

"Have you ever tried to get in another cosplayers pants, besides me?"

"No."

"Have you ever made lewd comments or forced someone into a sexual conversation just because you thought they looked hot in their costume?"

"Of course not…"

"Then what's the harm? You haven't broken consent, you haven't taken advantage, you're just a human with thoughts, perhaps more thoughts than some others if these vast, intense scenarios keep running through your head are anything to go by. You keep thinking someone is going to judge you and ruin you for something that is just natural and part of the human experience, even though you're more controlled and respectful of boundaries than, sadly, most guys are.

"You're not a bad guy. Stop worrying that someone might think you are. They can think whatever they like, just like you can."

The server comes and pops the bill on our table and moves along as I sit there kind of gobsmacked looking at Cam.

"You really think I'm thinking about this all too much, huh?"

"Yup. But that's par for the course with you," Cam says, snatching the bill away from me before I can look and putting his card down with it.

"I just don't want anyone thinking…"

"Stop worrying about it. People will think what they want. Sometimes, they'll air their opinions too, no matter how wrong they are. The end of the day, facts are facts. You and me, we're consenting adults, we met each other at a con, sure, but not as a creator and a fan, as just two gay guys who were up for some fun. And we keep having fun. There's nothing wrong with that, no matter what anyone thinks. Because they can choose to pick and leave facts as they want to make things look one way or another, but the end of the day, context is what's most important. And the context is, I like you, I wanted you, and you want me, and here we are."

"I want to kiss you so bad right now, you know that?" I sigh.

"Oh, I know. But after. Right now, I want to hear about *how* you sexualised me?" He gives me the impish look he wears so well, his bright yellow hair tumbling before on of his eyes.

"It was that Thunderman suit. The first time I saw you at my table. I ran my eyes up that costume, pulled so tight across you, and oh man, I felt like I could see every single inch of you."

"Heh, yeah, I forgot my dancer's belt on that one."

"You're what now?"

"My dancer's belt. You've seen it. The undies with the big white padded bit at the front?"

"Oh! I thought that was some kind of jock strap."

"It is, in my case. But the front kinda tucks everything away. Makes it so your dick and balls aren't basically pressed up to the spandex like a vacuum mould in the costume so everyone can tell what religion you are. You probably noticed it on newer male cosplayers, how their junk is super obvious, but on people who've clearly been doing it a while you can never tell. That's probably a dancer's belt."

"Huh." Makes sense. I had in fact noticed how less and less I was being affronted by an excitable member, always a little distracting when I'm sat at the table and basically eye level with someone's junk.

"But you noticed me, huh? And you liked what you saw?"

I gulp hard. "You know I like your body."

"Ah, but you also liked it before you saw what was underneath. Come on, it's me now, you can tell me. Did it make you hard, seeing me in that skintight outfit? Seeing my muscles and curves and other things through the fabric?" He runs his tongue across his lip casually, like he's licking up the last of the cream from his milkshake.

"Yes." I breathe out, and realise that I'm hard now too.

Abruptly, Cam stands from the table and puts a hand out to me. "Come with me. You've given me an idea."

I look at his hand offered to me. I look up at him. I squirm in my seat, my jeans thoroughly uncomfortable, and decide that standing up is just not an option right now. "Um, you may need to give me a minute." He takes a peek into my lap under the table, smiles and winks at me.

He takes my hand as we get closer to the canal, dragging me towards the sounds of revellers and drunken hen nights. Just before we get to Canal Street, where the street we're on connects onto it at it's halfway point, Cam stops and points me towards a shop door, which is oddly still open even at this hour.

"'The Clone Stop'? Why are we here, Cam?"

"You'll see."

He takes my hand again and drags me inside, where a skinny twink in a muscle vest looks up at us. "Evening," he says, cheerily. "If you guys need anything, just give me a shout. We're running a special this weekend too: any sale over £35 and you'll get a free 75ml bottle of lube."

The casualness with which he tells us the shops specials throws me a little as I start to take in the rest of the wares. Along one wall are shelves filled with dildos and vibrators of all shapes and sizes. Some are modelled after porn stars, with their like-nesses displayed on the packaging the copies of their packages are in. I'm a little embarrassed at how many of them I could name.

Next to it is a wall filled with straps, rings, loops and bands of all kinds of sizes and materials. Some are weighted, some are simple jelly looking rubber, and others still even have little spikes on the inside and I feel my testicles retreat inside me at the thought.

The racks are filled with clothing, ranging from brightly coloured to just plain black, with the distinction largely being colour is reserved for the more traditional material clothing and the black stuff is almost all leather, rubber and latex.

"Come on, down here," Cam smiles, guiding me down some stairs spiralling into an almost hidden basement.

Down there, there's more clothing, and the walls are lined with DVDs, covers ranging from the more discrete fantasy modelling shots to full on, balls to the wall pornographic action shots.

"Hi guys. You can try anything on, we just ask that you keep your underwear on, even if you're trying on a jock or anything like that. If you're not wearing undies tonight, boys, I'm afraid you won't be trying anything on."

"Not to worry," Cam smiles back at the other salesman down here, an older, broader guy, but you can tell that once he was just as lithe and smooth as the guy upstairs. "Got our pants on for now, and we know what we're looking for."

"We do?" I say, voice rising a little higher than I'd like.

Cam looks at me and smiles, and drags me over to the changing room. Well, changing area. It's more or less just a thick blue curtain hanging from the ceiling and railed into a rough circle, with a standing mirror inside. He shoves me in and leaves me there, as he heads off, rifling through the racks.

Before long, he returns thrusting a pink and white...garment in towards me. "Try this on. Let me know when you're ready."

I hold the hangar up and look at what he's given me. "Is this… a wrestler's uniform?"

"A singlet, yeah. Trust me, Arran. Try it on."

I um and aw for a moment, wondering how I'm possibly going to squeeze into this small looking thing, despite its tag saying XL. Hanging it on the mirror, I begrudgingly start getting undressed, remembering that, yes, I must keep my underwear on, and laughing in my head that this is the kind of place where that had to be said.

Getting the singlet on was both awkward and easier than I expected all at once. I had to work out exactly how it worked, essentially sliding my legs into the lower half like shorts, and then pulling the straps up and over my shoulders. There's a tension making me worried they might snap for a second, and then it's on. I look in the mirror.

"Oh wow," I mutter. Don't get me wrong...I'm no Cam. It clings to me, and I can see the roll of my stomach creating a gentle curve in the front. I turn to the side and my belly sticks out a bit, but the singlet is actually also holding me in some too. I follow my own curves and realise...I actually like seeing them. For some reason, I feel...powerful?

"You in it? Lemme see." Cam yanks the curtain open, so he and the cashier can actually both see me. Cam looks me up and down, biting his lip. "You look amazing."

"You think? I don't look too big in it?" I say, turning one way then another.

"Oh, something looks big in it, sweetie," the cashier calls over, smiling appreciatively. I turn and look in the mirror and realise I'm rock hard. Where my cock is pushed up against my stomach in the singlet, you can make out the line as it pushes back against the material.

Cam leans in and grabs my visible penis line and kisses me. "How does it feel?" He breaths in my ear.

"Like I need to fuck. Right now." I pant.

"Not here you don't. Come on now, lads, buy it before you get precum all over it." The cashier says laughing.

I get out of the singlet and Cam takes it to the till and pays, earning us a free bottle of lube too. The twink from upstairs winks at us as he hands it over, "Enjoy, boys."

In the hotel room, I'm kneeling on the bed, wearing the singlet. Nothing but the singlet. In the mirror, I smile, marvelling at how round my ass looks.

Cam comes out from the bathroom, wearing a lycra outfit of his own: it's one of his cosplays undersuits, but I can't tell which one. Right now I don't really care. He joins me on the bed, kneeling, pulling himself up close to me.

He wraps an arm around me, hand resting in the small of my back, "See. I knew you'd like this."

"What makes you think I like this?" I tease, nipping at his lip as he pulls away smiling. His eyes dart down to my very obvious bulge between us.

"Oh, I think it's pretty obvious." He grabs my butt and pulls us closer, until we're pressed against each other. I feel his cock get thicker in his suit, the movement causing our outfits to rub against us. I let out a moan.

"All this time, you just have lycra fetish." Cam bites my ear, his hands rubbing up and down my back through the material. I feel it shift slightly, but barely moving. My dick pulsates against the material, getting slightly wet at the end as Cam bites my neck.

"Unh, let me get this off again," I grumble, in ecstasy.

Cam stops me. "Oh no, we're keeping these on."

We fall down onto the bed together, kissing. I'm not sure how long passes with us rolling around and writhing over each other in our costumes, feeling our dicks rub against each other through the material as Cam grinds his hips against mine.

We feel up and down each others bodies, as if naked but not, but for everything we can feel of each other, we might as well be. Somehow, feeling all of it but not actually being able to see it all is incredibly hot, and it drives me wild.

I lay on top of him, panting into his mouth as I stiffly thrust my groin against his, feeling him rub against me, until suddenly and without warning, we both climax.

I roll off him, panting. We lay there in our spoiled costumes, staring at the ceiling.

"Well, now you know a new kink. You're welcome." Cam laughs, and I join in briefly, before rolling over and grabbing him.

"It's not just the fetish. It's not just that I like how this looks and how it feels," I say desperately. "It's also you, Cam. I'd have never had the confidence without you, never have gotten out of my own head. It's you too."

He looks at me, a slight smile playing at the corners of his mouth, before he kisses me. "Anything for you, Arran."

We get out of costume and lie there, naked, in each others arms for the rest of the night.

MANCHESTER ULTRA CON 2019
DAY TWO

I'm woken in the morning by my phone buzzing. I quickly check it and see it's a WhatsApp call from Chuck. These are rare, and he tends to prefer Zoom, but he knows I'm away at a show this weekend.

Cam rolls over with a grunt. It's just after 4am, so I move my hand around the floor in the dark, finding my clothes and throw a hastily discarded t-shirt and boxer shorts on, and head out the room door, grabbing my keycard on the way.

"Hey, Arran, good morning!" Chuck booms out of my phone at me, sitting behind a desk on my screen in a lushly equipped but starkly white office space.

I motion for him to lower his voice and whisper back in return. "Morning, Chuck. Sorry I didn't reply to your emails, but I was asleep."

"Oh shit," Chuck says, but no matter how much he drops his voice, that accent of his still echoes down the hallway, and I'm wondering if I should have grabbed trousers now too to head outside. "What time is it there?"

"Uh, about 4:25am, mate. Chuck, what's up, is something wrong with the book?"

"No, no, no, it's all good. We're just going to make a slight change to the release schedule is all. Wanted to give you a heads up is all."

"When's the release now? Is it sooner? Michael is still drawing the third issue, I thought you wanted three in the bag first..."

"No, later. We're going to launch just before Speech Balloon. You're going there, right?"

"Er, yeah. I have a table."

"Awesome. Okay, so plan now is the new series of *The surREALS* will drop about three weeks before Speech Balloon weekend, and we'll make a big splash at the show. Don't want to count our chickens yet, but I think we can pull some nice surprises there, you'll love it."

"Okay," I mutter, leaning against the door. "Well, you're the one with the experience, Chuck, so I trust you. Thanks for letting me know."

"Sure, buddy, no worries at all. Now, hey, I don't wanna keep you up, you got another day of con, right? Go get back to bed. Sorry again for waking you, man. Speak soon!"

And with that the image cuts to black and he's gone.

I straighten back up and slot the key in the door, and slowly push it open and try to sneak in. I have the t-shirt flying across the room to land on the floor again when I'm startled.

"Everything okay?" Comes a gravelly moan in the dark. All pretence of stealth leaves me in a sound that can only be described as something between a llama going through a very wakeful castration and a small, camp toad being trodden on, as I launch myself, ankles still tangled in my boxers, across the room and land roughly on the foot of the bed before bouncing off onto the floor. "Jesus, you really are a jumpy bugger!" Cam says, holding back a snigger as he sits up in bed to see where I've landed.

"I'm okay. I'm okay." I gather my breath back and kick off the boxers. "It was just Chuck."

"What the hell is he calling for? Does he not know the time?" The mirth in Cam's voice leaves quickly, completely replaced with irritation.

"Yeah, it's okay. Nothing really. They're just pushing back the launch of *The surREALS* is all, and he wanted to let me know 'face to face', so to speak."

"Ah, damn, Ar. You were looking forward to making a big deal of it in a couple months at London though." The tone shifts again, to one of sympathetic pity, "Didn't you already pay for some marketing in the brochure?"

"It's fine. I'll…see if I can get a refund or something, I guess. Or maybe just change up the ad. We'll make a splash at Speech Balloon instead. Let's just get back to sleep."

"Well," Cam starts, and throws the sheets off him revealing his naked body in the dim light of the room. But I've adjusted now, and I see him. "I was thinking, since you're, well, 'up'…"

I look down and realise I really am 'up' now.

"Oh well," I sigh, "Might as well." And I leap into the bed making him to squeal and laugh.

The Sunday goes as you might expect: more families, but overall fewer people walking around. Those that are here though are more keen to spend money, and while it doesn't seem as busy through the day, everyone is buying more before the wonderland of comics wonder wraps up and disappears for another six months or so.

It's around 2pm when my phone buzzes with a fresh email from the Comixpedia Press Team. Since signing up with the publisher, I've been on the press list too so I can get an idea of how they'll market the book.

"What's that?" asks the spiky haired mercenary with an unfathomably big sword next to me. And no, that isn't a euphemism, it's Cam in his latest cosplay (although with Cam, kind of a euphemism too).

He's stopped by the table to get a drink and well-earned

breather from the show, where he's undoubtedly been stopped all day to get photos with eager gamers.

"Comixpedia are releasing a brand new book. By Zack Nelson. Wow."

"Wow, that is quite the get." Zack is kind of a big deal in comics these days. He just got off a nearly five year run on *Batman*, and he's widely credited with bringing the Dark Knight up to the modern age, mixing the grim darkness that has swamped the character for decades with the overblown comic stylings of the Silver Age.

"Yeah. It's dropping July 17th." I mutter.

Cam sits up, a dark shadow falling over his eyes, caused by more than just the insanely structured blonde wig on his head. "Wait, wasn't that your original release date?"

"Yeah, it was…" I know it's nothing, and I know that of course I'd get moved but…

"That's really shitty, man. How can they just shift you along for some new book like that!" Cam's indignant anger burns through as he looks over my shoulder at the phone.

"Come on, Cam. It's Zack bloody Nelson. Of course they'd want to give him the big summer launch date for San Diego Comic Con, it'll be huge there. I'm just a newbie. Come on, you know it makes business sense." I am aware that I'm explaining this to myself just as much as I am Cam.

"I guess. Still sucks though. And Chuck could have been honest with you this morning about the reason for the move. It's not like you would have blown the story early," Cam must realise I'm being a bit quiet. He turns me to face him, and I look up at him under his obnoxiously huge blonde spiky wig. "Hey, you okay? I know it's shit, but you'll be fine with the new date."

I'm still feeling some kind of way, some way I don't know how to describe myself yet, but I smile at Cam's reassurances. "Yeah. Yeah, it's fine. Not like they ditched us entirely. Hell, the last cheque for the advance went through last week, and I paid the guys up to date and have a bit left over. What say we hit Canal

Street tonight after the show? Have a bit of a drink and night out?"

Cam looks at me with worry on his face, and then smiles and strokes me shoulder. "Sounds good, Ar. Hey, maybe we can find some Manchester twink to join our party, eh? We could use a scrappy little rogue to get involved." He grins, and the possibilities running through my head already distract me. My brain derails thoughts of me, Cam and a mystery guest star pretty fast though when another implication from Cam's attempt at double entendre hits me.

"Wait…who's the tank in this party? Am I the tank? Are you calling me a tank?!"

Cam is watching my table while I go and have a wander of the show floor. It's rare that I get the chance to do this, and Cam said he doesn't mind. I think he could see that as much as I was trying to let the sudden change to my schedule not get to me, it still kind of is.

I'm barely paying attention to the various stalls and cosplayers I pass, which feels rude, but my head just isn't in it.

Cam knows some of it but not all, because I know what he'd think. Or at least, that's what I tell myself.

But this isn't the first time something like this has happened. There's been format and layout changes that Chuck and his team have sprung on me and Michael a couple of times, each new sudden change causing me a mini panic as I try to rush to get it sorted as best I can. Of course, what's worse is I can't often get it sorted myself.

For all the years I've been making comics, I still find the technical side of things pretty complicated and hard to understand. So often I'm getting a message about a change that needs to be made fast that I actually don't understand, let alone know how to do, so I've had to rely on Michael most of the time.

Seeing as most of these changes have been involving file format, specs and sizes, it's really been more on Michael anyway, and I can tell he's getting a little frustrated with it.

I suppose Comixpedia Premiere's is still a new thing, and so a lot of the kinks are still being ironed out, but it doesn't stop it being a total ball-ache.

But it's more than that. This is actually the second time the launch date has changed, been pushed back, initially because Chuck said he'd like to get the third issue in the can first before announcing and releasing the comic. Which made sense, at the time.

Then there's the fact I got a bit of a gently angry call about my reaching out to some UK queer publications, to try and get some press for the book. Calling it passive aggressive doesn't feel right, but I was told how all these kind of things were being handled by the in-house press team, and that by 'jumping the gun' how I had, I could be stepping on their toes. After all, maybe they'd already reached out to those publications, and now I come off like I'm harassing them for press inches.

When I asked if they had in fact reached out to those publications, I didn't really get an answer. Chuck just smiled, and said, "Don't worry about it, Arran. We believe in *The surREALS*, we got this."

I'm sure it's nothing, I'm sure I'm just making a mountain out of a mole hill, but I really can't help but start to feel like maybe I'm getting the short end of the stick because I'm new to the publishing industry, as it were. And like, I get that, maybe I'm misinterpreting things, but...

"Hey, Arran!"

I turn, ripped out from my spiral by a Superman bounding towards me (not quite in a single bound). He's smiling at me, but right now I can't place him at all even though he looks like he knows me. Though that may be because he makes a very convincing Superman.

"Hey, man, long time! How've you been?"

"I'm good, thanks, really good. Tired now, it's been a long weekend." I continue scanning his face, and realise it does look familiar to me but I really can't place how or why.

"Ain't that the truth, I'm about ready to call it a day myself," he clocks the confusion on my face, and I scrunch up mine in an apologetic silent admission of guilt, "It's Vince, Cam's mate. We met at London last year."

"Oh my god, Vince, of course. I am so sorry, I am terrible with names. Faces I can normally work with, but all I was getting was Kal-El."

"Ha, I'll take that as a compliment! Guess I must be doing something right!" He smiles as he strikes the classic Superman pose, puffing out his chest and fair play, looking every bit the image of truth, justice and the American Way. "How's things going for you, though? Working on anything now you finished *The surREALS*? DC or Marvel snapped you up yet?"

Now it's my turn to laugh. "Nah, man, I'm not even on their radar! Or, well, as far as I know...Gertie, the artist, told me she spoke with an editor at Marvel, so they have read *The surREALS*, but I've not yet had the call."

"Ah, they're loss, man. It'll come though, you're a good writer," he says with a friendly smile. We stand in slightly awkward silence for a minute, realising that we don't really have much else in common beyond Cam and comics, and my battery for social interactions is starting to run pretty low.

"Oh, though I am doing more *surREALS*. With Comixpedia Premiers. But keep that on the down-low, it's actually not been officially announced yet."

Vince lights up. "Dude, that's amazing news! When the announcement goes out, you let me know, I'll spread the word among everyone I know. Get you all those sales you need to make Marvel and DC finally sit up and take notice, yeah?

"I mean, you have to be stoked, right! This is a huge step towards getting out there in the big leagues, you'll get the book in so many new hands. I'm happy for you, mate."

I smile. "Yeah. Yeah, I am pretty happy. Feels like this can only be a good thing. Little difficult, and it's a whole new experience even for me, but I think this could be what I needed."

"Anything worth doing is hard, mate. And it's like you say, this kind of publishing is all new, right? You'll smash it, I just know it. Anyway, I gotta head and meet up with another mate. See you at London in October, yeah?"

"Yeah, yeah, sure. Later, Vince."

You know what. He's right. This is huge. This has been difficult for me, and confusing and frustrating, but then it's still awesome, and exciting and a massive step forward in my career.

I head back to my table and Cam finally pulled out of the spiral and thinking about how this could be just what I needed and what the future may still hold.

LONDON EXCELSICON
AUTUMN 2019 DAY ONE

"So…how do you want to do this?"

The inoffensively attractive man on the laptop screen asks his question, before the camera pans out to reveal the group of people sat around the table screaming in a mix of elation and surprise and even relief. Then a small man with an impossibly wide mouth starts listing actions as his Halfling bard rogue uses a magic performance number to explode the heart of a dragon that moments ago seemed poised to annihilate him and his party in a desperate and lengthy battle of swords and sorcery. Or in reality, dice rolling and mathematics.

"People really tune in to this every week?" I call in to the bathroom from the hotel bed.

"When they're not taking breaks, yeah. Some people just listen to it as a podcast." Cam calls back.

We decided to save some money and split the hotel costs by sharing a room this time. I mean, end of the day, we'd probably end up spending all our time in one room anyway. He apologised in advance for how he might wake me as he had to get up early to get his costumes together, especially this one today.

Cam's cosplaying as one of the characters out of this YouTube series, where a bunch of semi-famous professional voice actors and YouTube comedians play Dungeons & Dragons. Apparently this is the second campaign, the previous one running for nearly three years, and among certain circles, these folks are becoming household names as the success and popularity of their broadcast tabletop adventures take on a life of their own.

I have to admit: Dungeons & Dragons, or D&D, is something of a geekery blind spot for me. My only experience of it was being taken to a game of it by my cousin, where her boyfriend was a player. He was a weirdly intense guy, and to my young mind it meant this dark room, with a bunch of people reacting to things that weren't actually happening or in any way visible took on a slightly disturbing tone. That my cousin would eventually run away with him and barely talk to the family ever since just cemented it as 'something I don't fuck with' for the longest time.

However, watching a few episodes of this on the ride down and this morning, I have to admit, I can kinda see the charm. As a storyteller, there's something deeply impressive about watching these people, fellow creatives even if the chosen discipline is different, essentially create narrative on the fly that is both compelling and at times moving. Some of the action sequences can get a little tedious with all dice rolls and quick mental arithmetic to work out multipliers and damage points, but these guys are all very good at what they do, and they manage to make up for it by creating genuine tension in their performances.

Cam got excited to introduce me to them when I said I knew nothing about these people who had been announced as the big Guests of Honour as it were at Excelsicon this summer, or how the internet went wild on their announcement, so he's been filling me in on the history, lore and fan elements that surround it.

"Hey, did you hear back from Chuck at all?" He calls from the bathroom as I make sure my money box is loaded with change for the day.

"What about?" I ask, bemused.

"Well, you said something about some new pitches, right?"

It's true. Technically, the next arc for *The surREALS* is already scripted, and it's just going through art, colours and letters. In fact, four out of the five issues are completed, the fifth well on its way now too, so it's been feeling like I didn't have a whole lot to do. Chuck had been saying for a while that Comixpedia would be up for new pitches and new books from me, so I sent a few ideas along.

"Nothing yet. Chuck thinks it's best to wait until the launch of the new series of *The surREALS* first. Get the launch for that right, and then think about what's next, you know?" I call back. It was a shame, because it's left me a little at a loss. I could look at starting something new independently, but I was kind of hoping to keep everything under a publisher now. It sounds weird, but to do otherwise feels like a step backwards somehow.

"Huh. Okay…" Cam trails off.

"What? I think he's got a point," which is not technically a lie, I do think he does even if I would love to get something to get going on now. "You think he's brushing me off?"

"No, not necessarily. It does sound kind of reasonable, I just… well, you said he asked you to come up with some new ideas and now he's saying to wait is all." Even shouted out from another room, and with Cam trying to hide it, his concern is unmistakable in his voice. I stamp down on the little flame of frustration in my head before it can burst out.

"I mean, I can't see why he'd lie to me, Cam. We're about to launch a new book together."

"Sure. You're right. Hopefully he likes the pitches when issue one drops next month. He's coming to Speech Balloon, right?"

"Yeah. Comixpedia are hosting the party this year."

"Cool." I wait and see if there's going to be any more to this conversation, an edge of dread tickling at the back of my brain. "Okay."

There's near silence in the hotel room as I look towards the bathroom doorway, part wondering what Cam is really thinking.

"Okay," he says as he walks out of the bathroom, "I think I'm going to need a hand if we're going to get to the convention centre on time for you to set up."

He stands there, stark naked, blotchy green from the shoulders up. His hair, this time, is a violent purple, with streaks of lilac, which he's had cut short into cropped back and sides and spiked on top. A few spikes bent artfully 'absent-mindedly' down in front.

If it weren't for the fact his face was green, you'd be forgiven for thinking he'd forgotten his cosplay and was about to Emperor's New Clothes it to the con, but making a change up from lycra and foam armour pieces, Cam is going a makeup route. And I don't think it's going well, as he looks at me imploringly, holding a green tinged sponge in one hand and the other held out in a casual cry for help.

Of course, the green only distracts me for so long, as my eyes wander down.

"Why are you naked?"

"I didn't want to risk getting body paint on my armour, and I'm starting to get flustered, which will just make me sweat, especially if I'm at all warm, so I just...look, can you please help me?" He rattles out in exasperation.

I get up, chuckling, thinking what a weird sight this would be if anyone walked in right now, following him into the bathroom. Around the sink is a mess of body paints, a set Cam got off Amazon for this particular cosplay, a few sponges and brushes, and our usual toiletries. The sink is already stained green around the rim.

"Okay, what do you need me to do?" I say, snatching up one of the sponges ready to get to work on my exasperated and attractive canvas.

"Just get dabbing green on me. You do my arms while I work on my chest. Oh, and dab, don't stroke it on, because-"

"Because we don't want to leave streaky lines. The canvas may be different, but it's not my first time painting, don't worry." I interrupt, already lightly pounding green paint over his right bicep.

"I thought you usually hired other people for the artistic stuff."

"Okay, ouch. What I do is artistic in its own way too, you know," I flash him a half smile to let him know I'm not really offended. "And I dabble with the art too. I'm just not very good, and I want all my stuff to look its best, so I get outside help."

"Fair," he says, and we continue coating his torso in green body paint in silence for a while, the only noise being the excited yells and gasps of shock of the game players on the laptop in the adjoining room.

"You know," I muse aloud, after a while, "If we took some of the yellow and dabbed that on top of the green in patches, we can create highlights and pick out areas. It'll make it look more natural, like this is your own orc skin."

Cam looks at me in the mirror with a raised eyebrow. I dodge the eye-line of his reflection and continue dabbing away at him.

"It's basic colour theory," I think, "And, um, I kinda…" I roll my eyes and shut them before making my big admission. "I sometimes put makeup application videos on while I'm working. I find something oddly relaxing about them and sometimes I wind up paying attention to them and pick up some things."

Cam stares at me in surprise, before a smile starts to play at his lips. "You're telling me I had my own personal amateur makeup artist here the whole time and you were just letting me blunder about this on my own?"

"Look, I'm no Trixie Mattel, but I think I picked up a thing or two is all."

"Well, have at it, queen!" He laughs, before suddenly breaking into complete sincerity. "I trust you."

I squirm with the sudden admission of vulnerability and safety, warmth creeping to my face that I try to ignore, turning quickly to get mixing with the body paints. "Look, it's not exactly the same, this is hardly foundation, eye shadow and blusher, but I think I know what to do."

I pick out some highlights on his cheekbones and head, before creating a softer yellow by adding white and dabbing that on the crease of his eyelids, his temples and the tip of his nose. I grab a soft tipped brush and blend it out a little, before also mixing a darker shade of green to deepen the pockets of his cheeks and along his hairline. I take a step back, and Cam leans into the mirror to inspect my handiwork.

"Arran, this…this is really good! Damn, dude, I look freaking amazing!" Cam gushes, and I feel a wave of pride flush through me, surprising myself.

We get back to it, covering Cam in the base green, and then I go back over picking out elements to give the illusion of depth. I use a lot more yellow along his chest, then the darker and lighter shades too to emphasise his natural musculature, which is as casually impressive as ever.

I'm on my knees, dabbing away, when I all of a sudden become very aware of Cam's penis. Understandably so, as it starts to rise.

"Um, just how far down do we need to go?" I ask, my eyes darting between looking up at Cam's face and sideways at his semi-erect cock.

"Uh, well, I am going to be wearing trousers, so technically we don't need to go any further."

"You, err, seem to be enjoying this quite a bit though," I joke, and as my breath falls over him, Cam shivers. He's now fully erect and right in my face. "Well, I suppose it would be a shame not to go for total veracity in our art." I start dabbing body paint past his Adonis Belt and into his groin, gently.

"We…we don't have time…" he breathes down at me.

"Shhh." I continue about my work.

After covering his groin, which is freshly neatly trimmed as Cam likes to do before any of our weekend trips, I slowly stroke the paint soaked sponge along his shaft. I hear his breath shudder at my touch, but I don't look away from the task at hand. Cupping his balls in my hand, I gently smooth the paint over the sack, back up to the underside of his cock, until the whole thing is evenly green like the rest of his torso. I peel back his foreskin gently, watching a glistening drop of precum emerge from the tip before teasingly giving it a soft kiss. Cam moans above me.

"There." I say, standing up and slapping his ass as I leave the bathroom.

"What? You can't-! Arran!"

"It's like you said, we don't have time, I have a table to be manning after all. Chop chop now, get your clothes on." I smirk at him, as I swing my backpack over my shoulder.

After he's dressed and we're leaving the room together, he leans in from behind and breathes into my ear, "Oh, I am going to get you back for this later."

***

He definitely got me back later.

The con was a really good day, to be honest. Surprisingly busy for a Thursday at the show, but the D&D group were doing a panel, and I guess they're more popular than I imagined because they definitely drew the crowds.

At the end of the day, Cam met me back at my table as I covered everything with a sheet for the night. He hangs out with me as I get everything settled when Michael Marcher, the DM (or Dungeon Master, if you're not in the know I guess) and essentially the face of the group's growing celebrity, came and stood next to us and started talking to Theresa, my table neighbour.

Theresa Simmons proved to be a very charming neighbour, having flown over all the way from Florida to be at the show, as she's done art for the YouTube table top gamers.

Cam, if he weren't painted green from head to toe (and then some), would be white as a sheet. His eyes are wide and fixed, barely able to leave the back of Marcher's head. I realise he's fanboying out again, and I decide I can play with him some more.

"Theresa! Aren't you going to introduce us to your friend?" Cam shoots me a quick, fleeting glare and I swear I hear a whimper escape his throat, before returning to his flop sweat.

"Oh hell, where are my manners! Michael, this is Arran, I met him today but he's a big voice in the comics community, seriously. He's gonna be a hit, I know it. And this is..." she looks over at Cam and raises an eyebrow. "Well, I figure you already know who Michael is, huh?"

"This is Cam, and he's not usually so shook, I promise you." I shake Michael's hand, who takes mine with a gentle grip and a warm smile as he says hello, before turning to Cam. Cam barely stammers out a 'hi' when Marcher just grabs his hand in both of his and leans in.

"Great Guldred cosplay, man. Pleasure to meet you." He smiles, and turns back to Theresa who is ready to go and the pair head off out of the convention.

"Thanks," Cam stutters out, before turning to me. "I could kill you right now, you know."

"What, after I just made you get over yourself and meet your D&D hero? I rather thought you'd rather do something else to me." I give him my best devilish grin, well practiced and mimicked from him.

He grabs my hand and marches us out, leading me all the way back to the hotel room. He shuts the door and immediately pounces on me.

The next few hours are a blur. Our clothes get thrown around the room. The poor white bedsheets of the hotel are not streaked with green and sweat after Cam pins me to the bed, before either of us even has the chance to shower the day off us, and is pounding me like he's both deeply in love and furiously mad all at once. It's carnal, animal, and I love it.

Oh, how I love it.

LONDON EXCELSICON
AUTUMN 2019 DAY TWO

"Why the fuck is my asshole green?"

I hear Cam laughing before he pops his head around the bathroom door to see me inspecting my arse in the mirror, a clear green patch covering me from between my cheeks outwards.

"Don't worry," he finally says, wiping tears from his eyes. "I checked, it's non-toxic and safe for ingestion."

"Is that's what it's called when it goes up your arse too?" I yell.

He joins me in the shower and helps me make sure that I am free of green everywhere, as I do him. And of course being together in the shower leads to other things, but we have time today. Cam's doing a much simpler cosplay today and just throwing on his Spider-Man suit, which is actually my favourite Spider-Man suit again, the Ben Reilly as Spider-Man look from the 90s. After all, aside from the cartoon, that was *my* Spider-Man.

"Ready for another day?" He asks as he buckles on his 3D-printed web-shooters.

"Yeah, I'm feeling pretty good about it, today. Yesterday was reasonable enough and the show feels fuller than ever this year, so I'm thinking I can get a few full runs sold."

As we're walking in, I check my phone and find some emails came through overnight from Chuck and the team of Comixpedia.

"Everything okay?" Cam asks when I've been quiet for a while.

"Yeah, it's fine. Just more spec changes for the pages. It's the tech-y stuff which I never really understand, but Alan will be able to handle it. I'm just going to give him a heads up before he sees the email and explodes." Alan is the book's letterer and formatter and he handles a lot of the file specs when putting the book together to send in to Comixpedia. Comixpedia keeps making these small, but apparently significant changes to the file requirements, which has left Alan feeling kinda pissed about the whole thing to be honest, just like Michael was with all the art set-up changes too.

If I'm entirely truthful, it's pissing me off too. Even though I know I can't handle it and the best thing to do is delegate it, I can't help but feel a wave of anxiety every time they send a new email asking for *another* change.

"Is it not all going okay?" Cam asks, and I can hear the worry in his voice again.

"Oh, it's going great. Michael is already well into the fifth issue, would you believe it? It's amazing what you can do when you're given an actual advance and budget." I'm not even joking with that last part. Before, it took me, like, six years to complete a six issue story arc, between saving enough money for printing and paying Gertie, preparing for handling shipping or Kickstarter rewards and things, it just seemed to take so much time and so long. But with an actual budget behind me, and being able to pay Michael, Alan and Tara (our colourist) in a speedier fashion, and stresses of PR and marketing off my shoulders, it's been a whole different beast.

"It's just the line is still new and I guess they haven't worked out the kinks, so we're getting a lot of them."

"I thought you liked kinks?" Cam butts my shoulder with his.

"Depends on the kink." I shoot back as we come up on the

entrance to the ExCel, where we'll have to part ways to find our respective entrances.

"Dinner tonight?" Cam asks.

"Definitely. I could use a nice chill dinner after skipping it last night."

"Sorry about that." He pulls down his mask so I catch a flash of smile before it's hidden by red lycra and giant bug eyes. "See you inside!" We hug and head towards our separate entrances.

The Friday is somewhat oddly quieter than the Thursday, but Theresa tells me it's because the D&D group are doing a live recording of one of their episodes after the con today, so most probably have tickets for that.

Not to worry though as it's still really busy, and as it's an unseasonably hot day today, I'm kind of glad for it to not be so rammed. Cam checks in a couple times, including bringing me a bottle of water knowing that yet again I had forgotten to bring anything to keep myself hydrated. Always taking care of me, that one.

"So how long have you two been dating?" Theresa asks after Cam leaves.

"Oh, Cam and me? Oh, we're not dating, as such."

Theresa looks at me with a raised eyebrow, looks to where Cam had walked away and then back at me, looking even more puzzled. "You sure about that, honey?"

"We've known each other for over a year now, but we're just close friends. We don't live near each other, we pretty much only see each other at comic con weekends."

Theresa leans back in her chair and folds her arms. "Uh huh. Just comic cons then?"

"Well, he's come down to see me in Swansea a couple times too." Or is it 'come up', I wonder to myself. I've always sucked at geography, and all of a sudden I feel like I'm unsure where Cam is from, though we've definitely talked about it.

Theresa leans in to me, beckoning me to get closer, so I do. "Y'all are fuckin' though, right?"

I shoot back into my seat, back straight as a pole, as I hem and haw trying to think how to answer this. Is she judging me? Is she insinuating I'm being improper? Should she be asking that at all?

"Calm your tits, Arran, it's none o' my business really. I'm just saying, I see you light up when he's here, and I see him wanting to look after you, and if you guys ain't already a thing you should make it a thing, because you're good together from what little I've seen."

"But…the distance.." I offer, feebly.

"Well, god damn, you Brits and your 'distance'. You realise your country ain't a speck of spit compared to places like mine, right? My husband lived two states over from me when we was courting, and god damn if we didn't make it work."

"You live with each other now though, right?"

"'Course, but we didn't right away. Not saying it's easy none either, but it's worth it." She takes a sip of her iced latte, which is mostly just watered down coffee now that the ice has melted. She makes a face at it, and then turns back to me. "He's worth it, ain't he?"

I take a moment to think, by which time someone approaches my table. I welcome them and let them know a bit about the series, then let them browse with a smile. They linger for a little bit before finally picking up the first issue and making the sale. When they leave, I turn back to Theresa, who's already waiting on my answer, "Yeah. Yeah, I think he is. But I'm not sure *I* am."

"How so?" She says, tilting her head quizzically.

"I guess…I guess I'm so focused on making this thing," I gesture towards my comics, "a *thing*. I worry that I don't give him enough time now as it is, and if we made it something more…official, I'd be going in knowing I'm underperforming right away."

Theresa nods her head, letting me know she follows. "I get

you, kid, I do. But this gig, for all the collaboration and whatnot, it's a lonely one. You can't be all about it and nothin' else, because you have no idea what you'll be missing. Not everyone waits for you to be ready.

"Take the comic. Did you wait until you knew, one hundred percent knew, that it would be really good before you went and made it a reality?"

"No. I mean, I guess I did a little at first. I often think 'what if I started sooner, where would I be now?' But even then, when we did start, it's not like we knew what we were doing."

"An' I bet looking at your first issue now, there'd be things you'd do different."

I grab one instinctively and make a face like someone just kicked my puppy in front of me. "I don't think it's that bad…"

"Sure it ain't, I had a flick through before you got in this morning, it's a good comic. Is it perfect? Nah, and I think you know that."

She's right, of course she is. Knowing what we know now, Gertie and I would probably come at it a little different. The one scene is pretty much an in-joke for my old university friends, we just lucked out that it played out pretty accessible to anyone. And while we're both stupid proud of it, we both know it could be better. "I guess so, yeah."

"But if you'd waited to be perfect, without actually doing the damn thing, you'd never have made anything at all. Same goes with your man there. It won't be perfect. It'll be damn near hard at times. And maybe you aren't perfect right now for it. But you ain't ever going to get perfect if you ain't ever going to actually do it."

"Huh. I'd never thought of it like that."

"Not a problem, kiddo, happy to help." She smiles then sips her brown milky water and scowls. "Now I'm gonna go see if I can't find me a good damn coffee in this glorified airport of a place. You want anything?"

"I'm good, thanks. Seriously. Thanks." I wave as she walks off, then sit back in my chair and let my mind sink in on itself, wondering if I'm holding us back and what we could be for each other.

"You okay?"

Cam asks me that and I suddenly realise I've been pushing my chicken katsu around my plate for…how long?

"Yeah, yeah, I'm good. Sorry, guess I just spaced out there for a second. Been a long day." I force a smile, then drop my head back down towards my plate, realising I don't really feel at all hungry.

I guess I'm not very convincing. "You sure? You've barely said a word all night. What's up with you?"

Sighing, I push my plate forward, figuring I'm done with my food. "Nothing. I just have a lot on my mind is all. I guess it's pushed out my appetite."

Cam eyes me with suspicion. "Did it not go well today? I mean, you know that's fine, right? It's going to be busier on the actual weekend anyway, so that will make up for it."

"No, yeah, you're right. It was fine today, just a little slower. But it will be totally fine." I take a long draft of my lager.

"You want me to help you on the table tomorrow? It's probably going to be pretty busy."

"No, no, it's okay. I don't want to ruin your day…"

"You won't be, I'm happy to help."

"But you didn't come to help me, you came to enjoy the show, to do your cosplay, you don't have to change your plans for me."

"I really don't mind. Might make a nice change of pace anyway…"

"No. Seriously, I'll be fine." I realise that came out a little harsher than intended. "Honestly, have fun at the show, I'll manage fine. Won't be my first time swamped in comics fans, manning the table alone." I smile at him with my most genuine fake smile I can muster.

Cam pauses. "...Okay." He puts his chopsticks down and reaches a hand over towards mine on the table. I flinch, but stop myself from pulling away. But he notices. "Babe, what's going on? The truth now, because you're kind of freaking me out."

I sigh, realising I can't keep up the pretence any more. "It's just something Theresa said, that's all. It's playing on my mind, and I dunno, it sent me into an anxiety tailspin I guess."

"What did she say?" He looks at me with such care and worry and...love?

"She warned me off throwing myself into the work too much. I guess it's plain to see I don't let myself have much else besides the comic." Cam strokes his thumb across the back of my hand, and I feel my lip tremble. "She thought you were my boyfriend."

Cam stops stroking, and he looks at me with a renewed interest, a change in his posture, barely perceptible to anyone if they hadn't come to spend so much time with him, to spend so much of it just looking at every perfect millimetre of that frame. "What did you tell her?"

"Well, I said we're not boyfriends. I said we're just good friends, like."

He pulls his hand away from mine.

"...Okay."

"Hey. Cam...did I say the wrong thing?"

"Well, we've not said anything either way, so I guess not, not really..." he says, eyes not meeting mine.

"Then why do I feel like I just hurt you? What do you tell people I am to you?"

He pauses. "It's never come up," he says eventually. "People have never really asked. I guess why would they."

Now it's my turn to feel hurt, and I don't know where this burn is coming from. "Really? But, you come visit pretty often... and we spend pretty much all our time together at comic cons..."

"But you've never come to Brighton to see me. And at comic cons, I spend most of the time with my cosplaying friends. The time we spend is in the evenings, at dinner, in the bedroom..."

"Don't say it like that. It makes it sound…"

"What? Sordid? It's fine. It is what it is. But no, no one asks if you're my boyfriend…"

"Do you want them to?"

He doesn't say anything. He just looks at me and I can't tell if his expression, which he's trying to keep stoic to mask how he's really feeling, is hurt or anger.

Finally, he just says, "I'm not interested in what other people ask or think. I'm just interested in how *we* feel about it." I can tell what that 'we' really means…I can feel the 'you' in it.

"…Okay."

We get the bill, pay and leave. We walk through London, barely saying a word. We sit opposite each other on the Underground lines, looking at each other, but no sound passes between us.

We meet his friends at the hotel bar. We talk to them, individually, but barely a word to each other. After a while, I head off and share a drink with Mitchell before heading up to the room.

Cam comes in shortly after. He strips off and gets into bed with me.

"Good night." He gives me a lingering peck on the cheek, before rolling over and putting his head to the pillow, back to me. I follow suit, lying on my side, facing away from him. I watch the lights of the night that play on the floor underneath the heavy blackout curtains and suddenly feel alone, in this room with this man who I know I hurt today, but I don't know if I'm the one to make it better.

"Good night." I say, to no one in particular, and close my eyes.

LONDON EXCELSICON
AUTUMN 2019 DAY THREE

I don't know how much sleep I got last night, but I wake up early, as the sun starts streaming through the curtains, warming the back of my head as I'm looking at the back of Cam's. I guess I rolled over in the night to face him, but he's still facing away from me.

I lie there tracing the lines of his back with my eyes, absent-mindedly, as my thoughts race. Why can't I just tell him how I feel about him? Why do I keep hurting him? What is it that makes me hold back?

But the answers come into my mind just as fast: an array of possible futures collapsing into each other, where I move to Brighton to be with him but it doesn't work out and I'm stuck in this strange town with no one else to help me; where he comes to Swansea and he gets bored of me and resents me for having made him come all the way to me; where I'm not there for him because I'm plugging away at making this whole writing thing become something to support us both, but in his loneliness he finds someone else and I'm left alone; where-

"Hey," Cam looks me in the eyes under heavy lids, struggling to stay open. I guess I didn't see him turn, didn't feel him roll

over, but now he faces me, the inches of the mattress between us feeling like miles.

"Hey. I didn't mean to wake you."

"You didn't. I...didn't sleep great." He frowns, a sadness there that is more than the anger at me from the night before. Something has been lost, but something added too. Regret?

"Look, I'm sorry..." I trail off. I'm not sure what exactly I'm sorry for. I mean, I know, but it feels like so many things, that I can't roll it into one sentence.

"Me too," he says, frowning. "Look, Arran, I like you, okay? I want to be with you, and I want you to want that, but if you don't-"

"I do!" Cam's eyes widen as I interrupt him, and a smile draws across his face. "But I don't know if I can be what you need right now." The smile fades as fast as it came.

"Look, Cam, I l- I like you too. So much. These times together...I think I look forward to this time, in bed with you, more than I do any other part of the cons now. But the cons are still a business trip to me. It's still me trying to make a reality of this dream of mine, and I just don't know if I have the bandwidth to be the man you deserve right now."

"But with Comixpedia...?"

"But with Comixpedia, things might finally be on the right track. I might finally be making my first real steps in this industry, and who knows where it will lead. And when I'm settled into my path, when I'm not hustling around the clock to build a career, I can be there for you. The way I want to be.

"The way you deserve." I edge closer to him in the bed, and caress the smooth jawline, roughened slightly by the night's stubble growth. He leans into it, sliding ever so slightly closer.

"Well, I'm glad the sex is still something you look forward to at least..."

"Hey. Hey, it's more than that. That's not what I meant. I meant *this*. I meant being with you, naked as the day I was born, completely open and vulnerable, just holding you and being held in return. This is what I want, all the time."

"Then why don't you say that? You say you're open, but I swear, you're still a puzzle to me…half the time, I don't even know what you're really thinking. If you even see any future for us."

I do. I see thousands, every minute, and every single one of them I crash and burn. I either ruin it or lose him, but I don't dare tell him. "I see a future. I want a future. I'm just…I'm not able to see how to get there yet. There's too much happening, and I'm… overwhelmed. But when this next series is out, once I start getting taken seriously by the publishers and the industry, then I'll have more energy to focus on this."

Cam looks at me, and for a moment I think the anger from last night is going to come back. But then he pushes into me, our naked bodies pressed together in an embrace. There's something different though: it isn't filled with heat and passion, or the softness of something more that I've been too scared to voice out loud. There's something desperate about it. Something frightened and longing, and wanting nothing more than safety and security.

We lie there for ages, just holding onto each other as if for dear life. I press my forehead to his, and then make our lips touch, gently. He answers with a kiss, deep and a sigh passing between us.

"Okay. I can wait a bit longer. I think you're worth it."

I look at this beautiful, sexy, wonderful, kind man who thinks, for reasons I cannot begin to fathom, that this struggling, frightened waste of air is 'worth it' and a giddy elation fills my chest before just as quickly being enveloped by a cool and steady dread. Because I'm *not* worth it. Not really. I never was.

We got ready in a kind of comfortable silence, but with the weight of things left unsaid between us.

Walking to the ExCel, Cam in Jedi robes (he wanted an easier day today, he says), me in whatever came out of the carry all first, we're still quiet. But we walk close together. The temptation to take his hand is strong, but I don't know if I've earned that, or if I'd be leading him on.

As if written by a lazy writer, the heavens open just as we reach the entranceway, parting our ways. The grey sky filled with the promise of thunder, a break in the long heat wave of the summer and early Autumn, pouring down upon us now. I watch Cam head under the shelter towards the fan entrances, and throw him a half-aborted wave when I realise he isn't looking back.

I have no time to linger on feelings: the con today is a monster. Like the middle of Times Square at peak rush hour, the show floor and the hall outside it are ram packed with people, making movement around a tedious and arduous affair. Every three steps you have to stop as the people in front of you have stopped suddenly to view a table, say hello to friends or take photos of a cosplayer.

I look out when I can to see if any of those cosplayers are Cam, but I don't see him. If he passes at all, I can't say I saw him.

"Hey, you okay today, kid?" Theresa looks up at me from her seat, eyes filled with questioning concern under her green bangs.

"Yeah, yeah, I'm okay. It's just hella busy and, well, I didn't get much sleep is all."

"Oh, big night with the man, eh?" She grins up at me and winks.

"Actually…" I slump into my chair, "we kind of had a fight. I mentioned that you thought we were boyfriends, and how I responded, and well, it kind of turned into a whole thing…"

"Oh my god, Arran, I am so sorry, I never shoulda said a thing. I never intended for this to happen, I feel like such a tool."

"No, no, it's not your fault. I think it's been building for a bit. And, well, it's *my* fault. Because I can't commit."

She looks at me with an almost motherly concern. Then a fan in leaves and tree branches approaches and raves about her art. When she's done talking to them and they leave happily clutching a print signed by Theresa, she turns to me again with the same look.

"Look, I get why you feel you can't commit. And this gig is a lot, and it can take up all your head. But we're not talking about your head here, are we, kid? It's your heart."

"And what if I ruin it? What if I spend so much time making *this* happen, that I forget to be there for him, and then…"

Theresa sits back, straightens her shoulders and takes a deep breath. "Listen, Arran, we barely know each other, and far be it from me to stick my beak in again and risk causing more drama, but…are you even there for him now?"

I feel my head swing on my neck like a swivel, I feel the tense of anger flash across my face, my mouth dropped open to unleash something but then…it evaporates on my tongue. "I guess not. You know, I've never gone to see him at *his* place. It's always mine or at comic cons…"

Theresa crosses the distance behind our tables and rests on her heels as she takes my hand in hers and looks up into my eyes. "This industry, it's a dream, I know. But let me tell you the truth of it: it is horribly unkind. The system is broken, designed to churn you up and spit you out once it's had the best years of your life and creativity from you. And you're already giving it yours before you've even been fully swallowed by this beast called comics. When you 'break in', whatever your threshold for that is because you already broke in, kid, you're doing it; when you get where you *want* to be, it's going to be a constant race onto the next thing and the next, and you can wait until the quiet spell all you like, but in comics…it ain't coming.

"It's a heartless and monstrous thing, and the only thing that will keep it worth doing for you is your unexplainable love for it, no matter what it takes from your mind, your health, your stability.

"But if you have someone with you…someone to help you weather the storm. To sing your praises when an editor has given you nothing but changes and revision notes for a week. To remind you of all your wins when all your pitches are shot down. Someone to hold your hand and let you just vent and rage about how fucked up it all is. The strength that will give you cannot be sniffed at, kid. Trust me, if it weren't for Hobie, I'd have dropped outta this game years ago. May still do someday. But knowing I got him with me makes whatever that uncertain future looks like feel worth trying."

The sting of tears hits my eyes as her words sink in. Already I can feel some of what she's saying. Comixpedia's revised plans, the way every message feels like a last minute, all hands on deck emergency, the way I'm on my own on this side of the Atlantic, trying to run a team to make this thing happen. I feel the truth in what she's saying, I do, but at the same time, I know I'm not ready. That I'm spinning so many plates and if I add another, the most precious, valuable plate of them all, they'll all just come crashing down.

"Um, I'm so sorry to interrupt..." We look up to see Princess Peach (or is it Daisy? I can never remember) standing over us, parasol in hand, and a small purse too. Within seconds, me and Theresa re-enter sales mode and get back to manning our tables, and the rest of the day flies by in a non-stop stream.

I don't see Cameron until the hotel bar after the show, where I meet him.

He didn't wait for me at the ExCel.

Cam had gone back to the room to shower and change, so when I saw him at the hotel bar he was already back into his 'normal' clothes. I see him with his friends, some of whom are still in cosplay, some not, and walk up to the bar instead. Once I manage to grab a drink, I walk over to the group and kind of hover awkwardly, not sure what to say for a while.

"Hey, Arran. Squeeze on in," says Brian, pushing up the couch to let me in. Cam just takes a swig of his drink and closes his eyes, as if to say it's fine, so I join them.

After a slightly tense quarter hour, conversations start flowing more freely between me and the group, and Cam and the group. Never with each other.

After an hour and a half or so passes, we haven't said a word to each other, but are laughing and joking, so no one would know there's this hidden tension between us. I make my excuses and head to the bathroom.

It's while I'm standing at the urinal going about my business that the worst thing to happen while you're pissing happens: someone tries to spark up a conversation.

"Hey, Arran! It's been a long time!" comes the voice behind me.

I look over my shoulder, still mid-stream, and clock a tall, brown haired lad in spandex. His cosplay is something I don't entirely recognise but know enough to know it's from some anime or other. I think one about a superhero school? I keep hearing its name come up, but I can't for the life of me think what it is right now, I'm a little preoccupied. I should check it out though, I figure.

"Um, hey. Um, just give me a minute…"

"You might not recognise me, I look a bit different these days."

I shake off, zip up, and turnaround to my unexpected urinary guest. Sure enough, he doesn't look immediately familiar. The kid (he's definitely much younger than me) is kinda cute in a gawky way, crazy messy hair, and I get the impression he was a skinny kid once, but he's not now. He's all broad in the shoulders, and the spandex costume is making it clear that he's actually ripped. It's then it suddenly hits me.

"Of course I do. Alex, right? It's been, what, a whole year?"

"Yeah, it's good to see you, man," he beams, excited that I remembered his name, and honestly, I'm a little surprised myself - I'm awful with names, especially for people I haven't seen in forever, but I still see some of his posts pop up occasionally on

TikTok and instagram. Though I hadn't realised he'd gotten this hench. "I'm surprised you recognised me."

"Oh, come now. You've filled out a bit, sure, but I never forget a friendly face," I lie as I make for the sink to wash my hands.

It's then I notice that his beaming happy expression turns slightly, looking more like an awkward worry.

"Hey, can I talk to you? About Cameron? I mean, you can tell me to mind my own business or whatever, but…"

A part of my brain panics: where is this going? Is he going to judge what me and Cam are doing? Is Alex secretly homophobic and I never picked up on it? Does he think I'm a creep for doing whatever it is I'm doing with a guy nearly a decade younger than me? "Uh, sure…but I reserve the right to call a 'mind your own business' if I think it's too personal, I guess?"

He nods, as if steeling himself up for something, bites his lip and takes a deep breath. "Why don't you let him in?"

"Excuse me?" I say, wiping my hands in the disposable hand towel, pausing mid dry as I'm genuinely at a loss.

"Look, it's pretty obvious to anyone with eyes that you guys have had some sort of argument. You've barely looked at each other at the same time, but whenever the other isn't looking, you look longingly at the other with this pained expression like something out of a bad 00s teen drama." The words come tumbling out of him like a dam broke, and I just stand their agog at the deluge.

"And I know you two love each other, it's so obvious to anyone with sense. But from what I can tell, Cam makes all the effort to come see you, trying to go to the cons you're going to be at. He told me he visited you in Swansea a couple times too, you know, but have you ever made an effort to go see him?"

"Hey, now…" I trail off, because I can't deny any of that.

"But I can tell you have feelings for him too, or you wouldn't be hanging around with us lot looking vaguely miserable. So if he loves you, and you love him, why the hell are you keeping him at arms length?"

Alex finally stops, and pants catching his breath again. I'm staring at him wide eyed until, with a sigh that empties me from toe to head, my shoulders slump and I fall backwards and lean against the sinks.

"I don't know. Okay? I don't know. I figure..." I pause as I check through the rolodex of reasons I think I have to hold Cam apart from me, at least for now. "I figure I'm just scared."

"Scared of what?"

"Well, what people would think? I'm just starting my career, finally, and like, if people knew I was...being intimate-"

"You can say 'fucking', I'm not *that* young."

"...if people knew I was fucking, I was...dating, a cosplayer, who's so much younger than me, what if it wrecks my career before it starts?"

Alex looks at me with a mix of empathy and confusion. He tilts his head to the side. "You guys aren't the same age?"

"What? No, I'm like ten years older than him, man. Wait, how old do you think I am?"

"I dunno, twenty-eight?"

"You're my new favourite." I say to him, completely deadpan.

"Look," he says, holding back a smile, "What does it matter what anyone thinks anyway? What, you think you'll get 'cancelled' because you're dating a younger guy? That's bullshit. 'Cancel culture' is bullshit, anyway. Most of the people claiming to have been 'cancelled' are still making millions to this day. And honestly, I don't think this is cancelling activity anyway."

I push myself up from the sinks, brushing a hand through my hair. "I dunno, kid, people seem pretty judgemental online when we're talking about age differences. And add in the fact he's a cosplayer, I'm a comics writer, there'll be a lot of conclusions made..."

"So? The people who matter know the truth. Who cares what some strangers in, I dunno, Minnesota think about your relationship? So what if some people think it's weird, or dodgy, or whatever...you two know the truth. Your friends know the truth. That's all that matters."

I feel my breath quickening, like I'm being caught in a lie, and I'm not sure why I'm panicking. "It's a bit different for gay guys, Alex. When it's a straight couple with an age difference, the woman gets the short end of it, whether they're the older or younger in a couple, but most of the time nothing serious will come of it. But when it's gay guys, it's all how the older guy must have groomed the younger guy, the younger guy doesn't have any agency, no matter how old they were when the relationship starts, and that kind of rhetoric? It follows you, it's really dangerous."

Alex smiles, then nods his head towards the door.

"Dude, I'm pan, I'm not oblivious to that at all. But again, what some strangers online think doesn't even matter. You can always delete the app, you don't really need it. This is all just an excuse, you know." I almost try to argue, but he jumps back in. "Come on, we've been gone a while. The guys'll think you started railing another cosplayer."

I follow Alex out the door, aghast at the change that has come in this kid in just one year. Not just his body, gone from the stick thin, scrawny kid of old to this new broad, tight muscular young man; but also the timid kid who was so excitable and almost starstruck last year is now schooling me in relationships, making smutty jokes and cutting right through all my shit.

"You know, you were honest about one thing: you are scared. And maybe you need to think about why you're really scared, because if you want to make this work out, you gotta name that fear to beat it."

"How the fuck did you become so bloody insightful, you bastard? What the hell happened to that scrawny little kid with the ill-fitting Spider suit?"

"Ha! Bunch of things. Gym, university, therapy and more money. You'd be amazed what each can do. I recommend therapy the most, to be honest, man. Now stop being a pussy and go get your man."

I look Alex dead in the eye, and he returns my stare, smirks and then pokes his tongue out at me and throws up a peace sign. Then he heads to the bar.

I look over to the group and see Cam mid conversation with one of the girls, and my feet are moving before I realise. I sit next to him, take his hand in mine, prompting him to stop and turn to me and before he can say anything I kiss him.

I want to say something stupidly cliche like the room goes quiet, and the world falls away, but it doesn't. The only silence in the room is from us, our lips locked, the room not even paying any attention to us at all. We part and I put my forehead to his.

"I'm sorry. I suck."

"You do. But then I like that."

"Bloody hell, Cam, you always turn it to filth."

"You love it."

"Yeah. Yeah, I do."

LONDON EXCELSICON
AUTUMN 2019 DAY FOUR

The weekend has been such a mixed bag. On the one hand, this may be the best sales I've ever done at a comic con, which was both unexpected and very welcome. It's been the busiest show, with crowds turning into just an amorphous blob of skin, spandex and nerd in places.

But emotionally, it's been a rollercoaster. Me and Cam felt like closer than ever at the start of the weekend, but by the end of it, things have felt the most fragile this...whatever this is has ever been.

Last night, we started speaking to each other again. The rest of the night we sat next to each other and held hands through most of it all. I read something somewhere once about there being different kinds of 'love languages', and I kind of thought it was asinine bullshit. Now, I know mine is definitely physical touch. Just that skin to skin contact, his smooth soft hand wrapped in mine, made me feel so relieved and at peace. Is that what love is?

We spent the night in each others arms, and decided we'll talk about where we are after the con, so I wouldn't be too stressed for the show. Again, always thinking of me.

Thing is, it didn't really work. I spent the whole show

wondering what he'd say to me and whether I've fucked this thing up; but also wondering just what I want out of this. Is Alex right? Am I scared of something? If so, what? I mean, I know I want Cam but why does it feel like in my head that it's either Cam or my career? How do they interact with each other? I'm not sure I have the answer even by the end of the show when I'm saying goodbye to Theresa and head out to the front entrance to meet Cam in the quad.

We don't even get dinner, we just head back to the hotel room. He walks in ahead of me as I close the door behind me and then lean back against it as the lock clicks into place, Cam turning to look at me, hands in his pockets.

"So…"

"So."

We stand there for a minute, each having so much to say but unable to find the words, and honestly, my mind starts racing trying to figure out just what I need him to know first.

"Look, let's just sit down and relax." Cam, ever the wise one, motions to the bed, and then kicks off his shoes and sits on it, crosslegged, by the head of the bed.

I kickoff my own shoes and match his seated pose from the foot of the bed, and let the stress of the weekend drop from my shoulders, letting out a huge sigh.

"I know I've been a bad partner. I know I've hurt you with how unthinking I can be, and for that I truly am sorry, more than you can ever know."

"I know you are, though. That's the hardest part." Cam shifts his balance, and grabs one of those ridiculous cushions the hotel puts on top of the pillows, the kind that just get thrown off the bed before you get in and have no real use. Except it seems maybe they do: they make for good comforters, Cam clutching it in his lap, arms wrapped around it.

"I know you don't want to hurt me, and I know that you're sorry about it, and yet…here we are."

The expanse between us on this bed feels like a widening chasm, and I don't know how to get across.

"I…I just feel so…overwhelmed, all the time. Cam, I really do love you, and I hate that you don't know that. But I think that's why I hold back - I'm not ready to be the good partner you deserve yet. My head is just filled with all these scenarios with the cons, and Comixpedia and *The surREALS* and I just…it's all I'm doing to keep on top of it all, and I worry if I went and made things official like you want, now, I'll just mess it up."

"But I can help you. You don't have to be doing it all alone."

"I know, and you do. You have no idea how much you help me…"

Cam snorts derisively. "Getting you off isn't the kind of help I want to be seen for."

I reach across the distance, ignoring the sting of his words because I know the barb is coming from a place of pain that I'm kind of responsible for. On my knees, I become a bridge across the gap and touch his face and make him look at me.

"You are so much more to me than some booty-call. I hate that you might think that, but I need you to know, right now, that I want you not just because of the fun we have in the bedroom…"

"And the bathroom, and the beach, and the bar toilets that time…"

"Hey! I want you, Cameron. All of you, all the time." I crawl up, kneeling in front of him, making me the taller one for once, and Cam looks up into my eyes. "I don't know that I can be everything you want or need right now, but I want to be, and I want to be soon. I just need to get passed this book launch, get my foot in the door of this industry finally, and then I can make sense of it all. And then I'm all yours, I promise."

He looks up at me with those beautiful blue eyes, and I see a fear in them, but then he gives me a watery smile and I think maybe I see some hope shining through. "You promise?"

"Cam, I want you, and I want to be there for you, like you've always been there for me. But I just need to get into the eye of the storm in my head first. Can you let me do that? Can you wait for me?"

Cam bites his lip, and I gasp as all of a sudden he reaches up and plants them on mine, and I feel myself sighing into his mouth as all the tension I had melts away.

Breathless, he pulls back and keeps my eyes locked on his as he unbuttons my shirt.

"I'll wait. But not forever. You're worth it, Arran Wilson, you really fucking are, but you need to get your shit together soon because I can't be kept in this Limbo forever."

He lifts slightly off the bed as I pull his jeans down passed his knees. "I won't, I need you, Cameron Perkins, and I won't risk losing you, I swear. I just need to get passed this hurdle so I can give you my everything."

Cam moves to his knees, his hand rushing behind me and under my pants, until I feel his fingers press against my butt. "Good. Though I kinda think I've had it all already, haven't I?"

I grab at him, stroking slow and firm, thrilling at how much his body shudders at my touch. "Oh I want you to take more."

"Okay, Mr. Wilson. Show me exactly how much you need me."

And for the next three hours or so, I do.

We lie in the bed in a state of post-coital bliss, vibing on each others passion and desire for one another, facing each other covered in sweat and more.

Cam fixes me with his gaze. "We needed that, to break the tension. But I mean it, Arran...I won't play second fiddle to your career forever."

"You're not..."

"Just promise me, after the book launch, with your foot in that invisible door you keep talking about, we'll make *us* a priority for a change. That I won't just be your naughty little costumed secret."

I look him dead in the eye. "I promise."

I kiss him, and then he rests his head on my chest, I feel his breathe among my chest hair, and in that contentment I didn't even realise I had already fucked everything up.

The drive up to Leeds from Swansea is an absolute nightmare every time, and I'm saying that as someone who never drives and is always driven.

Thankfully, Gertie and Emma drove over to mine and spent the night, so we're all going up together, so there's plenty of company, catching up and tunes to keep us entertained.

We've made this trip so many times before, but this time feels different. Gertie is now a Marvel artist, and my first book with a publisher launched just a few weeks ago, making this Speech Balloon the first one since that huge milestone dropped.

"Excited?" Emma looks at me over her shoulder with a smile, almost like she can sense what I'm thinking.

"Yeah. Yeah, I kinda am. It's so weird..." I mutter, glancing back out the window in the backseat, as the traffic continues to crawl forward. No matter when we leave, we always seem to hit a major traffic jam as we approach the city.

"Weird how?" Gertie asks, as she slaps the steering wheel as some bellend cuts her up to get into our lane.

"I dunno. Like, we just launched, and Chuck says initial sales are great, though I have no idea how many that is..."

"That's pretty standard, sadly. Marvel don't tell us the sales figures on books either. Unfortunately, that seems to be standard industry practice." Gertie flips off another bellend. No matter how calm and chill she is most of the time, Gertie is a kind of aggressive driver I guess.

"That's good to know. I guess. I'd rather know how many copies are selling, I'm used to that now. But Chuck says it's all good, and thinks this weekend will be huge somehow, but like, I've been doing this show for years now, and its not like I actually have copies of the new books to take, being all digital first.

"So I'm going up to this show I've done a half dozen or so times before, with the same title I've always had, even the same issues I had last year, but I'm not just a self-published, independent guy now. I'm working with a big publisher, my name is on the billing as a guest..."

"Shame they couldn't cover your table for you, though. Even though you're a guest." Emma frowns.

"Eh, Speech Balloon is a non-profit, I wouldn't be surprised if some of the other smaller, newer creator guests had to do similar, especially if they live in the UK."

"Enough about that," Gertie pipes up, looking back at me in the rear view mirror, "You excited to see Cam?"

"Yeah. Oh yeah, I am." I smile into the mirror at her, and when her attention returns to the road, I let it drop and return my gaze to the cars outside my window.

I am excited to see him. We've talked almost every day since Excelsicon. And I mean that, talked. Not sexted or cammed. Or rather, not *just* those, I guess.

I am.

But I'm also weirdly nervous. A trepidation that worries me in its existence within me, especially related to Cam. It's my own fault too...I can pin it exactly, without fail, to that promise I made him.

Because while I know I love him, and I want him to be happy, and he makes me so happy, I also know I still don't feel ready.

This milestone got hit, sure, but things don't seem any more clear, the path ahead no more settled, and there's constant information coming in, or worse, not coming at all, leaving me to let my mind wander. And we all know that's never wise.

About a week after the new series of *The surREALS'* first issue dropped, I messaged Chuck about some new pitch ideas to try out, like he said. But he came back and said let's talk about it at Speech Balloon. He's going to be here too, and it's so much better to do it face to face, apparently.

So I got that ahead of me. And finally making a commitment to Cam. Like I promised.

I just need to get it all straight in my head first.

"Hey, we shouldn't be too much longer now. We'll set up and then head to the Clayton. Is Cam meeting us there?" Gertie breaks me out of my reverie, and I realise it started raining, grey sheets pouring down from the darkening skies.

"Uh, yeah. He's already there actually. Train got in two hours ago now, so he checked us both in already."

"So we should give you guys twenty minutes before heading out for dinner, is what you're saying?" Emma grins like a Cheshire Cat over her shoulder.

"Ha ha," I throw back derisively. "We'll only need ten. I'm not as young as I used to be." I stick my tongue out at her as she makes a face of disgust, and Gertie pulls us into a much emptier lane and we sail into the city.

The next morning, we head into the show and see the venue halls for the first time since the final touches were made by the Speech Balloon and Comixpedia staff. That's when I notice the sign as we're walking in.

"Oh my god, did you know they were doing this?" Cam gasps, eyes wide. I gave him my spare exhibitor pass so he can come in and out easier with us, instead of waiting until later.

We're looking at the sign for one of the exhibition halls

entrances. Every year, Speech Balloon names the halls after a well known comic series, or something related to one of the big guests. We're currently looking at *surREALS Hall*.

"This is nuts!" Emma exclaims, bouncing next to Gertie who's actually looking kind of dumbfounded.

"I had no idea. Chuck said there'd be some surprises, but I wasn't expecting this." I beam. I don't know why, it seems silly. It's just a temporary venue hall name, it's nothing major. But it feels major. It almost feels like I made it.

Cam moves to go into *surREALS Hall*, but looks back when he realises that I'm not walking with him. "What's up? Shouldn't we get settled in? Doors open soon."

"Yeah, totally," I say, "It's just...I'm not in this hall. We're in Comixpedia Hall." I let out a sigh, but I'm still smiling nonetheless. This still feels awesome.

"Oh. That's kinda weird." Cam says, walking back to us.

"I dunno. I guess the hall names get decided after the floor plan. It's cool."

"Well, I'm still going to get a photo of you with it, come on."

I head over the the sign and pose there awkwardly, as is my go to stance in photos. Then Cam comes over and takes a selfie of us both in front of the sign, framing us into the corner so the name isn't obscured at all. Looking at the photos, I love the selfie more. I look so much more relaxed, just kind of serene with this smiling dork next to me.

We finish set up just as the doors open and the first crowds come in. It's a pretty steady day, and everyone is so enthusiastic about the comics on show here, it's really energising. Most are making a beeline for *surREALS Hall* though, as it turns out that's where the big name creators have been set up. Which is cool, they all genuinely do work their way around back through the other halls and get back to us too, and I've even had a few people congratulate me on the new series.

Sadly, a few have said they were hoping to pick up a copy here, and they look a little crestfallen when I say that it's currently digital only. It's a shame, but I get it: everyone has their preferred way to read. I let them know the hope is for a print release eventually, when the new series is finished, and they smile and let me know they'll look forward to it.

A little niggling part of me thinks how it might not happen if the digital versions don't sell well, but I brush it aside. It's in the contract, and some people won't change their reading habits, it's just a fact of business.

"Arran, did you see the main entrance?" Cam is wide-eyed as he approaches holding two fresh, steaming cups of coffee. We'd come through a side entrance to the building this morning, and I haven't really had a wander round yet, so had no reason to see the main entrance.

"No, why? What's up?"

Cam squeezes in between tables, sets the coffee cups down and turns to me, grabbing me by the shoulders.

"You need to go see the main entrance. Now. I'll watch the table. You just go."

I give him a quizzical look before making my own way out from behind the tables, looking back as I follow the flow of the crowd to the main doors to see Cam waving me on and grinning like an idiot.

Walking through some double doors into the large glass foyer, I look around, expecting maybe some crazy cosplay, or someone holding an owl (that actually happened once), but I can't see anything. Then I feel my phone buzz in my pocket. It's Cam.

Look up

I look up, and that's when I see it: a massive drop banner for the event, this massive image that is the first thing anyone coming in will see…and it's *The surREALS*. Comixpedia must have forked out for some serious advertising budget, as the banner proclaims the new series out on their platform now, and their status as proud sponsors of Speech Balloon. This info surrounded artwork of the team, from one of our big splashy guest cover artists, standing heroically and welcoming every single Speech Balloon attendee to the show.

I feel my mouth hanging open, staring up at this incredible thing, my hand moving of its own accord to snap some pics of it so I can remind myself later that, yes, this was real.

"Told you there'd be some surprises, buddy!"

I turn to see Chuck beaming back at me, wearing dark sunglasses despite the grey, overcast sky. He puts his hand out and I greet it with mine, as he then proceeds to crush it and shake it profusely.

"What do ya think?"

"I'm speechless, Chuck. Honestly, thank you so much, I don't know what to say."

"Ah, it's nothing. We just really believe in *The surREALS*, and it felt only right. Plus, hey, we gotta sell this book too, yeah?

"Look, I'll catch you later. I have a meeting at the booth now. Party later, yeah?"

"Uh, yeah, yeah, sure. I'll be there," and as he walks away, "Thank you!"

He waves a hand back at me, shouting over the crowd, "You're welcome!"

I head back to the table in a daze. Cam greets me with a smile as I drop into the chair next to him.

Meeting his gaze, I finally close my jaw. "That is so cool!"

Cam smiles, "I knew you could do it, babe. I'm so proud of you." He takes my hand in his and I smile back at him, all my worries lost in the moment.

The party is in full swing when me and Cam walk in. It's been a good day, and a real highlight for my career, and it feels like we have something to really celebrate. Cam gets us in some cocktails, and we join Emma, Gertie, Mitch and others. Raving about the day, talk turns to me, *The surREALS*, and how much the show is plastered in my book and how awesome that is, how happy they are to see me making this next big step in the industry.

And I'm feeling it. This is amazing. My characters are emblazoned, six feet high, the first thing anyone sees coming into the biggest, most well respected convention in the UK. My publisher is really putting a lot of energy and weight into advertising it, and making it a success. Making me a success.

Sure, I still don't know what's next. And we're almost wrapped on the last issue too, so after that, I really don't know what I'll be doing if I can't get these pitches picked up, but that's just par for the course, surely?

Here I am, in this moment, this is excellent. This is an achievement I've been striving for for a decade. And I did it.

So why do I still feel like something is missing?

Why can I feel that jolting fear of being lost?

"Hey, babe, you okay?" Cam leans in, making me focus on his eyes and bringing me back into the room.

"Yeah, yeah, sure, of course."

He frowns. "Arran, I know you. Come on, what's up?" He takes my hand and makes some excuses and drags me away to a quiet area just outside the food hall/convention party.

"I'm happy, I am. I swear," I start, but my voice breaks. "It's just...we're almost done on the book, and I have nothing else lined up. So I'm seeing all these things, and they're awesome, and amazing, and I love it and I'm proud, but I'm also...scared.

"I don't know what's next, I have nothing planned or set up, so part of me is thinking 'what if this is it?'. What if I've peaked now, and that's it, Cam?"

He holds my arms by the shoulders, stroking me gently with his thumbs in circles. He looks me dead in the eyes. "We've talked about this, you're letting your mind wander out of the now. Those places aren't real, don't let them distract from this right here.

"You keep thinking like a shark, like if you stop swimming for a minute you'll die. And that's taking you out of enjoying what you have, here and now."

"I know, but in comics, hell, all media, it's always the next thing, right? Like, if I don't wind up making anything for a year after *The surREALS*, won't everyone just forget about me? I just don't want to lose forward momentum when-"

"Cam! You're panicking about something that isn't even happening. How could anyone forget you? Just breathe with me."

He walks me through the breathing exercises he read about, and gets me to look at the good things that happened today. At the things that led to here. And it helps, it does, but...

"Babe, we need to talk about this, and I was going to wait until after the show, but I read this article about ADHD, and this guy who didn't get diagnosed until he was, like, forty-five, and it sounded so familiar. I think maybe it'll be worth looking into it, with a professional, maybe." He doesn't say this in an accusing tone, and while it's hit me out of the blue, it's clear he's been thinking about it.

"But I wasn't a naughty kid, Cam. I was hardly bouncing around the classroom. And no one ever told me I was back then."

"That's a really dated idea of what ADHD is, babe. There's, like, a whole spectrum of presentations for it, and I think you'd find you'd relate to a lot of it. I'll send you the article when we get home, and hey, we don't have to do anything about it, but I think it might be something, and I think maybe it could help you stay in the now, if we can confirm what makes your head go like this and get help, if you want.

"Whatever you want to do, I'll be there though. With you every step of the way." He pulls me into a big hug, and I can smell the booze on his lips, but I know all it's unlocked is a forthrightness, everything he's saying is coming from a place of love and care and I know he's telling the truth. He would be there. He'd be my partner. He'd stand by me through whatever is next. He could be my rock.

If I let him.

I kiss him, breathing him in, then we part. "I just think, right now, I'd feel better if I knew what was next for me, is all."

Cam purses his lips, then looks over my head back into the party. "Well, didn't Chuck say you could talk about the new pitches at Speech Balloon? Well, we're at Speech Balloon, and he's...right over there. Let's do this."

He looks at me with an expression of confidence, egging me on, and I feel it take root. "Yeah. Yeah, what's the harm."

We snake our way through the crowds, bumping passed comic creators losing their minds dancing in a rarely seen sense of abandon, carving a path towards Chuck until the man is dead in our sights, right ahead, whiskey in hand. The timing feels perfect, as the person he was talking to makes their exit and Chuck momentarily stands alone. Then he sees us.

"Arran! Hey, man, so good to see you! What a day, huh? *The surREALS* art around the halls is a total hit!"

"Yeah! And thanks again, Chuck, I really can't even begin to express all that means to me." I let him take a swig of his whiskey, as he nods and sways to and fro with the beat. "But I was wondering, about what's next? I was wondering if I could talk to you about those new idea pitches?"

Chuck smiles at me, as if weighing things up in his head for a moment. Then he places a heavy hand on my shoulder. "I think it best to talk about it after the show, man. There's a lot going on this weekend, it's maybe not the best place to talk about that right now. Let's put a pin in it until the third issue drops, a good halfway point in the series release, eh?"

I feel Cam nudge me from behind. "Oh. It's just, you said we could talk about it here, at the show. And you have been having meetings with other creators today, right? I heard a couple folks saying they'd been in talks."

"I can't really talk about those, man, you get it, confidentiality with the parties involved etc." he says, with a sympathetic smile cutting a hard line across his face. "And I get the excitement, I really do. We're really excited with the way things are going. I just think it's best to focus on this book, and then we can look at new things later, after this weekend. Let's focus on *The surREALS* here."

I feel myself crumbling under the weight of dread possibilities for my career. Will we ever get to talk about new pitches, is there a reason he keeps putting it off? "I'm just...I'm just a little concerned, is all. About the future, next steps. I don't have anything else on the books now, and we've almost put this series to bed. I was just hoping to maybe see about getting the next thing lined up so I'm still working."

Chuck exhales deeply, sets the whiskey on the table behind him, and turns back to focus on me, palms together like a prayer. "Look, Arran, I get it. I do. But it's really feeling like you're not appreciating the support we're giving you and *The surREALS*. Look at all the marketing, the banner out front today...we believe in the book, you can't deny that Comixpedia hasn't thrown its weight behind you."

"I'm not-"

"And you know you can always pitch with other publishers, we're not stopping you, but really, you gotta understand how much we're supporting you, and be a little more grateful for it."

I feel an arm envelop me and Cam's chest hit my shoulder, puffed out as it is as he surges to defend me. "Hey now, there's no need for this gaslighting bollocks, mate. You told Arran you'd talk to him about his pitches at the show, why are you changing the rules now? He's just asking to be heard out, and look at the future, he isn't denying anything you've done up til now."

I can hear the anger in Cam's voice, practically bristling like an angry cat's back, and Chuck can sense it too. That casual, well affected Californian smile drops, as do his shoulders, as he looks at Cam with a grim condescension.

"I'm sorry, and who are *you*?" The words practically ooze from Chuck's near-snarling lips.

"I'm his b-"

"He's my friend," I feel the words bubble and burst out of my throat in seconds, the aim to lighten the tension, the impact way heavier for Cam. "He's just a friend."

I turn and look back at Cam as his arm leaves my shoulders, and he takes a step back. He's looking at me with some of that anger leftover from his confrontation with Chuck, but also pain and betrayal. But worst of all, I see disappointment.

He continues to step back, until he turns and forces his way into the throng of dancers as I call after him.

"S-sorry, Chuck. I'll, err, see you tomorrow," I glance back at Chuck, as he picks up his whiskey and moves on in the opposite direction from me, barely paying any mind.

I push through the crowd, trying to find Cam, but he's nowhere.

People clap me on the back, congratulating me on the book or the big banner or the hall name, or something else I can barely register because right now there's only one thing on my mind and I've never felt so laser focused on anything.

I hurt him and I have never hated myself more.

I grab my coat from the seats, Emma and Gertie asking if everything is okay, and I wave them off as I burst out of the party and head down to the streets of Leeds outside.

The rain is beating down hard, and I'm already drenched through as I look up and down the street for any sign of Cam. I see a busker hastily grabbing up his gear and running to shelter, couples racing this way and that, men holding jackets over their girlfriends heads, a lone homeless man looking up into the sky and screaming at the downpour as it covers his face.

But I don't see Cam.

I head back to the hotel, foot tapping rapidly as the lift takes forever to reach our floor, I almost snap the keycard trying to get it into the slot in the door.

I step in and as the lights come on in our room, I look around as it sinks in.

He's not here.

I'm ringing out my soaked clothes and having a hot shower when I hear the room door open and shut. I turn the water off immediately, throw a towel around myself and head into the bedroom to find Cam, equally soaking wet, putting his clothes away into his bag.

I don't know what to say, unable to compute why he's madly throwing his things into his carry all, worried about where he's been and what happened to him, feeling sorry for letting him down and, I hate myself for it, a small ember of anger at what he did to Chuck and how that might have affected my standing with him.

"You're wet," I manage.

"Look who's talking," he throws back over his shoulder without looking at me.

"Please, Cam, stop. What are you doing?"

"I'm packing. I'm going home."

"What? How?" I ask incredulously, and feeling more than a little stupid for a question with such an obvious answer.

"On the next damn train I can get south," he growls, slamming the last of his shirts into the bag.

"Please, just look at me," I beg, "Don't leave me like this."

He spins on his heel, the bag toppling to the ground, the freshly inserted contents spilling out. An angry finger points right at me. "Don't you dare turn this around! Don't you dare make this about me doing it to you! You knew what I needed from you, you knew how I felt, and you still can't bring yourself to admit that you fucking love me!"

"That's bullshit, Cam! I do love you, okay? I love you! You need me to say it more often, please, I'll work on that, but please don't think I don't love you."

"I don't think that though," he says, calmer, but I can see the anger mixing with pain in his eyes, eyes that he still can't bring to look at mine. "That's what makes it worse.

"You do love me, but you won't do anything about it. You can't even bring yourself to just say that you do to other people. To letting them know what I mean to you. I'm just a secret. A fanboy that follows you around. A 'friend' and nothing more."

"You know you're more-"

"Of course I do! I have invested so much into being with you, I don't think you even realise. I've crossed the country pretty much every way I can, just to be with *you*. I've visited you, I have waited for you to be ready, and you promised me...damn it, Arran, you promised me..."

His last accusations hang in the silence between us, hovering over the bed we shared, another temporary one, one of many. And there's so much more I want to say to him, but I also know he's right. He's right, and I've been terrible, and I can't say anything back because my little neurotic mess of a brain is no excuse.

"Well? Aren't you going to say something? Aren't you going to *try*?" He asks, his voice breaking at the last words as the anger gives way to something worse: hope.

"What can I say? Anything I do will just sound like an excuse...and I can't excuse what I've done to you. You have no idea how much I want to, Cam, but it's all true. I've been a bad boyfriend, lover, partner, whatever the fuck we are to each other. I've sucked. And I told you I would, I told you my life feels...too much right now.

"I've been so focused on making this whole writing shit happen, and I don't have a guide for it, no one in this fuckshit industry really looks to help you, and you can't blame them, they're all too busy trying to make sure they'll still be relevant, that they'll still matter. My head is a mess, and I'm trying to make it in a world with absolutely no security, but I couldn't live any other way. But it's taking all I can to keep my head above the water, Cam, and I just...I need more time, to find a shallow, or a flow, or anything..."

Cam slumps onto the small couch in the room, his spilled bag at his feet. "But you just said, that's not going to happen. That's not just the comics industry, Arran," he looks up at me and meets my eyes for the first time since he came back, "That's life. It's messy, it's constant, and yeah, I know not everyone is built for the world as it is today. Social media is a constant barrage, and you can't handle it, but you're addicted to it and need it for your career too. Comics move so fast, and so much of it is by yourself, no matter how much of a collaborative business it is. But there's things out there to help, you just have to reach out for them, and you aren't, Arran.

"There's only so long I can stay in the water waiting for you to ask for help, or I'll be drowning too."

I walk over to the couch, kneel down and sort out his bag for him, zip it closed. I rest my hands on his knees, and look up at him, feeling the stinging in my eyes.

"What can I do? What can I do to make this right?"

"You know what you need to do," he says, resting his hand on my cheek.

I lean into it, the tears rolling freely down into the palm of his hand. "I—I just need a little more time, I just need to get my head right, I-"

"And there go those goalposts again..." he leans down and kisses me, and my tears flow with renewed vigour when I realise I feel his own fall on my face. He rests his forehead against mine, then stands, props his bag on his shoulder, and walks out of the room.

I sit there crying into the seat of the couch until I'm too hoarse to cry anymore. I fall to the floor when sleep finally takes me and lay there on the floor covered in nothing but a hotel towel and loss.

SPEECH BALLOON 2019
DAY TWO

I put on a brave face the next day.

It's the last day of Speech Balloon, and I've still got a book to promote. I smile, engage with the fans and passers by, and when people ask where Cam is I just say he had to go home.

I manage to get through until four o'clock in the afternoon before I cry again. Gertie and Emma have come over, demanding to know what the fuck is going on, and it's then that I break. I step behind my banner so no one can see me, as if a ton pull-up piece of plastic sheeting can hide me, and the two of them come around the table. Emma covers it as Gertie joins me and I tell her everything.

"I fucking ruined it, Gertie. I lost him." Sobbing I fill her in on what happened with Chuck, the times I couldn't bring myself to say exactly what Cam was to me, and how my messed up head and singular, tunnel-visioned focus on fucking comics of all things might have just cost me the chance at something genuine.

"Shh, shh, hey. Look, this sucks. And yeah, Arran, you fucked up. You think it's not a lot to juggle this career and a life outside of it, and a relationship? Of course it is, for all of us. Neurodivergent or not, it's difficult. And, by the way, I think Cam was on to something, you know, on the neurodivergence thing and I'm sorry I never noticed it or brought it up myself, I mean, come on. But I thought you knew?"

"Why would I know? I thought everyone's brain just worked this way, and when I realised how easy some people found remembering people when they haven't seen them in a while, or staying in touch, or reaching out, I just thought maybe I'm broken." I say, wiping tears and snot from my face.

"Ew, baby, no, here," she says, handing me a tissue from her purse. "You're not broken, and you might have broke this thing with Cam right now, but that doesn't mean you can't put it back together. You just need to do the work."

"But how?" I practically howl, before lowering my voice, as if everyone can't see my little melodrama behind the banner. "I feel so fucking tired all the time, and I thought I was getting some-where in this industry, but now I don't know. And if I don't have that, and don't have Cam, what the fuck do I have to show for the last few years of my fucking life?"

Gertie smiles sympathetically at me, wiping a tear from my eyes. "I'm going to ignore the absolute privilege of all you just said for a second, because I know your head is fucked up right now, and so is your heart. But I need you to hear me right now.

"You'll still have this amazing book that *we* made. And the new chapter you are only just now embarking on with it, and okay, things may look lost now, but you don't know where they'll be in six months. And if it comes to it, you'll start again, with a new book, a new Kickstarter, a new idea, because when you remember how to find it, you'll remember you have that drive within yourself to make this happen no matter what it takes.

"You have your health, you have your life. You have me, and Emma, and Mitch, and so many others, and you just need to remember that you have us and reach out now and again. When you're feeling low, when you need advice, hell, when you just need a wall to throw the shit inside your head against.

"And if Cam really loves you like he says, and I really do think he does, then I'm sure he'll come around…if you start pulling your weight."

I look at Gertie and blow my nose into the tissue, and she's right, I really don't see it now, but the weight of her words sit on my heart like a warm blanket, and comforts me somehow. Then my phone buzzes in my pocket, and my heart skips when I see it's Cam.

"I-it's from Cam. It's that article he was talking about. Nothing else. Just that." My heart sinks.

"Hey, don't look at it like that. It shows he's still thinking of you. If he didn't still care, he'd not send it. It's not over yet." Gertie smiles at me, and I weakly return it. "Now, come on. Deep breath. There's less than an hour left, then we'll go to the hotel bar and we'll drink and joke and focus on something else, and you can work on fixing your fucked up love life tomorrow, okay?"

I laugh. "Okay. Thanks, Gert."

"Hey, what are friends for."

At the hotel bar, everyone tries their best to get my mind off Cam and focus on the good things: the book deal, the launch, the show.

It works to some extent, but the sword I cut Cam with cut both ways, and the wound still stings, nagging at the edges of my attention. As I'm joining in conversations and laughing, I'm running through scenarios in my head, all the ways I could have ruined this forever. All the ways that this really is the end.

About three pints in, Chuck comes along.

"Hey, Arran. Can we talk, buddy?" He sounds apologetic and sober, despite the whiskey in his hand. We walk over to a pillar in the hotel courtyard, for a relative modicum of privacy.

"Look, I'm not happy how I spoke to your friend last night. Drinks were flowing, and emotions were running high, and that was no way to speak to anyone, so I wanted to say I'm sorry about that." He actually does sound genuine about it, and I frown.

"Thank you, I appreciate that, Chuck. But I think it was my own words that hurt him more, so don't worry about it too much."

"Right, right," he says, a little awkwardly, which I think is the first time I've seen him like that. Then it's like a switch flips in him and he returns to his usual, California charm. "And hey, we'll talk about pitches, I promise. I just really think we need to focus on *The surREALS* right now. Stick in the here and now. Don't worry about tomorrow, buddy, it's not going anywhere, it'll still be there once we have this all in the bag."

"Sure. Sure, thanks, Chuck. I'll, err, I'll let you get on with your night. Thanks for the apology, and if I don't see you, safe journey back to the States, yeah?"

"You too, my friend," and with that, our business is concluded and I head back to the others.

After a bit of time passes, there's a lull in the conversation. I wish there wasn't because I start thinking fully about Cam again, and before I know it, my thumb is hitting 'Send'.

> Chuck says he's sorry.

> I am too.

> x

I keep checking my messages for the rest of the night, and see after about half hour I'm left on read. And that's how it stays all night.

Just before I make my excuses to head up to bed, Gertie wraps me up in a big hug, which is big for her, as she's not overly fond of invading personal space.

"It'll be okay. He just needs to cool down. And you have work to do until then too. So just breathe, and let it happen."

"Yeah. Yeah, you're right. I'm sure we'll be back to talking in a few weeks, and then I can show him how much he means to me."

At midnight a few months later, I send him a text wishing him a happy new year for 2020…

…he doesn't text me back.

Mid-January, he finally texts me back for the first time since that day at Speech Balloon.

> Look, I know you want to try. But I need you to actually try.
>
> I don't hate you. I know it's hard, and maybe I did react too harshly, knowing what you're like.
>
> But I need some time to cool down and figure things out too.

> I know, I totally get it, and again, I am so sorry. And I swear, I will make it up to you.

> I just need some space right now. I'll see you at London, okay? We'll work it out then.

London, the show in March, not Excelsicon. Okay, that's not long. Not long at all. And when I see him, I'll make sure he knows I'm committed to fixing this.

LONDON EXCELSICON
SUMMER 2022 DAY ONE

The pandemic hit us hard in comics.

Maybe not as hard as it hit others, and I hate to come across like I'm belittling what people went through; what so many people lost. And there was some of that in comics too, but thankfully, not as much as one might think given how much of the industry is getting pretty old now, and how little healthcare is accessible to so much of it.

But so much of comics ground to a halt. Hell, even Marvel and DC stopped publishing for a couple months, and friends and colleagues found books of theirs long since announced and preordered getting cancelled as the publishers were forced to streamline their release schedule.

Independent publishers faced the greatest difficulties, with a couple smaller ones even folding, causing more losses. It felt like for a great many people, the omnipresent threat of COVID-19 was killing careers, jobs and comics almost as much as people.

I got hit too. Chuck had me send in pitches early February 2020, but just a few weeks later the first lockdowns started happening, and by the following month, Comixpedia's own release schedule ground to a halt, even as a digital only publisher. I checked in again in the June of that year, only to be told let's come back to it in September. In September I was told we'd look again in November, even though by this point they started announcing and releasing new projects, including one where the big name writer said they hadn't even started talking until the start of the pandemic. That felt real great, I can tell you.

The surREALS was doing okay, or so I'm told. I've still not seen any sales figures, even to this day. However, the book did finally get released in print. In a deal with a pretty big publisher called Blackstar, they released the whole series in one big book last August. Which was awesome, and everyone keeps congratulating me like this means I'm a big name now. Like my next book with a major publisher is assured.

It's not. It was part of my initial contract, it's just an earlier promise being fulfilled. I've not had a single publisher accept pitches from me since, including Comixpedia now. I'm basically back to where I was in 2018.

So I went back to the drawing board, as it were. Made a couple small projects with friends, wrote in a couple anthologies. Just to make it feel like I'm still doing something, even while my pitches for series and bigger books languish in a file on my computer, unread by anyone but me.

Comic cons obviously all got called off. So I never did get to see Cam again. He said he needed space, so I didn't text him. Once the pandemic shut it all down, I figured if he wanted to talk to me, to arrange some other way around it, he'll make the first move. I didn't want to overstep. I don't want to risk him ending it, definitively.

So it's with all this in mind that I find myself at the very first comic con in the UK since the pandemmy hit us all with a whammy to end all whammies. I try to make light of things again, it's how I dealt with the loneliness and overwhelming pressure and depression. As you might imagine, it's going swimmingly.

The landscape of Artists Alley has completely changed. Everyone basically gets a booth now, creating more barriers between everyone exhibiting to minimise risk. We're all in masks, and a few of us, myself included, even managed to find trans-parent ones, while others have bedazzled theirs so everyone can still have a bit of character. I've never had so much space behind and around my table, it's actually kind of amazing.

Crowds are smaller, as ticket numbers are vastly limited. But it's still busy. It's even mildly amusing seeing Spider-Men walking around, a full head to toe body suit on, but still wearing a violently turquoise or blue mask over their mouths. Hell, one thing that is really nice to see about comic geeks: the vast majority of them actually know how to wear the face masks properly, and do so respectfully and with no fuss. No noses sticking out, as ridiculously pointless as wearing your trousers with your knob hanging out over the waistline.

Thinner crowds or not, it's still busy, or as busy as it can be, and I find myself not just looking around giddily happy to see cosplayers and comic nerds again (tinged with an edge of nervousness as this is definitely the most people I've been around at one time now in years), but looking out for him. For Cam.

As I say, we haven't spoken. During the pandemic, he cut back on social media posts too. His Instagram got quieter and quieter, just sharing the occasional old cosplay photo. I'd like them, now and then, but tried to hold back from liking every single one.

Tried being the operative word.

But we've not really communicated at all in about two years now. So I stand here, selling comics, hoping against hope that he'll be here.

As I say, I made a couple new things during the pandemic, don't get me wrong. I wasn't just sitting on my laurels, pining after a gorgeous man. Of course not. That was just about sixty-five percent of my pandemic time.

I went back to basics. Did a couple small Kickstarters, some new one shot ideas, mainly. I figure I could show the breadth of what I am capable of as a writer, so I tackled some genres I hadn't before. Even did a little slice-of-life thing, which was hard. I much prefer writing the fantastical to the down to earth. Oddly, writing real life is hard, just like real life itself.

The day passes in a flash. A mix of it being genuinely busy, but also just being out of practice I guess. But one thing that is genuinely surprising, despite the reduced numbers, people are spending money hand over fist here. I think this is the most I've ever made in a single day at this show, and that's saying something. Probably the excitement of finally getting back to comic cons, people are excited to find new books and see new things again.

Not a single sign of Cam though.

LONDON EXCELSICON
SUMMER 2022 DAY TWO

I f the first day was busy, the second, a Friday, is something else.

The organisers timed this one right: the government extended the Bank Holiday, with most businesses (of the ones allowed to be open now anyway) having a half day or full day off today as well as the coming Monday.

As such, there's more people here than you might expect, even with the ticket limits. The organisers also made it so no one could have a whole weekend ticket, the idea being that if someone came for one day, caught the dreaded 'Rona, they'd then go home and wouldn't be back for another day to spread it further. Of course, they didn't stop people buying multiple days, so I doubt that's going to work as planned. It does mean that it's mostly new faces and outfits to marvel at today though, which is awesome.

I try again to keep my eye out for Cam, but to be honest, it gets so busy that before long I can't keep that up. It's all I can do to stay on top of all the customers coming to my table. It's nice to see so many people picking up the new titles too, and there's still plenty of love for the old copies of *The surREALS*. The collection, what few comp copies I was given, is almost gone, and frustratingly, none of the comic shop vendors at the show has copies, but I have a couple more to shift still.

I'm wrapping up a sale with someone when all of a sudden I hear a familiar voice.

"Hey."

I'm around the front of my table and throwing my arms around Cam before I can even register looking at him. Remembering where I am and the when and the 'oh god, semi-apocalyptic disaster' of it all, I pull back, still holding him by the shoulders to take him in.

He's got dark purple hair now, and he's wearing his specs. Oddly for him, normal clothes at an Excelsicon day, but he looks so good in his bootcut black jeans and a tight white t-shirt, a letterman jacket thrown over the top, like some kind of brightly coloured American Football high school jock.

"Oh my god, I'm so sorry, are we hugging? Are you hugging? I'm sorry, I just haven't seen you in so long, Cam, I had to. Fuck it, you wouldn't be here if you had the 'Rona, I'm hugging you!" I do so again. "I am so sorry, Cam-"

"Arran-"

"No, seriously, I cannot tell you how sorry I am about everything. You were right about it all. Hell, even the ADD as it turns out. I read that article, and yeah, it was *so* familiar to me. I took some tests online during the lockdowns and turns out it's exceedingly likely I have it, which is good to know. My local GP is crap about it though, won't even let me speak to a professional about it, says I'd have been diagnosed as a child if I was."

"But-"

"But they barely even talked about that here in the UK back then, I know. Fucking ridiculous. I figure I'll have to go private, when I can afford it, but trust me, when I can, it's the first thing I'm doing. I've been reading up on some management techniques in the meantime though, and they helped. So thank you, Cam. Thank you for caring enough to be thinking about me with that, you have no idea.

"And again, I'm so sorry, I just want you to know that, I will try my best to be better. For you. For me too, but also for you. My god, I fucking missed you so much, I just-"

"Ahem!"

I look over Cam's shoulder to see a slightly shorter, dark haired man looking at me with a raised eyebrow, and were half his face not covered by a mask, I imagine a pretty serious frown. His arms are crossed, and his body language just reads PISSED.

"I'm sorry, but you might want to check that cough out, sir." I say, giving him a well practiced smile that he is sure to read all the sarcasm from through my see-through mask (I really do love this thing).

"Arran," Cam says, pushing me back, and stepping back to join the throat-clearing random. "This is Justin.

"My boyfriend."

Excuse my melodrama, but in this moment, this is the worst part of the whole pandemic. "Oh. Oh, hello. Um, sorry for grabbing Ca-your boyfriend. Justin."

I move back around my table so it stands between me and Cam (and Justin) so it can stop me from trying to leap on Cameron again (and from throttling interloping Justin).

"Uh, sorry about that, it's just been such a long time, and I really have missed seeing Cam. Cameron. We're old-"

"Friends," Cam interjects.

I turn my head to him suddenly, the irony hitting me as surely as a long deserved slap.

"Yeah. Yeah, we're old friends."

"Of course, it's been a long time for everyone," Justin says, eyebrow lowered but expression nonetheless pointed, as he moves and puts his arm around Cam. "It's overwhelming whenever we get to see our old...friends."

"Sure, sure. Well! How you finding the con? Glad to be back in the thick of it?"

"Yeah, it's so great to see all the cosplay and everyo-" Cam starts excitedly, before Justin jumps in.

"It's a lot right now, huh. Not sure how comfortable I am with all these people in close quarters again." The venue, while enclosed, is the biggest convention centre on the European continent, and exceedingly well ventilated. "But Cam really wanted to get back into his old haunts."

"Uh huh. Not so much of a comic fan yourself then, Justin?" Cam bristles awkwardly, his lips squirming under his mask.

"Not really. I love the movies, of course, but the comics always felt impenetrable to me. Much easier to get into a good book, you know. But to each their own."

"Babe…" Cam nudges Justin, who looks to him and smiles under his mask, and then ruffles his hair.

"Anyway, it was so lovely to meet you, Aaron. Perhaps bump into you later." Justin makes to leave, arm around Cam, starting them both off away from me.

"Yeah, Jus-tin," (goddamn his name not sounding like anything else), "pleasure to meet you. Cam, it…it really was good to see you again. I hope…I hope you're happy."

"Yeah," he sighs, his eyes staring right into me. "Look, why don't you join us for dinner tomorrow night? We were going to go to that new place on the Dock, with all the outdoor seating. I could book a table for three?"

I glance at Justin, who looks impatiently from Cam to me and back again. "I'd love to. Tomorrow it is, then. It's a date!" I smile over at Justin, and wave at them both as they walk away.

When they turn the corner out of sight, I slump into my chair and hold my head in my hands. Fuck.

And then, the ADD brain starts concocting scenarios and part of me thinks this isn't over yet. I saw that body language in Cam, I didn't make it up. I know this isn't over yet. I know it.

LONDON EXCELSICON
SUMMER 2022 DAY THREE

Saturday is insane. A mad rush all day, and I'm pretty certain there's more people in here than there should be, but at this point, everyone doesn't much care. As much precautions as can be set are being observed, and everyone has been desperate for something like this, especially the exhibitors. The last few years almost ended careers, probably did for some to be honest. So, forgive us if we seem to be abandoning all sense and logic, but we are needing this right now and we're not going to let it go.

Needless to say, the day goes by like no ones business. A twelve hour day, but it easily felt like six. Sales were constant, and I am feeling flush physically and financially, all my sales being by card due to COVID measures, so money whizzing directly into my accounts.

After the show I rush back to my hotel, have a quick shower and freshen up. Operation: Win Back Cam is in full effect, so I shave, trim (everywhere), put on my best cologne and my best outfit, before heading over to the restaurant where I'm meeting them.

Cam waves me over to their table as I approach the restaurant. Thankfully, May is already scorchingly hot and dry (only thankfully as this means the restaurant's al fresco dining policy will be fine, not in the further example of ecological calamity we're living in), so there wouldn't be any chance for the weather to ruin the evening. I'm in some tight pink denim shorts, a muscle vest in black, with a pink and green vertical stripe shirt casually thrown over the top. During lockdown number one I got heavily into fitness routines and workout YouTube videos as a way to distract me and stop me from slobbing out on the couch too long. Lockdown two, I started looking at broadening my fashion horizons, which mainly meant changing out my wardrobe for a lot more colour when I could afford it.

As such, I'm feeling good about how I look, making sure I am making the most impact on Cam as I can.

I approach the table and notice Cam looking me up and down. "Hey, Arran. You look great!" Point number one towards victory.

"Thank you, Cam..eron. It was long overdue, but I finally got to looking after myself better. You look absolutely amazing too, as always." I smile, and wink through my sunglasses before taking them off, as if the dark shades would have hidden it from certain prying eyes.

I sit down before finally remembering to greet Justin. "Evening, Justin. How was today at comic con for you. Not too boring, I hope."

I expect some other wry, backhanded comment from him about comics, but instead I get...contrition. "I, err, had a much better day today, actually. It was really fun to see so much new stuff I'd not considered before. And, um, I really have to apologise for my behaviour yesterday."

"Oh?" I act surprised (but only partly acting, because I am a little surprised, as he seemed so determined to be a douche about what I do yesterday).

"Yeah, I probably didn't come across as very friendly, and I was kind of judgemental. I think I was just thrown when you greeted Cam, and it made me jealous. I know how much you meant to him."

Cam looks sheepish, and looks out to the water over the dockside. "Oh, he told you about-?"

"No. Not in so many words. But it's obvious to anyone with half a brain when he talks about you, and when you two saw each other yesterday. Half a brain and half a heart." Oh, so he talks about me (two points!).

"Yeah, it makes one wonder, when a relative stranger to you two as a pair can see it so easily, how you managed to let that slip through your fingers." There it is.

I look from under my brow, trying to throw a casual air, interrupting Cam as his mouth flies open to admonish Justin, but I beat him to it. "And how long ago did you two meet? Lockdowns ended, what, a few months ago? So I'm guessing sometime after that, that's why you maybe don't know that much about us."

Cam's face spins to look at me with the same flash of dismayed affront he shot at Justin a second ago. "Oh, we've been living together for over a year now. Started dating after the first lockdown and when the second one was being announced, we figured why be alone through it all again, and shacked up together. We've been together ever since." Justin smiles back at me.

"You…you live together?" I fall back in my seat, the revelation blowing me back. Minus one for the mission.

"Yeah. And, well, I guess he didn't tell me much about what you were to each other because, well. We all like to try and forget our mistakes, don't we?"

"That's it!" Cam says, throwing his napkin onto the table, as all heads in the restaurant turn towards us. "Justin, stop being a jealous dick. I am with you and I love you and it doesn't matter what me and Arran were to each other, because we're just friends now." Then he rounds on me. "Or at least I hope to be, if you would stop trying to goad my boyfriend out of, what? Some misguided sense of revenge?"

"I-" I start.

"I don't care, it stops now, whatever is going on in that head of yours. It's not going to happen. You can save the fantasies for your books, where they're welcomed. Not at this goddamn dinner table."

Justin and I hang our heads in shame. Cam stands there, panting heavily, and trying his best to slow his breathing as the dining public start to return their attention back to their own meals (but not before one girl in gigantic shades clicks her fingers and yells "Yaaaaas, kweeeeeen!" over at Cam).

"I'm sorry, Justin." I mumble, as Cam takes his seat again.

"Yeah, I'm sorry too. Can we start again?"

"Sure. Sure, I'd like that."

The rest of the dinner goes off relatively uneventfully. The food is delicious, and conversation, actually sparkling. Turns out Justin isn't actually that bad of a guy when someone isn't threatening to steal his man. He's a financier out of London, and he and Cam met just before the first lockdown at a work function, them being in somewhat similar circles. He's actually a bit of a Trekkie, so he does have some nerd cred, though he doesn't understand why Cam spends so much money on cosplay, insisting he could probably have afforded his own home if he didn't spend so much.

Of course, I know why he does it. I understand.

Cam, for his part, has actually been doing really well. Gone up a couple grades in the accountancy firm, setting him well on the path to seniority already. Great pay bumps, apparently, but I can tell there's more he's not telling me, and I think I know: he's not enjoying it. He's not happy there.

Part of me loses myself in a fantasy that this unhappiness is with Justin too, and that their perfect sounding little domestic cohabitation is on the rocks, and will fall apart soon and me and Cam...

I kick that part of my brain down and bring my full focus back into the now. I notice Cam flick his eyes down at my finger tapping against each of the tines of my fork in turn and repetition, a fidget to keep me present. I throw him a quick smile to let him know I'm okay and I'm here again.

I update them on the last few years and my endeavours, and as Cam congratulates me on the big book release for *The surREALS*, I have to be honest.

"Ah, don't congratulate too much. You were right. The contract, jumping into bed with Comixpedia, it was a mistake. It wasn't best for me, or at least, not for *The surREALS*. Perhaps if I'd taken a different idea to them, something that was one and done, and I could move on from. But they're not taking my calls, as it were, haven't for some time. Too busy chasing all the big stars out there. I hear they're even trying to tap Chris Claremont now, you know? The rights to the series are locked in with them for, like, seven years. So I can't do anything with it now."

"Arran, I'm so sorry. I know how much *surREALS* meant to you." Cam rests his hand over mine across the table, making Justin glance sideways at us and then gulp down his water hard to keep from saying anything.

"It's okay. I mean, it's not. But I guess it just pushes me onto other things, other avenues. Anyway, the book is doing okay, so I'm told. Still not being given actual sales numbers, but I see it about a bit. So hopefully, it really is going out and doing numbers. And maybe I can pick it all up again when I can...assuming everyone hasn't forgotten about it by then."

"Oh, I'm sure it's doing great," Justin interjects with a cough, prompting Cam and I to retreat our hands back to our sides of the table. "For instance, I know Cam rushed out to get a copy as soon as it released."

"You have a copy?" I ask Cam, my vision feeling a little watery all of a sudden.

"Of course I do," Cam goes to reach out to me again.

"It's a tough business, the creative industry. People have it bad all over. My friend got a gig with this animation studio though, maybe you should look into that." Justin pipes up, and Cam stops and places his hand in his lap. I nod politely at Justin and assure him I'll look into it.

It was all going fine and then, as the sun started going down on our now much more civilised dinner, Justin had to ask me whether I'd met anyone during or after the lockdowns.

"Well, no, not really, Justin. Kind of trapped in my little bit of Wales all on my tod, if I'm honest. And I was holding onto something, hoping maybe. Maybe I could get it back."

"Arran-" Cam starts, choking up as he says it.

"No, no, don't worry about it. Not on you, I just-you know me, ever the dreamer," I slap a hand on the table, "Well, guys, I don't know about you, but I'm really beat, and maybe the sun has got to me a little more than I expected in the couple hours we've been out here. That or the wine. Thank you for the lovely evening, I really hope you won't think bad of me for cutting out now. This should more than cover my part of the bill." I throw down a few notes, then make an immediate beeline for the exit before they can see the tears welling up, cursing myself that I let myself hope against hope that after all this time, we'd just go back to how we were.

I'm around the corner and halfway down the street before I hear the footsteps running up to me.

"Arran! Stop! For fuck's sake, you can't just run out on me again like that." Cam pants as he catches up to me. Poor choice of words.

"Run out on *you* again?" I spin on him. "Who was it who ran out on us in the pouring rain at Speech Balloon instead of sticking around and trying to work it out?"

"Hey!" Cam stands to his full height, his mood immediately shifted. "Don't you turn that on me! Don't you act like I hadn't been fighting for us for ages by that point, only for you to throw some new imaginary obstacle or end goal in my face every single time."

"Well, it's fine! Didn't take you long to move on, did it! A little lockdown and then you're moving straight in with the first guy you could."

"Fuck you, Arran! You left me on my own! I haven't heard a word from you since January 2020! You didn't send me a single text all through that first, lonely lockdown, but you know who did? Justin. Justin was there for me."

"You said you needed space! I was honouring that! I was waiting for you to message me and let me know…" I trail off, too weak to keep this up. The tears roll down my cheeks as I look back to Cam's face and realise he's crying too.

"I didn't think you wanted me anymore. I hoped against all hope, but my brain showed me all the different ways you didn't want me now, and I just…

"I didn't want to push you away, more than I'd done so already. I thought…I thought you still needed space from me, that's why you didn't call. Text. Anything…I thought maybe…"

Cam falters, lips quivering as a tear falls down his cheek.

"I should have messaged you, I'm being an idiot. It's a two way street, I didn't have to wait on you to make the first move, after how I left things…"

Before we know it, we're in a hug. I sob into Cam's shoulder.

"I missed you so damn much, you know that?"

"I know, I missed you too. But-"

We pull away, but as we part I brush my hand along his cheek and press my lips to his gently, before looking him in the eyes.

"Do you love him?"

"…yes."

I latch onto that pause, and not the answer. "Do you still love *me*?"

"Arran, that's not fair-"

"That's not an answer."

"Dammit, Arran," he pushes me back and half turns to head back to the restaurant. "Of course I still love you, Arran. I think I always will, because I think I loved you after that first night when all we were was two horny nerds fucking in a hotel room. But I *knew* there was something there and I held on, waiting for you to reach it with me and hold onto it too. But you never did." He walks away from me, taking one last look, tears staining his face, before he turns his back on me.

"I couldn't wait for you forever, Arran. And you shouldn't wait for me."

And with that, for all intents and purposes that matter, Cam is out of my life.

LONDON EXCELSICON
SUMMER 2022 DAY FOUR

Sunday flashes by, but not because of the crowds or the sales (though they're still seemingly non-stop, and I'm officially double my best ever show at this point): it runs by because my heart isn't in it.

My head is. I'm focused and I'm making sales, smiling and making all the right noises, but after last night I want to be out of here and back in my cave, buried under my pillows and reading a good comic and eating my body weight in chocolate cookies.

The one time things slow down for me is a moment when I swear there's a Spider-Man stood, watching me, from two aisles over from the corner. I go to wave, but think how ridiculous that is. It could be anyone. Cam said his goodbye, it's time to move on.

This con romance or whatever the fuck it was we had, I guess it's over now.

SAN DIEGO COMIC CON 2031
DAY ONE

The first day of San Diego Comic Con should be relatively light for me.

I have an interview with io9 around lunchtime at the Omni, and a signing at the Marvel booth for an hour around 3pm, and then that's pretty much it. I'm going to grab a drink with James, one of the editors at DC to talk about maybe coming and doing something with them as part of their next universe-shaking event, and I'll grab some dinner and then, well, the evening is mine.

I take my time in the mirror and shave my face to look as fresh faced as I can. I'm no spring chicken anymore, but also Wales doesn't get as much sun as California, so I think my Welsh forty-six passes for a Californian thirty-odd okay still. But it's only my second time at San Diego Comic Con and I still like to make an impression.

I take my PreP and Focalin, and apply a generous covering of factor fifty sunscreen. I made that mistake the first time here, using a factor thirty to start, and by the end of the first day I was red as a lobster from head to toe and had to find a CVS in the morning for actual medicated aftersun lotion. But I've been here in California for a week now, and I haven't burned yet. Tanning nicely though.

Started off in Los Angeles, where I stopped off to see Pavel and caught up. Spent the night in his bed before hanging out with a bunch of other gay comic creators by Jonah's pool. Figured why not get a small holiday out of this trip.

It's not all been fun and games though. I've had a couple meetings, the most interesting being one on the WB lot. There's some interest in turning *Red Dahlia's for Sunset Lovers* into a movie, which is surprising, as it's not even something I consider my best work. Still, has a pretty loyal fanbase and it did decent numbers, so might as well start somewhere, right?

I get dressed, throw on my shades and pop in my Null noise reduction earplugs, and I head down in the elevator to the lobby, and bump into Gertie and Emma. I haven't had much chance to see them since their wedding, what was it, three years ago now?

"Gertie! Emma! Hey!" I make a parody of a jog over to them.

"Arran! Oh my god, look at you! You're staying at the Hyatt too?" Gertie smiles, throwing her arms around me as I duck under her wide brimmed hat.

"Yup. Aren't all of us comic folks? How're things? It's been ages." I say, giving Emma a peck on the cheek.

"All good! We just wrapped on the last Marvel gig, and I'm going to be working on something hush hush with Scott Snyder at his new imprint. I'm really excited about it."

"And we just set up the new studio at the house, so she won't be working in the basement like a goblin anymore," Emma laughs, nudging her wife. "And Cookie is getting herself a little brother when we get back."

"You're adopting another cat? Are there pictures?"

We spend about five minutes in the lobby laughing and catching up and looking at photos of their cat (soon to be cats), mildly interrupted by a barrage of nods and waves from all the other writers, artists, editors and execs from the comics industry just checking in when I say let's go get a coffee.

We head into the hotel restaurant, and largely ignore the absolutely gorgeous breakfast buffet in favour of three cups of coffee and just sit around a table and catch up for a bit. We talk about the last three years, projects both professional and personal, and our lives.

It's not that we grew apart or distant in that time, but life has a tendency to get in the way, no matter how important someone is to you. These connections are so important, and I learned a long time ago that whenever the opportunity presents itself you should latch onto it, even if only for five minutes.

"Well, we better get going. Someone has a panel at 11am, and we haven't even got into the convention hall yet." Emma shoulders her large handbag, undoubtedly stuffed with various sunscreens, fans, bottles of water and more.

"It was good to see you, Arran. We have plans tonight, but will you be at the hotel bar later?" Gertie asks.

"And miss the opportunity to see you guys get trashed on overpriced cocktails again? Of course I'll be there!" I kid, and wave them off as they head out the backdoor, for the quieter path towards the convention centre.

I decide to head out the Hyatt lobby into the San Diego sunshine and walk down the main pathway to the front entrances of SDCC. The crowds are filling the streets of San Diego already. This convention really is something else, and I honestly think everyone should come and do it, no matter if they're a comics fan or not, a nerd or not, this is an *experience*. I've been to so many busy conventions, but San Diego Comic Con literally takes over the whole city.

I follow a group of fans into the building crowds, going with the flow of human traffic, mixing with excited people of all identities, and so many adopting the identities of their favourite characters. With my shades down, I'm relatively anonymous, but when a cosplayer dressed as the heroine from my last indie mini-series spots me, I of course pause for a selfie. I thank her for being a fan, and then move back into the flow, noticing out of the periphery of my vision a few looks as they try and work out who I am. One good thing about the comics industry, you can get pretty big in the books and still retain an element of anonymity, though not as much as it used to be.

As I approach the busy street crossing, I steel myself to move against the flow of people, as I push through to head across the street to the Omni. I'm early, but I learned fast at San Diego, if you want to get to an appointment on time, you should prepare to leave early and be ready for any kind of obstacle.

Meeting one midway across the street, a man holds an actual snake around his neck, and I wonder if he thinks he's going to get that into the convention. I make a wide berth and take the first exit from the traffic I can, moving towards the Omni lobby entrance passed fans, pop up cafe's themed after the latest TV shows and streamers getting their live shows on early.

I set myself up on the rooftop terrace and read an email from my agent as I sip an iced coffee by the pool. Seems we may have a place for my first novel, at last.

Not that I'm moving out of comics or anything, I just decided it's long overdue time to diversify. And as much as I love the medium, the industry is a cantankerous bitch and I could use a break. So, book publishing, possibly some TV work. Some indie projects that I'll probably take up with Image or Vault, but who knows. I'm not saying no to more comics work, I'm just...going with the flow, I guess.

I set my phone down and look out across the sea of fans and cosplayers, studio pop ups and installations, the convention centre, the docks. I think about how long ago and not so long ago all at once, the idea of me just going with the flow, not fretting about the future and just letting it take me felt so difficult a thing to do.

But it was so easy in the end. All I had to do was ask for help. Not that finding the right places to ask was easy, or having access was. That took time and disgustingly, money. But once it could be reached. Once I could ask. The work didn't feel too much like work at all.

I remember my privilege: I have that access now, I can take the time I need without worrying about keeping the roof over my head, and the medication I'm on works and thankfully was one of the first we tried. My head feels centred, steady. The calm I was always looking for to finally focus on me, it wasn't found outside like I thought it would be. It was within. I just had to be open and reach for it.

Time was I'd have worried what people thought about me being vulnerable like that, or admitting I needed help publicly when I did. I couldn't give less of a shit what someone thought now. Social media is a useful tool, and it's a great connector, but that's all it is, and I stopped giving it so much of my life a long time ago.

"Arran? Arran Wilson?"

I look up to see a young man with gangly proportions, scruffy blonde hair and thick glasses standing over me, holding a tablet and a satchel bag over his shoulder, a Flash t-shirt on. I stand and offer my hand immediately, with a smile.

"Owen, right? From io9? Pleasure to meet you. Shall we do the interview here?"

"It's been a wild ten years for you as a creator, hasn't it?" Owen starts, as he clicks the recorder on the dictaphone app on his tablet.

"Ha, you could say that."

"Did you always know you'd be here, now, back when you started?"

"Oh, no. Oh god, I was a mess when I was just starting, and I'm not afraid to tell you that. I don't think any of us, in comics, know what we're really doing, where we're going, or where we'll end up. We have hopes, dreams, sure. But the landscape in comics shifts almost as often as DC reboots its continuity, so you can never be too sure." I laugh.

"But you persisted. Why stick in comics if it's so hard?" Owen asks earnestly, and I wonder if he has aspirations outside of reporting someday.

"Because I couldn't imagine not *trying*. I won't lie to you, comics is a hard medium and an unforgiving industry. There are so few handholds on this climb, so it's disingenuous to call it climbing a ladder. And if, like me, you're neurodiverse, have depression, ADHD or anything like that, it feels especially hostile. I'd be lying if things didn't start really coming together once I had therapy and a confirmation and treatment for my ADHD.

"And this industry still needs to learn a lot, and improve. The way creators are, in the comics part of it all, often getting the short end of the deal is appalling. Our work is inspiring and leading to massive multibillion dollar rewards to some faceless exec somewhere up top at a studio somewhere, but we're barely seeing a dime of it, and far too frequently see nothing so much as a credit in the movies, TV shows and video games built off our hard work.

"But, perhaps I'm a masochist. I can't imagine being anywhere else," I lean in and go off record for a moment, "I'm sorry, Owen, do you mind if I smoke?"

"Oh, sure, no worries. If you're cool with it, I'll vape too."

"Of course, no worries," I say, fishing out a pack of menthol cigarettes and my lighter and sparking it up and taking a deep drag. "Filthy habit, I know, and I really wish I could get along with those vape things, but they do nothing for me. It's okay you don't mention my smoking in the article, yeah?"

"No worries." He smiles, releasing a pungent concoction of pineapple and cream cakes in a thick plume of smoke.

"Thanks. Anyway, sorry to interrupt, carry on, please."

"Okay. Well, let's start at the beginning. Probably fits well given those words on the difficulties of the industry, because *The surREALS* had a rough start at first, right?"

"Depends how you look at it, I guess. *The surREALS* started as an independent self-published book by myself and Gertie, our very first comic, and we'd been doing it for years before the

Comixpedia deal. But I guess that's what you mean, with how that all shook out?"

"Yeah. It must have been a blow when Comixpedia folded as an independent platform."

"Honestly, not really. At least, not in my case. Don't get me wrong, when Daintree came in and bought Comixpedia out, we all could see the writing on the wall. It was awful to see so many lose their jobs when the company was folded into Daintree's own e-reading platform, and that wasn't made with comics in mind so it undoubtedly stopped many projects in their tracks. There were a lot of good people at Comixpedia, and I'm just glad so many of them landed on their feet elsewhere.

"But for *The surREALS*, due to an oversight in the contract, the Daintree buyout actually released the series from exclusivity, and it meant I got the rights back to do what I wanted with the series years earlier than I would have. If it weren't for that, we wouldn't be six seasons into the series and looking at some exciting prospects for the future of it…elsewhere."

"Oh, that feels like a tease," smiles Owen. "We'll come back to that. But is that to say that the making of *The surREALS*, from independent self-published to the book we know today was without difficulties?"

Memories catch me off guard for a moment, and I pull the cigarette to my lips instinctively and take a deep drag.

"I wouldn't say that," I whisper as I let out finally, tendrils of smoke puffed out the corner of my mouth. "It was very difficult, emotionally. I was, am, very invested in that series. It means so much to me, so that was a very tough time. I made a lot of mistakes, and it very much was what set me on the path to getting the mental health help that I needed, if I'm entirely honest."

"You're always very open online, some might say that's what makes you popular. Others might think it's too much, and it's entertaining parasocial relationships."

"They might," I say, taking one last drag of the cigarette and then stubbing it out. "But to be blunt, to them I'd just say 'fuck 'em'. Fear of how people might perceive me, or react to my actions, is what held me back from seeking the help I needed in my life. I spent so much time constantly being guarded because of how others online or in articles may perceive me, it meant I…lost important things in my life. It's not worth it, honestly. I prefer to be open and honest, and I think that's an energy that would serve us all better, not just in the comics industry."

Owen nods along, making extra notes and checking his questions. He asks a few more questions about *The surREALS* before moving on to the next surprising stages of my career, like being picked up to do a few shorts in Marvel anthologies, the GLAAD award win for *Death Drop Racers*, to the "surprise" popularity of my run on *Thunderman*.

"It's rare that indie books continue past the original creators, at least not in their own lifetimes, but Gerry Horton himself passed the reins to *Thunderman* over to you when you did the reboot with Image. How did that feel?"

"Honestly, amazing. Gerry's work on *Thunderman* all those years was an inspiration to me, and formative to my own work, so for him to select me to take the character in new directions when he wanted to move on felt, honestly, immensely humbling."

"And you really did take it in a new direction. Still super-heroes, but your run became a deeply moving, deconstructionist take on the character and the idea of pursuing one thing in life so single-mindedly, at detriment to all other aspects of their life. His wife left him, his children became strangers to him, as he focused wholly on making the world a safer place. Where did that come from for you?"

I shift in my seat, bringing the cigarette pack back out. "Do you mind?"

"Not at all," Owen says, and I can tell he's making a mental note of some kind, and perhaps my smoking will turn up in this article after all. Ah well.

I light the cigarette and inhale it down into me again, before coming back up with something for this interview that I haven't shared before. "It came from a deeply personal loss that was entirely, and unreservedly my fault. I can make excuses about how I wasn't managing my ADHD or mental health back then, or that I was in a really tenuous point in my career, but that's all they are: excuses. I made choices and it lost me something precious.

"When Gerry gave me something precious of his, that was also precious to me, it seemed only natural to write about losing something so important to you because you're trying too hard on one thing and not learning to juggle the many things life gives you. I thought of my *Thunderman*, and I went from there."

Owen looks taken aback, and I run my tongue across the back of my lips, tasting nicotine and, I admit, smug satisfaction before I take another pull on my ciggie.

"Wow. That's…that's a lot. I'm sorry to hear that."

"Nothing to apologise for, it is what it is. Hopefully, others might learn from my mistakes perhaps, but as ever, I feel the best way to do that is to be open and share. It's what I learned from those mistakes, and a mantra I live my life by now."

The interview continues a little longer, talking about some of my Marvel work, and I drop what teasers and hints I can, bearing in mind embargo and NDAs, but otherwise, I think Owen has a good overview of my working life over the last decade. Perhaps even a bit more, to be honest.

He smiles broadly and thanks me profusely as he shakes my hand, telling me what a fan he is of my *Thunderman* run. Again, I thank him for a great interview and allowing me my little vice at the table.

I let him leave before I make my own way into the convention centre, following the flow of the throng into the building this time, and make my way to the green room, where I have a nice chat with Eddie from Dark Horse, and shoot the shit with Mitch who's out here with a film he worked on, before heading to the Marvel booth.

The interview dragged up some things I hadn't thought about in a while, and I feel the itch in my head but ignore it, the Focalin is just having to work overtime today. I'll drown it out with nicotine later, but for now, I have books to sign.

———————

Later that night, at the Hyatt bar, I settle in to conversations with my friends and colleagues I've made along the way on this journey.

Sadly, the Bar Con is still a thing, and conversations about business occasionally pop up. I wish I could say I wasn't guilty of perpetuating it, but I have to get gigs too, and would be lying if a few hushed conversations about potential pitches or setting up meetings with editors didn't come up. The drinks with James from DC earlier went great, so I think I'll be doing a pitch for one of their smaller characters they're hoping to build up in their new event next year.

The good thing now the drinks are flowing is so are the smokers, and occasionally I leave the relaxing chill of the air conned hotel bar for the closer warm night air of the Hyatt smoking area. I catch up with colleagues from past projects, and even meet a few new ones, and hopefully we can work on something together.

The networking gets a little much though, so I head back inside to the bar. Getting a good cider in America, I quickly learned, is like finding a leprechaun's pot of gold, so I stick with whiskey sour and turn to leave the crowded bar, leaving a tip.

"Arran?"

I bump straight into Kenny, who's been waiting to be served behind me. "Kenny, man! Dude, it's been years! How you doing?"

"Yeah, yeah, good, man. Much better. Hey, can I join you?"

"Of course!" I say, and go find us some seats while I wait for him.

Kenny hasn't really been in comics circles now for years. His meteoric rise did what all space rocks do eventually: burned up and crashed. More specifically, the work that that rise was really putting him through did a number on him, burning him out, and from what I gather, he had a pretty bad breakdown.

Kenny comes over and joins me, and we chat a bit about what we've been up to the past few years. He's drinking a soda, I note, but otherwise don't ask him about his problems that saw him leave comics. The most we get onto it is when I find out he's still working in creative projects, but he moved over to the gaming and animation sectors, working in writers rooms, and not pushing himself to get ever bigger gigs. It may mean his name doesn't get the spotlight treatment so much, but it has done wonders for his mental health.

The burnout he went through is pervasive in comics, and a lot of creative industries, if I'm honest. But it's especially bad in comics, as there is so little security or recourse for help. When it hit Kenny, his meltdown was quite public, and burned a bunch of bridges, but led to a very positive and open discussion online about mental health provisions and the way this industry pushes talent. Not that much changed at all, and not that any of it helped Kenny.

But he does seem a lot better, and I'm so happy to see him in a much better place now, even if it does feel a loss to not have him in comics anymore.

"Hey, man, I gotta hit the head, and then I think I might call it a night. Got a much busier day tomorrow, so probably should rest up." I stand to make my exit, and head towards the bathroom as Kenny wishes me a good night and good luck for tomorrow.

I'm washing up in the bathroom when the door goes and in walks Kenny again.

"Hey, man, I know you're heading to bed, but can we talk quickly, before you head up?" He sounds earnest and mildly anxious, and I've not seen that in him before.

"Of course, Kenny. What's up, man?"

Kenny paces in front of the cubicles, before striding over to the sinks, wipes it down with a hand towel and hops on the edge, facing me.

"Okay, years ago, in a bathroom…nowhere near as nice as this, I think I gave you some really bad advice and I needed to apologise."

My mind goes back a decade to another hotel bathroom on another continent, and another Kenny.

"I remember." I say, not letting any emotion into my voice.

"I don't know if you're still with him, or if you're not, and if you're not I hope what I said didn't end up being a catalyst for wrecking it, but all that shit about thinking about how people might look at what you have? It's all bullshit.

"It's thinking about that shit, and constantly pushing for the next thing in an industry that, frankly, doesn't give a flyin' fuck about you or how you're feeling that made me blow my whole fucking life apart, and I don't want to pass that toxicity on.

"It was wrong of me to say that. What someone else thinks about *your* life is none of their business and none of yours, and I shouldn't have suggested you pay it any mind at all. I'm sorry for that."

I think back on that night, and how it messed me up, and part of me wonders if I should hold Kenny to account for it, but then I remember: it was my choice to pay it any attention. To let it worm its way inside me and between me and Cam. Kenny didn't do that, I did. And he was as much a victim of this toxicity as anyone, and he's already paid so much for letting it consume him.

I move over towards him, and he gets off the sink looking at me with an expression like he doesn't know what I'm going to do. I hug him.

"Thank you for saying that, honestly. I accept your apology unreservedly. Anything that happened between me and Cameron was not your fault, do *not* carry that. You're alright."

A muffled sob sinks into my shoulder, and then Kenny pulls away, wiping his face clear of tears long held back finally released. "Thanks, man. Really."

I figure it must be part of his recovery process, and don't ask questions, just accept the moment for what it is and that it happened. "Look, I'm going to head up, but I want you to know, you have a friend in me. If you ever, *ever* need to talk, I may be on the other side of the world, but I'm also just on the other side of the phone."

"Thanks, dude. I appreciate it. Now, hey, you get on. And hey, good luck tomorrow!"

"You too," I say back as I leave the bathroom, and I mean it for every tomorrow to come.

SAN DIEGO COMIC CON 2031
DAY TWO

Today is a whole lot busier, and if the Focalin was struggling to keep up before, today it's having a real challenge.

I started off with a panel on being queer in comics, then a signing at the Image booth, before doing a panel for the next Marvel event I have a book in.

It's all going great, it's just a bit non-stop, and by the end of my signing hour in the Artists Alley stands, I decide I need a break.

I head out towards the back exits, where great big concrete steps lead down towards the dockside paths. The steps are a well used photo op position for cosplayers, and also a bit of a sun trap, so it's a great spot to stand and watch the cosplayers in their amazing costumes pose for mass photoshoots.

I lean on the railing, looking out over them towards the water, still and serene in the distance, slowly smoking my cigarette to savour it. I focus on my breathing and past the sound of cosplayers, the gentle lapping of the water against the dockside.

"That's a really bad habit, you know."

The first thing which strikes me is the voice is British, which is not unusual even here, but it's far less common. But the second thing, riding into recognition in my head as fast as the first, is I know the voice. I spin around, disbelief not letting me hope it can be true.

But sure enough, standing in front of me in full Star Lord garb, helmet on, jacket off, slung over his shoulder, is a familiar outline. I know the trails of those muscle lines by memory. That confident stance, and playful head tilt. Like something straight out of the past as much as the costume looks straight off the movie screens.

"Cam?"

He takes off the helmet, and as his dusty blonde hair falls in curls down his forehead, I see the man who could have been my whole world a decade ago. We fishes glasses out of his pocket and puts them on, smiling at me. A few more lines than before, but still, he feels like the boy I knew all that time ago.

I throw my arms around him without a second thought.

"Cam! Oh my god, it's so good to see you!"

"Arran, I'm glad I found you at last."

I kiss him on the cheek as I pull back, and am amazed to see him blush, "'At last'?"

"Ha, yeah," he says, brushing his hair back and holding the back of his neck. Is he nervous? "I've been trying to see you at your signings all day, but the lines were so busy, I just couldn't get to you."

"You've been looking for me?"

Cam smiles at me, and breathes steadily. "Yeah. You're kind of the main reason I came here."

Now it's my turn to get flustered. "You're kidding, right? You can't have spent all this money just to come see me?"

"No, no, of course, it's Comic Con too, come on," he laughs. "But knowing you were going to be here too, after all the achievements you've made, I had to come and see you in your element.

"I'm so proud of you, Arran."

I hold back a tear and just smile at him, before throwing my arms around him again.

"I'm so glad you're here, Cam. I really appreciate you saying that, and I missed you so much."

We part and stand together a little awkwardly, as I finish my cigarette. We small talk about the flights over, what we watched on the plane, the con itself.

"You here for the whole weekend?" I ask, hopeful.

"Yeah, actually. And a couple days after," he looks like he's psyching himself up for something, and I just cannot understand this nervous energy coming from him. "Look, Arran, I was wondering, did you want to get dinner, maybe? Catch up properly? Bit like old times?"

"Of course, me, you and Justin?" I ask, trying to not let on that it's been on my mind the whole time he's been standing here.

"Just us, actually. No Justin." Okay. No Justin. No real answer to the question I really was asking, but just the two of us.

"Well, I have the Eisners tonight, but how about tomorrow night? I know this really great place, a bit off the beaten track from here, should be less busy, but I could book us a table?"

"Sure. Sure, man, I'd like that. You have my number, I've not changed it. You still have my number, right?" He sounds momentarily concerned, as he puts on his helmet again and picks his jacket back up.

Of course I still have his number. "Sure. I'll text you the details. See you tomorrow?"

"Totally. And hey, good luck at the Eisners!" He backs away without turning a few steps, before bumping into a Storm, apologising, and walking into the convention hall.

And just like that, my head is filled with Cam all over again.

"Earth to Arran, come in, Arran."

I realise I've been swirling the wine in my glass for five minutes straight as I look across the table to Gertie. I bumped into her and Emma when I came into the Hilton for the Eisner Award ceremony, and we hopped on the first table we could find.

"Sorry, I was miles away."

"I could see that. I know these things are pretty damn boring, but you should probably pay more attention when you're actually nominated. Especially when your category is coming up." Emma jokes, mocking a small quiet applause in my direction.

"Oh, come on, I'm not going to win. James has got this in the bag. Again." I laugh and sip my wine.

"So what's got you so distracted then?" Of course gossip will be more interesting than sitting in a hall waiting for names to be called out. My leg bounces through it all, I'm paying attention as much as I can to it, but concentration gets more difficult the longer you're just sat around a table. So why not add a new distraction for us all to share.

"Cam is here." I say, and then down my wine.

"What? Cam Cam? Here? In San Diego?" Gertie looks dumbfounded.

"In the Eisners?" Emma says, head spinning around wildly so fast I swear it's going to come off her neck.

"No, Eisners, yes, San Diego," I fill in before she could auto-decapitate. "I bumped into him earlier. Apparently, he came here for me."

"What the hell does *that* mean?" Gertie asks and honestly, I am as lost for an answer as she is.

"I wish I knew. But it's good to see him, nonetheless."

"Was he with anyone?" Emma ventures, tentative.

"Not when I saw him. He said Justin wasn't going to come to dinner tomorrow, but he wasn't clear if that meant Justin wasn't here."

"Dinner? You two are getting dinner together? When? Where?" Gertie's investment in this is the most animated I've seen her all night.

"Tomorrow, this place I found last year called Karl's Brewery. Great food, enough off the beaten track that it won't be filled with con-goers, we can talk."

"About?"

"I dunno. How we've been? What we've been up to?"

"Anything else?" Emma asks, looking at me through her fringe.

I think for a moment, pouring myself another glass from the bottle on the table. "I don't know. I mean, it's been, what, ten years? Nine? We've lived different lives from the ones we knew back then, what else would we-"

"Arran Wilson!"

We all stop and swivel our heads towards the stage. The C-List celebrity they brought out to read this category, Best Limited Series as the screen suggests, holds an open envelope and beams out into the crowd as the room erupts in applause and the tables around us yell congratulations towards me.

I stumble out of my chair, take a last sip of my wine before walking towards the spotlights and just think 'what the fuck is happening?'.

SAN DIEGO COMIC CON 2031
DAY THREE

Saturday rushes by, which my aching head is thankful for. Doesn't matter how many Advil I threw down my throat in the morning, the sheer amount of wine I consumed while clutching the metal ball of the Eisners' trophy in my one hand could probably kill a small animal.

Congratulations continue to swoop in throughout the day, as fellow creators pass me by, whether they know me or not. I'm grateful for them all, and that my *Thunderman* run got that recognition is beyond anything I could have ever dreamed of, but my head was focused on one singular thing all day.

I smoked a whole packet as my brain whirred through all the countless possibilities this renewed connection to Cam would bring. What is this dinner about? Does he want to reconnect? Is it just a friendly meal together as we both find ourselves in a strange city?

Nothing starts settling down until I see him standing there, outside the restaurant. His tall, muscled, fine frame as stunning as ever, his calm confidence as disarming. Wearing tight jeans with a silk shirt tucked in, a wild pattern of geometric coloured shapes filling it in. And that smile. I've missed that smile.

"Hi," I smile back as I approach him, standing just far enough back to hold back any urge to try and touch him and make sure he's real.

"Congratulations on the award, Arran! I knew you could do it." he throws his arms around me, and I can't help myself but take a deep breath in of him.

"Thank you. Shall we?" We head inside, and get settled at our table, ordering drinks, including a cider for myself, as this is the one bar in the whole city I've found that serves it.

We make some small talk to start, and it's awkward at first, but sweet. He's been following my work, and tries to pick up everything, but admits I got a little too prolific in the last couple years for him to keep up.

"Ha, that'll be the ADHD, I bet. Can't stick on one idea too long." I joke, and he smiles knowingly.

"It's so good to see you, Arran. It looks like life has been treating you well."

"I guess. I can't really complain, anyway." I fiddle with a boneless chicken wing, almost too nervous to look over at him.

"So, the comics have been going great, Mr Award Winner. How about everything else?"

"Pretty good too, to be honest. Got my shit together. In therapy, and on medication for the ADHD, and it's helped a ton. Had to wait until I could afford to go private, but thankfully gigs started picking up and well, here I am. I moved out of the flat a few years back, into a bigger one. Finally got myself a proper kitchen, so I get to try out all the recipes I had been filing away over the years."

"And anyone to, um, cook for?" Cam asks, a slight break in his voice.

"No, actually," Cam looks at me a little sad, tilting his head. "Oh, don't get me wrong, there's been a couple dalliances here and there. One guy who I thought maybe could be something, but we only lasted a couple months."

I look Cam in the eye, stop playing with my food, and just go for it. Being open. Sharing. Honest truth. "I just never found anything that felt like *us*, and well, I didn't see the point. If it couldn't be as good as what *we* had, then it didn't need to be pursued. I had other things in my life going on."

"Arran-"

"No, no, it's fine. It's not me neglecting the rest of my life again. And not like I'm holding out hopes again, not like before. I'm realistic. I just..." I trail off, shaking my head and turning the conversation around. "Anyway, what about you? Still with Justin?"

"Actually," Cam leans back, looking into the depths of his IPA, "we broke up shortly after I last saw you."

"Oh, I'm sorry, Cam, I hope-"

"No, no, it's cool. It wasn't working out. I'd just rushed into it because he was providing something I wanted and I didn't think about if I wanted it from *him*...or someone else. We were wanting different things and it just didn't work out."

We sit there, letting the words hang there, the pause in Cam's sentence weighing on me. I figure it best to move on, rather than see him upset, lost in broken hearts and plans.

"So okay, I'm guessing you moved out. What you doing these days? You know all about me, but how are things going at the firm?"

"*Actually*," Cam repeats, laughing. "I left that too. It just wasn't doing it for me anymore. So I quit, and tried something else. I actually became an accountant." He smiles that devilish smile that used to drive me wild, and still does.

"But you already were an accountant?"

"Mmhmm, but now I'm that other kind of accountant," he laughs, calling back to that initial mix up on a horny night all those years ago. "I figured I'd give it a go, and it did really well, and well, I realised, what I want out of life is to enjoy it. We only get the one life, so why waste it feeling stuck and forced into a role, when you could be having a bit of fun and living all these experiences, you know. So yeah. Now I'm a 'spicy' accountant."

I can't hold the pretence any longer. "I actually might have already known that."

Cam's eyes widen and sparkle, laughter filling them just like the air around us as he lets out a tinkling giggle. "You sneaky bugger, you're a follower?"

"Maybe," I smirk, like he doesn't know of course I am. "I just felt like it was a great way to support you."

"Yeah, yeah, you just wanted to see my cock again," he teases, a frumpy woman in a bedsheet masquerading as a dress and sunhat glancing daggers over at us.

"Well, it *is* a very nice cock, if you recall," I tease back, throwing a 'fuck you' glance over at the prude trying to shame us with her looks. I let her know there is no shaming us.

"Well, I definitely remember how much you liked it. Anyway, it does good for me, and well, I started making cosplay items for other people too, and I still freelance a little actual accountancy on the side. It just means I'm not tied down to any one thing, and that freedom has really been...exhilarating?

"It made me realise something: that sometimes, you just have to go out and grab the things you want, throwing caution to the wind, hoping it will all work out in the end, because if you lock yourself in to planning for a future that may never come it will just leave you with all these regrets, you know. And I don't want any regrets in my life."

I put my hand on his on the table. "I think I know what you mean. You know-"

"I know," he says, rubbing the back of my hand with his thumb. "And, well, I did regret the way things were left between us. The way we haven't really been in each others lives, not really, all this time. And I wondered..."

"Yes?"

"...did you want to get out of here?" Cam smiles, that spark in his eye.

"Oh, you have no idea."

We practically run into the Hyatt lobby like school kids, laughing as we burst into the elevator and have to stifle our giggles when we bump into a Wolverine cosplayer and TV actor in there. We're corpsing on the ride up until our fellow passengers get off, and then we're all over each other before the doors have fully slid shut.

We're kissing each other like the other is air and we've been underwater for a lifetime. Our hands wander wildly, over shirts, under pants, through hair and down the back of my neck as Cam pulls my head back and sucks on my neck. I gasp as the lift pings my floor, and we rush to my room.

We fall through the door, laughing, before scrabbling back up and running into the room, taking clothes off with every step. By the time I'm resting one knee on the bed and turning back to him, Cam is grinning like an idiot, his dick hard and pulling at the jockstrap he's wearing. "Nice Lycra undies there, Arran."

I smirk back at him.

"Well, I have to get my kicks in somehow. Thanks for teaching me what they were."

He laughs as he rushes over, pressing up against me, rubbing against each other through what little clothes we have left. But that little is still too much. After all this time, I want it all.

I kiss down his neck, hearing him moan, down his chest, my tongue brushing his nipple, my hands gripping at the straps around his waist and pulling them down. He pops out with a bounce, and I take a second to admire this beautiful thing before burying my face in his crotch, breathing in the scent of him.

Cam moans as he falls back onto the bed, and I pull him forcefully towards me, raising his legs over my shoulders and caressing his balls with my tongue.

"Arran, please, please just fuck me," he pants out, but he has to wait.

I take my time, kissing and licking, his ass, his thighs, his balls, his shaft. I stand, and as I lean over him, I pepper him with pecks, my lips lingering wherever I feel him tremor most, and I remember still how to find every spot.

As I kiss his lips, I play with his asshole with my hand, feeling it relax as I massage slow circles around. Cam moans into my mouth, making me harder and harder, until I pull back.

"Are you sure?"

"Arran, please, *fuck me*," he begs.

I yank down my pants, my own cock falling forward with the freedom from the material, already wet in anticipation. I get on my knees and Cam wraps his legs around my head, pulling me in to his ass as I rim him.

Standing, I spit on my hand and massage it onto my dick and slowly push inside of him.

It all comes flooding back to me, memories of sweaty nights in hotel rooms half a world away, tantric desires spent gasping each others names, a history of lust and more than that, all pushing me harder into this moment.

We rut and moan and shout, and more importantly, laugh like this, losing ourselves in the moment and everything that came before. But we make it last. Before I finish, we stop and we lay in the bed, joking about past fucks, reminiscing about old jokes and kissing each other again.

Cam takes his turn, and fucks me as he holds my head down into the pillow, making me gasp with each thrust.

We're at times rough, at times tender, but always smiling, always in the moment, until panting, sweating and utterly spent, we lie together, filled with each other, like nearly ten years hasn't passed between us, and we're the same horny idiots we always were, before all the mistakes, all the fuck ups, just two guys who love every inch of each other, inside and out.

As we lay there, the San Diego sunset streaming through the window across us, Cam brushes my hair from my eyes and says, "I have never stopped loving you, Arran Wilson."

I kiss him, "Ditto, Cameron Perkins."

We stay like that for hours, until the streets outside the window sound quiet again, as con goers, creators and more all have made their escapes to their hotel rooms.

We cuddled, and kissed, and fucked and just stayed there, in the moment, not worrying about what came next.

Until Cam had to go back to his hotel room. He needed an early start for his costume tomorrow, and he'd need to be in his hotel.

I throw on the robe and walk him to the door, one last kiss in the doorway as he says goodnight.

Then my mind races.

Outside, dressed and chaining cigarettes, I wonder if maybe this was one last hurrah, if that's all I want it to be, if that's all he was after. Should I have asked him to stay? Is that the right thing to do? I wasn't lying, I've never felt about anyone the way I feel about him since, but is that enough?

I light another cigarette and blow smoke into the heavy San Diego air.

SAN DIEGO COMIC CON 2031
DAY FOUR

"So, how did it go?"

Emma and Gertie look on with interest as I join them back at the table, a loaded plate of breakfast goodies in hand. I need to get my energy back.

"It was nice. Just like old times." I say, noncommittally.

"Just like old times? *How* like old times?" Gertie raises an eyebrow as Emma chomps on about three rashers of bacon cooked in that crispy American way all at once.

"*Just* like old times." I smirk, sipping my orange juice.

"What does this mean?" Emma just about manages to make clear through a mouthful of bacon, Gertie shooting her a look and pushing Emma's coffee cup towards her. Emma washes down her food dutifully. "Like, are you guys back together, or…?"

I poke at my scrambled eggs with my fork. "I doubt it. Come on, it's been nearly ten years. It's probably just two guys who meant the world to each other once getting one last booty call in."

Gertie grabs me by the wrist, making me look at her. She locks my gaze with her eyes that are looking fierce and determined. "Booty call, my arse. There isn't a booty good enough on the planet that will make you travel halfway around the globe after ten years just for the chance to tap that again. I don't care how good you think you are, Arran.

"This meant something, and you can either choose to fuck it up again, or you can actually try and make it work this time."

"But it's been ten years, Gert. Our lives might not even fit like they used to anymore, it might-"

"So. Fucking. What."

We eat the rest of our breakfast in near silence, just small talk. They fly back home after the show tonight, wanting to get home to Cookie and their impending new sibling as soon as possible. I have a couple more nights before I fly back.

When they leave me to my third cup of coffee, I let my mind wander through all the possibilities, but I steer it, I push it into focusing on the ones where it could work. I sit there pondering how to make it work.

I still have commitments today, so I find myself on the Breaking Into Comics panel, as the show is drawing into its final hours.

These kind of panels pop up at nearly every con, or at least, every con here in the States. They're always well attended, but not just by aspiring comics creators, but just general fans, with maybe only a third of the room ever actually wanting to make comics themselves. Worse, if it's one of the big publisher ones, there's a contingent who are expecting an easy answer to get them right in there with Marvel or DC to write their *Superman* or *Spider-Man* story, when that is just not how it works.

If I'm bluntly honest, I find these things for the most part utterly useless and even a bit tedious. Because there is only one way to 'break into comics' - make comics. There's so many different avenues and ways to do it, and more coming all the time, that no one action plan exists. And as much as that was something I desperately wanted when I started, with my head it would have made things so much easier, I have a) learned that such a thing doesn't really exist, and b) just got on with it anyway.

The panel is relatively entertaining this time though, the host asking good questions, and there's a good mix of us up here for a change, instead of being a row of five white, straight cis men. The room is packed, with even a few folks standing around the edges of the room, just about visible over the lights shining in our, the panelists, faces.

We get to the audience questions section, and my heart sinks with dread. These things are always at best a mixed bag. Most of the time it's an endless line of fans asking publishers what the next Hollywood superhero movie plan is, no matter how many times it is uttered that the publisher and movie production studios are separate entities that barely speak to each other, let alone the latter revealing plans to the former in a world of ceaseless spoilers and clickbait hounds.

Occasionally, you'll get one or two genuinely interesting questions and responses, but often it's just "who would win a fight between etc etc."

That said, these kind of panels can have interesting ones, so I try to keep myself looking engaged, slowly turning my water glass to keep me in the moment.

A young woman in a *Spider-Gwen* cosplay comes up to the microphone, and asks her question.

"You've talked a lot about what got you to where you are now, and the right moves and a little of the wrong moves. But I was wondering, is there anything you really regret on the path you took into comics?"

"Excellent question. Arran, do you want to start with that?" I can only assume the host picked me because they saw how I stopped in my tracks and looked straight out at the girl. The question hit me hard, touching on a recurring theme from this weekend, and even this whole comics career ride I steered myself on.

"Arran?"

"Sorry, sorry, yes, sure," I stumble, pulling the mic closer. I look out at the sea of fans in the room, costumes, props and masses of swag, picking out characters in my head until I see him: Thunderman.

"I *do* have a regret, absolutely. And perhaps it's the most important lesson I learned in this journey trying to 'break in' to the comics industry, and I'll share it with you, though I don't know if you want to hear it.

"My regret is simply this: that I didn't walk away from comics at the times when it was needed."

A murmuration of surprised gasps and shocked whispers flows through the crowd, and even the panellists next to me cough, choking on their water, startled by my answer.

"Don't get me wrong, I don't mean that I wish I stopped making comics. I couldn't if I tried, I want this so much. But I became so singularly minded on making this happen that all other things in my life fell away. I was not the best of friends, probably not the most attentive of sons, and…

"…and I let the love of my life slip by me, because I was too scared to try and work out how I could be a good partner as well as a good comic creator. I kept waiting for one thing to fix into a settled path, to slot into place like a track of a train set, that I could just let it run in the background and move on to the other parts of my life then and give them focus in turn. But in doing so, I neglected the most important thing to me, and I broke his heart.

"I *absolutely* regret that. I was a fool to do so, because that's just not what life is. It comes at you all at once, and it never lets up, and you can't just let an aspect off the hook and roam around like a Roomba to do it's own thing and expect it to still be there when you finally look back. You have to work at *all* of it, at the same time, and god, yes, that is so hard.

"But it's life. And it's worth it. And if you ever have the chance to fix what you broke, you should take it, because regrets aren't worth anything but ashes on the tongue. Don't make this gig your everything, but if you do find yourself with that regret…don't let it stay that way."

I look out towards him. "Don't let *us* stay that way."

The room is silent. Slowly, smatterings of applause start, as the host doesn't know quite what to do. "Err, thank you for that, Arran, that was….well, that was that. Um, I'm not sure we have time for anyone else to cover that but how co-what are you doing?"

I'm stood up, because so is Thunderman in the crowd. My Thunderman. I make my way around the panel table, behind the host who looks at me in bewilderment, as Thunderman pushes down the aisle, down the line to the microphone, meeting me as I jump down from the small stage into his arms until our lips lock and the room bursts into thunderous applause.

"Hey," I whisper, as tear-stained cheeks bulge in a smile at my Thunderman.

"Hey," replies Cam.

That night at the Hyatt bar, we're the talk of the town.

'Comic writer snogs cosplayer at Comic-Con!', 'Long lost lovers reunite on the show floor', 'The Con Affair' and a sundry other more vile clickbaity headlines flood the digisphere as tweets and threads and posts galore spread the news. There was even one TikTok that managed to get a really good angle of our reuniting and set it to *The Only Exception* by Paramore that made me cry (I bookmarked that one).

Kenny comes up to us at one point and gives Cam a massive hug, completely surprising him, and I promise to fill him in on it all later. Gertie and Emma even manage to see us before they head to the airport and make us promise to come see them at their place and have a good proper catch up. Cam agrees, saying it's solely to meet the cats, of course.

We haven't talked about logistics, we're a little too high on how it all went down, I don't know if I'll move to him or he'll move to me, or if we'll just make the long-distance work for now, but whatever, that's not important right now.

What's important is that Cam's here with me, and he's holding my hand and I'm holding his, and I don't care who sees, because he's with me and that's all that really matters.

I spend the night introducing him to colleagues and editors, people in my weird and crazy life of comics, and he stays engaged and interested, between giddy kisses and playful nuzzles when no one's looking.

"Hey, Arran, buddy!" Chuck rocks up, whiskey in hand, and grabs my hand to shake before I can return his greeting.

"Hi, Chuck. How're things going? Moved on from Daintree, I heard." Chuck makes a micro expression of pain at that last part, one that by now I'm trained enough to see.

"All good, left them soon as I could and good I did too, they really made a mess of things. It's good I saw you, actually! I'm starting this new project, a whole new platform, and I think you'd be perfect for it-"

Cam clears his throat, and Chuck finally acknowledges the stunning man in full Thunderman cosplay on my arm. "Ah, sorry, I'm not sure we've met before?"

"Actually, you have, Chuck. This is Cam, my *boyfriend*. My partner. And we're actually kind of celebrating tonight. Been something of a really good weekend. So perhaps another time?"

Chuck looks dumbfounded as we turn and move away, towards some laughing artists I know who are normally good for a joke and a cheeky joint. "You have my email, Chuck, drop me a line sometime maybe."

Eh, business is still business. We can check it out together later.

We spend the night laughing and joking with friends old and new, as we fill people in on our story, or what we think is best to share (Pavel, of course, wants all the sordid details, and we give them to him and where to find Cam's 'accountancy' page, let him enjoy *that* later), until the night starts wearing down. Then we're just a core group of writers, artists and partners sitting around a table on soft couches chatting about life and putting the world to rights.

As everyone starts making their moves to bed, Cam decides to spend the night with me and we head up to my room, and we just talk, and kiss, and hold each other until sleep takes us, in each others arms.

———

I wake in the night and find it's not a dream: Cam lies on his side of the bed, the light linen sheet loosely tangled between his legs, one arm strewn backwards, hand still resting among my chest hair.

Despite the ever present air con, San Diego is exceedingly warm, and we are after all British. Spooning was not going to be too plausible for long, but even pushed apart in our somnambulant movings, we still have to maintain contact, a touch, to be sure that the ground is back beneath our feet.

I look over at the back of his head, sandy blonde even in the lightening darkness, and smile.

A thought comes over me, and the smile fades. I sit with it in silence, realising sleep will not take it away from me. I decide I cannot let it lie here, with us, with all my hopes.

Gently, I lift Cam's hand and place it on the pillow as I slide off the bed. I throw on some black linen shorts, a t-shirt, and reach into my jacket pocket and leave.

———

I'm on my third cigarette in front of the Hyatt when Cam comes and joins me.

"Hey, what you doing out here? The cravings that bad?" I know he knows it's more than simple nicotine pangs, because I know this man truly knows me, no matter how hard I didn't let him.

"I just…I just needed to think."

Cam comes over and pulls my hand away from my mouth, cigarette still held between my fingers, and looks me in the eyes.

"Hey now, stay with me. We're together, whatever is burning through that head of yours, that's mine to carry too."

I look at him, his concern finally beating small worry lines in the marvel that is his face, and I hate myself for thinking 'I did that', as if my own foibles are greater than the rend of ever-marching time.

But he's right. I know now, he's right. I let him in, and if it's too much, then I guess I'll finally know…

"I just…are we rushing back into this? We've not seen each other for nearly ten years, and now we're going to try and make a go of it? Are we mad?" I pace away from him, as the words tumble forth.

"So what if we are? We can be mad together."

"But what if…what if it doesn't work? What if I push you away again?"

"Do you want to?"

"Of course I don't, I don't ever…" I spin on my heel, facing him, looking ever so slightly upwards at those brilliant blue eyes, "But I know I'm a mess. I may know what it is now, but just because it has a name now doesn't make it easier. It doesn't mean I won't feel overwhelmed. That the chaos of my life, my career, this world I throw myself into even though it's every structure is designed to be as hostile as possible to anyone who doesn't know how to play it's silly little games…

"How can I know I won't wreck this? How can I know how to make sure it works?"

Cam's hand on mine, keeping the cig from me, gently stroking the back of my hand with his thumb. "You can't. And maybe *I'll* fuck it up. Maybe we'll just grow older and grow distant. Maybe whatever passion we still have for each other will run it's course, and in four years time, or one, we'll turn around and realise we're not meant to be after all."

With his other hand, Cam holds the side of my face, my stubble prickling against his smooth skin. "But at least we'll have tried. And through all the messes, all the hiccups, all the disasters, we'll always be able to say that we finally gave it an honest go and it wasn't meant to be but oh god, it was fun while it lasted."

Subtly firmer, he pulls me in, our hips meeting, his eyes locked on mine, the gentlest smile against his lips, and I realise his eyes glisten with tears as golden rays of the rising Californian sun start to peep through the towering buildings above us. "And I know your head is a mess, because it constantly runs the disaster scenarios. But what if we work out? What if we're finally the happiest we could ever possibly be?"

He leans in as the tears start to fall down my face.

"What if, when all is said and done, we'll be sitting together, in some room of our own, hands still held as we watch the sun rise then, just like we do now?"

He kisses me. Deep and slow and tinged with longing for all the lost years between us, and those that we may still have together. I feel the cigarette drop from my fingers as I grab the back of his head and pull him in harder, kissing back hungrily, letting him know in this language without words that god, yes, I want to try for that.

We part, smiling at each other and head back into the Manchester Grand as the day dawns around us. With my other hand, I take the cigarette pack and crumple it and all inside, and throw them in the trash.

A few hours later, we check out of my hotel and leave the city as it pulls down every single sign of Comic Con's presence.

And for once, the comic con may be over…but we aren't.

AFTERWORD

Hi. Hello. Howdy! Thank you for reading my first novel. You're the best, an utter legend, a true friend etc.

Now, I'm going to clarify and answer some questions I'm sure you have after having read the story, most of which can be boiled down to one question to be honest: "did any of that actually happen?"

Well, dear reader, let me assure you that I have been single and alone for some fifteen years now. I have also been making comics for some fifteen years now, thereabouts. Make of that what you will.

In all honesty, the reason the story is set in the world that I've been a part of for a big chunk of my life is the most basic teaching tip of writing: 'write what you know'.

I know comic cons. I know the comics industry (to as much of an extent that any rising creator in it does). I know having a dream career that always feels a little out of reach. I know having an unhealthy relationship with social media. I know being a little too singularly focused to the detriment of the rest of your life. I know the gay scene and hook up culture and trying to find a permanent love in a world of fast love. I know all these things and slapped them together into a little fantasy of a spicy romance story for you all to enjoy.

But the end of the day, I can only tell you that. You'll decide what you believe, what you think did happen and didn't. That's all up to you, and I invite you to enjoy your imagination - it's a wonderful place if you let it be.

As for the other question you probably have: "does it all work out for Arran and Cameron?"

Again, let your imagination take over. Hopefully, it can be a wonderful place.

ACKNOWLEDGMENTS

I would like to say a massive thank you to all of my test and beta readers. Tom, Michele, Morgwn, William, Ben, Craig (heck, everyone who checked it out!) - you were all a massive help, and I really appreciate it.

To Helen too, even if it did prove too spicy for you when you got about ten pages in. Gave me a giggle, and your assurances that I can really write really do mean a lot.

To all my fellow comic creators who have been an inspiration and keep me going even when I feel like I've hit a brick wall. I know we all hit it from time to time, but each and every one of you inspires me on the crazy little topsy turvy world of comics.

To every single person who read my comics and helped me and supported me, I keep making comics because of you.

And lastly, my family - you've always believed in me and even when it seems tough, you think I can make it through. I couldn't without you in my corner. Thank you for that.

ABOUT THE AUTHOR

Joe Glass is an award winning writer based in South Wales, UK. He's mostly known for his work in comics, including the Gayming Mag Award winning LGBTQ+ superhero series, *The Pride*, and the Gayming Mag Award/Ringo Award/GLAAD Award winning anthology, *Young Men in Love*, which he co-edited and wrote for. He continues telling queer stories for all readers, because why the heck not.

X x.com/josephglass

instagram.com/joeglass

tiktok.com/@joeglasscomics

threads.net/joeglass

ALSO BY JOE GLASS

Comics & Graphic Novels

The Pride Omnibus

Young Men in Love

Glitter Vipers

Acceptable Losses

The Miracles